Leave This Off The Books

ARDEN JOY

This book is a work of fiction. Any references to historical events, real people, or real places are used fictitiously. Other names, characters, places, and events are products of the author's imagination, and any resemblance to actual events, places, names, or persons, is entirely coincidental.

Cover Illustration © Cover Ever After
Distributed by Simon & Schuster

ISBN: 978-1-998672-02-8
Ebook: 978-1-998672-03-5

FIC027020 FICTION / Romance / Contemporary
FIC027250 FICTION / Romance / Romantic Comedy
FIC027000 FICTION / Romance / General

#LeaveThisOffTheBooks

Follow Rising Action on our socials!
Twitter: @RAPubCollective
Instagram: @risingactionpublishingco
Tiktok: @risingactionpublishingco

To my husband: who gave me everything I needed to make my dreams come true

Content Warning from the Author

I was once asked at a panel why I loved to write romance. My answer was that, at its core, romance allows us to explore the hardest parts of life in a way that feels safe, because at the end of the day we're guaranteed that happily ever after.

So, while this retelling of Shakespeare's *Much Ado About Nothing* brings all the traditional elements of a rom com that (I like to think) would make old Willy himself proud, it also includes some incredibly difficult situations—including stalking, domestic abuse, and violence.

These are topics that are close to my heart and ones that I don't take lightly. I know that in reality, the scars left by these traumas don't fade overnight the way they can in a story. And while I don't pretend to have all (or any) answers, I do hope that these pages will inspire a modicum of belief in the power of love, resilience, and the possibility of a future where the past no longer holds all the power.

If you've lived through anything like what's in these pages, please know you're not alone. If this book brings up anything too heavy, take care of yourself first. The story will be here when you're ready.

And if you are curious to get into Abby and Freya's love story, then you can get their version of events in *Keep This Off the Record,* the other half of the Much Ado About Love series!

Thank you for reading and enjoy!

xoxo,

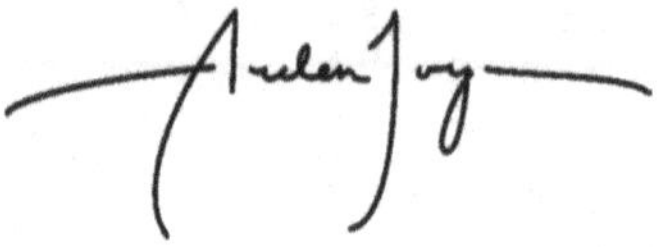

If you or someone you know is experiencing abuse, contact the **National Domestic Violence Hotline** at **800-799-7233** or visit **thehotline.org** for support.

For international resources, visit **speakyourtruth.today** to find help in your area.

Leave This Off The Books

Chapter One

Naomi

NAOMI: O.M.F.G.

RILEY: Here's my cup. Pour me some tea.

Naomi wasn't even sure where to start with filling in her friend. Her high school reunion had gone in every possible direction except the one she expected. And she needed to tell *someone.*

"I don't feel so good." Her best friend, Abigail Meyer, who sat beside Naomi in their Lyft, made an *urp* sound, and her naturally pale skin somehow became a shade paler.

"Should I be pulling over?" the Lyft driver asked, casting a nervous glance at them in the rearview mirror.

"No, we're fine." Naomi smiled assuredly at the narrowing eyes in the reflection. "Trust me. She hasn't started turning gray yet." She was confident, mostly confident, that they would make it home without any incidents. Having been best friends with Abby since the first day of

Hebrew school meant Naomi was no stranger to holding Abby's hair back after one too many drinks. And vice versa.

But they were in their thirties, at their fifteen-year high school reunion, and it had been a minute since she'd had to do that.

She returned her attention to her phone.

NAOMI: Everything has gone sideways. I actually flirted with someone. And then Abby threw a drink on Freya. Now she's very drunk in the car ride home.

RILEY: Ok - listen. You cannot TLDR something like this. I need you to start AT.THE.BEGINNING. and give me all the details.

"The beginning" was the moment they walked in the doors of Northwest High, and their alumni class president handed them their name tags and reunion programs.

"Have fun, ladies!" the class president had said with an enthusiastic wave.

While Naomi had been trying to smooth out a crease in her nametag, Abby had tugged at her, pulling her off to the side near some lockers.

"She's here," Abby said in a hushed voice.

"Who?" Naomi asked in a normal volume, looking around to see who might be near enough for Abby to whisper.

"Look!" Abby held up the program and pointed at a line in the evening events.

ALUMNI OF DISTINCTION AWARD

Freya Jonsson

Senior Correspondent, Nightly Global News

"You promised me she wouldn't be here!" Abby hissed like an old radiator being overworked on a frosty winter day.

"Promised" was a strong word. Naomi had relayed information. Information that had been hastily acquired and was now proving to be faulty.

When the invitation for their fifteen-year reunion had arrived (because, true to their class personality, they couldn't get it together in time to put together a ten-year reunion), Naomi had done a quick search to see if there was any chance that their former classmate, Freya, would be attending. Her latest post was a picture of her in Germany, which, according to the caption, was part of a story she was doing on the refugee crisis in the EU. This is what Naomi had told Abby as part of her argument to convince her reluctant BFF to RSVP yes to the event.

Naomi hadn't particularly cared if Freya attended the reunion. Freya, who had filled the role of popular cheerleader in high school, had not run in her social circle back in the day, so their interactions in high school were minimal at best. Most of those interactions involved her pulling Abby away from a heated argument with Freya. For four years of high school, Naomi couldn't understand what was happening between Freya and Abby. Like two pieces of flint, they seemed completely unable to pass each other without sparks flying. Naomi hadn't even figured out the combination on her locker on the first day of high school before she heard the two of them yelling. The whole thing was so out of character from the kind, sweet, funny Abigail that Naomi had known most of her life, and when she asked Abby about it, she couldn't get a straight answer other than, "She started it."

"I guess her social media isn't giving real time updates of her location," Naomi had replied to Abby.

That was something she hadn't considered but probably should have. Freya was more than a reporter for one of the largest news organizations in the world; she was something of a celebrity. Despite being just over thirty years old, she had become a household name. Not only a well-respected media personality who would go to the ends of the earth to find the truth, but also a bestselling author, a frequent guest on the couch of popular late night television shows, and influencer-level social media presence who was known to post heart-melting cuddle pics with her fluffy dog, garnering nearly a million likes each time. So, she probably didn't habitually post her exact whereabouts to the public. Oops.

"C'mon, we're here to see old friends and have fun," Naomi had continued. "Don't let Freya get in the way of that."

"I won't." Abby shrugged, a small dismissive movement that belied some irritation at the suggestion. "It's not like it matters either way. I wasn't expecting it, is all." Naomi couldn't tell if she meant it or if she was saying it to convince herself. Maybe a little bit from column A and a little from column B.

"Exactly. She might not even show up. Maybe she'll accept the award over video or something."

Abby gave a little snort. "That would be so Freya." Yep. There was definitely some column B in there.

"Good," Naomi had said, pushing open the double doors to the gym. "We've got four drink tickets between us, so let's get us some cheap reunion-grade alcohol and

mingle."

The small gym was packed, with easily more than a hundred people in the room. Despite the crowds, the bar was easy to spot. The two folding tables covered in black plastic tablecloths had a line a dozen people deep.

"Was that Mikey Weinberg we walked past?" Abby asked as they inched forward in line.

"You spotted him too? He's definitely cleaned up."

"Cleaned up? He's looking gooooood." Abby nudged her.

"You interested?"

Abby let out a guffaw. "He's a little too ... penis-forward for me."

Now it was Naomi's turn to guffaw. Her laugh came with a baritone echo, and it wasn't until the person in front of them turned around that Naomi understood where it was coming from.

"Sorry, didn't mean to interrupt your conversation," the owner of the laugh said. He was svelte, with sandy hair and rich brown eyes and a fair complexion that gave him a youthful, almost cherubic appearance. Not her type. Not usually, anyway. But there was an unexpected flutter in her stomach that caught her off guard. "That was just not something I was expecting to hear in line for a drink at a reunion."

"Yeah, dicks aren't my thing," Abby said, shrugging unapologetically the way only Abby could. Naomi adored Abby's ability to be unabashedly confident in who she was, but it could sometimes catch newcomers off guard.

This guy didn't bat an eye, though. "Having one myself, I can honestly say I don't blame you." He chuckled.

"I like you," Abby said. "Why weren't we friends in high school?"

"Oh, I didn't go here. I'm a guest. My name is Will, by the way." He extended a hand.

"Abby." She took it and they shook.

He nodded, and then his eyes fell on Naomi. "And you are?" His smile, an amused smirk, warmed to something a little richer. The flutter in her stomach went from a butterfly wing's soft flap to a hummingbird's buzz.

"Naomi," she said. He offered his hand and she took it. She felt a rush of heat at his touch and looked down to ensure that her olive skin hadn't turned bright red.

"And what brings you here?" The space between his eyebrows cinched together slightly, and he let go of her hand. "I mean, besides the reunion. Obviously. And the drinks. You're in line for a drink, clearly. God, for a journalist, I'm not very good at asking questions." The awkwardness was unexpected. And adorable.

"You're a journalist?" she asked.

He nodded. He may have released her hand, but his eyes continued to hold on to hers. "Associate producer, technically. Right now. I assist the real journalists with everything they need to put their story together. It's not particularly exciting."

"Really? I think it sounds incredibly exciting."

"I mean, I love what I do. Sometimes, it involves traveling to exotic places, meeting celebrities, or working on breaking news stories. But that's one percent of the job, and the other ninety-nine percent involves researching, editing, making phone calls, and sitting in meetings. That kind of thing. And then there's no guarantee that all that work will amount to anything. I've put months into stories that have ended up shelved because of a lead that fell through or because the studio didn't like the direction it was going. As I said, not super exciting. Like this very long explanation you didn't ask for."

Naomi offered a reassuring grin. "It's interesting to me, at least. I don't know anyone working in journalism, so this is all new to me. You said studio—does that mean you work for a television station?"

He nodded. "Nightly Global News on the WNO network. Not sure if you know it?"

Of course, she knew it.

She knew it quite well for three reasons.

One—even though she, like most people her age, did not get most of her news from TV, it was one of the most famous news programs on one of the most famous television channels in the United States.

Two—the WNO television studio was located in Chicago, two blocks from her office, and as she passed it every morning on her walk from the El.

And three—it was where Freya worked.

"I'm familiar," she said as noncommittally as possible, a sudden squeak in her voice.

"Yeah. My boss is here to receive some alumni award, actually." He scanned the room with his eyes as if trying to find her in the crowd. "We have to catch a flight tonight for an interview in London. She wasn't going to come originally, but I convinced her it would be good for her to at least stop by and see some old friends. She works a lot. Too much, really, so I try to help her have a little fun now and then, too. All part of the job, I guess."

Naomi gave a surreptitious glance in Abby's direction. She expected Abby to have some retort about Freya at the ready, but instead, she only had a placid, unreadable smile on her face, like a store mannequin on display in the window. Or maybe she got interrupted before she could say anything because at that moment someone—was that Dana? Daniella?—a person possibly with a D name Naomi vaguely recognized walked up to Abby.

"Abigail Channing, my yearbook compatriot. How are you?"

"Devan Landry!" Abby said without hesitation. "You were the only one who appreciated my layouts."

Right, Devan! Naomi hadn't been on the yearbook committee, but she'd heard all the stories from Abby. With all the pranks the two had pulled together, they would have a bit of reminiscing and catching up to do. Naomi had known Devan well enough to join in on their conversation, but in her peripheral vision, she could see that Will's gaze had moved from Devan back to her. And she didn't mind enjoying those eyes on her for a few more minutes.

"I did Mathletes when Abby was in yearbook," she said, facing him again.

"Mathletes!" Will let out a laugh. "That's ..."

"It's okay, you can say it. That's extra nerdy. I also went to math summer camps."

"That's a thing?"

"Yep! And I went every summer, for all four years of high school."

"So let me guess, you became a ... math teacher?"

"I thought about it. But I don't like people enough. I prefer quiet, sensible, and drama-free numbers. Which is why I became an accountant."

"I can't say I've ever heard numbers described as 'drama-free' before."

"Exactly my point. Numbers mind their own business—you don't hear about them. They do their job, and life goes on."

Will seemed to consider this. "Unless you start cooking the books. Then numbers become a problem."

"Sure, but then you're dealing with people again. The numbers aren't lying, the people are."

Will smiled at her, a wide grin that made distracting dimples appear. "You're making me seriously consider a career change."

Naomi wasn't a giggler. She wasn't a hair twirler either, but somehow her mouth let out a titter, and her finger found its way into her dark hair, which she was definitely looping in circles.

The line moved and they took another step forward, placing Will at the front. "Can I buy you a drink in exchange for some more accounting talk?" He flashed his two drink tickets like a magician revealing his cards.

More flutters in her stomach. She hadn't been sure if he had been politely passing the time while they were in line, but now it seemed like this was more than small talk. Like maybe he was feeling something too?

A part of her brain reminded her that the whole thing—having a stranger, who was crashing her high school reunion with his boss / her best friend's high school nemesis, spend a drink ticket on her at a folding table bar —was kind of preposterous. A part of her wanted to thank him politely and send him on his way. But another part of her wasn't ready to end this conversation quite yet. It had been so long since she had felt anything even slightly akin to a flutter that she had started to doubt that she could feel it again. But it turned out she could. And now she wanted to feel it a little bit more.

What the hell.

"Okay," she said.

The pleased look on Will's face brought a smile to her lips.

"What can I get you?" the bartender asked as they approached.

"I'll have ..." Will bent down slightly to read the list of drinks. "The Naughty Narwhal. I take it the Narwhal is your mascot?" he said, turning to Naomi.

"Go Narwhals!" she replied, giving a less-than-enthusiastic fist pump. Then, "A white wine for me, thanks."

Abby was still talking to Devan when the bartender set down her drink. Naomi picked it up and gave Abby a little wave. "I'm going to go right over here." She indicated a general direction with her glass.

Abby paused her conversation long enough to nod. Her eyes flicked ever so briefly to Will, then back to Naomi, seeming to piece the scene together. If Abby had any opinions about her drinking with someone connected to Freya, she wasn't letting on. She *had* said Freya's presence here didn't matter, so maybe she didn't harbor any feelings about Will working with her. After all, Abby wasn't one to mince words—if she had feelings about something, she would usually let someone know pretty quickly. And on the rare occasions that she didn't, Naomi had known her long enough to be able to decipher her expressions.

She stepped away from the bar and motioned to a small, empty spot along the wall next to a blue and white balloon arch.

"How's your Narwhal?" she asked as Will sipped the blue concoction.

His face puckered, and he nodded with tightly pursed lips.

"That good, huh?"

"It's very sweet," he said, inspecting the contents of his plastic cup. "But then, I'm pretty basic when it comes to my drinks. A simple IPA is all I need."

She decided to give him a little test. Again, not that she was remotely in the market to date anyone, but it couldn't hurt to do a little test ... for fun. "My introduction to drinking was Manischewitz wine during the holidays, so my tolerance for sweet drinks is pretty high. You ever had it?"

"My good buddy from college invited me to his house for Passover. That was my first time drinking Manischewitz. This little Midwestern goyim was not prepared for four very full glasses."

Okay, he wasn't Jewish. But he was the kind of goyim who was able to casually throw around the Yiddish term for someone who wasn't Jewish. Not that it mattered. Because she wasn't looking for a relationship. Or a fling. "It's fair to say it's an acquired taste."

There was a sudden flicker of playfulness in his eyes. "It's a taste I'd be open to acquiring."

The flutter in her stomach plunged lower. She hadn't had *that* kind of flutter in even longer.

Naomi had never really had to flirt. She'd married her high school sweetheart and after a tumultuous marriage and an even worse divorce, she hadn't had much interest in seeing what else might be out there for her. Trying to flirt with Will now wasn't like getting on a bicycle again. It was like trying to ride a unicycle for the first time. Through a ring of fire. While juggling kittens.

The wine helped a little. But as it turned out, she didn't need much help. She kept waiting to feel awkward, for uncomfortable silences, but they never came. Instead, the conversation flowed and the distance between them continued to shrink.

"Yeah! If you like the Green Mill, you should definitely check out the Jazz Showcase," Will said, a sheepish look overtaking his face. "Maybe I can take you, sometime?"

He had put a hand in his pocket and when he pulled it out, he held a business card between his fingertips. The first awkward silence passed between them as she looked at the card, unsure what to do. She wanted to say yes and she wanted to say no. She wanted more of what was happening between them, but she didn't want all the things that came with it.

No, she thought. She wasn't ready for anything beyond the safety of flirting under harsh, unforgiving, fluorescent gym lights.

Was she?

A distinct laugh cut through the chatter in the gym, breaking the spell of her indecision.

"I have to admit this isn't far off from how I imagined you'd end up. The sad, lonely drunk at a bar." That voice. It was unmistakable.

Freya Jonsson.

Something else was unmistakable too—the tone of her voice. Naomi had heard it before, many, many times during her high school career. There was only one person she could be talking to.

She turned to face the bar, and there was Abby, her back to Naomi, squaring off with Freya as if it were Freshman year.

"I'm not—" Abby said.

"Let me guess. You live alone. With your cat." It seemed that fifteen years hadn't softened Freya one bit.

Her personality wasn't the only thing that hadn't changed. She looked like a Barbie who had simply switched outfits. She had the same platinum blonde hair, pearly white smile, and perfect milky skin that Naomi remembered from high school. Only now, she was Journalist Barbie in a tailored pinstripe suit with Christian Louboutin heels instead of Cheerleader Barbie in a blue and white uniform with pom poms.

"Yes, but—"

"I knew it!" Freya laughed.

This couldn't have gone worse.

Somehow, those two had not only found each other but had found themselves right back in their teenage feud.

Back in the day, the only thing that would break up their arguments was the period bell. Or Naomi. Unlike Freya's friends, who attended these clashes like ringside seats, Naomi would never get involved but would, gently, guide Abby away. Since no one would be late for any classes, Naomi was probably their only hope for disrupting this age-old dance before it turned into something embarrassing like a school talent show performance gone wrong.

She looked back at Will, who was also watching the situation unfold, his expression an understandable mix of bewilderment and concern. She wondered if she should attempt to give him the Cliff Notes version of what was happening. But when she glanced back at the bar, she could see Abby's shoulders had crept up towards her ears and she decided he would have to wait for answers.

"Sorry," she held up a finger. "Give me one second."

She walked the handful of steps across the gym to the bar.

"Abby?" She put a light hand on her friend's shoulder. Abby turned and Naomi didn't miss the flush in her cheeks and haze across her eyes that suggested she was less than sober. Abby had a nearly full glass of blue liquid in her hand and three matching—and very empty—cups sat on the bar behind her. She and Will had been talking longer than she'd thought. She was going to need to get her friend some water, STAT.

"Oh. My. God." Freya put a hand on her stomach as she laughed. "And there she is, right on cue."

"Hi, Freya," Naomi said in a neutral tone. She wasn't, had never been, intimidated or impressed by the other woman. Her haughty act always felt contrived, like she was putting on a show, one that Naomi wasn't interested in attending.

"Abby," Naomi repeated, giving Abby's shoulder a gentle squeeze. "Can I steal you for a second?"

At the sound of footsteps, Naomi looked over her shoulder to see Will come up beside her, his face maintaining the look of confusion.

"Ah." Freya sighed. "Honestly, this is exactly how I imagined it. You, peaking in high school—if we could even call it peaking—and ending up as an old cat lady who is still obsessed with your 'friend' from high school."

Abby looked back at Freya, her eyes dark. "I am not—"

"Freya, um, I think they're getting ready to start the program," Will said in a hesitant voice that suggested that while he didn't know what was going on, he was gathering that it would be best to help Abby and Freya separate. "Maybe we should head over to the stage."

"Finally," Freya said to Will and then back to Abby. "It's certainly been a pleasure. For me, anyway."

Naomi had to stop herself from making a shooing motion with her hands. *Off you go*, she wanted to say. Maybe she should have. Maybe she could have stopped Freya from tossing in one last dig.

"See you at the next one, then? I seriously can't wait." The derision in her voice was unmistakable.

Naomi saw it out of the corner of her eye. A single flick of the wrist. And then a splatter of blue liquid from Abby's cup flew directly onto Freya's very expensive-looking suit.

"*Ohhh*," Naomi said as droplets of blue rolled down Freya's jacket. She covered her mouth to hide both her astonishment and her amusement. Freya had clearly come looking for a fight. And though she'd gotten one, Naomi couldn't think of a time she had seen Freya clearly speechless.

Before Naomi could decide what to do, Abby let out a single, braying laugh.

Freya found her words. "Really?"

Abby's laugh grew louder until she was nearly howling.

It was becoming clear to Naomi that she didn't need to get Abby some water; she needed to get Abby out of here. Which was for the best anyway. She'd already made things weird with Will when she didn't take his card, and she couldn't imagine it getting any better after all this. A swift exit now would allow them both to fondly remember their brief, magical encounter together.

She put her hand back on Abby's shoulder. "I think we're going to, um, head out now; come on, Abby. Let's go this way."

Abby, still cackling, let Naomi lead her towards the exit. "Don't be mad, Naomi." Her words had a definitive slur around the edges. "You can't be mad. I had to. I finally got to show everyone that *I* am the one who will get the last word. Sorry, Principal Baxter, no detentions today! By the way, I kind of had a lot to drink."

"I noticed," Naomi replied, gently.

"I don't know what happened. I was talking to that cute bartender, and she was making me these tequila cocktails." Abby gripped her arm and said softly, "I think I had like four."

"Well, then I believe we know exactly what happened," Naomi said in a motherly tone. "You had four drinks. On an empty stomach." Naomi fished her phone from her purse and requested a ride.

"I've made better decisions in my life."

"You have."

"But the bartender was, like, so hot, Naomi. How could I say no to her and her southern accent and her tattoos? And then suddenly ... boom ...

Freya." They had reached the doors to the school and stepped out into the thick Chicago summer night air.

"Yeah," Naomi said. "And then suddenly ... *boom* ... a drink in Freya's face."

"I can't believe I did that." Abby cackled.

"It's definitely not how I pictured things going," Naomi said.

"Hey, remember when I said you shouldn't be mad at me?"

"I do."

"I give you permission to be, like, a little mad at me. I kind of ruined the reunion."

"It was time to get going anyway. But it's definitely a night I'll never forget." Of course, there was Freya. But also Will. It was truly *Some Enchanted Evening,* and she had met a stranger across a crowded room. And their brief meet-cute encounter had showed her that maybe there was a chance for love again someday. Maybe she would let Abby talk her into downloading another dating app sometime. Maybe she was ready to try again.

Their car pulled up and they both got in. As the car began to drive, Abby leaned against the window. As the minutes dragged on, the silence began to weigh on Naomi. She needed to tell someone what had transpired. And there was only one person who would truly understand.

She pulled out her phone.

NAOMI: O.M.F.G.

RILEY: Here's my cup. Pour me some tea.

NAOMI: Literally everything has gone sideways. I flirted with someone. Abby threw a drink on Freya. Now she's very drunk in the car ride home.

RILEY: Ok - listen. You cannot TLDR something like this. I need you to start AT. THE.BEGINNING. and give me all the details.

"Naomi," Abby said, dropping her head onto Naomi's shoulder. "I'm beginning to suspect this wasn't my finest hour."

"At least it will make for a good story."

"No," Abby said, drawing out the vowel. "It's a bad story. Very bad, embarrassing story. You can't tell anyone. Promise you won't tell anyone."

"Ummm ..." Naomi looked down at her phone.

"This one goes in the vault," Abby said.

NAOMI: *I've been sworn to secrecy. You'll have to live off the crumbs I've given you. And don't say a word to Abby!*

"Okay," Naomi said. "Into the vault it goes."

Chapter Two

Will

"Napkin, honey?"

Will, who had been watching Naomi lead her friend out of the gym, looked at the pile of napkins the bartender was holding out to Freya. By the time he glanced back again, Naomi had vanished, leaving only the swinging double doors of the gym as evidence that she had been there.

Should he follow her? Or should he stay here with Freya?

The internal debate was so heated that he felt like he was going to break out into a sweat. Although it was also getting a little warm in the crowded gym.

He certainly hadn't planned on meeting anyone at his boss's high school reunion. In fact, he hadn't even planned on coming in. He'd intended to wait in the car and clear out his active volcano of an inbox. But at the last second, Freya had suggested he accompany her.

"I feel bad enough dragging you to this," she had said. "At least come in and use my drink tickets."

Standing in the corner of someone else's high school reunion didn't exactly top his list of fun ways to spend an evening. But he didn't want Freya to waste her few precious moments not working, being worried about him. So, he'd agreed.

It wouldn't be all bad, he had told himself. After all, he was curious to get an opportunity to see another side of Freya, to learn about her life outside of Nightly Global News, and maybe even get a glimpse into what she had been like in high school.

Will had been an Associate Producer with Nightly Global News for a little over three years, and most of it had been spent with Freya. According to the job description, he was supposed to rotate working with the NGN correspondents, but after his first story with Freya, he never left her side. It wasn't intentional, more of a natural progression as he consistently volunteered for her segments, and she constantly requested his assistance. Eventually, it became an unspoken expectation within the newsroom that Will and Freya were a package deal until last year, when it became part of his contract.

Freya fascinated him. She approached the world and people in a way he had never seen before. At first, he thought that was because he was a farm boy from Indiana who didn't know much about big media personalities, but over the years, he came to understand it had nothing to do with him and everything to do with her. She was razor sharp and laser-focused. She could spend three days reading through hundreds of pages of police records to find that one missing piece of information everyone else had missed as easily as she could sit across from the most prepped and lawyered-up celebrity and still get them to share their darkest secrets. He had made *her* his job, as much as his actual job. It had become a sort of game for him, trying to learn what made her tick and how he could keep all the cogs moving so that she could get her work done. And he considered himself pretty good at it.

But who Freya was *outside* the role of Senior Correspondent for Nightly Global News, now that was an entirely different story. He thought he got glimpses of what else lay behind those arctic blue eyes on occasion, but he was never quite sure because she was as good at hiding her personal life as she was exposing others'. What she thought or felt, beyond the scope of her professional life, was almost never expressed, no matter how hard he tried to get a peek behind the curtain. So, the opportunity to possibly see another facet of Freya was too good an opportunity to pass up.

Except not even a million AI simulations could have guessed what he had seen. Not that he had seen much. Only a few seconds. But the fire in Freya's eyes was undeniable. Not only her eyes, her entire demeanor had been engulfed in flames like a meteor hurtling towards earth. This was a woman who had listened to a serial killer detail his gruesome crimes without remorse and had barely blinked. What could Abby have done to elicit such a reaction? And, equally, what could Freya possibly have done to incite Abby to throw a drink at her? Freya could be difficult at times, but she would certainly never do anything to risk an errant tweet or TikTok about her. What could have happened?

It seemed like Naomi knew. The way her head had turned when she heard Freya laugh, the determination with which she walked over to them, and the familiarity in how she handled extricating her friend only added to the puzzle he couldn't quite solve. He wanted to ask her to put the pieces together. Truthfully, he wanted to ask her a lot of things. Like had she planned to take his card before they got interrupted? Could they go to that jazz show sometime? Could she explain how she absolutely knocked the wind out of him when he turned around and saw her for the first time?

But she had left, never once pausing to look back.

Naomi was witty and funny and gorgeous and in only a few minutes had left him wanting to chase after her. He continued to consider it as he stared at the gymnasium doors, still swinging in her wake. But the seconds dragged on, and so did the reasons why he shouldn't. Chasing down a woman he hardly knew was only romantic in the movies—in real life, it was plain creepy. Besides, he was here in a professional capacity. He wasn't necessarily on the job at this moment, but he would be shortly, and, in the meantime, he was with his boss at *her* reunion. The same boss who was standing across from him, soaked in cheap, blue booze for reasons of which he still wasn't entirely sure.

The right thing to do, he decided, was to stay with Freya. He would make sure she was okay and then later he could figure out if there was anything he could do about the Naomi situation. Maybe there was a non-creepy way to find her. Or maybe even Freya could introduce them.

He took the napkins from the bartender. "Here, let me," he said, turning to Freya. He looked again at the mess and realized he wasn't sure what to do with the napkins. Wiping off liquor of the front of your boss' suit hadn't been covered in their HR training on the rules of touch at work. Also, while he considered himself close to Freya, he could count the number of times they had had any form of physical contact on one hand, and most of those were accidents.

He took the stack of napkins and patted uncomfortably at her arm.

He was grateful when Freya took the stack from him. "I'm fine; it's just a drink," she said, picking up where Will had left off. "I'm pretty sure cleaning drinks off my clothes was not in your job description."

Will shifted uncomfortably, trying to decide the best course of action. Freya wasn't a big fan of having people care for her. He usually had to do it surreptitiously, by finding little ways to help her that didn't look like that was what he was doing. Like today, for instance, when she was looking particularly tired and he went to "get himself" coffee as a pretense to buy one for her too. Or last week, when she commented that her back was hurting after a long day at the computer, and he ordered her a lumbar support pillow and told her that the station had sent out ergonomic supplies to all their shows. Or three years ago, when he figured out that June fourteenth was her birthday but also National Bourbon Day, which happened to be her favorite drink, and had since made a point to give her a bottle of bourbon as a birthday gift disguised as a silly holiday gift.

He considered himself fairly adept at reading her, even when she didn't have much to say—which was often—but in this moment, he couldn't glean anything from the tone of her voice or her expression. Was she hurt or angry? Embarrassed? Did she need a minute alone? Did she need someone to help her laugh it off?

She disliked being asked those kinds of questions even more than she enjoyed being cared for. But he felt like he had to go for it. So, he did. "Are you ... okay?"

"Yep." She kept her eyes on her task, but the slight tinge of annoyance in her words was the first indication of how she was feeling. Still, she kept things light. "Good thing I wore black, huh?"

"It's just ..."

She cut her eyes to him for a moment. "It's *only* a drink, Will. I'll be fine."

"I think what your friend here is trying to say is, we're all dying to know what just happened," the bartender said, the New Orleans accent drawing out each word. When Freya looked up at her, she lifted her hands innocently. "Now, I know it's none of my business. But I work a lot of these reunion-type events and that was a first for me."

"You're right. It is none of your business," Freya snapped.

Will's eyes widened in astonishment. Freya could get testy, but she never snapped. Even she seemed taken aback by her reaction, and she cleared her throat before saying in a much friendlier, much more *Freya* way, "To be honest, you know about as much as I do. Um, what was your name again?"

"Caroline, but Lena is fine."

"Lena. Thanks for the napkins, by the way." Freya's body language and tone had completely shifted now, and she smiled at Lena. "I think I was able to get most of it off me before it soaked into my jacket too much. As I was saying, I wish I had more to tell you. I came over here to get a drink, we exchanged a few words, and then ..." Freya set down the napkins on the bar with finality.

"Oh, I get it." Lena threw the napkins away. "You two dated or somethin'? Bad breakup?"

Will remained still, like a hunter trying not to spook a deer. Lena was asking questions no one at Nightly Global News would dare ask, not even him. Freya's private life was strictly off limits. Could this nosy but disarming bartender get something out of her?

"No, Abby and I didn't date. There's no history." No dice. *Nice try, Lena.*

"Oh, these two have history," someone said behind him.

Then someone else added, "Can you say, 9021-oh my God, drama?"

Will turned to see two women walking towards them, blond ponytails poised high on the top of their heads and swishing like excited cat tails with each step. Freya must have known them because her lips pulled into a smile, and she gasped, but they seemed oddly disinterested in her. Instead, they walked past Freya and set up camp directly between him and Lena.

The first woman, whose nametag read, "Hi, my name is: Penny Davis," waved them closer with her finger. "Listen, you want the *goss*?" He did, in fact, want the goss. He couldn't help it. This felt like a once-in-a-lifetime opportunity that he couldn't miss, and he leaned in.

"It's simple," the other woman, Ashley Brown, according to her nametag, said. "In high school, Freya here was a queen. And little Abby over there was jealous. It was so obvious she wanted to be popular."

"Exactly," Penny said.

Ashley made sure Will and Lena were paying attention before she continued. "She reminds me of those yappy little chihuahuas that always bark at the bigger dogs."

"Oh my God, exactly. And Naomi was always hanging on to her like a bad case of fleas. The whole thing was bizarre."

Will involuntarily pulled back. A bad case of fleas? He couldn't claim to know Naomi very well, or at all, really, but that portrayal of her caught him off guard. Then again, he told himself, Ashley and Penny did seem to enjoy the hyperbolic side of life.

"Yeah, it was so sad. But also kind of entertaining. Like four years of binge-watchable, so-pitiful-you-can't-look-away, d-r-a-m-a." Ashley looked to Penny for confirmation. "Pen, stop me if I'm wrong."

Penny shook her head. "Nope. Can confirm that is one hundred percent accurate."

Freya laughed, but something about it told Will that she wasn't enjoying their little performance as much as she was letting on. "Will, meet Penny and Ashley. My absolute best friends from school who know a little something about drama themselves. You two haven't changed a bit, have you?"

"Not where it counts!" Ashley said. "We're as pretty and as catty as we were freshman year."

"If I had a drink, I'd cheers to that. But I got interrupted," Freya said.

Penny gave a very serious nod. "Oh, we know."

Ashley placed a hand on Penny's shoulder. "Why do you think we made a beeline over here? Not that we weren't excited to see you anyway. But that kind of upped our timeline for coming over here."

"You saw it?" Freya asked.

The solemnity in their eyes was gone, replaced by scandal-hungry eyes. "Are you kidding?" Penny said. "Abby drink-slapped you. Everyone saw it."

"*Everyone,*" Ashley said.

"I wish I could say I was shocked. But I'm not," Penny's attention was back on giving Will and Lena the *goss*.

"No, not in the slightest," Ashley confirmed, even though no one had asked. "If I were on the reunion committee, I can tell you I would have lost her invitation, that's for sure. It seemed inevitable that she was going to do something to try to ruin this for you."

The bartender let out a high-pitched *phew.* "Guess I dodged a bullet then, as I was about to give her my number."

Will looked at the bartender, grateful he wasn't the only one finding himself in this situation. "I was about to give my number to Abby's friend. Things went, um, south before we could."

"Okay, what?" Ashley said.

"Um, no." Penny aimed her finger first at Lena and then turned to Will. "And no."

"No?" Will echoed, feeling a little more deflated each time the duo took another shot at Naomi. He would probably never see her again, but it would be nice if she could at least remain a happy memory.

"Weren't you listening? Yappy chihuahua's fleas? *That's* Naomi," Ashley said.

"I'm sure Naomi is a perfectly nice human being," Penny said. "But if she's stayed friends with Abby all these years, imagine what kind of Stockholm Syndrome she must be living with."

"Wait a minute." Ashley's eyes grew as wide as an anime character's. "If you were going to get Naomi's number, then that means you and Freya aren't here together."

There was nothing between him and Freya, never had been and never would be. She was a superior, a colleague, a mentor, a friend. Freya didn't even seem like she had the time or inclination for romantic relationships, and his respect was too intertwined with a healthy dose of fear to make room for any attraction. But he didn't want any of that well-defined boundary to be spoiled by insinuations that could plant seeds of concern in Freya's mind. The sudden rush of discomfort forced the words out of his mouth too quickly. "Us? No, no, no." He knew as soon as he said it that he had made a rookie mistake. Ashley and Penny's pupils dilated to saucers, thinking they were on the trail of some more *goss*.

He knew better than that. When it came to people's perceptions, vehement denial was as good as an admission. The best thing to do was to answer a question with a question.

Freya, of course, didn't miss a beat. Before they could get a word in, she laughed and said, "You think I'd bring a date in a T-shirt?"

He knew what she was doing. She was matching Mean Girl for Mean Girl. Setting herself up as the meanest of all. But Penny and Ashley couldn't see the wires behind the illusion. His graphic tees, in this case an image of the Dunder Mifflin logo from *The Office,* were an ongoing joke between them. In the early days, she had side-eyed his laid-back style, a direct contrast to her flawlessly curated appearance. She probably still didn't love it, but somewhere along the way, her disapproval had softened into amusement and teasing. And so, he kept collecting shirts, but now each one was carefully placed in the hopes that they might earn a reluctant smile.

Either way, her plan had worked. Ashley and Penny tried to laugh off their mistake like it had all been a joke.

"No, of course not," Penny said.

Now that she had them off balance, Freya set about putting the record straight. "Will is my Associate Producer. We're heading out to London tonight for the G7 Summit right after I accept this award. He offered to wait in the car, but I said he should come in and have a few drinks."

For the first time, Penny and Ashley had nothing to say.

"Speaking of the award." Freya reached into her purse. "I need to head over to the stage. But it was a highlight to see you both. We should catch up soon! Lena, it was wonderful meeting you." Her hand came out of her purse with a bill folded between her fingers, which she tucked into Lena's palm. Then, without another word, she turned and began walking away. Will followed after her, but behind them, he could still hear Lena.

"Did you mean to—ma'am, this is a hundred dollars."

Of course, she'd meant to. She was always one step ahead of the story. She was counting on recency bias to change the narrative around what had transpired when Lena, Penny, and Ashley told their friends what had happened. Gregarious and generous, Freya Jonsson was the type of person who tipped a bartender at her reunion one hundred dollars. That's what they'd remember. The drink incident would only be folded in as part of the story, rather than the main attraction.

Freya didn't stop, didn't respond. She only gave a *toodle-oo* wave of her fingers. Will had to make full use of his long legs to keep up with Freya. "Your friends seemed ..." He wanted to say something kind but was having trouble finding anything genuine. "Nice." The way he said it almost came out like a question.

"They were right about one thing: they haven't changed one iota. They're still as shallow as a kiddie pool."

"I mean, they're your friends, so I wasn't going to say it, but ... yeah. I mean, who says 'the goss?'"

She gave him the first genuine smile he'd seen from her all night. "They were good friends to have in high school."

If all those things were true, then maybe everything they said about Naomi wasn't. Maybe there was still a chance. "You think they were right about Naomi too? She seemed pretty ... amazing."

Freya didn't even look at him. "I don't know," she said brusquely. "But it's too late now anyway, isn't it?"

His sigh was silent, but deep. She was right. It was too late. Which was probably for the best. Dating the best friend of Freya's high school nemesis probably wasn't going to end well. Still, he couldn't help but feel a little crestfallen. "Yeah, I guess so. It's too bad. She seemed like something special."

Chapter Three

Naomi

A voice ripped Naomi out of a deep Saturday morning slumber. "You told them."

She let out an involuntary squawk. Even with her eyes closed and her brain barely awake, she knew the person in her room was Abby. She and Abby lived down the hall from each other and had been each other's emergency keyholders since first grade, when they exchanged spare keys to their diaries. Which is why it wasn't unfathomable that Abby was in her apartment. But there appeared to be no screaming, no sirens, no smoke ... nothing urgent that would constitute this rude awakening.

Clutching her sheets, she rolled enough to be able to see out from under her arm. Abby stood in her bedroom doorway, hands on her hips, looking like she was the lone survivor in a horror film. She was still in her dress from last night, only now, it hung in a haphazard, tangled mess, much like the remnants of her messy bun.

Directly behind her stood Riley Tahara, their already strikingly tall and slim frame amplified by an all-black ensemble of skinny jeans, a fitted black shirt, and high-heeled boots. Their thick, wavy hair, dyed a frosty blue, brushed up against their flawless, flaxen skin, which was uncharacteristically lined with distress. Light distress, but distress nonetheless.

"What is happening right now?" Naomi asked. Given that she had texted Riley only moments after Abby threw a drink on Freya, she was pretty sure she knew exactly what was happening. But she was hoping there was a chance she was wrong. Or that she could at least buy herself enough time to wake up so she could defend herself properly.

Abby indicated behind her with a slight nod in Riley's direction. "Riley broke into my apartment and woke me up in the middle of an ungodly hangover sleep because of you. So, now you are facing the consequences."

Riley gasped like a maiden whose honor had been besmirched. "I did *not* break in."

"Did I invite you in?" Abby asked, looking behind her.

"What am I, a vampire?" Riley asked. "Besides, you gave me keys. I assumed that was an invitation."

Abby's eyes rolled so hard Naomi thought she was going to get vertigo. "I gave you my key last week because Naomi and I were both out of town, and I needed you to feed the cat."

"Yes, and I made a copy then. You know, for emergencies."

"Please," Abby gestured towards Naomi. "Enlighten Naomi as to what the *emergency* was that brought you into my apartment at 6:58 a.m. On a Saturday."

"I never got to say what it was because you were busy jumping to conclusions about God knows what."

"I know what," Abby said. So did Naomi. But who was going to be the first to say it?

Riley continued, unperturbed by Abby's interruption. "As I was *saying,* I needed to tell you I'm in love. It happened last night. I stayed late at work doing some last-minute fittings for a Fassi runway show we're doing next week. And then I stayed even later doing ... was it Ethan? No, Evan. Well, whatever his name was, he was a Greek god, wrapped in a Roman god, smothered in the nectar of the gods." Riley worked for Fassi, a large clothing chain store, but the way they talked about their job sometimes, it seemed like they spent more time with the models than they did with the clothes.

Abby spun to face them. The movement was probably supposed to be a dramatic, TV-courtroom-lawyer, *gotcha* sort of spin, but she lost any authority when she wobbled so hard she nearly fell over. Naomi guessed that, given the night Abby had had, she was either ridiculously hungover or possibly even still a little drunk. "That was last week, and his name was Eric."

"I mean, fine," Riley said, finally cracking. They muttered softly, "Maybe I also wanted to hear more about how you *Real Housewife*'d a star."

"Like I said," Abby said, returning her accusatory glare to Naomi. "You told them."

Naomi pulled herself up to seated, keeping the sheet tightly wrapped around her—more for a sense of protection than propriety. The urge to confess was becoming untenable. She was a terrible liar, but she loved tuning into the Abby and Riley show.

The origin story of this trio of friends hinged on Abigail. Abby had become friends with Riley first, during college. But it hadn't taken long for Naomi and Riley to meet and for the three of them to become inseparable. Still, Abby and Riley had a dynamic that was their own and part of what Naomi loved about their little threesome was watching their fast-paced and sometimes utterly ridiculous repartee.

In an effort to hold out a little longer, Naomi bit down on the tip of her tongue, a habit she had forced herself to learn sometime in the sixth grade after she finally figured out that her parents were not actually psychic but were picking up on the fact that she unconsciously nibbled on her lips anytime she tried to withhold any information. She trained herself to bite her tongue instead, and by the time she was in seventh grade, she had mastered her new lip-nibbling-prevention skill well enough to see not one, but two R-rated movies. Unfortunately, there was one person who knew her too well.

"I see it, Naomi! I see you biting your tongue. The jig is up. Admit you told Riley."

Naomi released her tongue. It was no use. "Riley!" she moaned. "You swore you wouldn't say anything!"

"I didn't!" Riley said. "I showed up with coffee. I handed Abby the coffee. Literally the most innocent and friendly thing a person can do."

"So," Abby said to Naomi. "Let me get this straight. You're yelling at Riley for not keeping a secret when you swore to me last night you wouldn't tell a soul?"

"Says the woman who used her spare keys to break into my apartment because she's mad that Riley used theirs to break into hers." Naomi was really struggling to keep a smile off her face.

Now it was Riley's turn for the dramatic courtroom gotcha. This one came without any wobbling and ended with an equally dramatic finger point at Abby. "Ah ha! J'accuse!"

Naomi's smile was starting to turn into laughter and there was nothing she could do about it. "I'm sorry, okay? But I had to tell someone. It was killing me!"

"Laughing while you apologize is not super convincing." Abby pouted.

Resigned to the fact that she wasn't going to get back to sleep, she decided to accept her penance. "It's hard to do anything properly without coffee. Can I please go make some before we continue this?"

"Yes. Please go make some." Abby put such emphasis on 'please' that it sounded more like she was begging than giving permission.

"Oh no, you don't," Riley said. "No more delays. There is perfectly good coffee in Abby's apartment that I brought specifically to facilitate this conversation. Naomi, you can have mine. Now let's get a move on."

Even though Abby's apartment was mere steps from hers, that was still a few more steps than she wanted to take this early in the morning. She did her best to give Riley the evil eye as she walked past them, but Riley was entirely unmoved. This was in part because she was a foot shorter than them and she became significantly less intimidating when she had to practically put her head between her shoulder blades to glare at them.

"Come on now, chop chop," Riley said, clapping their hands like a farmer directing sheep to the pen.

Seconds after she was prodded out of her apartment, the door next to hers squeaked open and a single, scowling eye peered out. It was the signature look for Mrs. Pachenkis, her seventy-eight-year-old neighbor who had lived in this building long before, as she had growled at them on multiple occasions, "You yuppies came in and made my rent go up." It didn't seem like Mrs. Pachenkis had any friends or family, only pets, including a very talkative parrot and a pair of cats that made a habit of bolting out when she was glaring at her neighbors from the crack in her door. Naomi had tried to befriend Mrs. Pachenkis over the years, but her gestures had been vehemently rebuffed.

Now she simply did her best not to give Mrs. Pachenkis any reasons to complain to the building manager. At the moment, the extreme tilt of Mrs. Pachenkis' brow suggested that Naomi had failed this morning, and when she looked down, she realized why. In Riley's haste to get them out the door, Naomi hadn't even changed out of her oversized T-shirt that almost, but not quite, made it to her thighs. She debated going back and changing, but by that time, she was out of Mrs. Pachenkis' view and nearly at Abby's door. She'd need to borrow pants from Abby for the walk back.

Naomi had barely touched the mezuzah on Abby's door frame before Riley was interrogating them.

"Story. Now," they said.

Borrowing some inspiration from Mrs. Pachenkis, she gave Riley the best eyebrow raise she could muster.

Riley met her look with one of confusion and offense. "What?"

She settled into the sofa, covering her legs with a blanket. "You are in so much trouble. This doesn't seem like appropriate behavior on Shabbat." Naomi was the daughter of an Israeli Jew who had fallen in love with an American Jew studying abroad in Israel and, after a whirlwind romance, had followed her back to Chicago.

Her family was both as devout and as liberal as the Venn diagram would allow. For her, that meant she was fully steeped in the traditions of the Jewish faith but was also given permission to live life, and Judaism, in whatever way was right for her. What had grown out of that was a deep, abiding love for Judaism and the intricate tapestry of history and culture that provided community, guidance, and grounding in all areas of her life. And like a beautiful tapestry, her Judaism was not rigid, but soft and flowing and able to change with the needs of the moment. Which meant that sometimes she would honor Shabbat by going to temple, sometimes she would only light candles at home, and sometimes, she would use Shabbat as a way to get out of trouble.

Unfortunately, once again, Abby knew her too well to let her get away with that. "You're right. Which is why you were home lighting candles instead of out drinking and cavorting last night."

"Cavorting!" She had forgotten about her brief encounter with Will until right now. She was not expecting that same flutter to tickle her as the memories queued up of his funny banter, his engaging smile, his gentle brown eyes, his very ... inviting ... lips.

"Spoilers!" Riley's voice brought her back to the present. "You have to start at the beginning,"

Abby scoffed and wordlessly walked down the short hallway in her apartment to the next room. Abby's apartment was identical to Naomi's, with the living room, bedroom, bathroom, and kitchen all connected by a single hallway.

Riley took a seat next to Naomi, clearly settling in for story time, and Abby's cat, Lancelot, made a beeline for the couch, his eyes set on Riley's lap.

"No, no, Lancelot," Riley said, scooting back as Lancelot leapt onto the armrest. "I hate to rain on your parade, good looking, but I'm in all black and you're in all silver and never the twain shall meet."

Abby reappeared holding two cups of coffee. "Are you tormenting Riley again?" she said to Lancelot as she leaned over Riley to hand Naomi one of the cups. Naomi could tell from the absence of any heat on her hand that drinking the tepid coffee was going to be a willful act of necessity and not one of pleasure.

Naomi tried to get Lancelot's attention. "Here, Lancey, come snuggle with me." When that didn't work, she picked him up and set him directly in her lap. He seemed to consider his options before padding in a circle and lying down.

"Enough distractions!" Riley, now safe from the dangers of cat hair, was back on task. "I'm ready. Fill me in."

Abby sighed and began. "Freya emerged from the depths of the netherworld and started doing that thing, that same goddamn thing she did in high school, where she picks apart and belittles my entire life. And I was a few drinks in."

Naomi was compelled to interject. "A few? I believe you told me you were four, *tequila* drinks in."

"Oh, sweetie," Riley said. "You've never been able to handle your tequila."

"I'm aware." Abby rubbed her temples for emphasis. "So yes, my tequila-soaked brain made a decision. A less-than-stellar decision. A decision I'm comfortable putting away in a vault and not talking about ever again. But if we're locking it all in a vault, then I get to add how amazing it was, that after all these years, I finally, *finally* got to put Freya in her place. For the first time in my life, I left her speechless. It felt so good. And now we close the vault door forever."

"You may think it was a less-than-stellar decision, but you can sleep soundly knowing that you have made many seasons of reality television stars very proud. And now that I am comfortably sated in my need for gossip, I decree it is time to go shopping."

Although she didn't have her phone with her, Naomi had spied the "100+ messages" notification from her work e-mail app as she was dragged out of bed. "I really need to work today," she said.

"On a Saturday? What kind of totalitarian regime do you work for?"

"An accounting firm that is in the middle of the busy season."

"Naomi," Riley said with solemnity. "The three of us—we've gone through something big together. Fingers were pointed, and lies were stripped away. Now we need to heal together. And there's no better way to heal than through shopping."

"I really should—"

"Excellent! I'm glad we're agreed on that."

It wasn't that she couldn't say no. It was that she didn't want to—and Riley knew that. She was on the tail end of fiscal year audits for a number of her company's biggest clients and had been working until the wee hours of the morning every day for weeks. Being at the reunion last night, however fleeting, had given her a taste of freedom, and she craved another helping. She'd pay for her rebellion with some even later nights to make up for the missed hours, but for now, she would let Riley talk her into playing hooky for a few more hours.

"I'm sorry, do I not get a say in this shopping trip?" Abby said. "I could have plans. Or work."

"Abigail Meyer," Riley replied. "I know you well enough to know you would never book clients during the sacred hours reserved for hangovers and the walk of shame. Besides, I peeped your calendar when I met you at your office for lunch yesterday, so I know you've got nothing planned."

After some more coffee, cajoling and, finally, a cab ride, the three friends were at their destination. Or perhaps more accurately, at Riley's destination. The small, treelined street of boutique shops was one of their favorite spots for one-of-a-kind fashion—the only kind Riley would be seen in. While Naomi didn't have the same predilection for eye-catching outfits, shopping trips with Riley gave her a chance to browse and occasionally indulge in a piece if something caught her eye.

As she and Abby were perusing jewelry and Riley was somewhere ensconced in an aisle of skirts, a jaunty piano rendition of "Poor Unfortunate Souls" started emanating from Abby's purse. Having been the one to suggest that ringtone, Naomi knew that it meant an incoming call from Abby's younger sister, Rebecca Rhein. Six years their junior, Naomi had known Becca since she had been born and loved her like the annoying little sister that she was.

Abby took her phone from her bag and answered it with a brisk, "Hello?" There must have been no answer because she said it again, this time more sharply. "Hello?" After another few seconds, she pulled the phone away from her ear and hung up.

"Pocket dial?" Naomi asked. Like Sisyphus, condemned for all eternity to roll a boulder up a hill, Abby had been sentenced to the burden of a life of receiving pocket dials. As someone with a name starting with *A,* she was often the victim of unintentional calls from unlocked phones.

The phone began to ring again. Abby answered Naomi's question by accepting the call and then holding the phone close to Naomi's ear so she could listen. Sure enough, it was the familiar sounds of a pocket dial: indistinguishable, muffled noises of life from behind fabric.

As soon as Abby ended the call, it was ringing again. Abby threw her hands up. "I swear on all that is good and holy."

She stabbed her phone like she was trying to skewer it. Naomi watched as she declined the call and then, like she was playing a reverse Uno card, turned the tables and dialed her sister. Her phone had barely reached her ear before she started talking. "Rebecca, can you please, for the love of God, lock your phone? Or at least, change my name so that I'm not your first contact? You pocket-dialed me again!" Naomi could hear Becca talking but couldn't make out what she was saying. "Yeah, well, do you have any idea how annoying it is to have a seventeen-minute message from the inside of someone's pants?"

Whatever Becca was telling her was causing every muscle in Abby's face to twitch. Abby's expressions were coming too fast for her to try and translate. Naomi's curiosity got the best of her and she mouthed the word "speaker" at Abby.

Abby obliged with a tap on her phone. "—someone getting murdered," Becca was saying. "Or at the very least, someone having sex. Isn't that possibility worth it? It would be worth it to me."

"I accept your apology."

"I am not apologizing for what my phone did without my knowledge. Although this does work out perfectly, since I was planning on calling you anyway."

A look of suspicion drifted across Abby's face. "Where are you? It sounds like you're standing in the middle of a runway."

"I might as well be. I'm over in Bucktown."

"Bucktown? What are you doing there at," she looked at her phone, "10:30 in the morning on a Saturda ... oh, please tell me you weren't doing what I think you were doing."

"Umm ..." came a squeaky reply.

"Becca! You told me you ended it with him! I thought you were going on the straight and narrow!"

From the moment she arrived on the planet, Becca had made it clear that she had a singular goal: to be the star of whatever room she was in.

She loved being the topic of conversation, loved being in front of the camera, loved having all eyes on her, but most of all, she loved being loved by boys. The minute she was able to understand the concept of a boyfriend, she had one. And then another one, and then another one ... until right before she graduated college when she did something entirely unexpected: she got engaged. Quiet, unassuming, and unremarkable, Peter Rhein was not a high school quarterback, a professional kitesurfer, or a NASCAR driver—a mere sampling of some of her previous beaus. He was the CFO of Lynch Mortuary Services, one of the nation's largest funeral home supply companies.

No one knew exactly why she picked Peter. Riley thought it was because of the number of zeroes on his paycheck. Abby thought it was because Becca had wanted someone to take care of her after graduation. But Naomi thought it was because to Peter, Becca was an A-list celebrity. Whatever the reason, everyone, including Naomi, had hoped that she had found her continually running show in Peter. But, the ink on their ketubah had barely dried before she was on to the next program.

"I did! And I was," Becca said. "But then I met Amos. He's a dancer for the Joffrey Ballet. You'd love him, Abby."

"Does the wedding band on your finger mean nothing to you?"

"Sure it does! Just ... not ... all the time."

Riley, who had been gathering clothes on the other side of the store, waved at them. "Ready!" they called, gesturing towards the dressing room.

It was well established that shopping with Riley included serving as Riley's judging panel for potential purchases, and Naomi dutifully headed towards the dressing room.

"Coming!" she heard Abby say.

"Who are you talking to?" Becca asked.

"Riley."

As Naomi entered the dressing room, Riley looked at Naomi. "Who is she talking to?" Riley selected a booth and entered, closing the curtain behind them.

Naomi took a seat on a bench against the opposite wall. "Becca," she said, as Abby took a seat beside her.

"Is that Naomi I hear too? Where are you all?" Becca asked.

"We're in Wicker Park. And you're lucky," Abby said. "If you had woken me up with this news—"

"Wicker Park! That's perfect!"

"Apparently," Naomi said, well accustomed to talking to Riley in between the sisters' banter, "she was out philandering with another one of her—"

"Wait, what's perfect?" Abby said over her.

"You! Being in Wicker Park! Cause I told Peter I was out with you and—"

"You what?!"

Riley held the curtain open enough to peer through and attempt to continue their separate confab with Naomi. "Wait, she was out with another one of her boy toys? I thought she was going to—"

"So did I!" Abby interjected into their conversation. Riley clucked their tongue like a disappointed parent and then disappeared back into the dressing room.

Naomi continued, "From the sounds of it, she's not only back to it, she wants to use us as an alibi."

"What!" Riley practically squawked.

"No! It's not like that," Becca said. "I told Peter I was going to hang out with Abby. I didn't say when or where or how long. So, I want to see you for a few minutes. At least that way I won't be lying. I'd feel so guilty otherwise."

"Your sense of morality is a shining light in this dark world," Abby said, sardonically.

The curtains slid open, and Riley appeared in a pair of neon yellow pants for their first judging session. Naomi wasn't a fan, and she could tell from Abby's face that she wasn't either, but she left it to Abby to find the most Riley-appropriate way to give the thumbs down.

"I don't know," Abby said. "These pants don't say goddess of the sun to me."

Riley looked into the mirror, taking in the feedback. "Hmmm ... goddess of the sun, goddess of the sun ... you're right, I am not a goddess of the sun in these pants." The curtain swung shut again.

Abby looked at her phone, then Naomi, and then muted the call. "I've officially hit that hangover zone where I'm caffeinated, exhausted, hungry, and nauseous at the same time. I literally cannot with her today."

Naomi put her arm around Abby's shoulder to give her friend an empathetic but gentle squeeze. "Then I think it's in your best interest to get some food and give in to your sister. Tell her to join us for some brunch."

Abby gave the kind of exhale that said, "I don't love it, but it's the best solution given the situation." She unmuted the call. "Okay, fine, Becca. We're going to get brunch and you can come."

"Yay!"

"Meet us at Tragically Hip on Milwaukee. From the looks of it," Abby tilted her head to look at the pile of clothing on the floor of Riley's dressing room, "We'll be here for a while. So please ... don't rush." She hung up, adding a groan to round out the image of her misery.

"When Becca gets here," Riley said. "I am going to give her a piece of my mind about this whole affair business. Don't get me wrong, I'm all for a little extramarital excitement, but only when I'm the extra in the marital. Either that girl needs to end it with Peter or get her throuple on, because this sneaking around is ridiculous. And frankly, it's stressing me out, and I am not willing to waste my limited facial elasticity on her."

"I think you telling my sister to have a threesome is not really the best route to take here," Abby said to the dressing room curtain. "How about you let me handle it?"

"You're acting like she would listen to either of you," Naomi said, chuckling.

At this, Abby's chin dropped to her chest. "Touché."

Riley had barely gone through one-third of their clothing selections when Becca arrived, as always, with a flourish. Her sequined top, mini skirt, and high black boots left no room for error, or even, it appeared, breathing. "Oh, you are such a darling, Abigail. What would I do without you?" Her hair, the same glossy russet waves that Abby had, was piled on top of her head in a top knot that bounced as she collapsed onto the bench beside Abby. "What a day it's been! Not quite what I was hoping for so far, but now that I'm here with you, I think it's starting to turn around, don't you?"

Becca lived by the motto *flattery will get you everywhere.* Mostly, she meant it as a directive for people around her. But she also wasn't shy about using it liberally with others because it did tend to get her where she wanted to go.

Like into her sister's good graces.

Naomi could see Abby's edges beginning to soften, even if it was against her will.

Becca noticed too and, apparently considering her mission accomplished, started moving on. "Hello, Naomi!" Naomi waved her fingers hello at Becca and smiled. If the Abby and Riley show was good, the Abby, Riley, and Becca show was even better. "Hello, Riley!"

A buzz from her back pocket pulled her away from the conversation. She considered ignoring it, but then it buzzed a second, third, fourth time in rapid succession. She slipped the phone out, expecting it to be from one of her colleagues giving her a hard time for being offline. But it was from an unknown number. And the first two words made her feel like the air had been sucked out of the room.

UNKNOWN: Hi Kiwi.

She and her ex-husband, Simon, had started dating in high school, then taken a gap year together to live and work in Israel at a small Kibbutz right outside of Tel Aviv. Kiwi had been one of the primary fruits produced on Kibbutz Ein Shalom. She had always enjoyed kiwis, but farming them had turned her preference for the fuzzy fruit into a passion that bordered on obsession. She took every opportunity to eat as much kiwi as possible, never slowing down even after a full year there.

Simon teased her mercilessly for this, nicknaming her Kiwi, a name that stuck long after they left the Kibbutz. He even placed the engagement ring in a hollowed-out kiwi when he proposed to her, the night before they flew home to America.

Hi Kiwi.

Those two words could only have been from Simon.

Except Simon wasn't supposed to be texting her. She had a restraining order against him that laid out quite clearly that he was not allowed to be within 100 yards of her or engage in any form of communication.

But Simon had never liked being told what to do. Not when she told him to take out the garbage, not when she told him to go to couples counseling with her, and not when she told him to please, *please* stop hurting her.

He seemed to take pleasure in finding ways around the restraining order. Mailing letters that didn't identify the sender, writing e-mails from dummy accounts on public Wi-Fi IP addresses, and, like now, sending text messages from unknown numbers.

She forced herself to read.

UNKNOWN NUMBER: Did you go to the reunion last night? I didn't but I kept thinking about it.

Kept thinking about you. Thinking about all the good times back then. Remember when we won that dance contest?

Wish I could have been there and danced with you one more time. I miss you. I know I shouldn't but I do. I know you miss me too.

Three dots flitted across her phone, and then one final message rolled in.

I can see it in your eyes when I watch you.

The words burned into her vision, turning everything else around her into ash.

"You okay?" She heard Abby's voice like she was listening through a can on a string.

Wordlessly, she handed the phone to Abby.

If Abby said anything, Naomi didn't hear it. Distantly, she felt Abby's arm across her shoulders and then the sense of being guided out of the store and onto a bench. As she sat down, the sharpness of the fear that had stabbed at her heart was overtaken by a sadness as dark, deep, and heavy as a black hole.

Simon was a mistake she would never be allowed to forget. Every time she began to feel like her life was her own and happy days were possible, he would resurface to remind her that she would never be free. She might be divorced from Simon, but she could never separate from the consequences of their marriage. Those she would have to carry by herself. Forever.

That thought made tears pour out of her like a torrential downpour. The tears, like Abby's hand rubbing her back, were all too familiar.

After a while, Abby spoke up, "I know 'it's going to be okay' is the worst platitude in these moments, but it really is going to be okay. Not because of him, but because you're not alone. We're all here with you."

The pain in Naomi's chest eased enough that she felt like she could take a deep breath. How did Abby always know what to say? It was like she could hear the megaphone in Naomi's head. This wasn't the first time, either. Abby had been there for her since the beginning, since the first time she shed tears over Simon. Abby was the only one who had made her feel safe, instead of judged.

"Well, I don't know if Becca is ever really here for anything," Abby continued. "But Riley and I are here." She even knew how to make Naomi smile in moments like this.

"Sorry," Naomi said through her tears. "I know I shouldn't let him get to me like this. Especially not after all these years."

"Yes, I definitely think shaming yourself is the right call."

Naomi made a braying sound, a hybrid of crying and laughing. She covered her face, pressing her fingers to her eyes like a tourniquet, trying to stop the tears. "I wasn't expecting it, is all. I haven't heard from him in, what, six months? I had started to think that maybe ..." Maybe he felt like he had punished her enough and was done. Maybe he had finally gotten the help he needed to heal and move on. Maybe, just maybe, some part of him loved her enough to let her go. The Maybes were too painful, eliciting a fresh downpour of tears.

"I know," Abby said. And Naomi knew that she did. She knew all the Maybes that lived in Naomi's heart, and she held space for them, in silence, while Naomi cried.

As the storm inside her began to quiet again, she heard voices behind her.

"So, what happened?" Becca asked.

Abby stood up, presumably to run interference with her sister, and Riley took her place on the bench.

"You doing okay?" they asked. Riley had met her before she married Simon, but several years after the start of her relationship with him, long after she had become too lost in the maze of the relationship to see that there was anything wrong. Riley had been there for her too, in a different way than Abby, because their relationships were different, but had helped her in a way she would never be able to repay.

"I'm better. It caught me off guard."

Riley held out her phone. Naomi had completely forgotten she'd given it to Abby. "I searched the number. It came up right away on one of those text spoofing sites. There's no way to trace it to him."

An involuntary sigh escaped her lips. Naomi had long since given up trying to "trace" him or waste any effort trying to get help from the judicial system. Simon knew how to get around the legalities. Sometimes she wondered if that's the only reason he became an attorney, so that he could learn the laws and make the connections he needed to keep her under his thumb.

Abby growled. "Of course."

Becca appeared at her side. "You know what you need? You need one night of really good sex. After that, you won't even be thinking about this loser; trust me."

"Rebecca," Abby said, moving closer to her sister again. "I think you should—"

"Should what? Stop giving good advice? Please, Abigail, if there's anything I know about, it's boy troubles." She wasn't wrong.

Riley was nodding vigorously. "And don't forget me, I mean, if you think about it." They looked at Abby. "Of the three of us, you're the only one without any boy experience. So really, it seems like Becca and I should take the lead here."

"You know, Riley, you have a point there," Becca said. "The two of us—we're like the dream team of boy advice."

"You're right! We should have a podcast!" Riley said excitedly.

"Yes! Oh my God, people would lose their minds. We could call it, um, Dicks for Days."

"Ooh! Cock O'Clock."

"Why not go simple and just call it Penis, Penis, Penis?"

"Okay, we'll figure out the name later. But regardless," Becca swiveled her head to look back at Naomi. "Naomi, my co-host is correct. The only way to get over a boy is to get under another one. Or at least near one."

All three of them were looking at her now. If Becca's goal had been to distract her with discomfort, it was working. She, unlike Becca and Riley, didn't like being the center of attention. "I ... uh ... I suppose ..."

"Trust me, this is exactly what you need."

That was not what she needed. She needed the opposite. She needed to be alone, with a hot bath, a big mug of tea, and a crime documentary that had at least three spin-off podcasts that she could binge. She didn't need sex.

No, the solution was definitely not to be found in a pair of bright brown eyes and tousled, earthy brown hair and playful dimples and defined arms and warm, comforting voice and ... oh god, was she thinking about Will?

"Uh-oh. I know that look." Leave it to Becca to pick up on that. "You've got someone in mind, don't you, you naughty girl? Who is it?"

"Well." She stopped. This was absurd. She'd talked to him for maybe an hour. She didn't even know his last name—his nametag had only had his first name hastily scribbled across it. It didn't matter if she had someone in mind. The moment had passed. And she had decided she wasn't ready anyway, right? But she knew that Becca, currently watching her like a lioness about to pounce, wouldn't let her go without some kind of an answer. "I met this guy last night ..." she said, as vaguely as possible.

"Freya's minion?" Abby asked, her voice laced with the kind of horror usually reserved for finding a spider in the shower.

So much for being vague. So much for assuming that Abby hadn't noticed she'd hit it off with Will or that she didn't feel some type of way about his connection to Freya.

Becca clapped her hands together. "Perfect! Text him."

Naomi shook her head, ready to put this to rest. "That's the problem. He was reaching into his pocket to give me his card." She didn't really want to go into the whole part where he had actually tried to *hand* her his card and she'd frozen up like a deer in headlights—if the deer had also had a full-blown existential crisis. She could get the job done without going into that insignificant and humiliating little detail. "But that's when, well ..."

She clamped down on her tongue and peeked at Abby. The rest of that story was in the vault. And as tempting as it was to throw Becca off the scent by telling her about Abby's dramatic exit last night, and as likely as it was that Riley would let it slip sooner rather than later, she was going to honor her best friend promise to keep it a secret. She released her tongue from between her teeth and said quickly, "Suffice it to say, things got a little crazy, and I never got his info. All I know is he works with Freya at Nightly Global News."

She internally patted herself on the back for her nice sidestep.

"Freya from Nightly Global News? As in Freya Jonsson?" Becca said, and Naomi's imaginary back pat turned into a face palm. "As in *People*'s Sexiest Woman of the Year? As in the face that has brought many lonely people great happiness in their beds at night?"

"Yes," Riley said, not helping. "As in Abigail's archnemesis."

"She is *not* my archnemesis," Abby said, her tone edged with mild exasperation at the turn the conversation was taking.

"Wait a minute," Becca said. "*That's* the same Freya? The girl from high school she always used to complain about?"

"One and the same!" Riley said.

"You never told me that!" Becca directed her high-pitched accusation at Abby "You never told me that you were friends with a celebrity."

Abby crossed her arms defensively. "That's because I'm not."

"It doesn't matter anyway. Like I told you—no number." Naomi redirected Becca's attention back to her. "I don't even know his last name."

"Naomi, Naomi, let me show you how it's done." Becca took out her phone, presumably to begin some Internet sleuthing. Naomi felt like she should object. But her interest in taking a peek at his Instagram or even LinkedIn outweighed her rational mind. What harm could it do to sate some curiosity and enjoy the view one more time?

"Here we go," Becca said, smiling at her phone. Naomi leaned forward, expecting Becca to turn her phone and put his social media on display. But that's not what happened. Instead, she said, "Nightly Global News, main line," and before Naomi could even process what she meant, Becca initiated a call.

Chapter Four

Will

Will's phone jingled from somewhere underneath a pile of papers on the floor of his hotel. Problem was, he didn't know which pile of papers or even which room. The stacks of documents, ranging from background dossiers on officials to redacted statements from the FBI, reached from his bed to the cramped bathroom.

Last night, after the reunion, he and Freya had boarded an eleven o'clock flight for a brief twenty-four-hour visit to London to sit down for rare interview with Luna Mendez, an elusive environmental activist renowned for her efforts in championing indigenous land rights. Luna's hectic schedule, divided between frontline activism in remote areas and speaking engagements across the globe, made it almost impossible to get an in-person interview with her. But the G7 had presented a narrow window for Freya to capture her invaluable insights. A *very* narrow window that required everything to go as planned. Their overnight flight had landed at 4:00 p.m. on Saturday in London, 10:00 a.m. Chicago time, and they were booked on a return flight the following morning, which would get them back to Chicago Sunday afternoon before the start of a jam-packed week. It wasn't enough time to even get jet lag. It was only enough time to record an interview with Luna and head back to the airport. Will had stayed behind in the hotel to serve as ground control and ensure everything and everyone was where they were supposed to be in order to make this interview happen.

Being anywhere but home on a Saturday was par for the course for Will. He hadn't had a weekend off since he had started working for Nightly Global News. This was, partly, because he loved the work. But, also, because there was so much work to be done. And it didn't help that Freya never, ever, took a day off.

He didn't mind, though. He had started working at Nightly Global News the same day he had moved to Chicago so he hadn't had much time to build a life outside of the office that he could miss.

It also wasn't too far off from the life he'd known growing up on a dairy farm. Cows, like the news, don't take weekends or holidays. They don't even take the night off. Come rain, shine, snowpocalypse, or stomach flu, from early in the morning until late at night, those cows needed to be fed and watered, put out to pasture and brought back, their babies delivered, their health managed, and of course, they needed to be milked. Even though his family lived on the farm, and the barns were mere steps from their house, it hadn't been unusual for him to go a day or two without seeing his father. And while his father had been absent tending to the cows, his mother had been ever present tending to the business side of the farm and their home. If she hadn't been meal prepping for the week or helping him with homework, she'd been on the phone with suppliers or paying bills.

So, for Will, a job that never stopped felt—quite literally—like home.

He followed the music until he spotted some papers that were vibrating and lifted them to reveal his phone. The number on the screen was one he knew—it was the main line for Nightly Global News. It wasn't completely out of the ordinary to be receiving a call from his studio on the weekend. Nightly Global News was, as the name suggested, a nightly program which meant that the studio was staffed seven days a week. What was out of the ordinary was that the *front desk* was calling him. They only called if someone was in the lobby for a meeting or an in-studio interview or if he was having food delivered. For a millisecond, he wondered if he had accidentally ordered food when he fell asleep on his laptop in the airplane.

"This is Will," he said, answering his phone.

"Hi, this is Carli at the front desk, so sorry to bother you," a voice said.

"No problem, what's up?"

There was a pause that lasted a second too long, suggesting a flicker of uncertainty. "I've got someone who called the main line asking for you."

"Me?" Will tried to get his brain to rustle up some guesses as to who might be reaching him through this circuitous route.

"Yes, normally I would have sent them to your office phone voicemail. But they said it was an urgent issue regarding an interview and that they had misplaced your business card, which is why they were contacting the front desk. Do you want to be connected to them, or should I send them to voicemail?"

"No, I'll talk to them." His stomach lurched and he prayed this didn't have something to do with Luna's interview.

"One moment."

He settled onto a small, clear patch of floor. After only a few seconds of jazzy Muzak, the line rang and then, "Hello? Is this Mr. Quinn?" asked a woman with a voice he didn't recognize.

"Speaking," he said.

"Yes, how are you today?" She didn't wait for him to answer. "This is Naomi Hoffman's personal assistant, Rebecca."

Naomi Hoffman? He scrambled to connect the name Naomi Hoffman to Luna Mendez, but nothing surfaced.

Then, clear as day, he saw the nametag in his mind's eye.

Hello, my name is

NAOMI HOFFMAN

His anxiety transmuted into delight, like an alchemist turning lead into gold. He'd been playing whack-a-mole with thoughts about the woman at the reunion since they parted ways, but his adeptness at the game in real life did not translate into his internal world. He hadn't been able to stop himself from remembering tidbits of their conversation, that flirtatious glimmer in her eye, or how her soft, curly hair brushed against her neck in a way that he wished his lips could.

Was it possible the moment hadn't passed and there was still a chance?

Rebecca continued. "You met Ms. Hoffman at the—"

"Reunion," he said, unable to hold back.

"Yes, yes, the reunion last night."

"I had a really nice time talking with her, but things ended a little, um, abruptly." He cleared his throat uncomfortably. In his line of work, he was no stranger to talking to people's *people*. But it had always been in a professional capacity, and it felt more than a little strange to be para-wooing Naomi via her assistant.

"I see. Well, Ms. Hoffman was wondering if you would be interested in having dinner sometime in the next—"

"Yes," he said before she could finish her sentence. He couldn't have kept his cool if he wanted to. At least it was only her assistant on the other line, and he was saving a little face. He held out his phone and put it on speaker. "Let me check my calendar."

His calendar was a mess. It was always a mess, which was one of the main reasons his social life—and by extension, his dating life—was almost non-existent. Monday was back-to-back appointments that started with a staff meeting at 8:30 a.m. and ended with a call to a contact in Tokyo at 7:30 p.m. Then he was heading out of town on Wednesday to do some legwork for a story on the hidden impact of abandoned mining operations on small communities in the Appalachian region. That left only a small block of time on Tuesday, in between meetings that ended at 5:00 p.m. and an interview that started at 9:00 p.m.

As Freya had told him early on, "In this job, you have to make time for your life in between the work, otherwise you won't have a life *at all.*" It wasn't unusual to add in a doctor's visit or a friend's birthday party in the small, scattered moments when the interviews, calls, meetings, and deadlines paused just long enough to let something else in. Sometimes, when the situation called for it, he and Freya would even go along on personal outings together. Like, for instance, to a high school reunion. Which meant that doing something like squeezing in a date right before an interview was nothing out of the ordinary.

It could work. He could have a few hours with Naomi and then head straight to the interview. He briefly considered looking into another week, but the image of those gym doors swinging closed behind her filled his vision, and he decided against it. She had already walked away once;

he wasn't going to give her a chance to walk away again. "I've got some time on Tuesday," he said. "Any chance that would work for her?"

"Tuesday?" she repeated.

"Yes," he said. "Six o'clock?"

"Six o'clock?" she repeated again. "Could you hold one moment while I check her calendar?"

"Sure," he said.

She was silent for a moment. "Yes, it looks like she's available during that time."

Will fist pumped into the air. "Awesome. I can tell you where in a sec. Hang on," he said, pulling up OpenTable and then hurriedly putting in the date and time. On a Tuesday night, there were a decent number of options. "How about the Bella Luna. It's in the Fulton River District, on Halsted."

"Bella Luna. On Halsted." The repeating thing was getting a little strange.

"Obviously, she—or you—can reach out if that time or location doesn't work."

"Of course," she said.

"Can I text the number you called from so you have my direct cell?"

"Yes."

"Okay, I'll send it shortly. Sound good?"

"Yes, thank you."

"OK, well," Will hesitated, suddenly aware that he had no idea how to end the call. Should he say something nice about Naomi? Ask Rebecca to pass along a message? It felt weirdly like passing notes in middle school. "Um, yeah—just, please tell Naomi I'm really looking forward to it. To her. I mean—to seeing her, on the date. That's what I'm looking forward to."

He winced. He didn't consider himself a smooth talker, but this was bad, even for him. The lack of sleep, combined with the sheer weirdness of setting up a date through an assistant, had completely thrown him off what little game he had. Hopefully, Rebecca was the kind of assistant who would convey the message, not the delivery. "Anyway, thank you for the call," he finished.

"Have a wonderful afternoon," Rebecca replied, her voice not giving any hint as to whether she was smiling politely or rolling her eyes on the other end.

His screen went dark.

He sat on the floor, trying to decide what to do next. His stomach was a Gordian Knot of delight, excitement, and anticipation.

And after a little bit of time, he realized there was, perhaps, a little apprehension too.

"Naomi was always hanging on to her like a bad case of fleas," one of *The Shining* twins, Will couldn't remember which one, had told him.

"If she's stayed friends with Abby all these years, and it seems she has, imagine what kind of Stockholm Syndrome she must be living with," the other one had said.

Not that he gave their opinions any weight, but there *was* that whole thing with Freya and Abby, which he was now willingly putting himself adjacent to. What was he walking into?

And how would Freya feel about it? Never, in all the many long hours he'd spent with Freya—or the numerous challenging, frustrating, and sometimes downright infuriating situations they'd been through together—had he ever seen her act the way she did that night. He'd only caught a glimpse at the end, but it had been a nuclear blast—and Abby was ground zero. There had to be more to the story. But that was one interview Will was never going to get. Freya would seal off those emotions like a reactor in lockdown—impenetrable, untouchable, and off-limits to everyone.

By the time Monday morning rolled around, he had spent a significant portion of his weekend mulling over what, if anything, he should tell Freya about his date.

Now, as he sat at his desk, watching the appointment reminder on his computer countdown the minutes until he had to go meet Freya, he decided that he would wait to tell her until he knew if there was anything worth telling her. Freya wasn't into making a big deal about personal lives, so there was no reason to make a one about his. For now.

His appointment reminder was replaced with an alert for a new email.

From: j.hellman@regeringskansliet.se
Re: Interview confirmation details

Mr. Quinn,

Due to a change in the Prime Minister's schedule, your interview has now been rescheduled for 1930 hours on Tuesday. Please confirm receipt.

Jörgen Head of the Press Department, Prime Minister's Office

Sitting in his office, door closed, he googled to make sure 1930 was 7:30 p.m. and then let a series of expletives skate off his tongue. He had been trying to secure this interview for months, in preparation for the Prime Minister of Sweden's visit to Chicago to celebrate the anniversary of the sister city agreement between Chicago and Gothenburg. The Swedish press department had made no effort to accommodate him up until now, so he should have known it would be inevitable that they were once again changing things.

As he fired off his confirmation to Jörgen, he tried to decide what to do. He didn't want to cancel with Naomi. And maybe he wouldn't have to. Their date was at six o'clock, so a 7:30 interview still left him with some time to see her.

The appointment reminder on his computer flashed at him. *Now: Costa Rica Promos*

He closed his laptop with one hand, grabbed a printout of some copy he'd put together for Freya to record with the other, then walked out of his office and down the hall.

Nightly Global News was a labyrinth of hallways on the twelfth floor of the World News Organization Tower. WNO, which had its humble beginnings as a radio station in the 1920's was now a global entertainment conglomerate headquartered in a forty-two-story building in downtown Chicago. Although much of the WNO Tower was now used as office space, it still housed a few studios for a handful of their television programs, including a couple of sitcoms, some of their longest-running soap operas, and Nightly Global News.

He headed to the makeup room where they usually met for promos, but Freya was nowhere to be seen. After a few minutes of waiting, he strode over to her office at the other end of the studio. Her office was big enough that he had to walk in and check several areas before turning back around.

"Hey," he said to a colleague who was passing by her door as he was coming out. "Have you seen Freya?"

"Yeah," they told him. "She kicked me out of Editing Room B like an hour ago. Something last minute came up, I guess."

Everything in this business was last-minute, so he couldn't even begin to take a stab at what had sent her to the editing room. When he arrived at Editing Room B, he gave a quick knock before opening the door slightly.

"You in here?" The room was dark, save for several large screens illuminating a pair of silhouettes. He leaned in further to try to make out who he was talking to.

"Under duress," came Freya's reply. Her shadowy figure put a hand on the person next to her. "No offense."

"None taken." It sounded like Janet, one of the newer editors on staff.

He glanced up at the screens where Janet was splicing a video and removing sections with the urgency of a doctor in the ER. He only needed to see one frame to identify that the editorial surgery was taking place on an upcoming piece they were doing about Governor Hadley. A *finished* piece—or so he'd thought. "I definitely want more on that, but first you're late to record promos for the Costa Rica segment," he said.

"Damn, really? Okay. We're almost done here. Give me just two minutes."

It took one more reminder but eventually she burst out of the editing room. "I know. I'm sorry. Let's move," she said, the speed of her steps mirroring that of her speech.

Will hustled alongside her. "What was that all about?"

"Ugh, Brian stopped by my office an hour ago." She shook her head. "He'd seen the interview with Governor Hadley, and he said I couldn't include anything about the Amerilife Gas Pipeline on Native lands."

Will's muscles tensed in protest and he slowed down. Brian, one of the Executive Producers of Nightly Global News, was notorious for tweaking their stories. This change, however, was more than micromanaging. "You've got to be kidding me. That was fifty percent of the interview. And it was important. People need to know that he's going to—"

Freya motioned for him to pump the brakes. "You don't have to tell me. Or him. Because I definitely did. But he said Amerilife is a part owner in WNO, which I appreciate him failing to mention to me before we went ahead with this story. So essentially, that means that we can dig up whatever dirt we want on Hadley, but not about that."

He had a few choice words for Brian, but none that he would say out loud. He couldn't understand how Freya was so calm about this. Dozens of hours of work wasted because of carelessness, red tape, and greed. But he took his cue from her and tried to match her demeanor. "I'm feeling very," he clenched his jaw as he looked for a workplace-friendly word to describe his feelings, "conflicted right now."

She shot him a look that was sharp but contained a modicum of understanding around the edges. "Nothing makes you feel better about your job than learning it's partially owned by a company that has a well-documented history of violating human rights around the world, and then being forced into protecting a civil servant who is doing the same thing, does it? The good news is, it's over and done with. I've taken care of it. Bye-bye, Amerilife. Hello, Mimi." They had arrived at the makeup room, and she waved at Mimi, their resident makeup artist, who was resting on a chair, looking at her phone.

Mimi, tall, slight, and eternally exuberant, leapt up. "Jonsson, you are late, late, late." She guided Freya to the makeup chair.

Will glanced at the clock. "I could have done the edits. You've got a full day."

Freya waved him off. "I've been doing the 'Playcate the Old White Cis Men Upstairs' tap dance for years. I knew exactly what Brian wanted, so I figured it would be faster to do it myself and get it over with. And we'll live to fight another day. Just not about this."

Mimi was brushing something onto Freya's face. "I have no idea what you're talking about. But I can confirm that the tap dance is real and sometimes a necessary survival skill."

Will dropped into a nearby seat, feeling like gravity had doubled in the last few minutes. A wave of heat washed over him, a mix of indignation and confusion. Freya and Mimi's words stung, but they also confused him.

He had grown up surrounded by strong women. Not only his mother, but his grandmother, who had managed the farm before his parents took over. And his aunt, who was their closest neighbor and had raised two girls on her own after his uncle died. It was probably one of the reasons he'd been drawn to Freya, why he felt comfortable in her orbit. If there was one thing he knew how to do well, it was work beside a powerful woman. And he thought he did it pretty well. But was he really that oblivious to the power dynamics at play right in front of him? He'd never heard his family talk like this, but it made him wonder if he'd been missing something all along. Shame gnawed at him, battling with a defensiveness he knew didn't belong in the conversation.

But Freya had already moved on. "Speaking of a full day. Talk me through tomorrow. Are we good to go with the prime minister?"

If she was moving on, then so was he. Gladly. "Security checks are complete, and I confirmed with her team this afternoon. We're set to arrive at 1930 hours, which I pretended to know and then looked up later."

"7:30."

"Correctomundo," he confirmed with a finger gun, immediately regretting both his word and hand choice when Mimi's eyes widened in mock horror and she mouthed "Correctomundo?" back at him, her lips twitching with amusement.

"So, we'll leave from here at 6:45?"

Today was not turning out to be one of his favorite days. He'd decided not to tell Freya about his date with Naomi until later. But he wasn't going to lie about it either. His plan had been to simply omit that piece of information until it became relevant. If it became relevant. Which, of course, it did the first time he saw her.

"You think a little earlier?" Freya said, misreading his silence. "You're probably right, we need to give ourselves some wiggle room with traffic."

He had no poker face. Even a lie of omission was a challenge for him. He leaned forward, uncomfortably. "I was thinking we would go separately and meet there."

"Why, if we're both leaving from the office? That's more time wasted if they have to sweep two cars." Even when she wasn't 'on,' Freya was on. Once she got even the slightest hint that there was something under the surface, she'd start digging.

"I kind of have ..." he cleared his throat. "Something right before."

She was watching him in the mirror, cold blue eyes locking him into place. "Something?"

"Yes, a, um, date."

That was all it took to get Mimi on board. "Oh, details, please. That's more interesting than prime minister schedules. Now close your eyes." She said the last part to Freya as she leaned in with a long brush.

He wanted to be mad at Mimi for pressing, but if she didn't ask it he knew Freya would have. "There's really no 'details.' She and I met only briefly, but we hit it off and are going on a first date." Perhaps, if he downplayed it all, Freya would lose interest and move on. It was a long shot, but he held onto it.

Unfortunately, Mimi wasn't about to let him get away with it. "There's always details. Where did you meet? Who asked out who? What did you like about her?"

"We met at ..." he tried to think if there was any other way to say it, without *saying* it.

He didn't get a chance, though, because, as always, Freya figured it out first. Her eyes opened suddenly, forcing Mimi to pull back. "You're going on a date with Naomi?"

"Ooh, Naomi?" Mimi said excitedly. "Who is that? Close your eyes, Jonsson. We're short on time here."

Will couldn't stop a groan from coming out. *Here goes nothing*. "She called me," he said, still looking at her, nervously trying to read her expression even though her eyes were closed. Maybe he had nothing to worry about. Maybe she wouldn't have feelings about it one way or another. But the anxiety of not knowing made his words start coming faster. "Her assistant did, actually. Called the front desk, I guess. Anyway, she wanted to know if I wanted to go out—and I said yes. I don't know, it seemed like a good idea at the moment. Then afterward I started panicking because I remembered what everyone was saying and about what happened and now I—"

"Slow down, hon," Mimi interrupted his confession. "I feel like I missed an episode, and now I need a 'previously on' recap. And Jonsson, relax a little. I can't get this eyeliner on when you're scrunching your eyes like that. That's better. Now tell me about Naomi."

"We met, briefly, at ..." This had taken a bit of a turn. How much was he supposed to say? Freya didn't like people knowing any more about her than they needed to. While he wasn't sure how she'd feel about him seeing Naomi, he was confident that she wouldn't want him relaying anything about her high school, the people he met, or that other side of her he saw. "A thing. But then, another thing happened, and she had to leave before I could give her my number."

"That's a lot of ... things. But I think I'm following, sort of. So, then she found you; that's kinda cute, right?"

"I thought so. But her friend and Freya have kind of this, well," he couldn't come up with another word under this much pressure, "thing."

"There are so many things flying around. This story is turning into a Dr. Seuss book."

"There's no *thing*," Freya said, her tone commanding. Even with her eyes closed, she could take charge of a room. "We bumped into some of my friends from high school on Friday. That's where Will met Naomi, and where I learned that my high school girl squad was still stuck in high drama mode. They were trying to dig up high school gossip about Naomi to scare off Will. It was pathetic, honestly, don't you think, Will?"

Gossip to 'scare' him off? That could almost be interpreted to mean she didn't have a problem with him seeing Naomi. Almost. There was something else. Discomfort with the conversation centering on her personal life?

Mimi began applying lipstick, and Freya opened her eyes, looking directly at him expectantly. One thing was clear. She wanted him to confirm her narrative: there was no "thing." No story for Mimi to tell the next person who sat in her chair. "Uh, right. Exactly."

Thankfully, Mimi was oblivious to this footnote of their conversation. "What is it with some people getting stuck in high school? The best time of your life is being a pimply bag of raging hormones in a sea of confused half-adults? I will never understand it. You're still going to see her, this Naomi, right? To decide for yourself?"

"I guess. If it's okay with ..." he started to say, then trailed off. He wanted to ask permission, but asking permission would also suggest there was a "thing."

"Of course, why would it matter to me if you see her?" Effortlessly, Freya picked up the ball he dropped. "And it's no problem; I'll plan to pick you up after your date on the way to the interview."

She stood, indicating both her makeup and the conversation were done. He followed suit, handing her the printouts he'd been carrying. "I made a few changes since you last saw these," he said.

"Thanks," she said, glancing at the papers, then back at him.

He was tempted to push the conversation a little further but decided against it. If there was one thing he knew, it was that he couldn't force anything out of Freya. If she had more to say, she'd say it when the time was right for her. Besides, why push something when it might all be nothing? It was only one date, after all.

Chapter Five

Naomi

Naomi sat cross-legged on the floor of her living room while Riley laid out a series of outfits on the sofa. She had called Riley only an hour ago when she had come home from work and it had hit her that she had to plan an outfit for her date tomorrow.

When the thought first popped into her head, it hadn't seemed like a big deal. It was even a little exciting. Until, standing in the silence, one hand on each door of her closet, staring at her clothes, her brain was kind enough to remind her that she had never, ever, been on a first date.

Not an adult one anyway. When she had started dating Simon, they were in high school. They had known each other for months, and the closest thing they'd had to a first date was sitting alone at a table in the lunch hall. By the time they had the money and autonomy to go out on a *date*-date, the kind that included romantic restaurant meals over candlelight, Simon was telling her what she could and couldn't wear.

As she realized she had no idea how to dress for anyone but Simon, the clothes in her closet began to swim before her eyes and with it the rising tide of panic in her chest. She'd slammed the closet doors closed and called Riley who, without hesitation, came to the rescue.

The Fassi headquarters, where Riley worked, were located directly above the Fassi flagship store, which meant Riley only needed to take an elevator down eight floors to begin shopping with their generous employee discount. They arrived at her apartment later that evening with three potential date outfits.

"Now, keep in mind, I didn't have too much to go off besides what you've told me about him, his location choice, and the light amount of internet stalking I've done," Riley said.

Riley's presence and the bottle of wine they had brought with them had helped to calm her nerves some. "What did you learn? I was too afraid to look. What if he's not as cute as I remember?"

"Girl, you *have* to do your research so you know what things to bring up. And to make sure they're not an obvious murderer." They handed her a pair of forest green linen pants and a black body suit. "Start with this one." Riley turned around to face the wall as she changed.

"An obvious murderer? You mean like if they put 'I murder people' in their bio?" she asked, standing up and shedding her work clothes.

Riley patted their hair, the blue from a few days ago now accented with purple. "You mock, but I stand before you, a serial dater, still alive. Which I attribute, in part, to my system of weeding out murderers."

"Does it count as a date if you can't remember their name the next morning?"

"I remember their souls, though. And ... other, more material, parts of them. That's all that really matters."

"Okay, outfit number one. What do you think?" Naomi didn't even need a mirror. She trusted Riley more than she trusted her own eyes.

Riley turned around and gave her a thorough visual inspection. "I don't like it as much as I thought I would. Try this one next." They lifted up a pleated, burnt orange skirt and white crop top, handed it to her, and then spun back to the wall.

"So? What did you learn?" she asked again, beginning the process of swapping outfits.

"Not as much as I'd like, I'll tell you that. I can assuage your concerns by telling you that he is indeed pretty to look at. And he also does not appear to be an obvious murderer. But he's not very giving when it comes to social media ... which I hope is not an indication of how he will be in bed, by the way."

"Let me get through this date before we start thinking about what he'll be like in bed."

"You haven't thought about what he'll be like in bed?!"

Naomi didn't need to see Riley's face to know the shaken look of disbelief that was on it.

Of course, she had thought about it. She'd thought about all the places his hands might explore on her body and wondered what that gentle laugh would sound like when it turned into a moan. In fact, she hadn't been able to stop thinking about it. "How about this," she said, hoping to change the subject as heat started to spread up her neck.

Riley whirled and examined her, fingers resting on their jaw. "This could be the winner, but let's try the last one." They held out a maxi dress adorned with a large floral print and then turned away again.

"Did you learn anything else besides him being pretty and not obviously a murderer?"

"An Instagram with a handful of food pictures and a goldfish named Ferris Bueller that I'm guessing is his, based on the caption. A LinkedIn with only his current position at Nightly Global News and his undergrad—a Communications and Film BA from Indiana State University. And a Facebook profile with only happy birthday messages from which I was able to deduce that he is two years younger than you."

"This might be a good side hustle for you, Riley. You help people pick out their outfits and investigate their dates."

"Ooh, I am a fan of this. I dress you up and dress them down."

"I think you'd make a killing."

"Speaking of his current employment, I need you to make this last long enough that I can meet Freya Jonsson and pitch her to do a story about me."

"About you? She usually does pretty hard-hitting journalism."

"Oh, I can be *hard.*"

Naomi decided not to take the bait on that one. "I'm ready."

This time when Riley turned, their entire face widened with pleasure. "Bingo. Gives of come-hither vibes but in a subtle, Naomi kind of way." They put their fingers to their lips for a chef's kiss. Naomi opened her mouth to ask a follow-up question, but Riley was already on it. "Hair up, I'll lend you the earrings, and those white sandals with the chunky heel you've got."

Naomi smiled and walked over to Riley, putting her arms around them. Because of the height difference between the two of them, their hugs always made them both chuckle. But she didn't think about it this time as she pulled them in for a tight squeeze. "Thank you," she said. "You *really* helped me." She searched for the right words. How could she begin to tell them how they had helped her with so much more than picking the right dress? It was about Riley giving her the space to be the kind of woman who sits on her living room floor and picks the right dress. For most people, she imagined this wasn't a very momentous occasion. But for her, it felt like a baby taking her first, wobbly step.

Riley squeezed back. "You got this, girl."

She released them and looked up. "I ..." It took her a moment to finish her sentence. "Don't know if I *do* got this."

"Of course you do! What are you even saying?" They stepped back and gestured to Naomi. "You're stunning. Smart. Successful. And humble enough to ask for help when you need it, which is why you're also fabulously dressed."

Naomi smiled but couldn't stop the sigh from escaping her lips. "*And* a divorcee."

Riley shook their head. "Her Royal Majesty, Taylor Swift, practically built her career on singing about her exes. Having an ex is the in thing now."

"First of all, I think singing about your exes was in before Taylor Swift."

"Mmm, disagree. But continue."

"Well, I don't think she's ever written a song about having never been on a date with anyone, much less slept with anyone other than her ex-husband who, by the way, likes to make an appearance from time to time and throw a chaos bomb into the mix."

Riley's head bobbed up and down, as if they were running through the catalog of Taylor Swift songs to make sure that was correct. "Perhaps not," they finally conceded. "Although who knows where her music will take us over the years. But T Swift aside, I gather you're trying to say that Will might not like you because of your past?"

Her chest tightened, leaving little air to get her word out. "Yes ..."

Riley took a seat on the armrest of her sofa. "Then, girl, he's trash."

When Naomi laughed, Riley held up a finger. "One moment." They reached for their phone on the coffee table and began tapping. After a few moments, the phone began to ring from the speaker.

There was a click and then her best friend's voice on the other line. "Hello?"

"Abby, what if Will doesn't like Naomi because of her ex-husband?"

Without hesitation, and with a fiery bite to her words, Abby responded, "Then he's trash!" Riley lifted their open palm towards her, as if to say "voila" but before they could say any more, Abby continued. "Wait, why? Did he say something to Naomi? I'm at my mom's for dinner but I can leave. Does anyone know where he lives?"

"Take a breath, Lizzie Bordon, we're not axing anyone tonight. I only needed some backup."

"Hi, Abby," Naomi said, throwing her voice towards the phone. "Everything is fine, I'm having a ... moment. You know. Wondering if this date thing is a good idea."

"Naomi! Hi! I—no, I'm on the phone with Naomi," Abby's voice suddenly sounded further away, like she was covering the microphone to address someone in the room with her. "No, she's fine, she—"

"Naomi, honey, what's going on?" It was another voice Naomi knew well, Abby's mother, Deborah, who had always been a second mom to Naomi growing up. When Naomi's parents had moved to Michigan after she'd graduated college, Deborah had taken an even bigger step into the role.

"Oh my God, is this about Will?" Becca had entered the chat.

Naomi glanced at Riley with an amused smile. Trying to have a conversation with all three Meyer women was like trying to fly a plane through a tornado.

"Is Will that young man Abby was telling me about?" Deborah said. "The one that you're going on a date with? He sounds like a doll. Too bad he's not Jewish but I'm sure he'll convert when you get married, right?"

"Mom, please," Abby said. "Can you let Naomi have a first date before you start planning their wedding?"

"Yeah, Mom," Becca said. "We're trying to get Naomi laid, not married."

"Oh, well, that's different," Debbie replied. "No need to worry about conversion if you're only in it for the penis."

"Mom!" Abby scolded.

"Just because you don't like penises doesn't mean we can't talk about them."

"*Thank* you," Becca said.

"Would you please ... " Abby made a grumbling noise and then started again. "Riley thought it might help—"

"Riley is there?" Sometimes it was impossible to differentiate Deborah and Becca's voices.

"Hi, ladies," Riley said. "Would either of you care to weigh in on why there's no reason in the world a man wouldn't want to date Naomi?"

"Not date—are you crazy?" That was definitely Deborah. "Naomi, you're perfection. Who is telling you you're not?"

"No one," she said. Then added, "Me. I'm the one. I got a little in my head about Simon and what Will might think when he finds out—"

"Simon!" Debbie practically spat the name. "Yimakh shemo. May his name be erased. That horrid man is part of your past, but he isn't a part of who you are. And if Will or anyone else feels differently then they're ... what did you call them, Abby?"

"Trash."

"There you have it. Trash. Any man would be lucky to have you as a wife."

"Or a one-night stand!" Becca shouted.

"Exactly. Or a one-night stand. Got it?"

"Yeah," Naomi said, not quite as enthusiastically as everyone probably hoped. "Given my taste in men, he probably is trash."

"Your taste in *man*, singular," Abby said. "One mistake. It was a big one but that one choice didn't write your entire future."

"I don't know if I'm ready to find out if that's true or not."

"I feel like we're getting too caught on Will's character," Becca chimed in. "You don't need him to do a deep dive into your personal life. Only into you."

Abby went next. "However your ... relationship with Will unfolds, I think Becca has a point. This is a first date—you don't have to tell him your entire life story. You can get to know him more and decide if he is someone you trust enough to share that with. It's your life and your decision, and you can open up to him whenever you're ready, even if it takes a while. But it for sure doesn't have to happen tomorrow."

"You're not on an episode of *Married At First Sight*, so you've got plenty of time," Riley managed to get a word in.

"Why don't you bring him over for dinner? I'm a great judge of character," Deborah said.

"She's not bringing a first date to your house, Mom," Abby said.

"Why not?" Deborah said, sounding offended. "What's so bad about coming here?"

Over the sound of a new argument, Riley said loudly into the phone, "Thank you, ladies! Love you, kiss kiss!" and ended the call. "There you have it. You've got this."

Her ears still buzzing from the cacophony of the last few minutes, Naomi looked down at her dress and inhaled deeply. Then, exhaling, she looked up and said, mostly believing it, "I got this."

Chapter Six

Will

Despite his optimism that twenty-four hours abroad wasn't long enough to throw off his internal clock, Will had still been plagued with jet lag. At least, that's what he was telling people when they caught him yawning.

Whether it was as a result of his insomnia or a contributor to it, much of the last two sleepless nights had been spent replaying his conversation with Naomi and thinking about their upcoming date. He'd dated and even fallen in love before, but he'd never had such an instant connection with someone that left him with so many questions he couldn't wait to get answered. Would he feel that connection again when he saw her? Would *she* feel it? Was it possible they could have anything deeper in common than the electric buzz of pheromones? What would they talk about on their date? Would they kiss at the end? What would her lips feel like against his? That last one, in particular, his mind had been happy to repeatedly explore and even attempt to fill in the blanks.

He had gone to bed early last night, determined to get a good night's sleep so he wouldn't show up to their date looking like a zombie. But his brain had not complied, instead turning those questions over and over again like a rock tumbler smoothing them until they shone.

Eventually, he gave up on trying to sleep and headed for the shower. Standing in front of his closet afterward, he bypassed his usual rotation of graphic tees and hovered uncertainly over the button-downs he rarely touched. His fingers landed on a pale pink one, crisp from disuse, and then paired it with dark jeans. When he arrived at the office—two full hours before Freya—he dropped into his chair and gripped a mug of coffee like a life raft.

"A shirt with actual buttons?" Freya remarked when she walked into his office later that morning and found him at his desk, nursing his second cup of coffee. "You must really be trying to impress her."

He was. But he still wasn't one hundred percent sure he should tell Freya that yet. Instead, he gave her a smile and then a rundown of what was on the agenda for the day. As always, it was jam-packed, the hours blurred together, and before he knew it, he was stepping through the doors of the Bella Luna—exhausted but running on adrenaline.

He had been to the Bella Luna once, which is why he had picked it for their date. When he'd first moved to Chicago, his parents had come for a few days to help him get settled in, and they'd all gone out to dinner here the night before they left. But he had begun to worry that with the passage of time, his memory, or the restaurant management, had changed the space.

He was relieved to see that it was a carbon copy of the image he had in his mind: cozy, with the kind of warmth that made the noise of the city feel far away. The dozen or so tables were small and unassuming, each draped with a simple cotton tablecloth and topped with flickering votives. Soft music drifted from hidden speakers, blending with the murmur of conversation from the handful of occupied tables around the room. The air carried the unmistakable scent of roasted garlic and fresh basil—just as it had the night he'd been here with his parents. And, bonus, it had the same dim lighting, which would, hopefully, hide the dark circles under his eyes.

He had barely checked in with the host when he heard the door open and he turned around to see Naomi.

Like the restaurant, she was exactly as he remembered and, just like last time, she took his breath away. Only more so now than last time because she wasn't here to get a drink at a reunion. She was here, in a flowery dress that invited him to drink in every curve, to see *him.* Her thick, dark curls were pulled back, allowing him unfettered access to her velvety brown eyes that, even in the low lights, held a rich intensity that pulled him in.

"Hi." He wanted to slam his fist into his forehead. *Hi?* He'd spent so many hours thinking about this date, and he'd never thought about what to say to her when he saw her.

She smiled at him. "Hi," she said softly.

"The host said we can sit anywhere we want. I thought that table by the window might be nice?" He pointed towards the table he had in mind.

"Lead the way," she said.

"It's nice to see you," he said as he began walking. "I'll be honest, I was pretty excited when you—well, when your personal assistant called."

Her laugh came tinged with something else. Nerves about being on the date? "Yeah. I mean, well, she's not really a personal assistant, per se.

She helps me with some of my—" her words and steps stopped abruptly, almost like she had slammed into an invisible wall.

He stopped too, looking back at her and then following her eyes. She seemed to be looking at a table with two women. One of the women wore a large-brimmed hat. It was an odd choice in the shadowy ambient lighting, to say the least. Perhaps that was the cause of Naomi's sudden distraction? Or maybe she'd just lost her train of thought, derailed by a moment of first-date nerves? Or maybe ...

"Do you want to sit somewhere else?" he asked.

"No, no!" she said, her attention snapping back to him. She kept walking. "Sorry, as I was saying. She's someone who, um, you know, helps me out from time to time."

"I'm glad she helped you out on Saturday." As they arrived at the table, he gestured for her to choose her seat.

"Me too," she said, her bare shoulder leaving a wake of electricity as it brushed his outstretched hand when she walked past him to her seat.

He sat down across from her and flattened his palms against the table, feeling like he needed to ground his racing pulse, the lingering spark from her touch still crackling through him. "I should let you know I can only stay an hour, but I promise it's not some excuse to get out of the date. An interview with the Swedish Prime Minister got rescheduled, last minute, for tonight at 7:30." He hadn't figured out a way to tell her without sounding like a dick so he decided all he could do was put it out there as quickly and bluntly as possible.

She cocked her head, a coy smile tugging at the lips. "Wow, the Swedish Prime Minister! You know, most people have a friend call and pretend they're sick or something."

Her joke, and a feeling of relief that she wasn't upset, made him grin. "What can I say? Go big or go home." A server came by and handed them menus. "Do you think they make the Blue Narwhal here?"

When she laughed, all the questions and what-ifs that had kept him up at night disappeared. All the answers were right here, in the moment, illuminated by her smile. "I think that was a one-night-only Northwest High special."

He put his hands up, a gesture of mock despair. "Oh, the humanity!"

"You like IPAs, though, right?"

"You remembered," he said, a tickle of pleasure running through him.

"I didn't get much information about you, so the few details I learned stuck in my head."

"Well, I'm honored to have been given some shelf space in your head." *If you only knew how much shelf space you've had in mine,* he wanted to add.

"How about you hit with me some more facts?"

"Ladies first."

She accepted the offer.

She told him about growing up as an only child in the city. And then he told her about growing up as an only child on a Midwestern farm.

She told him about her childhood dreams of being a veterinarian until she realized one tiny problem.

"I hate blood."

"Ooh, yeah, that's going to put the kibosh on a lot of jobs in the medical field."

"I was so disappointed when I realized being a vet wasn't like the toy veterinary clinic I had as a kid."

He told her his dreams of being a detective. "I'd run around with a little notebook, trying to solve mysteries. But on a small farm in Indiana, there aren't a lot of mysteries to be had. I think it was sometime in my late teens that I finally realized it wasn't mysteries I wanted, but stories. People's stories. Who they are and where they've come from, and how they got there. Solving people is a lot more fascinating than solving crime and usually involves a lot less danger. Well, sometimes. Anyway, that's when I decided I would go into journalism."

"All these years later, do you feel like you made the right choice? Like you are in the neighboring county to detective and it's where you should be?"

"Honestly, yes. I feel like I'm one of the lucky ones because I really love my job. I mean, I don't love every single moment, but there's nothing else I'd rather be doing as a career."

The food, the drinks, and the check became inconsequential as they talked about favorite movies, least favorite foods, dreams for the future, and even kids. She told him about the family she dreamed about having. "I always wanted two, a boy and a girl. Preferably, the boy first. I never had any siblings, and I always thought it would be nice to have an older brother to look out for me."

"Don't be so sure. I never had any siblings either, but I had two younger girl cousins whom I tormented endlessly. We're good friends now, but sometimes I still find myself apologizing to them for the hours of suffering I put them through."

"If you're good friends, I take it they've forgiven you then?"

"They have, except when it's convenient for them to bring it up to get something from me."

"I think that's more than fair. So, then, where do you land on kids?"

"My parents worked a lot, and I was an only child, so I spent a lot of nights having dinner by myself, and I always dreamed of having a big family that gathers around the dinner table for a chaotic, lively meal. As I've gotten older, I've realized that some kids have enough personality for multiple children, so it's not necessarily about quantity. I feel like I'd have to meet each kid first to decide if we should add another one."

Exactly like last time, the world around them and the space between them slowly disappeared.

And then, *exactly* like last time, Freya Jonsson's voice broke the spell.

Only this time, instead of a laugh, it was a yelp.

He and Naomi both turned to face the entrance just in time to see a woman topple backward to the ground, her arms swinging wildly in a pointless attempt to reclaim her lost balance. She crashed down with a dull thud, landing fully on top of another woman, who was already halfway to the floor. The first woman's wide-brimmed hat flew off and rolled across the floor, coming to a wobbly stop near the base of the host stand. It took a second for his brain to catch up with his eyes and make sense of what he saw. There, tangled together like a strand of Christmas lights, were Freya and ... Abby.

And from the look on their faces, they were both as flabbergasted to see each other as Will was.

They pushed away from each other and stood, Freya brushing out her suit as Abby placed the large hat back on her head. Large hat?

He struggled to follow what was happening while also trying to guess what had led them to whatever was happening. What was Abby doing here? Had she been the woman in the large hat sitting at the table that Naomi had stopped to look at? Why was Freya not waiting in the car? How had Abby managed to end up tumbling backward into Freya? And was there any chance that they would be able to laugh this off and walk away?

"Throwing a drink on me wasn't enough, I take it?" Freya snapped.

Will exhaled slowly. Guess not.

He sensed Naomi looking at him, and he looked back at her, not quite sure where to begin. "She was going to pick me up ... I didn't know ..."

"I didn't know either," she said, sounding somewhere between apologetic and exasperated. "I was super nervous about our date, and I think my friends decided to drop by."

"Friends, plural?" He glanced at the small crowd forming around Freya and Abby, who were still battling.

"Yeah. That's Abby's sister over there. And the really tall person is Riley." She pointed at someone who stood a foot above the rest of the crowd, their height made even taller by their platform shoes and the shock of pink hair pulled into a bun at the top of their head. "I'm sorry; they're really nice people but combined, they struggle with ... um ... boundaries. It's not always like this, though, I promise."

"This is about the award, isn't it?" he heard Freya say. "You're jealous of me, like you've always been."

He'd been worried about Naomi understanding that there were some boundary issues with his work life and personal life, but it seemed like maybe she would understand better than he thought.

"I promise it's not always like this with Freya either. I can actually do things without my boss. And when she does show up, it's never like ... this."

"Me? Jealous of you?" Abby said, her volume matching Freya's.

He stood up. Last time, the only thing that had separated Freya and Abby had been Naomi *physically* separating them. He got the sense that a similar intervention was going to be needed. "We'd better ... before ..."

Naomi nodded, pushed her chair back, and then hurried towards the two women.

"It's so obvious, Abby," Freya said, letting out a sharp laugh. "It always has been."

"Obvious to who?" Abby gestured out to what she probably thought was an empty space. But as her eyes followed her arm, it was clear that she—and then Freya—noticed their spectators. Both women took a sheepish step back.

Before he could move in, the person Naomi had identified as Riley walked up to Freya and held out a hand.

"Ms. Jonsson, it's a real pleasure to meet you. I'm Riley Tahara. They/them pronouns. I've always been a fan of your work. Real hard-hitting. Have you ever considered doing a piece on up-and-coming designers? It can be a real rollercoaster ride of emotions, you know. I think it would appeal to a wide audience. And if you're looking for someone, I happen to know a charming young person." Will wasn't entirely sure if Riley was trying to create a distraction to break the tension or to shoot their shot. Perhaps a little of both.

Freya gave Riley a firm handshake accompanied by a big nothing-to-look-at-here smile. "Thank you—Riley, was it? I'll certainly consider it." She released Riley's hand and looked at Will. "I came in here to let you know we're late."

"It's past seven already?" Will asked in disbelief. That explained why she was in the restaurant, but had the hour really flown by that quickly?

"7:09."

"Dammit—security won't let us in to see the prime minister if we're late. I'm sorry; I completely lost track of time. I'm ready to go, though." Will turned to Naomi. "I'm sorry I can't stay longer, it's just—"

"The prime minister, I know," she said.

Nothing about his time with Naomi had gone as planned. Not meeting her at the reunion, not her date-crashing friends, not whatever chaos was brewing between Freya and Abby.

But he knew without a doubt that it didn't matter.

He leaned in close and whispered, "I had a really great time tonight.. I hope I can see you again. Soon."

Having his lips mere centimeters from her neck made time slow down, even as his pulse quickened. The heat of her skin, the faint, citrusy scent of her perfume—it pulled him in. He wanted to close the distance, to kiss the soft, golden skin and follow the curve of her jaw to her mouth.

Instead, he kissed her cheek. The sensation lingered on his lips as he stepped back. And then, like yanking himself from a current, he turned and walked away.

Freya followed him outside, her heels clacking aggressively against the sidewalk. As she reached his side, he glanced at her, curious if he should say anything.

She answered his silent question by raising a finger. "Not a word."

Chapter Seven

Naomi

WILL: I'd love to ask you out sometime in the next week but my schedule is completely stacked. I'm heading out of town this afternoon but I've got a little time before my flight. I know it's last minute but since our offices are so close any chance you're free and I could convince you to meet me by the lake for a few minutes? I'll bring coffee.

Naomi's office didn't have any windows but the words on her screen made sunlight and birds and rainbows explode in her office. She read it again, then one more time for good measure and then closed it and pulled up her group text chain.

NAOMI: Will texted! He said he wants to meet for coffee right now since he's got a little time before he leaves town this afternoon!

She added a few screaming face emojis for good measure.

BECCA: After less than twenty-four hours? This boy is THIRSTY.

ABBY: He likes you in spite of us!

RILEY: I've been very clear about not being roped into the 'us' part of that disaster.

BECCA: What's your lip gloss situation?

ABBY: Where are you meeting him?

NAOMI: I don't know, I haven't texted back yet.

RILEY: What are you doing? Text him!

NAOMI: What do I say?

ABBY: Say yes!

RILEY: Yes!

BECCA: Tell him you're not wearing underwear

Naomi texted back yes, leaving out Becca's suggestion.

Twenty minutes later, she was seated, coffee in hand, beside Will on one of the wide, weathered stone steps that led down to the edge of Lake Michigan. The surface beneath her was warm from the midday sun, radiating a steady heat that anchored her against the lake breeze swirling around them. The water stretched out endlessly in front of them, shimmering under the sunlight in restless, glittering waves and behind them, the city hummed faintly, like a conversation happening in the next room.

Maybe because it had happened so fast or because there was something about Will that was different, but whatever the reason, she didn't feel nervous being here with him. She had barely known him a week, and this was only the third time she'd been with him, but sitting with him and talking about their day felt as natural as if they had been doing it for years.

"Let me see if I've got this right," Will said, pausing to take a sip of his coffee as if he needed to caffeinate before making his attempt at summing up the situation. "Becca, that's Abby's sister, decided to spy on us. And then Abby wanted to stop her, so she came to the restaurant but she was worried I'd recognize her, so she decided to wear a giant hat. And your friend Riley was told not to come but did anyway, and Abby tripped trying to drag them from the restaurant and landed on Freya?"

Naomi put a hand over her face. "That ... about sums it up."

Naomi had spotted Becca first at the Bella Luna. Mostly because Becca was smiling and waving at her. She only saw Abby when one corner of the hat lifted up enough for Naomi to see a flash of Abby's face before the brim dropped back down. But that one-second look at Abby's horrified face told her everything she needed to know. Becca, proud puppeteer of this meeting between her and Will, was crashing her date and Abby was babysitting—clearly, painfully, against her will. The only thing that had amazed Naomi about the whole thing was that Riley was nowhere to be seen. But she had assumed there was a one-hundred-percent chance that they would be making an appearance at some point. Which they had.

The rest of her guesses had been confirmed immediately after Will had stepped out of the door of the restaurant.

"*Sooo*," Riley had said to her, holding the "oh" until it sounded like they were going to break out into song. "I should probably get going."

She had looked at her friends with a blank stare. She knew the logical thing was to be upset with them.

But she wasn't.

It had been bizarrely comforting to see their familiar faces and to know that she wasn't taking this momentous leap on her own. And she knew none of them had had anything but the best of intentions—except maybe Becca, and even then, she was coming from her own version of a good place. Kind of.

And, just as importantly, despite the—and she was being generous here—hiccup, it had been a perfect date. The second Will had said hi to her all the noise in her head, the nerves and the doubts, the fears and futurizing, evaporated like dew on a warm summer morning. An hour together, as short as it was, had been enough to know that there was more to this than a little flirting and some butterflies. There was something there, something she wanted to explore. And when he leaned in to whisper goodbye and kissed her cheek before he left? The feeling of his body so close to hers, the heat of his breath on her neck, the sensation of his lips to her skin—she thought her knees were going to buckle right there, leaving her a lifeless doll on the floor.

Even though her friends, truly in spite of themselves, had not ruined her date and she wasn't feeling angry, she had decided that it didn't mean she couldn't string them along for a little bit and get a few drinks from them. She pointed at the table where Abby and Becca had been sitting. "Nice try. You all get to sit down and tell me exactly what the hell just happened."

Abby was instantly at her side. "I'm sorry, I'm *so* sorry. It's not what you think. I was trying to prevent a scene—not cause one. I didn't even want to be here. Becca made me."

"I did no such thing," Becca said as they all sat down.

"She was going to come, so I had to come to stop her. And then Riley showed up."

"Oh, no you don't. Don't drag me into this," Riley said. "Which, lest we forget, is literally what you did. You tried to drag me out of the restaurant. Which is what caused you to fall on Freya, by the way."

Naomi couldn't stop the singular laugh that escaped. "You seriously fell on her?"

Abby dropped her head onto the table. "Can you please accept my apology and my purchase of any alcoholic beverage of your choice?"

"I can," she had said. "But then I'm going to need you to start at the beginning."

Her friends had relayed the details to her, which she had now relayed to Will.

"That explains everything up to the point where Abby and Freya started fighting," Will said. It hadn't started this way, but somewhere during their conversation, the small space between them had disappeared. Naomi didn't even notice it happening, but suddenly she was aware of the warmth of his body, the gentle pressure of his arm, and the way his scent teased her senses, a subtle blend of spice and earthiness that made her feel lightheaded. She found herself having to work to focus on what he was saying. "What is *with* those two? Freya won't talk about it, but I guess that means nothing since Freya generally won't talk about anything outside of work."

"I don't think I'm going to say anything that's going to clear up your confusion. Those two have been like that since the first day of high school. I don't know what it is that sets them off."

"Huh," came the mystified reply. "I don't know about Abby, but with Freya, it's totally out of character. I'm completely baffled by it."

"Ehhh." Naomi laughed. "I wouldn't say it's completely out of character for Abby as much as it is a more amped up version of her character."

"I only met her briefly when she wasn't yelling at Freya, but I can see that."

The way he said that sobered her up.

"You got quiet over there."

"Oh, it got me thinking, is all," she said. Her heart began to flutter in her chest, pounding out a nervous rhythm that seemed to match the racing thoughts in her mind. "Are you okay with the fact that your boss is ... allergic to my best friend? Is that going to affect your job? I would understand if it did. If you didn't want to ..." She trailed off, unable to finish saying what he might not want to do. As if saying it out loud might make them true. Now it was his turn to be quiet. She held her breath, waiting.

Finally, he answered, "I wouldn't go so far as to say that Freya loves me, but I know she cares about me. I also know she's not one to beat around the bush. If she has a problem, she'll say it, so if she had an issue with *us*, she would have said something already." *Us.* The heavy thudding of her heart became quick skips. Did he see a future for *us?* "But I could ask the same of you. Are you okay with the fact that *your* best friend is, well, as you say, allergic to *my* boss? Is that going to cause issues between you two?"

She didn't need to pause to answer because she'd already asked Abby, and she could repeat back what she had been told. "Abby wants me to be happy. High school is a long way behind us—it might take a few tries, but she's an adult and will get her bearings."

"Good," Will said. He didn't look at her as he said this, but he reached over and took her hand, his fingers intertwining with hers and sending shivers down her spine. He gave her hand a gentle squeeze. "Because I really, really want to keep seeing you."

Naomi's heart bounced like a skipping stone tossed onto a lake, and she squeezed his hand back. "I really want to keep seeing you, too."

"I'd love to do something soon, but I'm gone until Friday and then this weekend is my parents' fiftieth wedding anniversary."

"Wow! Fifty years. I can't imagine." *At least I can't imagine fifty years with my ex.* She wondered, briefly, if she should add that last part and get the Simon thing out of the way once and for all.

"My folks aren't perfect, but the older I get, the more respect I have for them." He ran his thumb along the back of her hand as he spoke. "They really worked hard at finding ways to stay connected through the good times and the bad. It's definitely something I aspire to."

"Yeah ..." she said, chewing on her bottom lip, the indulgent feeling of his touch tempered by her thoughts. Could a man whose parents had a storybook marriage for fifty years begin to understand why she couldn't make it five years? Or would he see her differently after she told him?

"And while I know our first date was pretty exciting, I feel like going up to Indiana for the weekend to celebrate my parents' anniversary might be a bit much for a second date. Besides ..." He stopped, and when he started speaking again, his voice had taken on a richer quality that made her anxious thoughts grow hazy and indistinct, like watercolors bleeding together on wet paper. “I’d like to finally get to spend some time alone with you that is more than getting a cup of coffee for a few minutes.”

She looked up at him, the space between them nearly gone. “I’d really like that,” she said, not sure if she was referring more to spending time with him or his lips, which were now only inches from hers.

Will's hand, still wrapped around hers, gave a gentle tug, drawing her closer. Naomi's body responded instinctively, her head tilting up, her lips parting slightly as she met him halfway. For a moment, they hovered there, the promise and uncertainties of a first kiss hanging between the millimeters that separated them. Then, in a movement so gentle it felt like a whisper, Will's lips brushed against hers.

Naomi's eyes fluttered closed as she let herself get lost in the sensation, her lips parting to invite him deeper. The world around them dissolved, leaving only the gentle pressure of his lips and the soft caress of his hand on her back, pushing the thoughts of Simon out of her head like a bulldozer shoveling away debris.

She didn’t need to burden him with a past she wasn’t sure he even wanted to be associated with. What came next for them was still unknown, a cloudless sky full of possibilities. She didn’t need to bring on the rain clouds and lightning just yet.

Chapter Eight

Will

As they walked down the street towards his apartment, the sky lit by the early autumn sunset, Will laced his fingers with Naomi's. He continued to be amazed that even though it had been three months since he had turned around in the drink line to see her standing behind him, each time he touched her, it felt as exciting as the first time. And yet, he also felt a connection with her that seemed to span a lifetime, rather than only a handful of weeks. With his busy schedule, they hadn't seen much of each other during that time—at least not as much as he would have preferred—but with each passing moment in Naomi's presence, his heart grew more deeply entwined with hers.

Naomi glanced up at him, her cocoa-colored irises sparkling as her lips curved into a smile, small endearing crinkles appearing around the corners of her eyes. He squeezed her hand lightly in response and felt her fingers curl even tighter around his.

When they arrived at his apartment door, he released her hand and reached into his pocket, fishing for his keys. As he unlocked the door, he turned to look at her. "I realize we never discussed after-dinner plans. I was hoping you'd come in. Stay the night? Maybe the weekend? I'll have to work some, but you're welcome to stay here."

"I'd love to stay," she told him. "But I need to get ready for Rosh Hashanah."

"Wait, don't tell me." In the last twelve weeks, he had taken a self-guided crash course in Judaism. He knew a big holiday was coming up, and he searched his memory for the right one. "That's the ... Jewish New Year. It starts on Sunday, right?"

"Yep, at sundown. But back in college, Abby and I started our own tradition. We call it Nosh Hashanah. It's kind of like ... a Jewish Friendsgiving. Basically, a few days before Rosh Hashanah starts, all our friends get together, bring snacks and treats and hang out before heading home to see our families. It started with us bringing whatever we could afford from the dorm vending machine, but has gotten a little fancier over the years."

"Sounds like fun," he said.

"It is, except for the part where it's tomorrow and I'm hosting, but I haven't so much as looked at a recipe or attempted to get any decorations out of storage. I keep meaning to, but I've been a little ... distracted." She gave him a mischievous grin.

The smile left him no choice but to lean in and kiss her. "Do you want me to come over beforehand and help?"

"I thought you weren't going to be around, which is why I didn't mention it. Aren't you flying out to Zagreb tomorrow to help some countries that are doing something important?"

"You could steal my job, the way you summed up covering the final negotiations for a trade agreement between the EU and the Balkans that could change regional stability across Europe."

She laughed. "What can I say? It's a natural-born talent."

"It's an overnight flight that leaves around midnight. If your party starts at sundown, that leaves me plenty of time to come by. And not to brag, but I'm a pretty mean cook. Mean like the kind of food Gordon Ramsey makes, not the kind of person he is on TV. Or I could help set up. My mom hosted Christmas dinner every year so, I've got quite a few years of decorating under my belt." The words came out faster than his brain could stop him. Even though it had been three months of something so perfect and comfortable, it felt like the memory foam of relationships—it had still *only* been three months. That was when you started leaving a few things at their place. Not when you invited yourself over to be part of their inner circle for a holiday. "Or, like, I could do some shopping for you and drop it off. Or whatever." He tried not to wince at the blundering attempt to back out gracefully.

To his surprise and pleasure, though, she didn't let him. "I think that would be great. You don't need to help, but I'd love for you to come. It'd be really nice for you to be able to meet some of my other friends and spend some more time with Abby and Riley and Becca outside of, you know ..."

"Yeah." He knew.

The last time he had seen them, he'd also seen a side of Freya he still couldn't make sense of. The Freya he knew, the Freya he'd spent more hours with than away from since he started this job, *that* Freya had composure and control as immovable as a face full of Botox. The Freya he saw around Abby was like Godzilla, breathing fire and laying waste to cities. He wasn't religiously inclined, much to his Presbyterian mother's chagrin, but seeing the unrecognizable look in her eyes was the closest he'd come to considering demonic possession as a viable explanation.

"Even though I can't stay the weekend ..." Naomi tilted her head, a playful smile tugging at her lips. "I bet I can make up for lost time tonight."

As images of all the different ways they could do that flooded into his thoughts, he practically groaned. He leaned in and brushed his lips against a spot on her neck that he had come to learn was especially sensitive. "I bet you can, and I have a few ideas," he whispered, not missing how she shivered under him.

"Funny, so do I." With a playful giggle, she closed the remaining distance between them and pressed her lips against his.

He pulled her close, her body both excitingly new and becoming wonderfully familiar as his hands wandered up her back, tracing the curve of her spine through the thin fabric of her shirt. Naomi's fingers found their way into his hair, tugging gently at the strands as she deepened the kiss. As they fell into each other, they also fell backwards, their bodies instinctively seeking support. They bumped against the apartment door, causing it to swing open with a creaking sound.

Their laughter was muffled by their kisses, a refusal to part their connection, as they stumbled away from the door, tumbling onto the couch, an old leather relic from Will's college days, that creaked in protest as their bodies collided onto it.

The television suddenly flickered to life, no doubt from the command of the remote tucked somewhere underneath their bodies. He sat up and fumbled for the remote, but before he could find it, Naomi wrapped her legs around him and pulled him closer, whispering four of the most electrifying words he had ever heard, "Don't make me wait."

He didn't.

Clothes were discarded with reckless abandon, scattered across the living room floor like remnants of a forgotten life. Their bodies entwined, he moved with an urgency that echoed the intensity of the connection he felt every second he was with her. Gasps and moans mingled with the soft sounds of fabric rustling and the rhythmic creaking of the worn-out sofa until at last they lay exhausted together in a tangle of limbs, sweat glistening on their skin. Naomi rested her head against his chest as their breathing slowly evened out.

He ran his fingers through Naomi's hair, feeling the soft curls beneath his touch and then kissed her on the head, causing her to look up at him.

"What are you thinking about over there?" Naomi asked.

Will paused, his eyes meeting hers, and he couldn't help but smile. "I'm thinking about us," he replied, truthfully. "How it feels like I've always known you."

A blush crept onto Naomi's cheeks as she returned his smile. She nestled in closer, their bodies molding against each other. "I know what you mean. Have you ever heard the word beshert before?"

He shook his head.

"It's a Yiddish word that means, like, destiny. Before I met you, I couldn't really picture myself being with anyone again. But when we met at the reunion, it felt like it was supposed to be. Like you were my ... beshert," she said, tracing circles on his arm.

"You feel like my beshert too." He pulled her impossibly closer, sure that she could feel his heart beating faster as he let the words out that he'd been wanting to say. "And I think, I ... love you."

She pulled him in for a kiss that told him he wouldn't have to worry about her saying it back. "I think I love you, too," she said when she broke the kiss. "Actually, I don't think. I really do." She laughed, a giggle of delight that made him join her.

For a long time, they lay together, basking in the sweetness of their love and shared destiny, the silence only broken by the sound of happy kisses.

"Beshert," he whispered to her. But as he said it, her words echoed back to him. She couldn't picture herself being with anyone, *again?* They'd hadn't really discussed their past relationships and for a second he contemplated asking if she was referring to someone specifically. But he decided he was enjoying this moment too much. He wanted to stay here, with her, feeling like this for as long as he could.

He glanced at the TV, still on from before. "Can I convince you to stay right here and watch something for a while?"

"Sounds perfect."

He patted his hand around the sofa in search of the remote. "I'll watch anything except this," he indicated towards the TV with his chin.

"*Real Housewives*?" Naomi asked. "Abby and Riley watch that show religiously. They're total reality TV addicts as you'll discover when you spend time with them. But this is definitely one of their top favorites."

"I hope they'll still accept me when they find out how I feel about it," he joked. "It's nothing personal—that kind of TV doesn't do it for me. It's about a bunch of women manufacturing drama while the whole world watches." His fingers made contact with the remote, in between the cushions.

"I don't know if that's entirely fair." She shifted in his arms, her body suddenly feeling less relaxed than it had a minute ago. "Sure, the producers are editing it to make it more exaggerated, but I don't think you can say that the women are *manufacturing* it."

"Manufactured might be a strong word, but you can't deny that they make terrible choices and then act dumbfounded when it goes completely south," he replied, feeling the slightest pinprick of annoyance. His suggestion to keep them in their post-coital bubble had had the opposite effect for some reason.

Naomi sat up, leaving his skin cold from her absence. She brushed a curl behind her ear. "These women have complicated histories and relationships. Yes, they make questionable choices sometimes, but so does everyone."

The pin prick of annoyance had graduated to a spinal tap. Why was she making such a big deal out of this? He let out a little sigh as he tried, again, to explain what he meant. "There's a big difference between having complicated histories and making poor choices because of them," he told her silhouette. "And then to take it a step further and compound it by dragging everyone they love into it too?"

"You're saying you think it's better if they hide all their problems." Her reply, more statement than question, was sharp.

"No, honey," he said, with a modicum of surprise at her tone. Apparently, Naomi was a bigger *Real Housewives* fan than she was letting on to be getting this upset about it.

"Then what?"

"I'm just—all I'm saying is it's bad enough to create all these problems for yourself, but it's even worse to go onto a television show to shine a spotlight on it. Do you think all the people in their lives signed up to have their dirty laundry televised and scrutinized? If these women could put all their mistakes out there in some vacuum where no one else was affected, then I guess that's their choice. But that's impossible, and to me, it's unforgivable. Maybe it's the farm boy in me, but I'd run so fast if I *ever* met anyone like that. Are you really telling me you wouldn't either?"

"I suppose," Naomi said, her voice nearly a whisper.

He waited for her to say more, but the silence dragged on. He wasn't sure how they'd gotten here, and he was ready to leave the conversation behind. "I didn't mean to hate on something you like. I know reality TV is wildly popular, so I am in the minority. However, for you? I'd watch *Real Housewives*." Relationships were all about compromise and even though he'd get heckled for it back home if they ever found out, this was one compromise he'd be happy to make. "Maybe I haven't seen enough of it to truly appreciate it. It's still early, so let me get some popcorn, and we can make a night out of it."

The television flickered like a strobe light across her face, giving him glimpses of her expression—which seemed to change each time the light shifted. Finally, with what sounded like a hint of a sigh, she shrugged. "That's okay. Reality TV is more Abby and Riley's thing—I should get going anyway. Early day tomorrow."

"You sure?"

She looked back at him, her lips stretching into a smile. "Positive."

He watched, silently, as she stood up and went about collecting and putting on her clothes.

"I love you," he said, as she pulled on her jacket.

"I love you, too." She leaned in and kissed him. "See you tomorrow?"

He nodded and watched, a blanket of anxiety settling over him, as she walked out the door. He couldn't tell if it was his imagination, but it felt like her words, and her kiss, were a few degrees cooler. Was she really upset about his opinion on reality TV? Or was there something else?

This wasn't the first time he'd found himself asking that question around Naomi. Every once in a while, her demeanor would change for reasons he could never pinpoint. At least, that's what it seemed like. All those times, like tonight, he was never sure if something was wrong or if he was merely inept at understanding women, so he said nothing. He let their conversation replay in his mind, wondering if he might get a clue, but under the hypnotic glow of the television, he soon fell asleep.

He awoke to bright sunlight streaming into his living room and his phone pinging under an item of clothing on his floor. Half asleep, he searched his living room until he located the correct pocket with his phone.

FREYA: Brian is hounding me to get this in.

When you get here, can you bring those financial records you were looking over?

Actually, now that I'm thinking about it, we don't have time to include that part.

Maybe they'll let us do a follow up. Forget the records but if you could swing by the supply closet, I could really use some new highlighters.

And now I'm out of printer paper.

He skimmed the messages and then pulled himself out of bed. He hurried through his morning routine, slowing down only to choose his T-shirt: a simple yellow and white shirt that read, "Good God, Lemon," a phrase that had become an inside joke between him and Freya. He'd been saving it for a moment when she needed to smile, and this seemed like the moment.

His place was a fifteen-minute drive to the studio and he stopped for donuts and coffee on the way since it was clear that Freya had been at the office for at least several hours already, and he was quite sure she had not consumed anything since the sun came up.

When he arrived at the Nightly Global News studio, he found Freya in her office, scrolling through footage on her computer. She didn't look up at him, only pointed at her screen. "I want to include this section with Sandy talking about the Ford plant closing. But we're going to need to verify what she's saying about her father getting laid off."

She was dressed in forest green Lululemon yoga pants and hoodie. During the week, she was always dressed to the nines at the office. However, Lululemon was her uniform on weekends.

"When is the last time you ate?"

She shrugged and leaned in closer to her computer. "Didn't we have the employee rosters in one of these folders somewhere?"

In response, he set the coffee and pastries on her desk.

Her eyes went to the coffee, back to the screen, and then back to the coffee. Finally, she sighed and leaned back. "Okay, fine." She grabbed a donut and took a carnivorous bite. "But if this story gets cut because we sent it in late, I'm sending you up there to explain that donuts took us down."

"I'm willing to risk it," he said, taking a seat across from her. "Besides, that's never happened once. Have we gotten so close to the deadline we could have gotten it pregnant? Sure. But we always pull it off in the end."

She took a long pull of her Venti iced coffee, and as she did, her shoulders relaxed, and her grip on the cup loosened. She looked at him as if she were seeing him for the first time that day. "Thanks," she said, then took another bite of donut, her eyes flicking to his shirt and then up, with the smallest of smiles, "Nice shirt."

Internally, he fist pumped. "Thanks," he said, keeping his composure. He picked up a blueberry muffin and began to peel back the wrapper, glancing at her screen. "How long you been at this?"

"Brian caught me last night, told me we'd put too many resources into it, and if we didn't have something for him by this afternoon he was going to cut the story."

"You should have called me."

Freya swallowed the last of her donut. "I figured one of us should have a good Friday night. Hopefully, you fulfilled the assignment."

He couldn't stop his lips from parting in a smile as he thought about his evening.

"That good, huh?"

"We broke out the big L word last night. I've said it before, but somehow this felt different. This sounds so corny, but I feel like she's the one. Like—it's felt that way from the minute I turned around and saw her and ..."

An amused expression drifted onto Freya's face. "Did she have you at hello, Will?"

"Listen, you." He cinched his lips together to hold back the laughter. "I brought you sustenance, and this is how you treat me?"

She held up her hands. "I can only work with what you're giving me. And right now you're giving me some real *Jerry Maguire* vibes."

"That reference is so dated, it really softens the blow."

She wrinkled her nose at him.

"It's not like that. It doesn't feel like she 'completes me.' It feels like ... she compliments me."

Instead of tossing out a joke, Freya pushed back in her chair and put her hands behind her head, a contemplative look on her face. He wondered if she was about to give him a glimpse into her love life, a topic on which he knew next to nothing despite his best efforts. She'd never dropped so much as a morsel. He'd seen photos of her at premiers and fundraisers on the arm of a variety of tall men, most of whom had features that could cut glass. But she never talked about those men and certainly never brought them anywhere that he could meet them.

Would this be the moment that she finally let something slip? An anecdote or a piece of advice? He stopped chewing and bent forward slightly.

She looked up at the ceiling. "*Two halves have little choice but to join; and yes, they do make a whole. But two wholes when they coincide ... that is beauty. That is love.*"

He blinked.

When he didn't say anything, she returned her gaze to him. "Poetry," she said, her tone matter-of-fact. "Peter McWilliams. I read that a while ago, and it always stuck with me."

He resumed chewing, feeling slightly disappointed. "I never would have taken you for the poetry type, Jonsson."

"I am, but less for the romantic side of it and more for the exploration of the written word. I find it helps me think outside the box."

He filed that away. It wasn't a peek into her romantic life, but it was a useful tidbit into the private world of Freya. "Speaking of going outside the box, you don't happen to know anything about the Jewish holiday of Rosh Hashanah, do you?"

"My parents were atheists from Iceland, so I can't say that I do other than a general overview of the holiday. Why?"

"Naomi invited me—well, I kind of invited myself—to a Rosh Hashanah thing tonight. I was hoping you could give me pointers and also pick me up from her place on your way to the airport."

"Going over for the holidays? You two really are in love."

"Right? I thought maybe she wasn't ready to integrate the relationship into the rest of her life, but I guess if I'm coming over for the New Year, that must not be it. Now I have to be sure I don't make a complete ass of myself and make her regret it."

"Sounds like you've got some research to do."

"Let me guess. Not until I finish the research I need to do here?"

Freya pressed a hand to each cheek. "Aww, Will! You read my mind. Now who is completing who?"

He shot her an insolent glance before turning her monitor to face him. "Alright, alright. Let's get to it."

Chapter Nine

Naomi

In a little under three hours, Nosh Hashanah would begin. Somehow, Naomi had managed to prepare her signature Nosh Hashanah apple chutney challah, assemble an apple and honey cheese board, get the decorations out of storage, and clean her apartment enough to show her friends she cared. With the remaining time, she only needed to bake two dozen bumblebee cookies, set the table, and set up the holiday decor. Luckily, Abby, Riley, Becca—if she felt like it—and Will were on their way to help. She wanted to be excited about Will coming; she *was* excited. But under the excitement, anxiety bubbled up like a simmering cauldron.

This may be the farm boy in me, but I'd run so fast if I ever met anyone like that.

She couldn't blame him for feeling that way, but it didn't take the sting of his words away. Creating problems for yourself and then forcing someone to be a part of those problems *was* selfish. It was exactly the reason she hadn't told him about Simon yet. They were still getting to know each other and trying to decide if this was real, so she didn't need to rope him into something he might not even want to be roped into in the first place. When she had invited him to Nosh Hashanah, she had thought, maybe, if he spent time with Riley and Abby and got their official stamp of approval, then she would tell him. And when they said their first 'I love yous' she'd thought for sure the time had come. But after their conversation, she'd begun to wonder if she should tell him at all.

Afterall, it sounded like he didn't want to know. And if Will loved her as she was *now*, why did it matter who she was *then* anyway?

"Judging by the look on your face, you also saw Taylor Swift's new haircut." Riley's voice brought her back from her thoughts. They were standing in the doorway of her apartment, holding two grocery bags that appeared to be filled with a variety of liquor. "We need to enact martial law until it's fixed."

She smiled, in spite of herself. "I missed it!"

"It's absolutely tragic. All her people should be fired. All of them," they said, stepping towards her. "But if it's not a Swiftie problem, what else could constitute a look like that? Is it a boy problem?"

When she didn't answer right away, Riley gasped. "What did he do? Things were going so well!"

"They're going well!" she assured him. They were. This small problem, her problem, wasn't something they—and by extension, Abby, because it would inevitably get back to her—needed to worry about. She decided to tell the truth. Kind of. "He ... doesn't like *Real Housewives*. He said it's women manufacturing drama."

Riley's gasp increased in sound and duration. "Blasphemy!" they said, emphasizing each syllable. "I knew he couldn't be as perfect as he seemed, but who could have guessed it would be *this*."

"I know," she said, content that her semi-truth had done the trick. "I hope you'll be able to forgive him." She took the bags from Riley and set them down next to her cabinet turned makeshift bar.

They gave a dramatic sniffle and then placed a hand over their heart. "I'll never look at him the same, but I suppose I can move past it." Riley lowered their hand and looked at her, a solemn expression settling across their face. "You know, I've always thought that reality TV is a mirror to our own lives. We may not be throwing drinks at each other—well, Abby is apparently—but in our own way, we all have our own drama, don't we? Hopefully, Will knows that."

Naomi glanced up at Riley, curious if there was anything more behind that. Could they have picked up on what was really going on?

"Look who I found!"

She glanced up to see Abby walking in, followed by Will pulling a rollaboard suitcase behind him.

Will nodded. "It's true, she did. I didn't recognize her without her big hat." He looked at Abby, a smirk pulling the corner of his lip. Naomi had given him permission to tease her friends about their date crashing, but she hadn't expected him to start the moment he arrived. Her face must have registered her nonplussed expression because he quickly added, "Too soon?"

"Never," Riley said. "Good-natured ribs are our social currency."

Abby let out a hearty laugh. "They're right."

"Now that we're all on the same page about that, can I make some comments about your shirt?" Riley said, dubiously eyeing Will's Rosh Hashanah-themed shirt that said *Shofar So Good* above a drawing of a shofar, a curved ram's horn traditionally blown during the Jewish High Holidays, that he'd snagged at Target on the way over.

Will laughed. "You sound like Fre—" He stopped so fast, it almost sounded like he was choking. He swallowed and then turned to Naomi, lifting up his suitcase. "Where would you like me to leave this?"

"Hello, my darlings!" a melodic voice called out. Everyone turned. "My lord, there's a little nip in the air tonight!" Becca appeared, breathlessly, tugging off her coat and revealing a sleeveless, black and red corset dress. Flinging her coat on top of the coffee table, she glanced behind her and waved as if inviting someone to come in. Which was exactly what she was doing.

"You've got to be kidding me," Abby said under her breath as a statuesque man came into view. He pulled off his woolen cap and dark luminous hair fell across his shoulders.

Naomi had done her best to prepare Will for life with her friends, but she had thought there would be more of an easing-in process.

"Who did you bring to our party?" Abby asked.

"And what are you wearing?" Naomi added.

Becca dropped her arms at her side. "Well, Shana Tova to you, too." She rested a hand on her hip and adopted an air of annoyance. When no one responded, she gave a slight huff and continued, "This is the latest from Paris, and this is Marius. We met at the gym. He was my yoga instructor—I know what you're going to say: Becca, that's so cliché."

"Actually, that's not at all what I was going to say," Abby muttered.

Will stepped into view and greeted Becca's guest.

"I'm Will," he said with an outstretched hand.

Marius shook his hand but did not respond.

"He's taken a vow of silence, dear," Becca said out. Looking back at her sister, she explained. "It's part of his spiritual quest. Isn't it great?

Don't look so glum, Abby. I really think you'll like him. You know, once he's talking again. And in the meantime, enjoy the view."

Riley raised their hand. "I know I will."

"I need a drink," Abby said.

"That reminds me! Marius!" Becca spun around and scampered back to Marius, slipping her hand through his defined arm. "Did we leave the wine in the car? Let's get it."

Marius nodded and, placing his hand on the small of her back, he led her out of the apartment.

As the door shut, Abby exhaled noisily. "He can drink and sleep with a married woman, but he can't talk."

Riley smoothed their sideburns with their fingers and considered her question. "Who are we to judge what the spirits require?"

"I think the spirits are requiring all of us to get back to work," Naomi said.

The next few hours flew by as they hurried to finish preparations. As the sunlight faded, friends began to trickle in and soon her apartment was humming with happy conversation that was sure to draw a complaint from Mrs. Pachenkis before the night was over. Everything was going perfectly.

"This is a disaster!"

Naomi was in the kitchen loading more cookies onto a platter when she heard Riley shout from her living room. Moments later, Abby walked into the kitchen.

"Do we have any ice left?" Abby asked, walking to the refrigerator and opening the freezer.

"If there's nothing in there, then we're out," Naomi said. "Is that the disaster?"

Abby shuffled things around in her freezer. "Riley has some pomegranate cocktail they wanted to unveil, but it seems it's 'meaningless' without ice." She closed the freezer. "I guess I'm walking to the store to get more ice lest we are forced to consume meaningless drinks."

Naomi smiled and started down the hall, holding the platter of cookies on her shoulder, hearkening back to her days as a server.

"Naomi—" Riley was at her side.

"Abby is getting ice right now," she assured them, setting the dish on one of the folding tables.

"Oh, thank god. I cannot serve the Chosen People room temperature vodka *and* Prosecco in one drink. You all have suffered enough."

"That's very," she put a cookie in her mouth to muffle her sarcasm, "considerate of you, Riley."

Her back pocket buzzed. She pulled out her phone, and immediately her mouth went dry.

UNKNOWN

It could have been a wrong number; it could have been spam. But she knew. It was him. The honey-laden cookie in her mouth suddenly tasted like broken glass, and she forced herself to swallow the shards.

Clutching her phone in her hand, she made her way to her room and closed the door. She didn't want to look but she knew she had to. She wouldn't be able to mingle with her friends and pretend like she wasn't wondering what the text message said the whole time. After all, there was still a chance it was only spam. It was better to bite the bullet and find out.

She sat down on her bed.

UNKNOWN: Happy Nosh Hashanah Kiwi

A tight exhale squeezed out of her throat. Simon had been there for the start of Nosh Hashanah. He knew exactly what she would be doing at this moment because for many years, he was doing it with her.

Three dots appeared, and then another message rolled onto the screen.

UNKNOWN: I need to talk to you. Only a second, I promise.

Talk? He wanted to talk right now? Her stomach churned. Another buzz.

UNKNOWN: I'm downstairs. I'll wait.

The blood froze in her veins.

Downstairs.

He was downstairs.

Downstairs meant mere steps from her apartment. From Will. She couldn't let that happen. She couldn't let Will find out about Simon this way. She had to stop him.

She hadn't seen Simon in years. But her fear of seeing him was microscopic in comparison to her fear of the scene he could make in front of Will.

She stood up, only then realizing that her cheeks were soaked in tears. She swiped at her face and then took the deepest breath she could manage before walking out of her room. Will was at the bar with Riley, pouring an entire bottle of Prosecco into a large glass bowl.

She snuck out as quietly as possible, keeping her head down to avoid catching anyone's eye. As she slowly closed the door behind her, she noticed Mrs. Pachenkis looking out from her apartment.

"Keep it down in there," Mrs. Pachenkis ordered.

Naomi gave her a tight smile and waved.

The normally short ride down the elevator stretched like a walk to the gallows. She didn't know what he was going to say. Or do. But she knew that she had to do whatever it took to get him out of there as quickly as possible.

The elevator doors opened to the apartment lobby. Outside the lobby doors, illuminated by the courtyard lights, she could see Simon leaning up against the glass window.

With a slow, deliberate exhale, she attempted—and failed—to calm her nerves. Walking across the lobby, she pressed the doors open. In the dusky light, she could still make out his handsome features that hadn't changed even after all this time. A few inches taller than her, with a sharply defined face that was softened by chestnut brown hair and forest green eyes, Simon had taken her breath away the first time she met him and, fight it as she might, he still did every time she saw him, even today.

His mouth broke out into a broad smile when he saw her. He was wearing a pair of simple, brown chinos and a navy peacoat, both of which clung to his well-maintained frame as he pushed away from the window. "Kiwi! Wow, I've missed you." He reached out to brush her cheek with his hand. She turned her face from him, and he jerked his hand away. "Sorry, I forget I'm not supposed to do that anymore."

She crossed her arms and squeezed herself tightly, feeling like her seams were about to burst and she was barely holding herself together. "Not supposed to—Simon, you're not supposed to be within one hundred yards of me!"

The smile on his face disappeared as quickly as it had appeared. "You want to start things off like that?"

"I'm not starting—" She cut herself off. Trying to win an argument with Simon would never work. "This isn't a good time, Simon. You need to leave."

"I know all your friends, all *our* friends, are up there." His eyes flicked up at her apartment window, then back down. "But they can wait. We are more important than a party. More than anything. I've realized that. I'm back in anger management classes, Naomi. I'm seeing my therapist again. I stopped drinking. I came here to tell you I did all this for you. I know our marriage is over, and that's my fault. But I want to be someone who deserves a place in your life, even if it's only as friends."

She had heard variations of this speech dozens of times, but it still sent fresh ripples of pain through a part of her. The part that wanted so badly to believe that this time it was true and he had finally, really changed. "What if you called me next week? After the holidays?"

"No!" he said. He rubbed his hands against his face as if trying to wipe away a rage that was starting to brew. "You can't even give me five minutes?"

In that instant, she knew nothing had changed at all. The anger in his voice made her heart slam in her chest like a jackhammer, and she took a step back. "Simon, this isn't a good idea ..." she said, her voice hoarse as she started to fight back tears.

"Don't say that," he tried to say softly, but there was a sharpness to his words she knew too well. "Don't say that, love. You know that we were always meant to be together. And I know that any problems we've had were because of me. But I promise you, I'm different now. This ... this is the new me. All I want is a chance to show you I've changed. Won't you at least give me that chance?" He reached out and put his hands on her arms.

His grip on her felt like a noose tightening around her neck, choking the air out of her lungs, and she lowered her eyes, hoping to hide the unwanted tears that were starting to fall.

"The hell?" a voice asked.

They both followed the sound to find Abigail standing a few feet from them on the sidewalk. The bag of ice she had from the store was at her feet, and ice cubes were scattered around her like an impressionist painting. Relief washed over Naomi. Followed by shame. Abby would do what she had always done, what Naomi could never do for herself. Abby would protect her.

"Abigail," Simon said with a smile, as if greeting an old friend. He released Naomi's arms and smiled.

Abby didn't smile back. Instead, she thundered towards them, her body seeming to grow in size and ferocity with each step. She situated herself squarely between Naomi and Simon, bringing her face directly in front of Simon. "Leave."

The friendly façade vanished, and his eyes sparked defiantly. "Stay out of this, Abigail."

"Simon," Naomi spoke calmly, afraid that the situation might escalate. "Please, just go."

Simon looked back at Naomi with a snarl. "You still letting this woman run your life?" He turned back to Abby. "Stop getting involved in other people's business. Let her decide what she wants."

"She did decide what she wants, Simon," Abby said, her voice firm. "When she had a restraining order put against you. Now leave."

"You don't get to—"

Abby pointed towards the street and said loudly, "Go. Now."

They stood in silence, waiting, until after an eternity, Simon took a step back. And then another.

"I won't give up," he said before, thankfully, turning and walking away.

They stood together, not speaking, as he made his way down the street. When at last he turned the corner, Abby pulled Naomi into a tight hug.

"Are you okay?" she asked.

Naomi nodded into her friend's shoulder. "Thank you," she said.

Abby released her. "What happened? Why was he here? Why were *you* here?"

Naomi wished she could skip over this part. "It's nothing," she said. "He texted he was here, and I came down to tell him to leave."

"I can't believe he'd do that to you. I want to be more upset but I'm too happy that he screwed himself so royally. He was probably counting on getting you alone so it would be a he said, she said situation. He didn't expect me to show up and be a witness to his restraining order violation. Thank you, Riley, for your ice disaster. Naomi, this means we can finally report him to the police! We have proof this time!"

That thought hadn't crossed her mind, but as it did, her body tightened, forcing out a single, intense, "No."

Abby's eyebrows lifted, a look of consternation etched between her brows. "What?"

I'd run away...

"It's not that simple."

"What do you mean? It's incredibly simple. We call the police. Simon goes to jail. End of story."

She shook her head, wishing Abby would let it go. "You know it's never like that. There'll be reports and court dates, and even then, who knows if he'll actually go to jail? All it's going to do is make him angrier and more dangerous. And ..." Naomi stabbed her tongue between her teeth and bit down as hard as she could. She wasn't ready to have this conversation.

But Abby wasn't fooled. "I see what you're doing. Nice try," she gave a single shake of her head. "What are you not telling me?"

Naomi released her tongue and let out a sigh. "Will," she said slowly, each word dragging like it weighed a thousand pounds. "He doesn't know."

"Doesn't know," Abby repeated. "Doesn't know what? That you have a restraining order against Simon?"

"He doesn't know anything about Simon," she answered, her voice as beaten down as she felt. "He doesn't know I was married before."

"You haven't told him yet?" Abby asked, her volume rising with incredulity.

A rush of frustration coursed through Naomi, and she found herself matching Abby's volume. "If I tell him, then he's involved!"

"He's already involved!" Abby exclaimed. She blew out a measured breath and then said in a softer voice, "He was involved the moment you let him buy you dinner. I know we all told you to take your time, but we meant like a few dates, not a few months. Simon is a big part of your life. You can't leave him off the books like he's an accounting error. And Will deserves to know the truth."

"You make it seem like I haven't given this any thought!" she said, her words pouring out of her like acid, each one laced with raw emotion. "But I have. I think about it all the time, and this, what happened, only proves to me that I've made the right choice in all this. Right now, Will is upstairs, hopefully having a wonderful time at his girlfriend's party. But if I call the police, then it's over."

"I don't think he'll care if the party is over."

"Not the party, Abby! Everything we have is over; it will never be the same. Once Will knows, then ... then he's a part of it. He's part of the mess I made. I don't want him to have to live like me and be scared every time my phone rings or there's fast footsteps behind me. He didn't sign up for that when he picked me, and he doesn't deserve it."

"But—"

She wasn't done. "And, maybe it's selfish of me, but I want to have one wonderful thing that Simon can't get to. I love that when Will sees *me*, he doesn't see a person who stayed with an abuser, who covered for him, who loved him in spite of all the things he did. The Naomi he sees is the Naomi I want to be, and when he sees me that way, it makes me feel like I can see myself that way too."

Abby opened her mouth as if to speak, but nothing came out.

"You've always taken care of me," Naomi continued. "But I'm asking you to let me do this my way, Abby."

Abby watched her for a few seconds and then gave a resigned nod. "Okay," she said. "You're right. This is your decision."

This time, Naomi was the one who went in for the hug. "Thank you." Still holding on, she added, "Can we keep this between us right now?" She knew Abby's first instinct would be to go to Riley. But she couldn't handle doing this all over again, couldn't stand the thought of Riley looking at her the way that Abby just had. She didn't need another fight or the weight of someone else's worry pressing down on her. And she definitely didn't need to spend any time wondering what was being said in hushed conversations when she wasn't in the room.

Naomi could feel Abby stiffen, but after a moment, she said, "Okay."

Naomi gave her an extra squeeze and then let go. "Thank you for always being there for me."

"I always will be. Promise," Abby said. Her smile was warm, but her voice carried a sadness that settled in the space between them. "But we should probably head up or someone is going to come looking for us. You go ahead. I need to grab the ice." She turned and nodded towards the bag still sitting on the ground where she had left it.

Grateful to have a moment alone, Naomi returned to the lobby. She used the ride up to her floor to collect herself, pressing her hands to her face as she took slow inhales. She had years of practice picking up the fractured pieces of herself after a fight with Simon—locking them away, one by one—until she could move through the day like it had never happened. Even now, after all this time, she found that ability came back quickly. As the elevator doors opened, she felt the last few minutes dissolve and she put a bright smile onto her face as she headed into her apartment.

"There you are!" Will said before she had taken more than a step inside. "I was looking for you."

"Sorry," she said.

He examined her face with concern, and she stopped herself from patting her eyes to make sure they were dry. "Everything okay?" He leaned closer, saying in a quieter voice. "You were gone a while."

"Yep," she assured him. "I was checking in on Mrs. Pachenkis." She hated to lie, but she hated the questions more.

"Please tell me you've brought ice," Riley appeared next to Will. "We're down to Becca's wine, and it's atrocious."

"Has anyone ever told you that your voice carries?" Riley turned to see Becca, lifting a drink to her lips, her hazel eyes watching them with an amused look.

"Oh, sweetie," they replied, brushing a wrinkle from their skirt. "Just because I think your taste in wine happens to be appalling, that doesn't mean I feel the same way about the things that really matter, like your choice in shoes."

Apparently satisfied with this answer, Becca merely sipped her drink and smiled.

"You came back right in time. I have to head out," Will said.

"Is it already time to go?" Naomi asked.

"Yeah, Freya texted that she's here."

Naomi's eyes went wide. "Wait, here? She's *here?*"

Will nodded. "She's picking me up on the way to the airport. I figured that would be safe since even if for some reason she did try to come up, she'd have to be buzzed in *and* she doesn't even know your apartment number. We've got multiple layers keeping Abby and Freya apart." He chuckled. "I mean, Abby would literally have to go downstairs and stand in front of Freya's car to—

"Oh God."

Naomi ran to the window, knelt on the sofa, and looked down at the entrance of the building.

Will knelt beside her. "What are you—"

"*Look.*" Naomi pointed at the two figures down below. Even in the growing darkness of nightfall, it was impossible to mistake them for anyone else but Freya and Abby. Surrounded by ice cubes still littering the sidewalk, their hunched shoulders and sharp movements required no interpretation.

"You've got to be kidding me."

"What is the matter with them?" Naomi said, exasperated. "They're grown adults, not teenagers."

"I've been trying to figure that out myself," Will replied.

"What's going on?" Riley said, joining them on the sofa. They looked out the window and gasped. "Abigail, there you are, you Jezebel! Bring my ice!"

Becca had made her way to the sofa and sat down in the remaining free space. "I'm going to need narration. I'm not climbing on a sofa. Not in this dress."

"Hang on, who is she talking to? Is that—" Riley stopped as, with one fluid motion, Freya bent down, picked up one of the ice cubes on the ground and threw it at Abby. Riley slapped a hand over their mouth. "Okay. That just happened."

"Yep, we gotta go," Will said, sounding like a parent whose child is melting down at a playground. He sprang off the sofa and Naomi was right behind him.

As they raced through the doors of her lobby into the courtyard, they both heard Freya shout, "You think you're the only one who can throw things?" She leaned down to scoop up another handful of ice. "Think again." She stood up, arm cocked back and ready to fire, but faltered when she noticed her audience. Naomi expected to see a fierce, angry expression on Freya's face, but it looked more like a triumphant smile.

"Ooh, an encore!" Becca said, coming up behind her, the ice from her drink tinkling as she walked.

"I should have brought a drink too," she heard Riley say.

Having been through this twice now, Will seemed to know what to do. "I'll call you from the airport." He gave Naomi a kiss before positioning himself next to his boss. "Freya," he said in a cautious tone.

Freya blinked, almost like she was coming out of a trance. The pleased smile, however, stayed on her face as she turned to look at Will. "There you are. Ready to head out?"

"Sure," he replied and, without waiting for an invitation, walked to the passenger side of a BMW parked a few steps away. Wordlessly, Freya got into the driver's seat and moments later the car peeled away.

Once the car was out of sight, Abby turned to face her friends. "Okay, no. This time it wasn't me. I *swear*. I was picking up ice cubes and ... she was standing there ..."

When no one answered, she tried again. "And then she started ... I mean, I tried to be ... but then she was all ..." She pointed towards where Freya had been standing. "You should have heard ... what was I supposed to ..."

She paused, clearly waiting for someone to jump in, but after a few seconds, she gave up. "Not my fault this time!" she declared, breezing past the trio without meeting their eyes and marching towards the lobby.

As the doors to the lobby closed, Riley looked out at the now-empty sidewalk, their eyes flitting back and forth as if they were replaying the last few minutes in their mind. "It's so not like her," they mused. "There's something about those two that's not sitting quite right with me."

"How so?" Becca asked.

"It doesn't feel like normal fighting to me. There's an electricity like …" They hesitated, as if they were seeking to place a description with the sensation. "Like foreplay."

Becca swirled the liquid in her glass and took a gulp. "Don't get me wrong, Riley. I've been in more than one relationship consisting of nothing but fighting matches. But our arguments always ended in sex. Amazing, angry, torrid, sweaty sex. What's the point of all that," she indicated the scene of the crime, "if you're not going to end up in bed together?"

Normally, this kind of banter was a stress reliever for Naomi, but it wasn't serving as the balm it normally did.

"Everything is such a mess," Naomi moaned, tossing her head back.

"What? That little thing?" Becca asked.

That, she wanted to say, and everything that had happened with Simon. But she wasn't going to go there. Instead, she nodded. "My boyfriend's boss and my best friend are like bleach and ammonia." She rubbed her face in her hands. "I think they're both good people, and they don't mean it but like … *why*? Why does this keep happening? What is wrong with them? And what are we supposed to do about it?"

Riley cleared their throat. "I think it's becoming obvious what we do," they said. "Get those two love birds together."

Naomi hadn't thought anything could distract her from the emotional turmoil of the last hour, but somehow, incredibly, Riley had done it.

"What?" she said, in full disbelief.

Becca, clearly intrigued, stepped forward. "You're thinking," she said, following Riley's train of thought, "that this whole rivalry thing is really one, long, drawn-out game of foreplay?"

"Yes!" Riley said excitedly.

Becca gave a sarcastic chuckle as she considered this possibility. "If anyone could hold out that long, it would be my sister."

"Wait a minute," Naomi said to Becca, feeling like she was trying to stop a Domino chain that had been set in motion. "You're not actually buying into this theory, are you?"

Becca shrugged her shoulders. "Nothing can make a person more insane than a case of blue balls." She added quickly, "Not that I'd know. But I've seen its effects. This is assuming, of course, that Freya, you know, plays for that team. I mean, I know there have been rumors circulating online for years, but does anyone know for sure if she is actually partial to the ladies? You went to school with her, Naomi, you must have seen something, right?"

"Why are you even asking her?" Riley interjected. "I have the most finely tuned dyke-tection this side of the Mississippi, and I am telling you that Freya loves the ladies and, in particular, Abby, who also loves her back."

Naomi still couldn't make sense of it. "Even if that were somehow true, which I don't see how it could be, what does it matter? The only feelings they seem to be aware of are their hatred for each other, and I doubt us telling them otherwise would make any difference."

"Well, obviously we can't *tell* them. We're going to have to," Riley swirled their hand, like casting a spell, "encourage them to discover it on their own with the assistance of some behind-the-scenes work."

"Such as?" Naomi mimicked Riley's hand motion.

"I'm not sure yet. The details will come to me. Which leaves only one question. Naomi Hoffman, are you in?"

"In?" Naomi asked. "In what?"

"*In,*" Becca explained.

"Exactly," Riley confirmed. "In."

Naomi shook her head. "You can say it any way you want, but it's still only one word that requires more words around it."

"In on helping Abby and Freya unlock their true feelings for each other so they can have a happily ever after and then, by extension, so can you and Will."

Now that ... that was tempting. Whatever 'behind the scenes' work Riley had in mind, not so much. But a happily ever after for her *and* her best friend? If there was even a slight possibility that Riley was right, it might be worth exploring. "I'm not saying I'm in. I'm saying that before I could consider being in, I'd need Will to be in. And I really don't think—"

"Bup bup," Riley held up a silencing finger. "Your phone, please."

She reached into her pocket and then stopped. "Why?"

Riley stretched their hand out. "Phone, please."

Curiosity and exhaustion overpowered her ability to press further, and she handed over her phone.

Without hesitation, Riley unlocked her phone and began tapping.

"How did you know my—"

"You think Abby's passwords are the only ones I know?" they said without breaking stride with their fingers. After a minute, they handed her phone back to her. "Now, read," they commanded. She looked down.

NAOMI: This is Riley. I've commandeered Naomi's phone to ask you one question. If I were to say that Freya and Abby were in love with each other, what would you say?

WILL: I'd say I was sitting here thinking exactly that.

NAOMI: So then if I said we need to discreetly help them come to that conclusion you'd say…

WILL: I'd say, if it can be done we should try. But also, what does Naomi say?

The last message was typed out but not sent

NAOMI: Naomi says she's in

Naomi looked up at Riley. She had a lot of questions, quite a few concerns, and a handful of objections. But right now, she needed this. She needed her friends to come together, she needed a distraction, she needed a plan, even if the plan was only a side quest that didn't help her get closer to dealing with her own problems.

She looked back at the phone. And hit send.

Chapter Ten

Will

As Will escorted Naomi into the majestic Tiffany-ceilinged ballroom of the Chicago Cultural Center, he couldn't help but notice the way her eyes widened in awe. As she took in the crowd of elegantly dressed guests, the opulent flower arrangements, and the soft strains of a string quartet playing in the background, her lips parted into a silent "wow." After a few more seconds, she found her voice and said it aloud.

"Wow." She grasped Will's arm a little tighter.

Will guided her towards the table with the seating arrangements. "Table two," he read the number on the back of the name card. "We're right by the podium."

They weaved their way through the crowd and reached their table at the same time Freya did. "Hey there! Glad you made it," she said, hanging her purse on the back of a chair.

"Thank you for inviting us," Naomi said. "I've never been to a black-tie fundraiser before. My experience with fundraisers is mostly limited to school bake sales."

Freya pulled her chair out and sat down, her movements hinting at a tense undercurrent beneath the cheerful façade. "Thank you for coming. I'll be happy to have some friendly faces to look at while I'm up there emceeing."

Freya had made it no secret that her comfort with being front and center on camera did not translate to speaking in front of live audiences. Will knew that if she was openly talking about something she was afraid of doing, then it had to be pretty bad. Which is why he gathered that she must have really believed in the cause when she accepted the invitation to emcee at the Chicago for PAWS gala, the city's premier animal rescue fundraiser.

Now, he watched as she squeezed her fingers together so tightly he could see her skin turning white.

"We're going to get something from the bar. We'll grab you a champagne," he said.

The room was packed with the city's upper echelon making their rounds, so they worked their way to the back of the room, skirting the wall as they headed towards the bar.

"Do you go to a lot of these?" Naomi asked him, putting her arm through his.

"Never," he said with a laugh. "Freya does, but I'm not usually on her invite list. I think she's nervous because she has to—"

He was cut off mid-sentence when Naomi stopped short, her arm slipping from his. He heard the unmistakable sound of fabric tearing, which was then immediately followed by a gasp.

He turned to see Naomi's skirt, well, half of it, hanging on a doorknob of one of the large ornate doors leading out into the hallway and Naomi, eyes almost as wide as her mouth, looking down at her bare legs.

Quickly, he stepped in front of her to provide some cover while she tugged the remnants of her skirt from the doorknob.

"Oh my God," she squeaked. "Oh no! I can't believe this is happening."

As Naomi's face began to turn red, Will's mind raced as he tried to think of the best way to help her through her mortification. He could fumble through reassurances, pretend like this wasn't happening, or ... he could do what he did best.

Make her laugh.

It was a gamble—but he went with his gut, that flipping the script with some humor would let her reclaim the moment.

He leaned in closer and chuckled. "Babe, I know we were making out a little before we left, but you really couldn't wait any longer?"

And just like that, the flush of embarrassment was met with relief and amusement. "Did it work? Did I seduce you?" She giggled back.

"Baby," he said, lowering his voice slightly, "I am *so* turned on right now."

This made Naomi laugh even harder. Between giggles, they managed to extricate the remains of her skirt from the doorknob, and then Will offered his jacket to wrap around her waist.

"What do you want to do?" he asked. "Do you want to go? Or maybe someone can bring you another dress?"

Naomi rubbed her hand along her forehead as she tried to collect her thoughts. "You think we can salvage this evening? You're not too humiliated to be seen with me?"

Will planted a kiss on the spot she had been rubbing. "I always want to be with you. And besides, I'm confident everyone in this room is far too self-involved to have even noticed."

Naomi let out a short breath. "Okay. Well, let me text Abby and see if she can bring me something else to wear. I can hide out in the bathroom until she comes."

"I think I saw the bathroom right across the hall," he said, turning the offending doorknob and opening the door.

He helped Naomi get to the bathroom and then posted himself outside the door. After a few minutes, she poked her head out. "Abby's on her way. Can you meet her at the top of the stairs and point her in the right direction?"

He gave her a two-fingered salute and followed the long, curving hallway until he reached the marble staircase leading up from the lobby.

After about twenty minutes, he heard Riley's voice carrying up the stairs. "I've never been so speechless."

"I have a hard time imagining what could render you speechless," Will said when Riley and Abby came into view dressed in sweats and winter coats, a stark contrast to the opulent setting behind him.

"How about Becca calling to say Peter left her for cheating, and all she wants is to have him back?" Riley said, as if Will had always been part of the conversation.

Will's eyebrows shot up. "*Becca* said that? The same woman who came to brunch last week with her cycle instructor after spending the night with her contractor?"

"The same."

"That ... would ..."

"Exactly."

Naomi must have heard them talking because now she was calling out from the bathroom door down the hall. "Um, excuse me?"

"Sorry, I'm so flabbergasted, I'm failing in my duty to direct you to Naomi," he said to Abby. "The bathroom is right around the bend there, on the left."

Abby, holding a navy-blue dress, looked in the direction he was pointing. "I'll bring her the dress, and Riley can fill you in."

Riley didn't need the invitation as their fingers were already on his shoulder, inviting him closer. "This one was not on my Bingo card, for sure. Literally on the way over here, Abby's phone rings and it's Becca, and she's absolutely a wreck. She said that Peter came home tonight and said he knew everything about her affairs, and he was leaving. And then, she's going on and on about how the only thing she wants is to get Peter back and—okay," their voice dropped to a whisper. "I can fill you in on all that later, but now that Abby is gone, we need to talk."

He didn't need any more clues to know what Riley wanted to talk about. It had been a little over a month since Riley, using Naomi's phone, had texted him about his idea that confirmed something that had been simmering in the back of his own mind. Could all the fighting between Abby and Freya be covering up something else, something deep down that they didn't want to admit to each other or even to themselves?

He hadn't heard any more about it and had begun to wonder if perhaps this was a wild hair that had come and gone like one of Riley's fleeting hairstyles. But apparently not.

"Abby. Freya. You're still in, yes?"

"Still in," Will confirmed in a hushed voice. If Freya had unrealized feelings for Abby, which was the only explanation outside of an *Invasion of the Body Snatchers* situation that could make sense of her behavior, then helping her discover those feelings seemed like a win-win. He'd help Freya find love and, as a lovely bonus, it would make it so he and

Naomi didn't have to worry about any more run-ins between his boss and her best friend. "But Naomi isn't convinced." Naomi had texted back that she was "in," but he had quickly come to learn that she was in like someone slowly inching their way into an icy pool.

"You are though, right?"

"I feel like I shouldn't be. All evidence would suggest otherwise. But for some reason, what you said makes sense. Maybe this really is just two people in love."

Riley nodded with vigor. "It is, and honestly, I'm furious at myself that it took me so long to see it."

"You think there's something we can do about it?"

"Will. You've been a part of our little cohort long enough to know that I am never wrong."

"I'm not sure I'd go that far."

"Of course you would. Now listen, I've been letting this percolate, and I think I finally know what to do. It's ridiculously easy. See, what was tripping me up is that there's a snowball's chance in hell that either one of them was going to be receptive to anyone straight up telling them."

"I agree," Will said.

"Exactly. If these two are going to figure out their feelings, they need help figuring it out while *also* thinking that they have figured it out on their own," Riley continued. "But they can't know that we know that *they* know, so we have to let them believe they accidentally found out."

"I think I'm still following."

"I'm not," a voice behind them said.

They whirled around to see Naomi standing behind them, looking as stunning in her new dress as she did wary.

“Where’s Abby?” Riley asked in an exaggerated whisper, encouraging her to talk softly.

“I didn’t see her when I left the bathroom, so maybe she went to look around a bit.”

“Good, then I have a little more time,” Riley said. “Listen, this is what finally came to me, and it’s perfection. If we’re going to get Abby and Freya to realize their own feelings, they have to think the *other person* has feelings for them before they will let their guard down. Which sounds like an impossible problem, but I’ve come to realize the solution is actually simple. We let each of them overhear us talking about how the other one is in love with them.”

“That sounds anything but simple. That sounds complicated.”

“What’s complicated about making sure Abby and Freya are in the right place at the right time to listen to us say the magic words that will change their lives forever?”

“All of that?” Naomi replied. “Every word that came out of your mouth?”

Riley had managed to make their plan sound complex, but Will could see the heart of what they were getting at. And they were right. It was perfect in its simplicity.

“Riley’s describing what we sometimes call a strategic leak,” Will told her. “It’s when someone intentionally shares confidential information within earshot of a journalist in the hopes that it gets reported on.”

“Yes, that!” Riley’s voice rose slightly above a whisper. “Once the information leaks, they’ll realize how they really feel for each other, and the rest will play out on its own. I know it.”

"Okay, let's assume this 'strategic leak' is somehow doable. There's a lot of ways this could go sideways, and if this doesn't work, Riley, it could do a lot of damage," Naomi said.

"You've already made your reservations clear. But you know I'm right. We *need* to help them unleash their true feelings."

"On the off chance that's somehow correct, *how* could we even do that?"

"Oh, I've got ideas. Plans. But we need to strike while the iron is hot. I think we could do something in the studio. Can you manage that, Will?"

Will considered it. Since it was where Freya spent most of her time, it made the most sense to try it there. "It might be possible."

"Of course, it's possible."

They all froze, startled at the sound of footsteps coming towards them.

Abby was rounding the bend, inspecting them curiously. Had she heard what they were saying? Could this have gone wrong before they even had a chance to start? He tried not to let the panic show on his face as his mind skittered. He forced a casual smile, hoping it didn't look as strained as it felt.

"Where did you disappear to?" Naomi asked, a slight tremble in her voice. "I came out of the bathroom, and you were gone."

"I wanted a glimpse of the red carpet, and I ran into—" She didn't finish her sentence. At first, Will was worried she meant Freya, but he hadn't heard any yelling or seen any objects flying. "What are you cooking up for Becca, Riley?"

Will tried not to let his relief show as it swept through him, loosening the tension in his shoulders. Whatever Abby had overheard, she'd assumed it was about Becca—and not herself. The fragile thread of their plan was still intact. At least for now. "Why am I the subject of your inquisition?" Riley asked with an impressive amount of feigned innocence, given the close call.

"Call it women's intuition. Also, I heard you. You've got ideas, do you?"

Naomi tugged on his arm. "You know, we really should get back in there. Thanks again for saving the day."

He nodded and began to walk away, not missing Riley silently mouthing, "Let's talk soon" at him.

It, therefore, came as no surprise when this text from Riley appeared a week later:

RILEY: You. Me. Drink. Talk. Tonight.

WILL: Meet. Good. Drink. Good.

Whether or not Riley's plan worked, he would consider it a success because it had given him the opportunity to become part of the group on a deeper level than merely being Naomi's boyfriend. Now he was on the inside, working together to help one of their own. And the more time he spent with them, the more he realized how much he'd missed having friends and a life outside of work. He had been so consumed with his career he hadn't even noticed how lonely he'd become. But now he felt like a parched plant finally getting water, his dry roots drinking in the connection and camaraderie he'd been lacking.

Will was grateful to snag a little one-on-one time with Riley anytime, but especially tonight. Besides the fact that Riley was quickly becoming one of his favorite people on the planet, he had been hoping to chat with them in private at some point to see if he could get a little advice about

Naomi. His first instinct had been to talk to Abby, but something told him he should start with Riley. Perhaps they could give him a lay of the land and, among other things, tell him if going to Abby was the right call.

RILEY: I was going for more of a spy, Morse code thing than the caveman thing.

WILL: I will self-destruct this message after I receive my assignment

RILEY: Better. Meet me at the Jefferson Tap at 9?

WILL: I'll be wearing a single red rose.

RILEY: Great, now I'm going to have to change.

"Obviously, we're here to finish our conversation from the other night," Riley said the moment they were both seated at a table in the back of the pub where rows of gleaming beer taps and vintage sports jerseys added to the casual, laid-back vibe.

"I thought that might be the case. But no Naomi or Becca?"

"Well, Becca is a mess. And while there is most definitely a time and a place for that whole thing, this is not it." Riley began to peruse the menu.

"How's she doing? Besides, you know, being a mess."

Riley shrugged. "Abby thinks maybe this is forcing them to own up to how they feel about each other. Which is a hilarious observation, considering who it's coming from." Riley put the menu down. "As for Naomi, we need to focus. Not spend half the night quelling her anxieties."

"I think she's getting there. We talked about it this weekend, and I laid out why this is a low-risk, high-reward situation for me. That seemed to reassure her."

"Oho, I like it, Quinn. I like it." Riley looked up at a server who had made their way to their table. "McClelland, neat."

"Daisy Cutter IPA," Will said. He turned back to Riley. "McClelland, neat?"

"What can I say." Riley leaned back in their chair. "I like my whiskey like I like my men."

"Yeah, straight, apparently."

Riley clearly tried to give him an offended look, but the crinkle of amusement in the corner of their eyes was unmistakable. "I would have accepted rich or smooth." They crossed their legs. "Now, let's get down to it. How are we going to make this happen?"

Will nodded. "I've been giving it some thought since we talked last time, and I think I know exactly what to do. Freya has a TV in her office that only shows the video feed from the studio. All we need to do is go in the studio, presumably under the guise of me giving you all a tour, and accidentally," he put air quotes around the word accidentally, "turn on the feed and then have a brief conversation about how we've learned that Abby is in love with Freya. We'd need to make sure Freya is in her office and, ideally, not a lot of other people are around who might see it and come in to turn off the feed."

"Let me guess, that's a tall order."

"I thought it would be, but then I realized we're in luck. It's short notice, but Thanksgiving is this weekend and the whole floor is already clearing out for the holiday. By Friday, it will be a dead zone. But that's Freya's favorite time to work. She says she can get more done when everyone is gone. I'm thinking we go Friday night." When Riley didn't respond right away, Will scrunched his face. "Too soon to pull it off?"

"Are you kidding? It's brilliant. Brilliant!" Riley placed their hands on the table and leaned forward. "When we first met, I couldn't have imagined you had such depth to you. But I have to say, I think this is the beginning of a beautiful friendship."

"That's high praise," Will said as the server brought their drinks.

Riley raised their glass. "The highest. Well done." They clinked their glass to Will's. "Now, thankfully, while I was waiting for you, I started writing out an initial script for our little performance." They put their hand on a napkin resting beside their drink and slid it across to Will.

Will looked down at the napkin and saw lines of text scribbled across it.

"I obviously can't put this anywhere Abby could find it, so we're going to have to memorize it and then relay it to the women. It's not my best work, but I think it'll do."

Will read a few of the lines.

R: I wouldn't want to be Freya Jonsson for all the money in the world.

W: What? Why not?

R: Why else? She has the most beautiful, most amazing woman madly in love with her and she's too blind to see it!

He skimmed down a little further.

R: That woman is smitten beyond belief. And I'm not the only one who noticed this—ask her best friend and her sister.

Will looked up. "You think you can get Becca *and* Naomi to both follow a script? Naomi gets stage fright and Becca is..."

"Becca, I know. But they're crucial to making this believable. Don't worry about that, though. I can wrangle those two. You only job is to make sure we get this in front of Freya." Riley swirled the drink in their glass and then sipped. "I definitely didn't expect you to come so prepared; I thought we were going to be brainstorming for hours."

"What can I say, I like to keep you on your toes." Will cleared his throat. "But since we have some time ..."

Riley didn't miss the hesitation in his voice, and their eyebrows arched with piqued interest. Under Riley's gaze, Will took a healthy swallow of his drink, partly to calm his nerves and partly to give himself a few more seconds to finalize what to say. He wasn't as much worried about the answer, although there was a little bit of concern around that too, as he was about framing his question right. He didn't want Riley, or Naomi if it ever got back to her, to think he was having doubts about his relationship. He didn't have any doubts. Everything was crystal clear for him. Except this one smudge.

"I was hoping I could get some advice from you," he said. Advice seemed like the right way to approach this. Advice cast him in the light of seeking solutions rather than venting about problems, and he knew from personal experience that Riley would never turn down the opportunity to give advice.

Like the Grinch's heart, Riley's pupils grew three sizes until their irises became a black pool of anticipation. "I'm listening."

"Things have been going so great with me and Naomi," he said. "Better than great. I know it's only been a few months, but I'm already at a place where I can't see a future without her. I even found myself wandering into a jeweler to look at rings while I was out getting lunch the other day. I mean, not that we're going to get married anytime soon, but it's something we've discussed."

"Ooh!" Riley's hands fluttered together into excited claps. "You want advice on picking out a ring for Naomi? You've made the right decision coming to me. Let's talk budget because the Asscher cut I'm picturing for Naomi is going to run you at least 10K and then—"

Will made a braking motion with his hands. "I'm not there yet. And ten thousand? I don't know what you think I make, but we're going to have to ratchet down the expectations. Also, that's not what I wanted to ask your advice about."

Riley leaned back in their chair, reeling in their engagement ring enthusiasm. "Okay, hit me with your question."

"Well," he said, trying to gather his thoughts again. "Things are going great, like I said. But, sometimes, I don't know how to explain it. Sometimes it feels like there's something else. Something ..." He stopped again, wishing he'd spent more time figuring out the best way to articulate his feelings before broaching this with Riley. "Okay, it's like the reality shows you and Abby watch. You know how sometimes one of them gets a spin-off show?"

Riley nodded. "I'm not one hundred percent sure where you're going with this, but I'm loving the ride. Please continue."

"Sometimes it feels like Naomi has a spin-off that I'm not on. Like there's something else happening in the background that pulls her away sometimes. For example, we'll be hanging out, having an amazing time. And then suddenly she'll change and get distant. Or she'll step out to do something, and when she comes back, she's different. She says everything is fine, but I can tell something's bothering her. She'll be distracted for a while, but then the next day she's back to normal. It happened at Nosh Hashanah actually; maybe you noticed it. She disappeared, and when she came back, she seemed totally out of sorts."

"At Nosh Hashanah?"

"Yeah, remember she came back into the apartment after she went to check on Mrs. Pachenkis? You were worried about the ice, and then we got distracted by the whole, well, you know."

"How could I forget? It was my TMZ moment, and I failed to record a single second. When do I forget to take my phone with me? Never, that's when. I'll go to my grave regretting not getting that on video."

"You might not have noticed then. Or maybe you didn't because I'm imagining it. Or maybe this is just something women do. But you know Naomi well, so I thought maybe you could tell me if I'm missing something."

He expected Riley to devour his question like a competitive eater, but the voraciousness in their eyes had been replaced by a quiet thoughtfulness. "Have you asked her about it?"

"Not really? Kind of? I mean, I ask if everything's okay and she says yes. I'm not sure what else I'm supposed to do."

Riley gave a few short nods. "I see. Well," they paused briefly. "To paraphrase the immortal Phoebe Buffay, everyone is looking for their lobster. But Naomi? She's not a lobster. She's an oyster."

Will took a sip of his drink. "I have no idea what any of that means."

"You're telling me you wear those horrid graphic tees every day with random pop culture references on them, but you don't know about the lobsters from *Friends*?" When Will shook his head, they groaned. "Lobsters. They mate for life. It was a whole thing. But I always thought it was dumb. Because we throw lobsters in a pot of boiling water to eat, so who wants to be a lobster anyway?"

"Okay," Will said, a confirmation that he understood the words Riley was saying, not necessarily the meaning.

"I had a great metaphor, and you're killing me here, Will. My point is that Naomi is more like an oyster. She doesn't open up often or to a lot of people. But when she feels safe, you can get to know a part of her that is more beautiful than any pearl earrings at Tiffany. If you think she's not telling you something, my advice is to first throw the phrase 'is this just something women do' into the patriarchy vault of shame and never use it again. And then, ask yourself why. Why would she think you're not safe to totally open up to? Why would she think you couldn't handle her spin-off series? What have you done to make it clear to her that you can handle it?"

The questions rankled him more than he wanted to admit. "I've always done my best to show Naomi, hell, to all the women in my life, that I can be trusted with their ... pearls. This analogy doesn't have a lot of longevity. You get what I'm trying to say though, right?"

Riley nodded enthusiastically, and a sense of relief washed over Will that they were finally on the same page. "Absolutely. You're a *good* guy," they said. Except something suggested that wasn't the compliment it sounded like.

Will took another drink, gathering a little more liquid courage to ask the question he wasn't sure he was going to like. "But?"

Riley crossed their arms. "Good is nice. And nice is passive. It's changing your profile picture to show support for a cause. It's signing a petition on MoveOn.org. Listen, the world isn't safe for women. And if you're not disrupting that, then you might be a good guy, but you're not a safe one."

Will scrambled to follow what Riley was trying to say and what it had to do with Naomi and her secrets. "I disrupt it *by* being a good guy."

Riley snapped their fingers. "Bingo."

"Bingo, what?"

"Start there. Start with that premise, and it will lead you straight to your answer."

Will almost wished he'd never said anything. Things were murkier than they had been before he brought it up to Riley. Were they saying she was definitely hiding something that she didn't want to tell him? Or had Riley, in typical Riley fashion, gotten completely off track? Was this riddle about disruption and being a good person related to Naomi in any way, or simply an exploration into their different outlooks on life? Either way, it seemed like Riley wasn't the one who would shed any light on what was going on with Naomi, if there was anything at all.

Instead, he lifted his glass. "I will. Thank you."

Riley clinked their glass to his and then tipped their head back and downed the last of their drink. When they came back to center, any trace of solemnity had vanished, replaced with an unmistakable twinkle of mischief. "Then, my friend, we've got work to do. Let's get to memorizing this script."

Chapter Eleven

Naomi

Naomi tapped the taco emoji a half dozen times and then sent the message to Abby.

> ABBY: I'm leaving right now! I'm going to need an extra-large margarita. Becca is blaming me for not fixing her marriage.

This time Naomi went with a long string of drooling emojis.

> ABBY: Are you too hungry to communicate with words?

A line of one hundred emojis rounded out the conversation.

Except Naomi wasn't hungry at all.

She was too nervous to be hungry. Too nervous to type out full sentences. She took a deep breath and reminded herself that tonight was the last night of The Plan.

The Plan.

Riley had brought it up repeatedly since first suggesting that they should intervene in Abby and Freya's relationship, if it could even be called that. But when the talk never evolved into anything remotely concrete, she started to think maybe Riley had forgotten. And then, a little over a week ago, Riley and Will had appeared at her door, arm in arm with tipsy smiles and unsteady steps.

She knew that Will and Riley had been forming a friendship that existed outside of the friend group but until that moment, she hadn't realized it was already at the point of drunken, late-night schemes.

"We commence Friday!" Will had declared.

"Commence what? What are you two up to?" she asked.

"The Plan," Riley said ominously. "With Abby. And Freya. And ..." They finished their sentence by sticking out their tongue and emulating a very messy make-out session. For the next half an hour, the two of them stumbled over each other to explain The Plan, which involved an actual, well, *plan,* including set dates, times, and even a script.

The Plan made her anxious. She wasn't good at lying. She wasn't good at acting. She wasn't good at keeping secrets. She had struggled enough trying to keep quiet about Simon—although lately, he had made that a lot easier. Since Rosh Hashanah, he had disappeared. Despite saying he wouldn't give up, she hadn't received so much as an errant text message.

As the weeks passed and still no word from him, she found herself becoming more comfortable in her relationship with Will and her decision to leave Simon out of it.

The future with Will was bright, perhaps infused with the sparkle from an engagement ring somewhere down the line, and darkening it with problems from her past would serve no purpose except to hurt Will.

Of course, that bright future would be even brighter if it wasn't constantly interrupted by his boss and her best friend fighting like two beta fish dropped in the same tank. Which is why she had continued to go through with The Plan, which Will and Riley had separately, and then together in her apartment, assured her would be quick, painless, and with no bad outcomes.

Despite her reservations, last Friday night, she and Will and Riley and Becca had all gone to the WNO Tower under the guise of a spontaneous tour of Nightly Global News. Freya had been there, working late as Will said she would be, and after saying hello to her, they had walked into the recording studio where the news anchors sit and put on a performance that was "accidentally" piped into Freya's office.

"That woman is smitten beyond belief," Riley had said, midway through the script they had taught to the rest of the group as if they were passing down an ancient folktale. "I'm not the only one who has noticed this—ask her best friend and her sister."

Becca had even participated, saying that anything to do with Abby made her feel better about her own life. "Totally. Abby's been acting weird lately. Weirder than usual. For her," Becca had recited, going occasionally off script to throw a few extra digs at her sister. "Not eating, not sleeping, looking like she belonged on the set of a post-apocalyptic movie."

"Sure," Will had replied on cue. "That could be for a lot of reasons."

"True," came Becca's line. "Except Naomi and I asked her about it one night. Didn't we, Naomi?"

Her mouth had gone dry as everyone turned to her, expecting her to say her part. "She confessed the whole thing," she managed, desperately trying not to look at the red light on the camera that threatened to unravel what little nerve she had left. "That she was madly in love with Freya and couldn't think of anyone else."

With Part One of The Plan completed, now it was time for Part Two: Abby's Pocket Dial. It was simple enough. Unlike with Freya, she didn't have any lines. In fact, she didn't have to do much, really. She only had to go out to dinner with Abby and make sure she answered her phone when The Pocket Dial from Will, Riley, and Becca came in. There were only two small flaws in the plan:

A) She wasn't good at lying, acting, or keeping secrets
B) Abby could read her like Neo could read the Matrix

She saved the Excel sheet she had been working on and stood up from her desk, affording herself a full-length stretch before walking out of her office. She hadn't taken more than a few steps into the hallway before her phone rang.

"Are you prepared?" Riley said when she answered.

"You made me practice for two hours last night." She grabbed her coat from the closet in the lobby and headed to the elevator. "Considering my job is to go to a restaurant, I'd say I'm over-prepared. You're the one with the important job. Shouldn't you be studying your script with Will and Becca instead of checking up on me?"

"We're trying! But Becca is insisting we help her pick out her outfits for some kind of couples counseling session with Peter. I'm not sure I'm following everything she's saying."

"You think she's up for all this? With everything going on with Peter?"

"This is exactly what she needs. Don't worry about her. Worry about yourself. Make sure Abby picks up her phone and, for God's sake, don't under any circumstances do that little tongue bitey thing." They paused. "You're doing it right now, aren't you?"

She released her tongue from her teeth. "I still can't believe we're actually going through with any of this. It's not too late to back out."

"Naomi Hoffman. You've already laid half the trap, and you're about to go seal the deal. You're in far too deep. Now go and do Cupid's bidding. We're all counting on you."

Riley hung up before she could respond, so she said it to an empty elevator instead, "No pressure."

The restaurant, a ten-seat spot located in the garden unit of a lingerie store, was a few blocks from her office, so it was a short walk there. She and Abby had spent a good portion of their twenties devouring their addictively delicious yet somehow affordable food. In the last few years, particularly as she navigated her divorce with Simon, they had gone out less and less, opting for the safety that their sofas provided. Which is why she was more than a little bewildered when she opened the door to the restaurant and wasn't greeted by the din of a handful of customers but the roar of voices from a crowd of people. The entrance was so jam-packed, she had to shimmy her way to the host to put their name in.

There was one, perhaps only one, upside to this tragic loss of their hidden joint. For tonight at least, the chaos would hopefully distract Abby and provide her some cover.

"You're not going to believe this," Naomi said when Abby walked in a few minutes later. "It's a forty-five-minute wait."

Abby looked as dismayed as Naomi felt. "Apparently, it's not our secret spot anymore."

"I'm happy for them," she said, trying to give it a positive spin. "They deserve the success."

"Yes, yes, obviously good for them. But in the meantime, I'm devastated for us. I don't mind waiting, but what are we going to do when we're drunk and desperately need the yummiest tacos in the city right away?"

She smiled and shrugged. "Wait, like the plebs we are."

Abby mimed grasping the hilt of a knife with both hands and stabbing herself in the chest. "My heart." She moaned.

Naomi stared at Abby's hands. Her empty hands. Where was her phone? If it was in her purse, there was a chance she'd miss the call. She started to panic but then remembered they'd discussed this scenario last night. If Abby wasn't holding her phone, then she had to...

"You okay?" Abby asked.

Dammit. She needed to be more careful. She instinctively started to bite down on the tip of her tongue, but caught herself and opted for an effusive smile. "Oh, yeah. So what were you saying in your text? Why was Becca blaming you?"

Step one, get Abby talking and distracted. Her sister was easy bait.

On cue, Abby rolled her eyes. "I guess she and Peter finally went to see that therapist I recommended to her. Which, don't get me wrong, gave me this funny feeling I've never felt before. Something akin to feeling proud of her. I can't be sure. But then she needed to take time out of her day to tell me how terrible it was and make it sound like it was somehow my fault."

Three minutes to go.

Step two, ask to use her phone. "Uh huh, listen, could I borrow your phone for a second? Mine is almost dead and I forgot to check the, uh ..."

As predicted, Abby was too lost in her exasperation about her sister to care what Naomi needed the phone for. She unlocked her phone and handed it to Naomi without stopping. "Which is this fun thing we've been doing since their whole marriage ... debacle, if you can even call it that. She asks me to help her. Not really asks, demands. And then hates whatever I suggest. And I'd like to help her, I really would. She makes me want to pull my eyelashes out sometimes, but she's also my sister, and I only want her to be in pain if I'm causing it. But I've also never really understood what her motivation is. And I've never really gotten to know Peter super well, which I feel bad about. But I also felt so awful being around him when I knew what his wife was up to. But at the same time, I didn't feel like it was my job to tell him. Those two are an enigma, wrapped in a mystery, tangled inside one giant ball of dysfunction. All I have to say is, be glad you are an only child."

One minute to go.

Pretend to listen and scroll, pretend to listen and scroll and ... there it was. The phone lit up in her hand, and Becca's name flashed across the screen. Her heart was tapping out an Irish step dance as she held it up for Abby. "Oh. Oh, h-hey. Looks like Becca is calling."

But Abby didn't take the phone. "Oh, good. Either a pocket dial or she's calling to register another complaint. I think I'll pass."

"No!" she said it so loudly, she startled herself as much as Abby. She tried again, reminding herself this would all be over in a few moments. "No, um, it really sounds like she's going through a tough time right now. You literally just said you don't want to see her in pain."

Abby scrunched her face but, thankfully, took the phone. "You know, I don't feel it's proper best friend duty to throw my words back in my face and make me be a good person."

Naomi didn't reply. She only watched, breath frozen in her lungs, as Abby answered the call. Home stretch. "Hello? Hello?" she said again before confirming what Naomi already knew, "Yep, pocket dial."

Riley had told her to act interested in the call, to get Abby to listen in rather than hanging up right away. "What do you hear?" she asked.

"It sounds like Becca is at Riley's getting her version of a cup of sugar?"

Becca was supposed to pretend like she was coming by for clothing advice, but given how things had gone last time, it would come as no surprise to Naomi if Becca was already going off script. Abby paused and listened a little more before chuckling. "Oh my God. It's Will, too."

"That's right," Naomi said, like she was only now remembering. "Will mentioned he might hang out with Riley tonight."

"Either way, I don't really need to listen to her talk about how she's going to use sex toys with Peter from the ass of her jeans." That was definitely not in the script.

Abby began to pull the phone away from her ear.

Naomi grabbed her arm to stop her from pressing the disconnect. "Wait, wait," she said, quickly searching for something, anything, that would pique Abby's curiosity enough to keep her listening. "Aren't you curious to find out what Will and Riley are like when we're not around?"

Abby considered this. It might have only been a few seconds, but those seconds stretched into millennia while she waited. Finally, she nodded. "Alright, this might be worth it after all. It sounds like Will is about to spill some tea." She put the phone back to her ear and furrowed her brow as she began to listen more intently.

Naomi felt like a marathon runner crossing the finish line. She squeezed her hands tightly, to hold back the internal "whoop!" that threatened to come out. She'd done it. Now it was up to Becca, Will, and Riley.

And they must have been pulling their weight because Abby's mouth was slowly dropping open until it looked like her jaw was dangerously close to falling off.

Eventually, Abby lowered the phone, her face blank. Naomi had, of course, wondered how her best friend would react to overhearing that Freya was in love with her. She'd imagined a few scenarios, but none that involved Abby in total, stunned silence. She had expected laughter, possibly anger, even potentially a victory lap. But this was unusual. And curious. "So? Hear anything good?" she asked, hoping to get something out of her.

"I'm not feeling well all of a sudden," Abby said, patting her forehead and her stomach, as if she wasn't quite sure where the ailment was.

"Do you want to step outside? Get some fresh air?" *Talk about what's got you in such a tizzy?*

"I think I need to go home."

"Oh, sure. We can grab a cab and—"

But Abby had already turned and walked away.

Naomi watched her and then let out a little giggle. Okay, maybe that had been a little more fun than she had been expecting.

She waited a few more seconds and then walked outside. Abby was already gone.

She sent off a quick text to the group.

NAOMI: Abby heard the call and left. I'll head over now.

Her message got a thumbs up. It might have been the adrenaline, but the cold winter air didn't feel quite so frosty anymore, and she decided to walk. As she wound through the city streets, she replayed what happened in her mind for any indication that in might have actually worked, but she couldn't tell for sure. After half an hour, she arrived at her destination. It was Riley's favorite hangout spot and the post-The Plan meetup point: a goth-inspired café and cocktail shop. Through the window in the door, she could see Will, Riley, and Becca sitting at a table in the back, giant grins plastered across their faces.

Inside, only a few feet away, was everything she'd ever wanted. Not only a good man who loved her, but who loved and was loved by her chosen family. She couldn't help but grin too. Taking hold of the skull-shaped doorknob, she pulled open the door and was greeted by a welcome blast of warm air and roaring laughter.

Her friends looked up and let out some excited, if not particularly sober, cheers. "I'm with them," she said to the barista/bartender.

"You're here!" Will waved at her.

Riley patted the chair next to them. "Sit down and tell us everything!"

"Do you think it worked?" Becca asked, bouncing in her seat.

Naomi hung her coat on a nearby hook on the wall and then sat down, giving her companions a quick once-over. "Hang on a second, you weren't expecting me to meet you here for at least another hour. How are you all already drunk?"

"There may have been some shots involved," Will said, a chagrined look on his face.

"Shots? You don't do shots."

"With me, everyone does shots," Becca said, reaching across the table and patting her on the hand. "You know that."

She did, unfortunately.

"I took the liberty of ordering you a drink," Will said, pushing a midnight black drink in a martini glass towards her. She sipped her drink, the surprising sweetness harmonizing with the happy chaos of the table.

"Drinks later, news first," Riley said. "How did Abby take it?"

Naomi could only shrug. "She got this really strange look on her face and ... left. Not sure what that means."

"It means my plan has been perfectly executed," Riley said. "Almost perfect except for when Will and Becca both went off script."

"I told you I wasn't going to use words like 'thirst' and 'ache' to describe anything about Freya, *my boss,*" Will said.

"And I don't see how comparing my sister to a fictional character who slaughters innocent people was going to do anything but motivate her to see past her ego," Becca added.

"As I was saying," Riley continued, "Despite these mishaps, we've done great work."

"Well, cheers!" Naomi said, raising her glass. If nothing else, this adventure had brought them together and made Will one of the crew in a way she could never have managed on her own.

"But do we think it worked?" Becca asked as she clinked her glass. "Like if she didn't react, is that a bad thing? And Freya, too? It's not like she's done anything about it either."

Riley took a purposeful gulp and then returned their glass to the table with a *thunk*. "Absolutely, it worked. But if there's one thing we can be certain of, it's that we are dealing with two of the most stubborn human beings on the planet. Even if they know how they feel now, they're not going to *admit* that they have these feelings. They need a push."

"Wait, there's more for us to do?" Naomi asked. "I thought The Plan was done."

"It is. Because *we* can't do anything, but the right situation can. It's all about the game of chess we're playing with fate," Riley said, their eyes sparkling. "We've put the pieces into place, ensuring that when the right circumstances occur, they'll be ready and it will be checkmate."

Will lifted his drink. "You are truly the Grandmaster of love."

"As the great poet Taylor Swift said, love can be a ruthless game. So then I say to you, dear friends, if that's true, then let's play it to win."

Chapter Twelve

Will

Freya was yanking him down the hallway, which was a dangerous type of jostling when he was still in the throes of a hangover. He was impressed that Freya was so agile, given that thirty seconds ago she looked about as green as the smoothie he had unsuccessfully tried to consume this morning. He had convinced Freya to come out with him and Naomi the night before, in part to help Freya blow off some steam after a particularly stressful day and in part to nudge Naomi and Freya a little closer as friends. It had almost been a year since he'd met Naomi—give or take a few months—and he no longer felt like "the boyfriend" in her group but instead had been grafted in as one of the gang. It could never be the same with Freya and Naomi, mostly because he and Freya weren't really a "gang." But she was his closest friend here in Chicago, and while Freya and Naomi were on friendly terms, he had hoped to create a little more bond between them. Turns out all it took was an impromptu Thursday night out with some cocktails and a burlesque show at a speakeasy to accomplish that. Unfortunately, success also came with a hangover.

Which, apparently, Freya had the ability to partition at will when it required getting far enough down the hall so that Brian—who had accosted them in the hallway—couldn't hear them.

Brian, their least favorite Executive Producer, had stopped them first thing in the morning to kill yet another story. Will and Freya had already known that their story, a look at a conversion therapy camp through the eyes of a survivor, would be a tough sell to Nightly Global News. They'd spent weeks putting together what they needed to make a compelling pitch that would be worthy of, at the very least, some discussion. But after all that work, and in less than twenty-four hours, it was getting axed.

"This is network television, not cable. We need stories that are *family friendly*," Brian had told them moments earlier. The way he put emphasis on the words 'family friendly' gave Will images of a mob boss putting emphasis on the words "make a donation." It wasn't the first time Will had heard this phrase invoked over the years, and it hadn't taken him long to understand what it really meant. "Family-friendly" wasn't about protecting viewers—it was about keeping the studio in line with the religious and political interests that funded it. If a story risked upsetting the people who truly held the power at WNO, it wasn't just shelved—it was erased, swiftly and without question. Which is why he had thought the conversation was over until Freya's eyes flashed with the familiar expression she got when she'd remembered an important piece of information for a story.

As Brian turned to leave, she lifted her hand up to pause his exit. "Hang on, Brian. If you're looking for family-friendly, I've got an idea." Then she had grabbed Will by the arm and said, "Give us a moment. Don't go anywhere. I think you'll like what I've got in mind."

And then she was pulling Will towards an open conference room, saying, "Hear me out," in a hushed tone as she shoved him inside and shut the door.

He took a seat in the nearest chair, not only to show Freya he was in attendance for whatever presentation she was about to give but also to recover from the aftereffects of that brusque walk.

"Do you remember what you told me last night?" she asked.

"Yes." He had told her a lot of things, but he didn't need any more context to know what she was referring to.

In the handful of minutes Naomi had been out of earshot last night, he'd let it slip to Freya the secret he'd been keeping for several weeks: he had a ring and was going to propose to Naomi.

It was fast, he knew. But over the months, he and Naomi had discussed marriage—first as the fun hypothetical that helps build a picture of what a future could look like and then as a fact of a future that would someday come to be. Until, one morning, he woke up and knew for certain: the only future he wanted was one with Naomi, and he wanted it to start now.

He hadn't intended to say anything to Freya until after they got engaged but then, his tongue loosened by several bourbon cocktails, it somehow slipped out.

He had expected, for myriad reasons, including the Abigail connection and the fact that Freya was a woman so focused on her career that romance seemed like a nuisance, that she would offer little more than polite congratulations. But instead, she'd seemed enthusiastically elated.

And now, she was bringing it up again. Why?

"You told me you had the ring, but no plan," Freya said, dropping into the seat next to him and swiveling to face him.

"I have some general thoughts, but I ... am not really sure where you're going with this."

Freya placed her forearms on her legs and leaned in. "What if you propose to her on Nightly Global News?"

"I—what? Propose on—"

"Nightly Global News!" Freya sprang up from her seat like she was on the upward swing of a seesaw. He'd seen her like this, a bloodhound on the scent, but he had never been ... the scent before. "This is the part where you hear me out—and quickly because Brian isn't going to wait out there for very long. He has the attention span of a fruit fly, and we need to strike while the 'family-friendly' iron is hot. Here's what I'm thinking. We invite Naomi to watch you at work, and then when she's not expecting it, the cameras turn on her, and there you are on bended knee. Can you think of any grander gesture, anything more romantic than announcing your love for Naomi in front of millions of people?"

"Not off the top of my head, no. But—"

"But what?"

"You really think he will—"

"I do."

"And she will—"

"Yes."

"And we'll be able to—"

"Stick it to the man *and* get you an epic engagement? Yes. Listen, Brian wants family-friendly, but instead of pandering to the boys upstairs and doing some watered-down story, let's use it to get you a once-in-a-lifetime proposal."

Once-in-a-lifetime proposal.

It sounded crazy. But it also sounded like something Naomi deserved.

Freya wagged her finger at him and grinned. “I see that look on your face, Will. You know I’m right. Now trust me on this and let’s make it happen.”

Freya’s grin, like her belief in this on-camera proposal, was infectious, and he found himself nodding. “I suppose it can’t hurt to suggest it to Brian.”

“I love it,” Brian said after hearing Freya’s pitch. He snapped his fingers. “This is what I’m talking about, Jonsson. People aren’t interested in these woke exposés you’re always after. This is exactly the kind of out-of-the-box thinking that builds viewer loyalty. When they’re invested in the people making the news, they’ll trust the news. You get the vision.”

“Oh, I definitely get it,” Freya said.

Brian began to walk away and then said over his shoulder, “Let’s get this on the Monday night show!”

“Monday?” Will nearly choked on the word. “Freya, that’s in three days.”

“Will,” Freya said. “You’ve got the girl, the ring, and the plan. Give me one good reason you can’t propose on Monday?”

He had stood there, waiting. There had to be dozens of reasons why he shouldn’t. But as the seconds passed, not one came to him. He couldn’t think of a single reason not to ask the most incredible woman he had ever met to marry him as soon as humanly possible.

Seventy-two hours later, he stepped out of his car, patting the ring box in his pocket, and smiling at Freya. "Ready for this?"

"Me?" she asked. She pulled her navy-blue coat a little tighter around her as a gust of frosty spring wind swirled around them. "I'm only here for the ride. You're the one who has to pop the question. Speaking of which, are you nervous?"

Over the last three days, he had waited for the nerves, for the enormity of what he was going to undertake in such a short amount of time, to settle in. But it never happened. Every time he thought about proposing to her, it felt as certain as the sunrise. Even the lingering concerns about whatever Naomi might be keeping from him didn't factor into his decision. Whatever it was, she would tell him when she was ready, and they would figure it out together. Because there was nothing they couldn't overcome. "I would be nervous if we were doing this live. But since we can edit out the parts where I inevitably do something my future children will want to watch on repeat, then no. I'm really not nervous."

Freya had glanced down at her phone as he finished talking, which wasn't unusual in a business where multitasking was required. Her eyebrows lifted with her head following a few seconds after. "What about now?" She held out her phone.

To: W.Quinn@ngn.com
Cc: F.Jonsson@ngn.com
From: B.Green@ngn.com
Subject: Proposal

Got out of a planning meeting. The proposal segment idea polled well among a random sampling of viewers who said they want to see more behind the scenes content that shows the softer side of our company. Assuming you get the girl, NGN wants to see you through to your nuptials. Five-minute segments each night for one month. In exchange, we will cover wedding costs (budget to follow).

Keep me posted on the proposal.
B

"Oh," was all he could manage.

Freya retrieved her phone from his hand. "Brian has a way with words, doesn't he? Aside from feeling like your married life has become a commodity for Nightly Global News, what do you think? I told you they'd eat this up! I never imagined they'd eat the cost of your wedding too, but: free wedding. What are you thinking?"

Not a lot, actually. His brain, already at capacity with trying to put together a proposal in three days, couldn't quite hold onto the contents of the e-mail. "I'm going to have to get back to him on that," he said.

A Nightly Global News van pulled into a spot beside his car and Pete, a veteran NGN camera operator, hopped out. "Quinn! You look like a man ready to propose." He spoke with an endearingly thick, Chicago accent. He patted Will on the shoulder and then glanced around and said in a quieter voice. "Crap, is she here? Did I blow it?"

"Not yet," Will said, bottling thoughts of Brian's e-mail up like a wine that needed to age in a cellar for a few years before being opened. "We've got a few minutes."

"Phew. I imagine blowing your proposal would have put a little strain on our working relationship." He tugged on the sliding door on the side of the van, revealing piles of neatly stacked boxes, cords, and equipment.

"I'm glad you decided to wear a grown-up shirt on this momentous day and not one of those kiddie T-shirts."

Will tugged at the collar that pinched at his neck. "Don't kid yourself, Pete. I wore it for you."

Pete let out a bark of a laugh as he began to unload a large black case. "Okay, so before she comes—is the plan still the same?"

Will nodded. "Naomi still thinks she's coming to see me on the job. You're still supposed to act like you're getting set up, but really, you're recording."

"You gonna want a live mic?" Pete asked, leaning into the van.

"Yes," Freya replied for him. "We need to hear her answer loud and clear."

He pulled a large, hand-held microphone bearing the NGN logo out and, after fiddling with it for a moment, handed it to Freya. "I gotta say, Freya," he said, procuring a set of headphones and giving them to Will. "No offense, but this is a lot better than any of the other gigs you've put me on." He settled a camera onto his shoulder with the familiarity of an equestrian loading a saddle onto their horse.

"Offense, Pete. Offense," Freya said, smirking, then glanced up at a car heading towards them. "Oh, here she comes."

Will's heart started beating so fast, it felt like his entire body had begun to vibrate. The rest of his life was starting right now.

Naomi rolled into a nearby space and then made her way towards them. She was dressed in jeans and her favorite DePaul University hoodie, and he was confident she had never looked more beautiful.

"Hi," he said. He wanted to pull her in for a kiss, but he was afraid he wouldn't be able to kiss her like he wasn't about to ask her to marry him. So instead, he gave a small, awkward wave.

"Naomi!" Freya, thankfully, stepped in to help. "Will said you were stopping by to watch us record a segment. It'll be nice to have a little extra estrogen to balance things out for once." She jutted her chin towards Pete and Will.

"Don't mind me," Pete said, his eye pressed to the camera viewer. "I'm just getting set up."

Smooth, Pete.

"Thanks for letting me crash," Naomi said. "I have to admit I've always been curious to see what you all do, so I was pretty excited when Will said you'd invited me."

"It's nothing too exciting today, unfortunately. A quick interview, but it should still be fun. We'll be doing it right over there." She gestured to her left to a grassy expanse that led to the seemingly boundless Lake Michigan, its midnight blue water swelling with frothy waves. The grass gave way to massive stones, cut into rectangles that formed uneven stairs down to the water. It was one of his favorite spots in the city because it offered an unobstructed and remarkable view of the Chicago skyline. And it was also steps from where he and Naomi had shared their first kiss, which was why he had picked it for today.

Will tapped his pocket again as he watched Freya lead Naomi across the grass until she was standing near the rock stairs.

"Here we go, buddy," Pete said under his breath as they started after the two women.

It didn't shock Will that Freya hadn't needed any direction or assistance. She was fully in her role, acting as if she were setting herself up for an interview.

"How's that sounding?" she said into the microphone. It was only after Pete gave him a nudge that he realized she was talking to him. He put one of the headphones to his ear and gave her a thumbs-up. "It's pretty windy out here. Good? Okay. There we go."

Freya made a show of looking around before putting her microphone in her pocket. She took hold of Naomi's arms and nudged her until she was directly across from Freya. "Bet Will forgot to mention that we were going to put you to work when he invited you to come along today. Normally, Will has to be my interview body double, but today you get to do it!" She and Naomi laughed. "Now, if you could move a little to your left. See! You're a natural at this! Right, okay—so how's this looking?" She turned and nodded at Will.

"That's my cue," he said.

"Good luck," Pete replied.

He set the headphones down and did his best to walk quickly, but inconspicuously, around and behind Naomi. Freya was holding Naomi's attention, still enlisting her to work out the "kinks."

"Much better. Good, so let's see. Now then, I'm interviewing you and I say something like—So how are you today, Naomi?" Freya had taken the microphone from her pocket and was holding it towards Naomi. Freya's eyes remained on Naomi, but the smile on her face suggested that she could see that Will was in position and had pulled the ring box out.

"I ... I'm great, thank you," Naomi said, leaning in towards the microphone. "A little cold."

Freya nodded. "I see. And tell me, Naomi, have you decided whether or not to accept Will's proposal of marriage?"

"His what?"

He tapped her on the shoulder and as she turned, his colleagues, the skyline, the lake, and the entire city went silent. The only sound was Naomi, gasping, as he lowered onto his knee.

He'd written something down but now, looking up at her, the words were lost to the sparkle of her tears, which made his own eyes well up and his carefully crafted proposal fade away. "Naomi Hoffman," he began, hoping he'd find the right words. "From the moment we met, you have changed my life for the better. You make me happy in ways that I never even thought were possible, and I want the opportunity to spend the rest of my life making sure I make you just as happy. If you'll let me." He had to force himself to take a breath as he opened the box. "Will you do me the honor of becoming my wife?"

Tears of joy streaked her face as she said, "Yes, of course!"

He bounded up, pulling her into his arms and kissing her with unbridled excitement. Somewhere in the distance, he could hear Pete and Freya cheering. He broke the kiss so that he could put the ring on her finger, but that short time away from her lips felt too long and as soon as he could, he pulled her in close for another kiss.

"I think you can put the camera down now, Pete." He heard Freya say.

Naomi pulled back and whispered, "They're not really recording this, are they?"

"Well, actually," he replied. "I've got something else to ask you ..."

Chapter Thirteen

Naomi

As Naomi entered the room, she was greeted by a harmonious chorus of "Ooh!" It was the sound she would expect to hear when walking in wearing a potential wedding dress. The other sounds, the shuffle of the NGN camera operator moving in for a closer shot and the *click-click* of the NGN photographer capturing everyone's reactions, not so much.

Two weeks ago, she would have checked "single" on her tax form. But in only two weeks, that was about to change. She was going to be married. Except, she wasn't only getting married in two weeks; she was doing it all on national television.

She hadn't needed to give any thought to accepting Will's proposal, but accepting NGN's offer to film her wedding had taken a little more consideration. There were plenty of pros and cons to weigh, and she'd turned them over in her mind more than once.

For starters, she had never had any aspirations of being a celebrity of any kind, so the idea of sharing her wedding journey on such a public platform was incredibly daunting.

But having a wedding with a celebrity budget *was* certainly something she had dreamed of.

Then there was the issue that they wanted it to happen in a month. She would have eloped with Will a second after he proposed; however, trying to put together a television-worthy wedding in a month was an enormous undertaking.

But that celebrity budget meant she was going to have access to wedding planners, top-notch vendors, and, again, that very large budget to help make it all happen.

There was also the fact that the studio had warned them, perhaps more for Will's benefit than her own, that a Jewish wedding would invite antisemitism from every corner of the internet. Will was not converting, but he embraced her desire to have a Jewish life, starting with their wedding, and she knew that meant she was going to have to approach the internet and her various inboxes with care.

But she also believed in facing hatred with ometz lev, the Jewish value of a courageous heart.

And then ... there was Simon. When she had said yes to Will, she knew she had said no to telling him about Simon. For almost a year, she'd kept that part of her past locked away, growing only more certain with time that dragging Simon into their lives would do more harm than good. She was happy, Will was happy, *they* were happy. She didn't want to change that—didn't want to burden Will, hurt him, or make him see her differently. And it wasn't only that *she* didn't want to tell him, Will had all but told her *he* didn't want to know. He'd been talking about reality

TV, not this, but still. Whether or not he'd feel the same about her past, the possibility had only cemented her choice to remain silent on the topic of Simon.

Now, it wasn't just a choice—it was final. She *couldn't* tell him. If she did—after a year of silence, after promising forever—how could he not see it as anything but a betrayal?

No, that door she had already closed was now nailed shut. And for the most part, she felt relief.

She didn't have to wonder anymore if she should tell him, if she was making a mistake by keeping it to herself. The decision was set in stone, like the three flawless diamonds on her finger.

There was comfort in that certainty; in knowing she could move forward without the weight of what-ifs pressing down on her. She would honor Will's wishes, protect what they had, and keep Simon locked away in the past where he belonged.

She knew, however, that there was a chance that her being on TV would catch Simon's attention.

But it seemed more likely that her television debut would keep him away. He had only been able to do what he did precisely *because* he stayed in the shadows, so that no one, including the authorities, could prove or would even believe that someone like him was capable of the things he had done. Exposure was his greatest weakness, and being on TV meant she was stepping into the light, somewhere he couldn't follow. So, in actuality, it seemed like being in the public eye was probably the best way to keep Will safe.

When she weighed it all out, the choice became clear. Fear made up the cons, but the pros were undeniable—so she had agreed to put herself and her wedding on Nightly Global News.

NGN wasted no time and immediately began having a short "Wedding Special" segment each night at the end of the show. With only four weeks to plan an entire wedding, she and Will had been busy selecting everything from the chuppah they would get married under to the playlist of songs they would dance to.

And they had done it all on camera.

Heading into week three, it was time to pick wedding party attire and, in doing so, reveal the wedding party—something they could finally do because the studio had at long last approved their picks.

She and Will had been forbidden from discussing their wedding party until potential candidates had been vetted by the station. It seemed a bit over the top—it wasn't like she was picking the Vice President of the United States. But NGN was footing the bill for everything, including the $15,000 dress she was currently donning, so who was she to ask questions?

Those two weeks of waiting had been particularly grueling for Riley, who had channeled their anxiety into late-night texts to her and Abby.

RILEY: Naomi, if you love me, you'll tell me if Will picked me. TELL ME.

NAOMI: I love you but not enough to get slapped with a lawsuit for breaking my NDA.

RILEY: Are you prepared to get slapped with a wrongful death lawsuit? Because if Will doesn't pick me, I'll fling myself off the Michigan Avenue Bridge

ABBY: That bridge isn't very high. You'd probably survive

RILEY: The weight of my sorrow will drag me to the bottom of the river.

She knew, of course, that Will had picked them.

"I knew he was going to pick me," Riley had told her after they had found out.

Now, they were with Will and the other half of his wedding party—a cousin she had never met named Lucas—somewhere downtown getting fitted for tuxes while she was with her bridesmaids selecting their dresses and hers.

"I love it, but I'm not going to lie, this dress doesn't say 'do me,'" Becca said. She was lounging sensuously on a velvet chaise at the foot of the dressing stage, skimming through her phone.

"For the last time, Becca, just because you wore a wedding dress so see-through you wouldn't need to go through a metal detector at the airport does not mean that Naomi wants the same thing," Abby said.

"For someone who claims to be sex-positive, you are sex positively boring. And since you so kindly brought up my marriage, maybe you'd like to take the time to inspect all the grey hairs, AKA the only thing I've gotten from going to the marriage counseling stuff you suggested."

"I'm not—that's not—ughhh," Abby growled.

Naomi's original plan had been to have Abby as her one and only bridesmaid. But the execs weren't too keen on the idea of such a small wedding party and insisted she invite at least one more person. Becca was a natural addition, being as much family to her as Abby was. But that was also part of the problem. Trying to get the sisters to work together felt a lot like trying to get siblings to get along in the back seat of the car.

"I'm done listening to your marriage advice," Becca said. "I'm taking matters into my own hands."

"Fine by me," Abby replied. "You were the one demanding I give you the advice. Now, can we get back to Naomi? You look gorgeous but at the risk of being on the same page with my sister, it's not my favorite."

Naomi expected Becca to come back with a retort, but instead she gasped. "Oh my god, Naomi. Did you know your hashtag is trending?" She stood up and walked over to Naomi. "Look! #Wilomi! You have a couple name! This is it, girl. You've peaked. If society gives you a couple name, there's literally no higher you can go."

Naomi's cheeks grew hot. "No, we're not a big deal," she said, trying to sound like she was focused more on the dress than on the incredibly uncomfortable concept that they were a big deal.

But even as she denied it, she knew that they maybe, kind of, actually, were. She'd started to get an inkling of their rising fame about halfway through the first week when her Instagram account followers went from two digits to six, even though her profile had nothing more than about a dozen photos of meals she'd eaten over the last three years.

The next day on the drive to work, her phone rang, and it was a friend screaming to turn on 101.9 FM because The Morning Mix was taking a poll on their wedding band auditions (sixty-two percent of listeners agreed with their decision to go with the *Trixie Trio* rather than the flashier *Bebe and the Babes.* It felt nice to have some public affirmation).

Then last week, interview requests started pouring in. First, it was a local blogger. Then, a big-time bridal blogger. Then, a Chicago television talk show invited them on for an interview. When she got the call offering to fly them out for a spot on *The Tonight Show*, she realized things were getting really serious between her, Will, and the public.

The studio was thrilled about it. The five-minute segment at the end of the news became ten minutes, and then they added a thirty-minute special after the nightly news that bumped the *King of Queens* reruns. Sorry, Kevin James.

Trying to juggle planning a wedding in a month made her too busy to really think about her growing fame—or at least that was her excuse for not thinking about it. She was pretty sure if she thought about it too much, if she allowed herself to think about what it meant that she was "famous," she'd burrow under her covers and never come out.

"How about we try on the next one?" the attendant, a smartly dressed woman with an enormous smile named Valerie, said. Valerie offered her arm to help Naomi down from the pedestal.

For her first wedding, her gown had been a very simple tea-length white dress she'd ordered online from Mod Cloth. She hadn't even gone to a bridal store to try on wedding dresses, so this entire experience was new, including how bulky and heavy the dresses were. As she dragged herself towards the changing area, feeling a bit like Quasimodo climbing the tower, her watch tickled her wrist, alerting her to an incoming message. It was from Will.

As the text rolled onto the screen, she saw it was a group message to her, Riley and Becca. But no Abby. That could only mean one thing ...

WILL: Umm . . . so there's a slight change in plans.

RILEY: You all are going to love this

WILL: You know how I was going to have my cousin be my groomsman? The NGN higher ups made a last-minute call.

As the attendant began undoing the ribbons down the back of her dress, Naomi watched the bubbles on her wrist and waited.

BECCA: Who?

WILL: It's Freya.

And they want her to be the "best man."

Naomi gasped.

Valerie looked up. "Oh, sorry, am I hurting you?"

"No, no," she assured her and then looked back at her watch.

WILL: You understand what this means right?

RILEY: Freya and Abby have to walk down the aisle together after the ceremony.

BECCA: Freya and Abby have to walk into the reception together

WILL: Freya and Abby have to sit together at the wedding reception table

Thankfully, "OMG" was one of the pre-written responses she could choose from on her watch. She hit it twice, for good measure.

NAOMI: OMG

OMG

RILEY: OMG indeed. This is excellent news

No, this was most definitely not excellent. She looked towards the door—her phone was sitting on a chair on the other side of it. Should she try and get it? She pictured herself dragging her half-laced-up dress out the door to grab her phone and decided against it, instead tapping the talk-to-text. She whispered into it as softly as she could.

NAOMI: This is a nightmare!

"Sorry?" Valerie said, looking up.

Busted. "Oh, no ... I'm ... I'm texting on my watch." She pointed to her wrist.

The attendant gave a professional smile, but the veneer of 'ummm, ok' peeked out from her eyes. She gave a tug to the dress, and it fell to the floor in a shimmery pile. "You can step out," she instructed.

Naomi complied, keeping her eyes on the watch.

BECCA: This is going to get so awkward so fast. I'm here for every minute of it.

RILEY: You're all missing the point. This is it! Check. Mate.

It had been months since The Plan had first been enacted, and with everything else going on, she had almost forgotten about it. But it seemed Riley had not. They were still waiting for the moment that would set the rest of The Plan in motion. And they seemed to think her wedding was it.

WILL: You think this is going to be checkmate?

RILEY: Weddings are all about sex and desperation. What bridesmaid HASN'T tried to get laid at a wedding?

BECCA: Not me, that's for sure.

RILEY: Weddings are nature's pressure cooker. Add in the media component and the fact that they have to do all of these public activities together?

A series of bomb emojis filled her screen.

Naomi tapped the microphone icon, brought her watch to her mouth, and tried to say even more quietly:

NAOMI: I'm not really excited about the idea of bombs at my wedding.

Valerie, who was across the room gathering up the next dress, looked over but said nothing.

WILL: I think they'll be able to keep it together for the ceremony. It's not like they're going to go at it—one way or another—while they're standing at the altar

BECCA: Have you met my sister ...?

"Okay, here we go." The attendant knelt in front of her, holding open the top of a new dress. "Hop on in."

She stepped into the dress, and the attendant lifted it up around her in one motion and then held out the delicate lace sleeves. Naomi quickly slipped her arms through them so she could continue looking at her watch.

RILEY: The question is not whether they'll be able to keep it together during the wedding but whether they'll be able to be separated after the wedding.

BECCA: Also, if they do have an epic blowout at your wedding, imagine what it will do for your ratings. So really, positive outcomes all around.

RILEY: Becca is making some excellent points today.

The attendant was behind Naomi again, beginning the process of buttoning up her back. Naomi leaned in towards her wrist but didn't bother to whisper this time.

NAOMI: There's no way out of this?

Valerie probably thought Naomi was trying to get out of her marriage while trying on wedding dresses. She wondered if she should explain the situation to her. But she wasn't even sure she'd be able to if she tried.

WILL: I don't see how.

To be honest, I'm happy to have Freya as my best man. If it weren't for that whole "epic blowout" factor of course . . .

Yes, if it weren't for that one *tiny* thing.

RILEY: I'm not even worried. My plan is flawless.

"Done! What do you think?"

Naomi had been so busy following the drama on her wrist, she hadn't noticed that she was in a wedding dress.

And it was gorgeous.

"Wow," she said, looking at the dressing room mirror and rotating left and right, watching the waterfall of white glisten in the light with each turn. It was elegant but simple, sexy but tasteful. It hugged her in the places she wanted to be hugged and was forgiving in the areas she wanted forgiveness. And it was light; the silky skirt was long and full but not weighed down with all the heavy layers and crystal and beads and whatever else made those other dresses feel like there was an anvil in the pockets. Not that they even had pockets. She could picture herself *walking* down the aisle in this dress, rather than hauling herself and her dress down the aisle. "I kind of really love it."

"Ready to show it off?"

Naomi nodded, and Valerie opened the door to the dressing room.

The sounds of approval that greeted her as soon as she stepped out confirmed how she was feeling. She hopped onto the pedestal feeling as light as a feather.

"It fits you like a dream. How do you feel in it?" Abby asked, coming up beside Naomi. "Absolutely stunning."

"I would definitely do you in that dress," Becca said.

"I feel ... like a bride." She let out a giggle as she said it.

"Is this the one?" Abby asked.

Naomi looked at herself in the mirror. She saw herself standing in front of Will, promising to love him for all time, in this dress. She nodded, the joy manifesting as tears in her eyes. "It's the one."

"It's the one!" Abby repeated with an excited squeal.

The attendant bent down and arranged the skirt that was draped on the floor. "This is such a romantic train. And it bustles nicely too. It's a bit complicated to do because the lace is so delicate, but the end result is really beautiful." She looked at Abby. "That's usually the Maid of Honor's job. Are you up to the challenge?"

Abby leaned in to examine the constellation of tiny buttons on the back of the dress.

"You see," Valerie said, demonstrating. "These little loops on the end of the train pop onto the buttons up here on the dress, so that all that extra fabric is out of the way when it's time to bust a move on the dance floor. But it takes a little work to find each loop and get it to hook on properly."

Naomi watched in the mirror as Abby bent down and attempted to copy what the attendant had done. Whatever she was trying to do was not going well because within a few minutes, she was sprawled across the floor, bottom lip firmly planted between her teeth as she examined the dress like she was conducting a fragile scientific experiment. Finally, she looked up at Naomi and gave a pained grimace. "This dress is amazing, but did you have to say yes to a dress that has a Rubik's Cube for a bustle?" Abby glanced at the camera swirling around her and said under her breath, "They're going to love this, I'm sure."

"Don't worry," the attendant said. "They'll demonstrate it again at the fitting."

"I'm going to need more than a demonstration. I'm going to need a road map and a week to practice." Abby squinted. "I can't even see half these buttons."

"The fitting is generally at least a week before the wedding, but because of the," Valerie gave a small, polite cough, "Condensed timeline, we don't have that luxury. It'll take almost a week to get the dress in, so we'll be doing the final fitting two days before the wedding, and you won't have the dress until the day before."

"The day before?" Abby made another, unsuccessful attempt to slip one of the buttons through the corresponding loop. "Girl, you're going to be late for your reception because I'll be spending two hours trying to get these buttoned."

"Don't worry," Valerie said. "I've been doing this for years, and I know the foolproof way to ensure you'll be ready on the wedding day."

"I'm listening," Abby replied.

"The night before the wedding, get some drinks in your system. When everything gets a bit fuzzy, then practice. Then drink a little more and practice some more. When it's time for the reception, have a glass of champagne and watch your muscle memory kick in like magic."

"Now," Becca said, coming closer to inspect Abby's work. "This is solely a Maid of Honor thing, right? I'm not expected to spend my night—"

"You're off the hook," Naomi assured her.

"Thank God. I love you and all, but that's not really where I shine." She waved her hand in the general direction of Naomi's train. "But I do shine at being a cheerleader and coming up with great hashtags. Like ... hashtag bitches be bustling! Ooo, that *is* good." She turned her attention back to her phone, no doubt to get the hashtag trend started.

"Sounds like we have a plan for the night before the wedding, Abby," Naomi said. "You heard your sister. Hashtag bitches be bustling."

"God help me."

"Well then." Naomi laughed. "I'm ready to get out of this dress so you can start trying on bridesmaids' dresses!"

A woman with a clipboard and headset stepped out from behind the cameras. The camera crews that followed her and Will always came equipped with a producer, who—despite being called producer—served as a sort of director for the unfolding show of their lives. It seemed more than a little odd to have someone show her where to stand, interview her at random moments, and even instruct her what to say at times, but bill, foot, no questions. Will had explained to her that if this were a full-fledged reality program, they'd be paired with one, maybe two, people for the entirety of their time but since Nightly Global News was a news program and not in the business of reality TV, it was more like producer popcorn and they were getting whoever at the station was available. Today, they had someone named Natalie.

"While we wait for Naomi to change out of her dress, let's do some CCI's," Natalie said. CCIs, which stood for Confession Cam Interviews, had taken some extra getting used to. Stopping everything to give the behind-the-scenes interviews that revealed to the audience a peek into what Naomi was thinking and feeling was a bizarre experience, to say the least. "Abby, why don't we start with you?"

Natalie gestured towards a spot in the room where a few cameras and some very bright lights were waiting for her.

As Abby's interview began, Valerie helped Naomi down from the podium.

"Abby, how is dress shopping going?" she heard Natalie say, throwing Abby a softball question.

"Dress shopping is going amazing," Abby said. "Naomi found a dress and it makes her look like she belongs on the cover of a bridal magazine."

"Now I heard you all talking about the bustle. What was going on with that?"

Even from across the room, Naomi could spot Abby's side eye. "Well, it sounds like I'm going to need some extra practice. But we've got a plan." The door to the dressing room closed. Naomi would have to wait until tomorrow to hear the rest of the interview.

Chapter Fourteen

Will

Will lifted his foot off the brake to allow the car to roll forward a few inches before pressing it again. He and Naomi were making their way to the West Loop on a perfect Saturday afternoon, which is where everyone else in the city seemed to be heading too. "I just thought of something. I think this is the first time that—" Will looked surreptitiously at the two GoPro cameras suctioned to his dashboard.

"First time that ..." Naomi prompted.

"*Thaaaat*," Will gave himself a second to decide how to finish his sentence. "You-know-who and you-know-who will be in the same place since you-know-what."

"Ooh, good point."

"Do you think there will be any—" he tried, unsuccessfully, to mime a physical altercation while also holding onto the steering wheel. "Or—" he fluttered his eyes at her, in a cartoonish version of flirtation.

Naomi, rightfully, laughed at him. "Unless you know something I don't, there has been no ... indication either way."

Will shook his head. In all the months since they'd crashed NGN and strategically leaked a story about Abby's secret feelings for Freya, his boss hadn't said a word to him or even so much as hinted that something was amiss. For all he knew, she hadn't even overseen the entire production they had put on for her.

The walkie-talkie resting in the cup holder of Will's Prius crackled. "Rude," a tinny voice said.

His colleague, Annalisa, was riding in an NGN van a few cars behind them, listening to the entire conversation.

"Don't worry your pretty little head about it, Annalisa," he teased. "It has nothing to do with the wedding."

"Uh huh." Annalisa sounded unconvinced. "Anyway, has anyone told you what to expect for your bachelor/bachelorette party?"

Annalisa wasn't asking for herself. She was asking to get them talking for the cameras, which would be collected from the car this evening and edited for tomorrow's wedding special. As someone who spent nearly every waking hour in the vicinity of cameras, Will had thought that being in front of them would come naturally. But it had not. It required a kind of ambidextrous thinking akin to patting your head and rubbing your stomach. Like now, he didn't only have to answer the question, he had to make sure he didn't a) look at the camera b) talk to Annalisa or c) answer the question without repeating it first.

Will looked over at Naomi as he tried to keep the rules in mind. "I don't know what to expect at our bachelor/bachelorette party, aside from being told to dress up in prom attire from the era of our choice. Do you, Naomi?" He had gone full 1970's, and rented a powder blue tuxedo, complete with bow tie, cummerbund, and—most importantly—a chest full of ruffles.

Naomi had hit up a vintage store down the street from her office and had picked up a puffy-sleeved tea dress in a metallic pink not seen since the 1980's. She had done something to her curly hair to make it poof up like she had touched a live wire before pulling it up into a high ponytail at the top of her head. "Your guess is as good as mine."

NGN had put the wedding party in charge of planning the joint bachelor/bachelorette which, on paper, sounded like a great idea. In reality, though, Will had tried to figure out how he could explain to the higher-ups the dynamics of that group and why putting them all together might not work so well. There were Abby and Freya, who might start throwing things at each other or could potentially be in the throes of discovering intense feelings for each other because of a very elaborate prank. And then there were Becca and Riley who were ... well, they were Becca and Riley. Individually, they were a force to contend with, but together they could combine like Power Rangers to create a new form of unstoppable strength or in their case, chaos.

With Naomi's blessing, he had decided the best course of action was merely to do nothing besides hope for the best. "The invitation did say 'Set Sail for Love' so I have to assume it's some kind of nautical prom bachelor party mash-up." When Naomi didn't answer, he glanced at the passenger seat. She was hunched, clutching her phone and reading something with a peculiar intensity. "Everything alright?"

She looked up with a start. "Huh?" She locked her phone before setting it in her lap and smiling. "Yeah, some work stuff." But her smile, like the rest of her face, was taut.

It was that familiar, hollow expression that always left him with a similarly hollow feeling in his stomach. It wasn't about work. It was about something else. The something else he had never been able to decipher. And he had started to think he wouldn't need to. Since Rosh Hashanah, those incidents had tapered off. But here they were again.

Static, and then Annalisa, broke the silence. "Anything you're especially looking forward to?"

Naomi violated the Prime Directive and looked into the camera. "Do you think we could finish these questions when we get there?"

A long pause and then, "Sure."

Naomi turned her head to look out the passenger window and placed both hands over the phone like she was trying to stop whatever was in there from coming out. He'd already asked her if everything was ok. What else could he do but sit within her silence and, like the party they were about to go to, hope for the best?

"Looks like Freya is here," he said as he pulled in between the white lines of a parking space.

"Why don't you go ahead? I need to do some adjusting." She tugged at the tulle peeking out from her skirt.

He got out of the car with a nod and began walking to where Freya was sitting in her parked car, staring into her visor as she applied lipstick. When she didn't notice him, he raised his hand to tap on her window, but stopped, almost instinctively, to glance back at Naomi first. She didn't appear to be adjusting anything. Instead, it looked like she was taking a call.

He turned back to the car and rapped on the window a little more intensely than he meant to.

Freya jumped so hard Will was glad she still had her seatbelt on.

"Didn't mean to startle you," he said when she rolled down her window.

"You didn't. I'm a bit groggy from the trip."

"Yeah, I bet." In between the wedding preparation, the filming, and the onslaught of interviews, Will had not been able to do much real work, though he still did his best when he could. A week ago, he had finally gotten an email giving him the go-ahead from the San Jose Department of Corrections to conduct an interview with a death row inmate that was the focus of a story he and Freya had been working on around prison reform. This had been incredible news smothered in terrible timing. They had waited years for this interview, and time was, quite literally, running out for the inmate who deserved the chance to speak. Asking for an extension so that he could be filmed picking out kitchen appliances for his registry wasn't an option. But neither was leaving for three days. With no other alternative, Freya had gone with another producer and conducted the interview without him. He couldn't stop the breath of frustration from escaping. "I can't believe I couldn't come with you. We've been trying to talk to this guy for how many years?"

"Many."

"How did it go?"

"About as well as you might expect it would go sitting across from someone who knows they're helping to fight for something they'll never get to see. The courts have basically said that at this point, even DNA evidence wouldn't exonerate him because it wouldn't eliminate him from the crime scene. It's utterly incomprehensible. But, for a few hours, at least, let's not talk about work and enjoy your bachelor party, shall we?" She smiled at him, but even the red lipstick couldn't disguise the fatigue.

No, more than fatigue.

It seemed like there was an uneasiness underneath her cheerful front.

But he knew better than to ask, so instead he said, "Fine, but I want to hear more right after. I can't believe that's the end of the road. I just can't."

"Yes, later. Are you heading in?"

"Yes, Naomi stopped to ..." He turned to look back at his car. Naomi was still sitting in the passenger's seat exactly where he had left her, still clutching her phone to her ear. He looked back at Freya, trying to remember what he had been saying. "Um, do something with her dress. I'm not entirely sure."

Freya gave him a dismissive roll of her eyes before getting out of the car. He wanted to tell her that while, yes, he was not entirely sure about women and their dresses—including Freya's dress, which looked like it belonged at the Oscars, not a prom-themed party—in this case, his uncertainty was much more complex than that. He had thought, many times, about telling Freya about the nagging worry he had and asking her thoughts. But he still hadn't been able to make sense of Riley's advice, and the last thing he needed was more nebulous suggestions that only left him feeling further confused and incapable of handling things. It was, as he reminded himself often, probably nothing. Merely a Naomi quirk that he wouldn't even notice in ten years.

When Naomi joined them a minute later, slipping her arm through his and smiling up at him, he felt reassured in his decision. She was fine. And they were fine. And now it was time to celebrate.

The three of them walked to the entrance of the restaurant. While he had never been to the Beach Club before, there was a lot of buzz about the new "it" spot, so he wasn't surprised when he stepped in and saw the expansive and bright space that took its decorative cues of white, cream, and gray from the east coast beach scene. What did surprise him was everything else.

This wasn't a prom theme. This was *prom.* He was standing on a red carpet that went between an enormous life ring that had the words "S.S. Wilomi" at the top. There was a stage, with a band, and a dance area that had wave-shaped lights projected on the floor. There were streamers, balloons, flowers, and a banner that said, "Set Sail for Love." And there was a photo backdrop, if it could even be called that. It was a three-dimensional cruise ship deck with an actual winding staircase.

He knew that he should say something for the cameras that had, like vultures, begun circling him. He and Naomi, and he suspected the rest of the wedding party, were already mic'd, so anything he said would get picked up even if the cameras weren't close. But Naomi's squeak of delight about summed up all the words he had. He tried to imagine how they had pulled this all off in a matter of days, until his internal pondering was quickly answered.

"Yoohoo!"

Riley. Of course. If anyone could imagine this and make it happen, it was them.

Riley was relaxing, in a posed kind of way, on a wooden beach chair and sipping something bright pink from a tropical-looking glass. They wiggled their fingers in an invitation to join them. As he approached, Will could see Riley was in some kind of massive, nautically-themed ball-gown, and their hair, almost blindingly silver, was spiked up like waves billowing across the ocean. He should have known that Riley would never have been anything but extravagant when it came to dressing for prom.

"Welcome aboard!" Riley said.

Naomi let out another squeak, and Will started to wonder if that was all Naomi would be able to get out this afternoon. But then she said, "Riley, this is incredible! Way better than ..." She stopped so abruptly that Will did a quick visual sweep to see if he could spot something that had drawn her attention. But he didn't see anything, and she continued, although a little hesitantly. "My actual prom."

"I'm pretty pleased with how it turned out," Riley said after taking a long sip. "Especially since I basically had to do it by myself."

"Dirty, *dirty* lies, Riley. I helped." Becca entered Will's line of vision and he was sure if he had been drinking something, he most definitely would have done a spit take. She was dressed in ... nothing? In truth, it was a see-through dress with a handful of rhinestones that would theoretically cover enough to keep her from getting arrested. Becca had never really made a habit of leaving much to the imagination when it came to her clothing, but this eliminated any questions.

Riley, naturally, didn't bat an eye. "You put me in touch with some strippers."

"It's not my fault the studio refused to listen to reason! If no one is going to get naked, can you even call this a bachelorette party?" Becca was always, sometimes comically and sometimes uncomfortably, sexual. But it seemed especially dialed up today as she balanced herself on the armrest of Riley's chair and leaned back like she was taking direction from a Playboy photographer. "Speaking of getting naked—"

"That didn't take long," Will said.

"—has anyone seen Peter?"

"Peter?" Will repeated. And so did Riley and Naomi. Apparently, he wasn't the only one who hadn't expected to hear that she had come to the party with her estranged husband.

"The last I heard ..." Naomi didn't finish her sentence, instead looking over at Freya. He had forgotten about Freya. He wondered how much, if any, introduction into the world of Naomi's friends she had gotten during their party planning.

Becca seemed unperturbed at the idea of sharing her marital strife with outsiders. She looked at Freya. "It's fine, honey. My husband and I were having a little, you know, trouble. My MySpace of a sister had us going to couples counseling and group therapy and obviously none of that helped. And then I figured out what the answer was. See, I was looking to other people for something Peter could give me all along. The excitement and variety I was looking for? All we needed to do was roleplay. Well, and the occasional threesome, but mostly roleplay!" She punctuated her sentence by leaning back even more, as if it were possible to reveal any more of her body under that dress and making a seductive face at the nearest camera. She continued talking but kept her eyes on the camera. "So tonight, we're running with the prom theme. I'm the prom queen, obviously, and he's going to be a nerdy kid who always had a crush on me, and I'm going to pop his c-h-e-r-r-y."

Will tried not to laugh. "Out of everything, that's the word you feel you need to spell out?"

Becca didn't answer, which wasn't unusual. He had learned early on that at least fifty percent of what Becca said was for performance instead of conversation. "We rented a room at a seedy motel," she said. "I tried to get the same motel I used for my *actual* prom, but it's gone, tragically."

"Well, mazel," Naomi said. "I'm so happy that you and Peter found something that works for you. I knew you two would figure it out."

"Yes, congratulations on your," Will realized, too late, that he had approached his congratulations from the wrong angle and his voice lifted an octave as he tried to pull out of the verbal nose dive, "role ... playing?"

Thankfully, Riley was ready to bring the focus back to them. "Rediscovering marital bliss, while certainly a feat, is no excuse for abandoning me. As I was saying, I basically did this by myself."

For the first time, Freya spoke up. "I'm not even going to try to argue with that. I've been completely checked out for the last three days, so thank you, Riley, for taking on the lion's share of the work. And doing such a fantastic job." This was the most she had said about the party planning process, and it couldn't have been more Freya. She had navigated working within a close-knit friend dynamic that often required a decoder ring to understand. It also included someone who, not that long ago, she had been throwing ice cubes at—but could potentially be in love with or still hate just as much as before. But he knew she would never admit that any of that was challenging or even of note.

"What about Abby?" Naomi asked, before taking an hors d'oeuvres from a passing server. "Oh my God, this is fantastic."

Riley gave a pleased smile. "Wait until you try the coconut and pineapple spring rolls. And Abby? Well, she—oh here she is, right on cue."

Will turned with everyone else to see Abby coming towards them in a purple dress that was unmistakably 90's with a skintight skirt and low-cut peplum top.

"Sorry, sorry, sorry!" She shuffled towards them in a specific way that said
I-can't-move-my-legs-and-I-don't-want-to-trip-in-these-heels-and-please-god-don't-let-my-boobs-fall-out.

Women and their dresses.

Abby entered the circle between him and Naomi, practically flopping onto Naomi as she took in deep breaths.

While they waited, Will checked to see if he could notice anything out of place on Freya's face. But, unsurprisingly, she wasn't giving anything away. He took a quick survey of the group and saw they were all checking too.

"You okay there?" Naomi asked, turning her attention to Abby.

Abby straightened and exhaled. "Yes, sorry. I really thought I could get here in time to help set up. I tried to explain to the police that it was a false alarm and I had a party to get to, but they still made me go through the entire process."

"Your alarm went off again?" Naomi asked.

Will looked at Freya, wondering if he should catch her up on the fact that for reasons yet unknown, Abby's office alarm had been going off repeatedly over the past few weeks, but decided that she probably wasn't invested in any of their friend-circle conversation.

"I didn't want to bother you while you were getting ready for your party. But yes. *Again*."

"What is that, the second time this month?" Will asked.

"Fourth time in less than two weeks!"

"That's so scary!" Naomi said.

"At this point, it's mostly annoying AF. No one has any idea what's going on. The alarm keeps showing that the door is open, but it's not open and nothing is missing. The alarm company thinks it's an electrical short. The building super thinks it's a mouse."

"Now that *is* scary!" Riley said.

"I know! Can you imagine if it showed up while I was in my office?" Abby said, looking horrified.

Riley gave a little shiver. "Why don't you bring Lancelot to your office? Let him live up to his name a little and save a damsel in distress."

Was Will supposed to tell Freya that Abby had a cat named Lancelot? He wasn't sure what his role was here.

Abby laughed, but then her smile refocused into a scowl. "This is the last straw for me. The alarm company keeps promising me that they've solved the problem and it won't happen again. And then it does. And it's a huge waste of my time because I have to go all the way down to my office each time, talk to the police, inspect the place, and confirm to them and the alarm company that nothing has been stolen or destroyed. It's more than an hour out of my day each time, and I've decided if it happens again, I'm ripping the panel out of my wall and setting it on fire while I dance over its melting body."

The idea, however ridiculous, was intriguing, and Will contemplated how to pull it off. "You'd need like some kind of blowtorch to light—" He felt Naomi squeeze his arm, rightfully reminding him that perhaps Abby wasn't particularly interested in the mechanics of melting an alarm panel.

Plus, she seemed to have moved on from her alarm issues. "How are things going here? And also, *what* is going on here? Explain to me what kind of prom you three are dressed for?" She used her chin to indicate Becca, Riley, and Freya. Was he seeing things or had Abby held her gaze on Freya a little longer than anyone else? Will looked to Naomi for confirmation, but she was distracted. On her phone. Again. Her body angled enough that her screen was hidden.

"Oh, this old thing?" Riley added a hint of a southern twang to their words. "Just a little something I whipped up for the occasion. I couldn't find anything on theme that complemented my nearly invisible waist while making the rest of me as visible as possible, so I had to take matters into my own hands and alter a dress to my liking."

"I wanted to be as visible as possible, too," Becca said.

"I, er, missed the memo and tried to find something I owned that looked like what the kids are wearing today," Freya said.

"More work problems?" Will whispered to Naomi.

Naomi locked the screen. "Yep."

"Hi, everyone." Will's colleague, Max, walked up to the group. "Now that you're all here, let's get started. I've met some of you, but for those of you I haven't, I'm Max, and I'll be the producer for this evening's event."

One of the producers. For an event this big, he was sharing the workload with Annalisa. But he'd worked with Max enough to know that he never shared credit unless he had to.

"We've got about fifteen minutes before the other guests start to arrive. So, we'd love to get our CCI's in while we have some time. Who wants to go—"

Becca raised her hand like she was the star pupil in class. "Me! I love me some Confession Cam. Besides, I want to make sure there's nothing to interrupt me and Peter once we get, you know, started."

"It's honestly a wonder they can use any of the footage from Becca's interviews," Abby said as Becca left with Max.

"From what I've heard, they pretty much can't," Will replied. It had been amusing, to say the least, to hear his colleagues struggle to find any content with Becca that wouldn't leave Nightly Global News with a hefty fine from the FCC.

There was a short silence, and then Freya asked, "Only a couple more days until you walk down the aisle, you two. Are you ready?"

Freya's question had, obviously, been directed at him and Naomi. But it hadn't been obvious for Riley who answered first. "I would be a lot more ready if we weren't having this wedding at noon. On a *Monday*." They said Monday like they were doing a Garfield impression. "Can you explain to me how that is a thing that is happening? Who gets married on a *Monday* afternoon?"

"People who care about ratings do," Freya said. "These two have the biggest following with stay-at-home moms and viewers in Europe. Twelve p.m. central is lunch time here, and end of the day over there. Ratings are king."

"That explains a lot. The patriarchy is once again doing us in. If ratings were queen, I think we'd be approaching this a lot differently. Ooh, queens! That gives me an idea. Naomi." Riley's attention shifted to Freya, and the topic switched. "Let's replace your wedding guests with drag queens. And then that could be a spin-off show: Drag Queenzilla, where a bunch of drag queens crash your wedding and—is this making sense or have these Pink Bikini cocktails finally caught up with me? Maybe time to switch to the punch. Anyone else? You know what? Never mind; you're all getting one. Don't worry, it's a true prom and the punch is spiked."

"Hoo boy, Riley is going to keep us on our toes tonight," Abby said as soon as Riley was out of earshot. "Has anyone ever *un*spiked punch before? Because we might want to."

Naomi laughed before changing the subject. "We thanked Riley already," she looked to Abby and then Freya, "but I wanted to thank both of you for helping put this together. It's phenomenal and the party hasn't even started yet."

Freya gave a polite smile. "I wasn't kidding when I said Riley put this together. They are a good friend."

"We—" Abby began, then stopped. Will might not have paid much attention to her use of the word 'we' if Abby hadn't then glanced at Freya before starting over. Was something going on between those two, or was he reading into things? "I think, well, *my* only contribution was helping to come up with the theme."

"I loved it as soon as you told me. What sparked the idea?" Naomi asked.

"Some late-night reminiscing over wine," Abby said, definitely giving Freya some kind of look. Or was it? He cut his eyes to Naomi to see if she had picked up on it too, but she seemed lost in thought. Was it related to her "work" problem? His mind was spinning.

Just then, Max returned. "Okay, who's next?"

"That was fast," Naomi said.

"Becca got, um, distracted."

"Sounds about right," Abby said.

Will was tired of trying to guess what was going on in the three women's heads and was grateful for something else to do. "I can go."

Max nodded and pointed at him and Naomi. "Great. Let's have you two do this one together first, and then I'll have you each go separately."

The "confessional" was set up by the photo backdrop where a combination of production lights and stage lights were pointing at a pair of chairs.

"Alright, kids, have a seat," Max directed. Not that he needed to. They'd been doing Confession Cam Interviews nearly every day for nearly a month now. It had been uncomfortable in the beginning, and while Will still didn't love it, he was also starting to wonder what life would be like without having someone pull him away for a regular download of his thoughts and feelings. "Alright, guys, we want to keep this really short so that you can start to greet your guests and focus on having fun. Ready?"

Naomi and Will both nodded, and Max stepped back behind the gaggle of cameras pointed at them. "What do you think of your party so far?"

The party hadn't started yet. But he knew the drill. They wanted a soundbite they could overlay at any point during the segment. He glanced over his shoulder at the faux cruise ship behind him and then back at the camera.

Remembering rules one, two, and three, he began, "I think the party is absolutely incredible! I feel so grateful for our amazing wedding party who put it together. I'm a little worried that it's so good our guests might enjoy it more than our wedding."

Naomi laughed, the way only a fiancée can at a corny joke, and nudged him with her shoulder.

"Naomi, what's something special about this evening?" Max asked.

"This evening is extra special because I get to see so many of my favorite people under one roof," she told Max. "Of course, we'll see everyone at the wedding. But I feel like that's going to be different. We'll be focused on each other and getting married. This is only about having fun and hanging out."

"Speaking of your wedding, it's coming up in two days. You feel ready?"

Naomi exchanged a smile with Will and then said, "Are we ready for our wedding? I guess you could say that we're as ready as you can be when you plan a wedding in a month! I think the only loose end to tie up at this point is, literally, tying up my bustle. Y'all have been giving Abby such a hard time about that. But don't worry, she's coming over tomorrow night to for our hashtag bitches be bustling pre-wedding bustle practice and wine party."

Will still wasn't entirely sure what a bustle was, but he knew that Abby's struggle with it had taken on a life of its own on the Internet.

"Will, any plans tomorrow night?"

He shrugged. "I don't have any plans for tomorrow night. Our big party is tonight, so I'll be at my place, getting an early night so I can be ready for the big day."

"Aside from bustle troubles, Naomi, do you feel like you have any wedding day jitters?"

Oh, Max. Always looking for the drama.

"No, I'm not having any pre-wedding jitters," Naomi said, laughing off the question. "We made a lot of decisions in a very short amount of time, so I have absolutely no idea how the wedding is going to go. But even if it all goes wrong, it will all go right because at the end of the day, I'll be married to this guy. And I have no jitters about that."

"What she said," Will said. He wrapped his arm around her, his chest feeling like it was going to burst open, and birds were going to emerge and start singing. "I love this woman," he said with a grin that he couldn't have stopped if he wanted to.

Chapter Fifteen

Naomi

Standing in her living room in her wedding dress, Naomi stretched her arm out for a selfie. "Smile!" On the screen of her phone, she could see Abby flash a peace sign from her spot on the floor beside the train of Naomi's dress. After getting Abby's approval, she uploaded the photo to Instagram and typed out a caption:

The bustle party is on! I hope you all are lucky enough to have a best friend who is willing to spend two hours looking for tiny loops on a wedding dress so you can dance the night away. #bffs #bitchesbebustling #wilomi

She hit post, and immediately the likes and comments came flying in like a meteor shower. She still wasn't entirely used to the throng of excited, and sometimes fanatical, followers who hung on her every word. A month ago, what she posted online was seen—if at all— by a few friends who knew her well, could hear her voice in the words she wrote, and could envision her, the three-dimensional person, in the two-dimensional pictures she posted. But now, her words and photos were being consumed and dissected by people around the world who were creating an image of her in their heads based on tiny snippets of her life. It was terrifying. And enthralling. She knew that when it was over, she wouldn't miss it at all. And yet, she also knew she was going to miss it more than she cared to admit. Sometimes it was hard to imagine going back to a life where the world wasn't excited about everything she did. Sometimes she couldn't wait to return to the normalcy and privacy she'd enjoyed her whole life but never truly appreciated.

But tomorrow she would be married, the wedding special would be over, and so would the entourage of cameras, the whirlwind of interviews, and the clamoring of followers for her to share more, more, more …

"Everyone is commenting that we have to go live so you can show off your technique!" Naomi held out the phone to Abby.

Abby inspected the screen and laughed. "Everyone is obsessed."

"We can ignore them," Naomi said.

"No." Abby swept the phone from Naomi's hand and tapped at the screen. "No, no. We must give the people what they want. Besides, I've got this down. And while I don't quite understand the sudden, international fascination with bustling, I'm ready to be crowned champion."

"Oh boy."

Abby wasn't someone who sought the spotlight, but when it found her, she never shied away. So, it only made sense to Naomi that she had adapted quickly to her role as co-star. Abby never tried to take over, but when the moment was hers—like the world's sudden obsession with her ability to bustle—she embraced it without hesitation. And though she'd never admitted it, Naomi had a feeling she was having more fun than she let on. After a little bit more tapping, Abby said, "Here we go!" Naomi couldn't see her screen, but she assumed Abby had done the deed when she heard her say, "Ask and you shall receive. We are live because the time has come for me to restore my honor and show you all my newfound talent. Actually, I'm realizing I got ahead of myself. Our glasses are empty, so, first, allow me to hand over the reins to the beautiful bride so I can refill our wine."

Abby handed the phone back to Naomi, who smiled into the camera. The view counter was already well into the four digits and climbing. "Hey all! How is everyone doing tonight? I know you're all coming here to catch Abby bustle her way to fame, but to fill the time, I can answer a few questions while we wait for her to come back with our drinks." She watched the comments scrolling across her screen. It had taken a little practice but she was starting to get the hang of replying to people as their questions tumbled by like an avalanche. "Am I worried Will is going to see my dress right now? He's already seen it. It was too hard to keep it from him when it was all over social media and TV. I know, it sucks. But I think it'll still be special for him when he gets to see me wearing it down the aisle with my hair and makeup and everything. What time are we getting to the studio tomorrow? Oh my God, we have to get there at like four in the morning. So definitely going to be winding down here soon. Oh no, Yumi— you have to work tomorrow and can't watch it live? I know, Monday in the middle of the day is kind of a tough time. I didn't pick it. But I know NGN said they were going to put the replay up right away so hopefully you can catch it later. We don't have any surprises planned, so the good news is you don't have to worry about spoilers. You've seen all the preparations so there's nothing people will be talking about. Oh, thank you, WeedWaterWoo. I think that glow you're seeing is mostly from the wine, though."

"Speaking of." Abby appeared holding two very full glasses.

Naomi took the glass with her free hand and tapped it against Abby's glass. "Cheers!"

Wine emojis and "cheers!" rolled by.

"Yes," Abby said, replying to someone. "White wine *only* around a wedding dress. It was this or vodka, but we decided hard liquor the night before a wedding was not the way to go."

"What do you say, Abby, are you ready for your big performance?"

Abby took a large gulp of her drink and then set it down. "If I ever met my younger self, I'm not sure how I would explain this particular moment in my life. But sure, here we go!"

Naomi looked into the camera lens and gave her invisible audience a stern, but playful, gaze. "This is my best friend, so be nice." She handed the phone back to Abby, who had knelt beside her train.

"For starters," Abby said, holding the phone up to the lacy fabric near the bottom of the train. "I defy any of you to find one of the loops that will hook onto the buttons—which we will be getting to shortly. Keep looking. Give up? It's here."

With her free hand, Abby lifted a single thread hidden across the lace. A section of the train came with it as she pulled up. "But wait, now we have to find the corresponding button." She scanned the phone across Naomi's skirt. "Holler when you spot one. Go ahead. Nothing? Okay, here's one." Still holding the loop, she pointed at a tiny, lacy button the size of a Tic Tac.

"Now it takes two hands to get this little loop around the button, so Naomi, if you could." Abby returned the phone to Naomi, who kept it pointed at Abby while she carefully connected the two pieces together. After a few extremely low-stakes tense moments, she lifted both hands over her head in triumph. "Tah dah! There it is! I win! I win bustling!"

"Yay!" Naomi cheered. "Give it up for Abby!"

"And I only have to do that nine more times to actually bustle the dress!"

"Everyone is saying they had no idea it was so overly complicated," Naomi reported to Abby. "YourPalAl says we can send live images from Mars, but can't invent an easier way to get the train of a dress off the ground. I agree, YourPalAl. So now maybe you all should go make some memes about how amazing Abby is as penance for all your trolling."

"I also accept Venmo and wine as penance," Abby said with a laugh.

"And with that, I'm going to say goodnight. But I'll try to go live before the wedding and, of course, I'll be seeing you all tomorrow at noon when I get to marry the love of my life! Ahhh! Okay bye! Bye everyone. Bye!" She waved at the camera before ending the live and collapsing on the couch.

Abby joined her with a sated sigh. "On my deathbed, I will go peacefully knowing that I was mocked by the internet and then redeemed myself."

"I'm sure your grandchildren will sit around your feet and ask you about it."

Abby widened her eyes into a doe-like stare and said in a high-pitched voice, "Grandma, pretty please tell us the bitches be bustling story one more time?"

It wasn't *that* funny. But the combination of the wine and the pressure of the last few weeks made it the funniest thing she'd ever heard, and soon they were falling over each other in a fit of laughter.

The only reason either of them heard Abby's phone ringing was because they both stopped to take in a breath at the same time. Wiping her eyes, Abby picked up her phone from the coffee table.

"You've got to be kidding me." The laughter was gone.

Naomi pressed herself to seated so she could see Abby's phone. The screen said *SECURISAFE.* She put the pieces together quickly. "Is that your alarm company?"

"Yep. But they won't be my alarm company the minute we've put you in your 'just married' car. I'm over this, but I haven't had the time to get set up with a new company." She accepted the call and said began responding in a curt voice, "Hello. Yes, this is she. Uh huh, my code is 122119. Yep, I'm on my way." She hung up, making a guttural noise of frustration as she did.

"On your way? You really have to go right now?" Naomi asked.

Abby sighed as she stood up from the sofa. "It's the same old drill. They've already called the police, so I have to go."

"Do you want me to come with?"

"I appreciate the offer, but unless you're wanting to try out what it feels like to be a runaway bride ..." Abby gestured at Naomi, who looked down at the partly bustled wedding dress she was still wearing.

"It's not buttoned up in the back, I could—"

"Naomi, as your maid of honor, I absolutely insist that you do not spend your last night as a single woman going to my office and standing there while I assure the police for the millionth time that nothing has been stolen. You should go have a cozy bubble bath and then get into bed. I would be doing you a disservice if I let you do anything else. You, more than anyone, need to be well-rested for tomorrow. No one will be paying attention to me."

On quite literally any other night, Naomi would have been adamant about keeping her best friend company on her annoying errand. But tonight, the night before her wedding, she could let Abby convince her to stay in. A bubble bath and an early bedtime did sound extremely enticing, especially compared to the chilly evening spring air outside. "If you're sure ..."

"I'm sure," Abby said as she grabbed her jacket off the chair and walked to the front door. "I don't know what it says about me that of the half dozen times this has happened, this is not the first time I've had to go down there when I'm not entirely sober."

"It says it's happened a half dozen times too many."

"You always know exactly what to say." Abby opened the door. "Alright, I'll be back in probably a little over an hour. It's late, and you have to get up at an ungodly hour to get married tomorrow, so I won't be offended if you fall asleep."

Naomi gave her a salute.

As the door closed behind Abby, Naomi stood up and walked into her room, where she carefully shimmied out of her dress before placing it back on the bridal hanger she had ordered from Etsy, which was emblazoned with her name. With the studio covering all the major wedding expenses, she had been able to splurge on all the dreamy Pinterest extras that caught her eye, like custom hangers for her and her bridal party.

Given the number of people who had keys to her apartment, walking around naked was always a somewhat risky activity—not that any of those people with keys hadn't seen her naked before. More on principle than actual concern, she jogged into the bathroom and closed the door. Then, per Abby's suggestion, she started a bath.

As the steamy water began to fill the tub, she opened a drawer and pulled out a red satin bag containing a lavender scented candle, matches, a paper face mask, a sparkly bath bomb shaped like a unicorn, and a note that read, "Happy birthday! May your baths be extra bubbly, your face masks extra soothing, and your lighting extra flattering. Love, Riley." She had been saving their gift for a night when she deserved some extra pampering, and this seemed like the perfect occasion.

With the candle lit, mask on, and bath bomb frothing, she was about to step into the bath when her phone beeped. Her body reacted instantly as she read the word "UNKNOWN" across the screen. Her phone might not know who was texting, but she did. And she knew why.

She placed a hand on the edge of the sink for balance and, with the other hand, picked up the phone.

UNKNOWN: Hi Kiwi

After more than half a year of silence, yesterday he had started calling again. She had ignored him until, on the way to the bachelor/bachelorette party, she had started receiving a slew of texts from him. As she read them, knowing that not only Will but the cameras were watching, she tried to keep her body and breathing neutral, but it had been nearly impossible.

At first, her heart rate had skyrocketed out of fear, but then it had morphed into a flutter of disbelief and finally elation. It was really happening. She had been right. Going public with her relationship hadn't angered Simon; it had finally, truly changed him. After so many years of empty promises, things were finally going to be different. She had wanted so badly to tell Abby in that moment, to assure her that all her fears had been misplaced. But she knew she could never say a word. Abby had never known Simon like she had, and Abby could never understand the other side of Simon, the side that Naomi always knew would win out in the end.

UNKNOWN: You around?

NAOMI: Yes.

Her phone began to vibrate with a call. She took a deep breath and answered it.

Chapter Sixteen

Will

Getting married was quite possibly the easiest thing that Will had ever done.

Not that he was married yet, but with an hour to go before he would head to the altar, he was feeling pretty good about his wedding day.

Call time had been four-thirty in the morning, but when he arrived, he'd been informed that since his hair and makeup would take about twenty minutes, he could come back at ten-thirty. Everyone else, including Riley, was then promptly whisked away for an undisclosed amount of time, leaving him to enjoy a relaxing morning. After catching a few hours of sleep in the green room, he grazed the craft services table before deciding to take himself out for a heartier breakfast at a café down the street. Scrambled eggs, a stack of chocolate chip pancakes, three slices of extra crispy bacon, and two cups of coffee later, he still had several hours to kill. So, he went in search of the perfect bottle of champagne to pop with Naomi during their first few moments alone as husband and wife, which he found at a specialty liquor store a few blocks down from the studio.

By the time he arrived back at the studio a little before ten, he was feeling rested and relaxed.

"You can't go through with this wedding, Will." Riley practically pounced on Will like a feral cat as he entered their green room.

As quickly as Will's stomach plummeted to the center of the earth, it returned comfortably back into his body when he saw the nature of the wedding-stopping emergency. "Riley, your hair ..."

"It is unconscionable. An absolute violation of human rights."

This morning, Riley had walked into the studio sporting bleached silver hair with a long stripe down the middle dyed as yellow as a highlighter. Now, it was brown. All brown. Not brown mixed with another, less natural, color. Or even a natural color. It was regular, plain, and completely brown. And it had been trimmed and styled into a side part that made them look like they belonged in a 1950's commercial for dish soap.

"What happened?" was all Will could think to ask.

"What *happened*? I think you can see what happened. They told me there had been a last-minute decision to ruin my life, and I was contractually obligated to comply."

Will could imagine that the words "family friendly" came up at some point in the last twenty-four hours.

Riley drifted over to the mirror like a wayward ghost. "A travesty," they moaned.

While Will had never understood Riley's dedication to a fiber that grew out of their head, he had always done his best to show his support regardless. "I'm sorry."

Riley looked at Will and then back at the mirror, running a hand over their heavily gelled hair. "Abby says it's my most radical look yet. In some ways, she has a point."

Will came close enough to put a hand on their shoulder. "Tomorrow, you can change it to any color you want."

"Tomorrow I won't be on television in front of the whole world." Riley pivoted away from the mirror.

"To be fair, most people will be looking at—"

"Maybe this is for the best. I would have outshone you at your own wedding. Now I'll fade into the background for perhaps the first time in my life. I can't think of a greater gift I could offer you. But what a price I've had to pay." Riley collapsed on the sofa like a maiden in need of smelling salts. "It is a far, far better thing that I do than I have ever done before ..." Riley's muffled recitation of Canton's famous speech before his execution in *A Tale of Two Cities* came from somewhere under their arms.

Will stayed rooted to the floor, trying to decide what, if anything, he should do. This side of Riley was slightly outside his area of expertise.

The door opened and Freya walked in. She took in the scene and then turned to Will, her face making it unnecessary to voice her question as to what was going on.

"We're having a bit of a situation." He gestured to Riley. "Their hair. I'm not really sure what to ..." He trailed off.

Thankfully, she didn't need more explanation because she nodded and made an irritated growl. "I'd heard some rumblings that they wanted to tone things down. I told them not to touch a hair on Riley's head. Sometimes when I'm in this building, I wonder if I'm actually dead and don't know it because it seems like no one can hear me." She walked over to Riley. "Are you okay, sweetie?"

Will had never heard Freya call anyone 'sweetie.' But Riley certainly had a way of capturing even the hardest of hearts. Their quixotic, playful, and kind spirit made it difficult not to get drawn in.

Riley lifted their head. "My God, Freya. Your makeup. The way that tuxedo traces your curves. People are going to go blind looking at their screens when they see you and your rapturous beauty."

The effusive compliments probably helped too.

Freya's downward expression of concern lifted into a smile, and she wagged a finger at them. "You are terrible for my ego, Riley."

"I love a woman in a tuxedo. I guess it should come as no shock that you pull it off better than any woman I've ever seen. Although, let me fix that pocket square." Riley sat up straight and snatched the light green cloth from Freya's pocket and began folding it as if it were origami.

"I'm sorry about your hair," Freya said.

Riley kept their eyes on the pocket square as they let out a sigh. "My whole life, people have been trying to make me into something I'm not. But it's never worked." They handed the pocket square back to Freya. "I think your people upstairs will find I can still sparkle, even with brown hair."

"You are the sparkliest person I've ever met. And that's saying a lot."

Coming from Freya, that was indeed saying a lot. Will couldn't stop a smile from spreading across his face. In the few spare moments he had had over the last month, he'd sacrificed some of it to worrying about how Freya and Riley would mesh as his wedding party. But clearly, he had nothing to worry about.

Freya tucked the pocket square back into her pocket. "If we had more time, I would say we should go raise some hell, but I was sent here to tell you all that it's time."

Will felt a tremor in his core, a mixture of anticipation and nerves. During their dress rehearsal yesterday afternoon, they'd been told the station was expecting thirty million viewers to tune in. Trying to comprehend that many people had proven to be like trying to comprehend the sound of one hand clapping. It was impossible and anxiety-inducing.

"You alright there?" Freya's voice brought him back from his thoughts of thirty million people.

"So many people," he said, his mouth feeling a little dry.

"Be grateful you don't have to walk down the aisle in heels and a giant dress like your bride does. You only have to stand there and say, 'I do.'"

"You make a good point. I do get off pretty easy." He pointed at Riley, whose mouth was opening. "I heard it. We're keeping things PG today."

Riley looked dejected as they stood up, brushing the wrinkles from their tuxedo. "First my hair and now this. What's left for me?"

Will put an arm around Riley and led them towards the green room door. "The joy of watching your good friend marry the woman of his dreams?"

Riley exhaled loudly. "I suppose that's nice and all."

Will opened the door to find Max waiting for them, headset and clipboard at the ready. "Follow me," he said.

"Good to see you too, Max."

Max gave a tight smile and pressed a button on his headset. "Walking over now."

Freya's heels echoed on the tiles as they snaked through the hallways. "Have you ever been on this floor?" Will asked her. Rather than try to find a chapel that would hold not only guests but all the camera equipment, NGN had decided it made more sense to use a chapel that was already set up for that. Namely, the studio chapel on the thirty-first floor, which had seen television couples from soap operas, sitcoms, and even a few dramas tie the knot.

"Before you started, the station was doing some promo for a new show and they had me do an interview with one of the actors up here. I remember thinking it was more of a maze than NGN, and I see nothing has changed."

"Glad it's not just me."

Eventually, Max stopped in front of a door and pulled it open. "Through here, please."

Inside was another long hallway that led to a door at the other end. Only, unlike all the other hallways, this one was lined with cameras and co-workers. At the head of the parade was Annalisa, who greeted him with a smile. "Ready?" she asked, then nudged her head towards the camera behind her to indicate the answer should be directed there.

"I've never been more ready for anything."

"Actually, not quite. Aren't you forgetting something?" Freya patted the top of her head.

"Oh!" He reached into his back pocket and pulled out a sage green kippah. Naomi had given it to him right before they had said their good-byes yesterday. The small skullcap, traditionally worn by men during Jewish weddings, had been handmade for him and embroidered with their initials and the word beshert. "Thank you."

"Only doing my job," she said.

With a little assistance, he secured the kippah to his hair. As he walked down the hallway, he received some handshakes and messages of "good luck." Annalisa opened the second door and, with a deep breath, he stepped onto the stage. The chapel looked exactly the same as it had yesterday, except for the fact that every row was packed from aisle to aisle with people. He recognized some of them. His parents, of course, and a smattering of friends and family from back home. And Naomi's parents. But many of the faces were unfamiliar to him. There were Naomi's friends and relatives he hadn't met yet, yes, but also guests brought in by the studio—sponsors, WNO execs and board members, even sweepstakes winners that had scored an all-expenses-paid trip to Chicago to attend the wedding and get a picture with him and Naomi at the reception

As he walked to the spot marked with a small X in gaffer's tape beneath the lush floral chuppah, he thought about how it was more than a little odd to have people he didn't know sharing in this intimate moment of love between him and Naomi.

Then he remembered the thirty million people he didn't know who were also watching his wedding. He folded his hands in front of himself, squeezing them to try and distract himself from that thought.

Freya took her place beside him, seemingly unfazed by the audience, both visible and invisible. Finally, Riley joined them. Out of the corner of his eye, Will could see Riley repeatedly patting their hair like it was a sad puppy.

As the last few guests found their seats, a voice boomed from somewhere in the back. "Stand by, everyone. Chapel going live in five ... four ..."

Will inhaled a chest full of air and held it until the countdown reached one. As he exhaled, all the red lights on the cameras tucked into every corner of the room turned on. On a screen at the back of the room, the live feed of the Wilomi Wedding Special co-hosts faded away and was replaced with the image of the chapel. Of him, standing at the altar.

Even with the buzz of nerves, he felt surprisingly calm. The hardest part was over. He was here and he was ready. Naomi was waiting for him right outside those double doors at the end of the hallway.

The rest was only two little words.

He smiled at the guests, and their smiles bloomed like wildflowers across the pews.

Will turned his head towards Freya and Riley and said softly, "The last time I had this many people looking at me with such adoration, I played a donkey in my church's Christmas pageant."

"See, now I would have pegged you as more of a sheep," Freya said.

There was a rustle near the front of the chapel, and then Will heard his name. "Mr. Quinn!"

Will turned to see a man he didn't recognize in a navy suit standing in the aisle, waving his arms. "Mr. Quinn!" Will let out a chuckle as he tried to guess what the studio or perhaps his bride had up their sleeve. Was this man about to serenade Will with a song Naomi had written? Was this the beginning of a flash mob that would carry Naomi down the aisle? "Patrick from NBS."

The chuckle stopped abruptly.

Will glanced at Freya and then back to the door where Annalisa was standing, looking as confused as he was.

"NBS? Like the television station?" Riley said in a whisper loud enough to be heard over the hum from the guests probably asking the same thing.

"Yeah." Freya sounded annoyed but not concerned. "It appears he managed to sneak onto the guest list."

"Trying to get a little fifteen minutes of fame for his station?" Riley said. "I respect the hustle."

"This should be over in a second. Here comes security now."

Sure enough, two hefty security guards began a measured but quick march towards Patrick from their place at the back of the chapel. Patrick noticed them too and started making his way towards the front as he shouted. "What is your reaction to the allegations that Naomi is having an affair with her ex-husband?"

The murmurs stopped. His heart stopped. He had heard the words, but they didn't make sense. Naomi didn't have an ex-husband. Naomi would never cheat on him. Except ...

"What?" Will heard himself say. He didn't want to know more, but some part of him pressed on.

Patrick was nearly at the altar, with the security guards only steps behind. "The story broke seconds ago on NBS. Naomi was photographed in the arms of her ex-husband last night." He brandished a small tablet, raising it into the air, like he was Arthur pulling the sword from the stone, right before the two guards grabbed hold of him.

There it was again. Ex-husband. Why did he keep saying that? Will held up a hand. "Wait." The security guards paused but didn't release Patrick as Will continued. "Wait. What do you mean, Naomi's ... ex-husband?"

"Take a look for yourself." When the security guards wouldn't let him go, Patrick threw the tablet like a Frisbee. It landed on target, at Will's feet. He stared at it, his heart and mind holding his body captive. But he knew he had to find out.

He bent down, his body fighting him like a rusty machine, and picked it up.

The screen displayed a photo with a carousel of similar photos lined up beneath. In the picture, the sky was charcoal black, and the starbursts of light from the streetlamps nearly overpowered the image. But he could still make out Naomi's apartment in the background. More importantly, he could make out Naomi. He could see her unmistakable thick black curls and her DePaul sweatshirt. But not her face. Because it was pressed into a kiss with another man.

His stomach churned like an erupting volcano as he swiped from photo to photo, each one a more passionate kiss than the previous.

Suddenly, the tablet was ripped from his hand. "It's not me!" Naomi was in front of him, swiping through the photos with desperation. "I wasn't with Simon last night, I swear, Will!"

Will could barely find the breath to make himself speak. How could this be happening? "Simon? You know this man?"

She looked down at the ground, and he stared at her, begging her, willing her to say no. To say this was a mistake. Or a joke. But when she looked up, tears poured down her face in rivulets like rain on a window, and he knew it was none of those things. "He's ... he's my ex-husband."

A jolt of pain ripped through him, fury and heartbreak too intermingled to distinguish. "You were married before?"

"I'm sorry I didn't tell you sooner." Naomi was sobbing. "I'm so sorry. But I swear, I swear that's not me in the picture. I would never ..."

But she would. She *had.* She had lied. The rest didn't matter. Every second of their relationship was unraveling in front of him. Every kiss, every promise, every dream. It had all started with a lie.

Abby appeared beside Naomi and took the tablet. "This isn't Naomi." She said it as if she wanted to be certain but wasn't. It was obvious she wasn't because she was swiping and zooming and clearly looking for definitive proof that she couldn't find because it wasn't there.

Because Naomi had lied.

"Where did you get this?" Abby spat the words at Patrick.

"Those photos were sent to us last night from an anonymous source," Patrick said in a strong and professional journalistic voice as if this were some press conference and not Will's entire life being destroyed in a single moment. "There's more, too, if you keep going. We analyzed the photos and were able to confirm they aren't photoshopped, and the newspaper on the bench confirms the date."

Riley came into his field of vision. "It can't be her," they said, taking the tablet from Abby. "There's no way. Besides, you were with her, right? That was the plan, you were going to spend the evening practicing the bustle?"

Will looked at Abby, a flicker of hope that was quickly destroyed. "It was. We did ... except ... the alarm at my office went off again. I was there, talking to the police for over an hour."

Will had watched Naomi's live last night. Not a lot. He had done his best to avoid seeing too much more of her wedding dress. But enough to have seen her at her apartment with Abby and hear her excitement when she talked about getting married. He knew the way her eyes crinkled and her voice got almost sing-song when she was genuinely happy. That was the Naomi he had seen last night. Or had he? Did he know anything about her?

"Where ... where were you last night while Abby was gone, Naomi?" His throat constricted as he tried to fight back tears.

"In my apartment. I swear. It wasn't me. It wasn't me!"

Will knew he should be feeling something for her as he watched Naomi plead with him through her sobs. But when she reached for him, all he felt was bitter, icy pain and he recoiled from her as tears blurred his vision. "How? How can I believe you? You've been lying to me this whole time. How can I believe anything you've ever said to me?"

"No! Please! It wasn't me!"

She took another step towards him, and he backed away further away. The woman in front of him wasn't only a stranger. She was an assassin who had completed her mission. "I can't ... I can't do this."

"No!" He barely registered her cry as he ran down the aisle. "Please, Will! *Please*!"

He barreled towards the doors, shoving them open like he was Samson pushing the pillars of the temple down.

The corridors beyond twisted in every direction, a maze that seemed designed to trap him. Every hallway looked the same, every turn led to another indistinguishable stretch of tile floors. The polished surface of the floor reflected the overhead lights, making everything feel even more endless as he searched for an exit.

Stairs, elevator, a rope ladder out a window—he didn't care how he got out. He just needed *out*. Away from the lies. From the loss. From *her*.

He took a sharp right, then a left, nearly colliding with a catering cart as he searched for any familiar landmark. Another right, then a hallway that looked promising—until it led to nothing but a supply closet. He spun back around, heart hammering, retracing his steps only to realize he wasn't sure which way he had come from. Another turn. Another identical corridor.

He looked down the hallway on his left and caught a glimpse of two figures at the far end of the hallway, standing close, locked in something charged.

A fight?

Or a kiss ...

The flash of red and blonde hair registered.

Abby and Freya?

His curiosity was decimated by the realization that if it *was* them and they saw him, they'd try to stop him. Ask him questions. And he couldn't handle that.

So he turned the opposite direction before whoever they were stopped whatever they were doing and recognized him.

"Will, please, I'm begging you."

At the sound of Naomi's voice, he picked up his pace.

"Stop, please! Don't leave."

He spotted the silver frame of the elevator down another hallway and careened to the right. He pressed the elevator call button again and again.

"You don't understand. Let me explain."

As the elevator doors opened, he turned to look at her. "You think I don't understand? I understand perfectly. I understand that you're not who you thought I were. I understand that you played me like a fool." He stepped onto the elevator and hit the ground floor button. "I understand that we're done, Naomi."

The elevator doors, and his heart, closed.

Chapter Seventeen

Naomi

EOnline.com

Trending Now

Wilomi Wedding disaster! Bombshell details of affair and jilted groom revealed!

The Wilomi love story never really felt like reality television, but more like a window into the lives of two people living out their happily ever after.

That is until Monday afternoon, when the wedding ended with a scandalous accusation, a tear-soaked bride, and a runaway groom.

In a twist no one saw coming, the dreamy wedding of Naomi and Will took a nightmarish turn when a reporter from rival station NBS crashed the ceremony, brandishing photos that allegedly show the bride with another man the night before the wedding.

While the date and authenticity of the photos have been confirmed, one key fact has not been confirmed: although the woman in the photo bears a striking resemblance to Naomi, her face is never visible as her back is turned to the camera in all the pictures. The only person who has been identified is the man in the photo, who turned out to be Naomi's ex-husband, Simon Phillips.

Whether or not it is Naomi kissing Simon in the photos doesn't matter because not only did WNO and the fans not know about Naomi's previous marriage, Will himself was allegedly unaware of this hidden chapter in his bride's past. But upon finding out, the heartbroken groom bolted, leaving Naomi alone at the altar to chase after him, her pleas and tears captured by cameras as the stunned guests looked on.

TMZ reported earlier today that they have uncovered that Naomi had divorced her husband six years ago and had filed a restraining order against him a year later. The restraining order suggests a tumultuous history between Naomi and Simon, providing a possible explanation for the secrecy surrounding their marriage.

As the dust settles from the chaotic wedding day, questions linger about what truly transpired between Naomi and Simon. The scandalous twist not only shattered the dreams of the Wilomi love story but also opened a Pandora's box of unanswered questions. How did Naomi manage to keep this dark chapter hidden for so long? What led to the restraining order? And most importantly, does this spell the end for Wilomi?

On the latter, both Naomi and Will have maintained a stoic silence, refusing to comment on the allegations that overshadowed what was meant to be the happiest day of their lives. The absence of an official statement has only fueled speculation, intensifying the mystery surrounding the tumultuous events.

Continue Reading

Reddit.com/r/WilomiFans
LolaOKnows 1 day ago339 comments
Leaked Naomi Photos
Y'all. Got my hands on the Wilomi photos. LittleLink.com/193674b I dunno, what do you think? I mean it looks like her but at the same time you can't tell for sure, can you? There's no clear shot of her face so like ...

midsizedmanor
Yeah there's no clear shot because she's too busy putting her face into another man's face.

Lmnop164
It's literally the same sweatshirt she wore when she got engaged. Like this isn't rocket science. It's her.

Firefirefirefire1
I don't know if that's her or not but frankly I don't give a rat's ass. I always thought Will was the tag on the back of a shirt—useless and

cut off—and he proved me right at the wedding. He didn't give her two seconds to talk before he made it all about himself and ran off to lick his wounds. No wonder she needed to hide stuff from him. This girl is #TeamNaomi all the way.

Kellsbells48
Does it even matter if the photos are legit? Whether she cheated or not, she lied about her past. How can Will trust her ever again? How can WE? #TeamWill

Flipptyfl0p
Of course it's her. This is betrayal at its finest. Poor Will deserved better. #TeamWill

thisisanonme
Sorry but I don't buy it. Those photos are too blurry and it's all too convenient. I'm #TeamNaomi. I think there's more to the whole story.

Summertimegirls09
This is an Occam's razor situation. The simplest solution is the right one. We know that Naomi has curly hair, a DePaul sweatshirt, a secret ex she was hiding from us, and that she's a total see you next Tuesday. Ergo: it's her. All I can say is that Will dodged a bullet.

Kthanksbyeeee
I'm more interested in hearing from the main players regardless of whether those photos are legit or not. Their silence is deafening. Especially hers.

Wilomimademejoin
The only photo I care about is the one of Riley gasping when the reporter dropped the bomb. Would pay good money to have that on some merch.

View more comments

The Washington Post
Reality TV Breakup Sparks Fandom Frenzy: The Dark Side of Team Naomi and Team Will

In the wake of Will and Naomi's highly publicized breakup on national television, the digital realm has witnessed the unified Wilomi fandom split into two derisive factions known as "Team Naomi" and "Team Will." As these allegiances grew, so too did the intensity of the discourse surrounding the former couple. What started as passionate support has devolved into vitriolic personal attacks on the reality TV stars and even some cases of threats and doxxing that have required police intervention. This division among fans, while highlighting the fervor and dedication of viewers, has inadvertently cast a spotlight on the more sinister aspects of online interactions.

Dr. Katherine Reynolds, a noted cyberpsychologist, offers insight into the situation. "The phenomenon of dehumanizing celebrities online is not novel. However, the fact that it is becoming more prevalent is a concerning trend for our society. Fans often dismiss the need for basic human kindness towards celebrities, under the misguided belief that these individuals are impervious to the emotional ramifications of public scrutiny, which has been well documented to not be the case," Dr. Reynolds explains. "This dehumanization is then further exacerbated by the veil of anonymity online. Without having to face the victims of their verbal attacks, fans feel they have free rein to levy their most severe criticisms against public figures like Naomi and Will, without a second thought for the psychological impact such comments may wield."

As these dynamics evolve, it becomes increasingly clear that the narrative surrounding Will and Naomi's breakup is a microcosm of a larger issue that is not unique to them. A similar scenario unfolded with the British royal family members, Prince Harry and Meghan Markle. Following their decision to step back from royal duties and share their experiences with the public, the couple faced a maelstrom of backlash across social media platforms. Fans and detractors alike engaged in heated debates, often crossing the line into personal attacks. The situation highlighted how quickly public opinion could polarize and turn aggressive, especially when fueled by sensational media coverage.

You have reached your free reading limit. Subscribe now to continue reading!

Episode 259: Special Guest - NBS
He came, he saw, he slayed ... the romance, that is. But little did he know, he'd also slay the hearts of millions watching at home. Yes, you know who it is. You begged us and we delivered—in our latest episode of "Reality Hurts" the #1 reality TV gossip podcast, hosts Alex (Team Will) and Tina (Team Naomi) sit down with the hero of the hour, the mysterious

Patrick from NBS."

We've compiled all your questions and trust us, we don't give Patrick a chance to catch his breath. He tells us about the anonymous tip that led to the explosive you-can't-make-this-up wedding reveal, what it was like sneaking into the wedding (no, he doesn't tell us how, the bastard), and what it feels like knowing that #PatrickSlayingHearts is trending. Plus, so much more. You won't want to miss this.

Etsy.com

WorshipTheScreenCo *star seller* Sacramento California

42,045 sales

Featured Items

Riley's Iconic Gasp iPhone Case

Featuring the iconic expression that defined the Wilomi wedding disaster, this case not only protects your phone but will make your life infinitely better every time you look at it. We can't all be Riley but we can all take a little Riley with us.

Crying Naomi Unisex Jersey Tank

Naomi might have been left at the altar, but you won't be with this Crying Naomi shirt. This shirt gives you all the emotion of the Wilomi wedding but all the comfort of a 100% ring-spun cotton shirt.

Team Will 11oz Mug

ICYMI, this store is Team Will. Declare your allegiance with our "Team Will" mug. Whether you're a loyal supporter or simply appreciate some good drama, this mug is perfect for your morning or Irish coffee (we're not judging). Join the ranks of Team Will and let the world know where your loyalties lie with every sip.

Patrick Slaying Hearts Keychain

All hail the mysterious and mysteriously sexy Patrick from NBS. He took down Will and Naomi's love, but then took our breath away and left our hearts slayed. If you want to bring him with you wherever you go, then grab this Patrick Slaying Hearts keychain.

To: NaomiHoff2@gmail.com
Subject: Whore

You disgust me. How can you even stand to look at yourself in the mirror, knowing the damage and pain you have caused others? The world would breathe a sigh of relief if you were no longer a part of it. So do us all a favor and rid the world of your twisted existence. And if you can't maybe some else will do it for you.

Chapter Eighteen

Will

Will had traveled internationally often enough to have become accustomed to reading words that he couldn't understand. But he had never had that experience with words that were in English.

However, since his wedding day, he had found that his brain had become disinterested in concentrating on or comprehending words. Text messages, letters, articles, and, in this case, work e-mails were nothing more than a collection of jumbled lines in various shapes that he knew were supposed to have meaning but did not. Now, staring at an e-mail that he had been looking at for almost an hour, he knew he probably shouldn't even be back at work. Freya had told him to take at least a week off, with heavy emphasis on the *at least* part. And he had taken a week off. But that week had moved like molasses, not only infinitesimally slow, but thick and suffocating. Each second that passed felt like he was sinking deeper into the unyielding grip of a relentless abyss. To avoid the hounding press, the rabid Internet, the nosy public, and even his out-of-their-depth family, he had retreated to his bed. This left him with only his thoughts which, it turned out, were worse than all those things combined.

So, when his week was up, he skipped the 'at least' part and returned to work.

Because even though Freya gave him a disapproving side eye when he arrived that Monday morning, he knew she, of all people, would never try to stop him from working.

He suspected she was doing more than merely letting him sort of, barely, do his job. Not one executive producer had appeared at his desk the entire week, suggesting that she was protecting him too. He'd seen the dozens of missed calls from upstairs and listened to a handful of their voicemails, so he knew what they wanted. They wanted what everyone else wanted. They wanted him to talk. They wanted him to go through every moment of that day, no, of their entire relationship, with a fine-tooth comb and dissect it, looking for clues, for answers, for next steps. They wanted him to examine how he was feeling and explore what he was going to do next.

But he wasn't ready to do that for himself, much less for the public whose only stake in all this was likes, views, clicks, and plain old curiosity. The memories of that day weren't clear enough to dissect, though. They played in his head like a stop-motion video; soundless pictures that flashed before his mind's eye. The crowd. Riley and Freya smiling. Someone in the audience. The tablet at his feet. The pictures. Naomi running down the aisle. Her face as the elevator door closed.

It seemed, in exchange for understanding basic English words, his brain had been doing its best to keep him from having to relive that day. Seeing it in anything more than fits and spurts would have been as blinding as staring into the sun. He had to look away or be seared by the anger and betrayal. And the questions. So many questions. Why had she done this to him? Didn't they have something special that had been worth protecting? Why didn't she love him enough to tell him the truth? Why hadn't he been what she needed, what she *wanted*, enough for her to choose him over whatever had made her believe she couldn't? Had she ever really chosen him at all?

"You look like you could use a break."

Freya was standing in front of his desk. Despite not being able to focus on a single e-mail, he had no idea when she came into his office or how long she had been standing there. She was wearing red and gold Lululemon pants and a matching shirt, which told him he also had no idea what day it was because she only wore workout clothes to the office on the weekend, and he would have guessed it was Thursday.

He wasn't sure if Freya had meant her comment to be humorous, but he found himself smiling nonetheless. "Considering I haven't gotten any work done today or really this whole week, I'm not sure stopping would constitute a break."

"I didn't say what you should take a break from," Freya said, a knowing look on her face.

"Fair enough."

"Come grab some coffee with me." When he hesitated, she added. "Or a drink?"

"It's only eleven o'clock."

"On a Saturday. Of what might end up taking first place as being the worst month of your entire life. You still have a lot of life to get through, so it's possible you'll find a way to outdo this, but it's going to be a pretty strong contender to beat."

It felt strangely comforting to hear someone else say it out loud rather than only in the echo chamber of his own head. Maybe he needed more of that.

"I guess I could do with a cup of coffee."

"Great, I've got the perfect place in mind."

He pushed up from his seat and reached for his phone, where it was currently serving its main purpose as a paperweight. Since the wedding, his phone had been on silent, which had been his only line of defense against the constant stream of calls and texts and notifications from the studio, reporters, family, friends, and fans. Even Naomi. Though the latter had stopped coming in.

He carried it with him only to call Ubers, order delivery, and occasionally let his mother know he was still alive. His phone lit up as he picked it up, revealing stacks of notifications and reminding him of what was waiting for him outside his office. "I'm not sure we can go anywhere without getting chased down."

"That's why I reserved a conference room, and I've got Starbucks waiting for us back at my desk."

Will had always prided himself on being one step ahead what Freya needed. But it was moments like this that made him wonder if all this time she had only let him think he was.

"And before you ask," Freya reached into the pocket of her hoodie and produced a silver flask. "I'm also ready if you decide to take me up on that drink."

It was such a relief to laugh. A part of him had wondered if he knew how to anymore. Without another word, he followed Freya until they were settled into their makeshift café.

"Thank you for this. I didn't realize how much I needed it," Will said after his first sip. "The coffee, but also the ..." He gestured vaguely at their setup with his cup.

"I'm sorry I didn't suggest it sooner. I'm not very good at ..." Freya returned the vague gesture. "But that doesn't mean I'm not here to talk. Or listen. I'm sure you have lots of people to talk to, but I wanted to make sure you knew I was here too."

"I do, but I don't know what to say to any of them, that's the problem. I literally told my mom, 'no comment.' Which isn't a lie. I don't have a comment. A comment would suggest that I have something to say about all this, and I don't know how to form a single coherent thought around it yet. Which is absurd because it's been, well, considering it's Saturday and not Thursday, that means it's been two weeks." As the words started flowing, he looked down at his cup. "Are you sure you didn't sneak that something extra in here to get me to talk?"

Freya wasn't distracted by his attempts at misdirection. "Two weeks is rounding up."

"I guess, but—"

"It took you longer to grow a beard. Remember that?"

"I wish I could." Will chuckled. The beard had eventually grown in, but not before he earned the nickname Stubble Trouble from his coworkers.

"Stop me if this isn't helpful, but maybe you don't know what to say because you're trying to write the story before you've done the investigation."

"I'm not sure I totally follow."

"Everything that went down *at* your wedding?" Freya shifted in her chair. "You know, as a journalist, that's not really the lede, that's only the reason to ask, 'How did this happen?' Have you asked that yet?"

The question sliced through him like an icy gust of wind, so sharp it left him breathless.. He thought about the unanswered texts from Naomi asking him to give her a chance to explain. "I ... don't know if I want the answer to that."

"Because"

The words were already there, waiting for him to give them voice. "Because what if I find out that it's true and I only confirm that all of it, our whole relationship, was a lie."

Freya murmured in agreement as she sipped her drink. Or at least he thought she was agreeing with him, but then she smacked her lips and said, "But what if it wasn't?"

"How could it not be? You were there. You saw the pictures. You heard Naomi admit she had been married before. What am I supposed to ..." He put both hands over his face and shook his head rather than try to finish that sentence.

"Do I dare disturb the universe? In a minute there is time for decisions and revisions which a minute will reverse," Freya said. "T.S. Eliot described this moment, getting out of the inner turmoil and stepping into the courage to move forward, as disturbing the universe. Which is my point, Will."

At the sound of his name, Will pulled his hands away from his eyes. Freya was looking at him, her gaze as steady as her voice. "You have to take the risk. Disturb the universe and start asking questions. Yes, maybe it's all a lie. Maybe those photos are really her. And maybe Naomi played you from the beginning. But maybe not. Maybe she had a reason for keeping things from you, and there's more going on than you realize. I don't know which one it is, but as a journalist, it seems to me like there are too many loose ends and too many maybes. And there must be a part of you that feels the same way. Is the love you had worth giving up on before you get those answers? Is Naomi worth it?"

Will sat motionless, but internally, his mind was a battleground of emotions. From the instant he had met Naomi in line for a drink at Freya's reunion, everything had been effortless, like they had slipped into a kayak for two built exactly for them. The few bumps they had encountered had felt more like gentle waves rocking them forward. Now he had been thrown into treacherous rapids that he hadn't asked to navigate.

Was it worth it?

Something about that question reminded him of his conversation with Riley at the bar, the night they'd drafted The Plan. He'd always had the sense that Naomi wasn't ready to tell him something. But he'd never wanted to really know why. Even when he asked Riley for advice, he hadn't really asked what he could do, only if Riley knew what was going on.

Good is nice. And nice is passive.

That's what Riley had said to him.

Will had told himself he was confused by that answer. But if he was being totally honest with himself—and at this point, he already felt bad enough about himself, he didn't have much to lose—he had mostly been too focused on the pin prick to his ego to explore it further. It was the same feeling he'd gotten when Freya and Mimi had talked about the tap dance they had to do for the patriarchy. The insinuation that it was something he didn't know about rankled him, but not enough that he tried to understand.

Was Riley right? Was his niceness just passivity in disguise? Perhaps everything had been effortless with Naomi because he hadn't made an effort. Had they been riding in the same kayak all the time, or had Naomi been navigating the rapids alone this whole time?

The thought sat uncomfortably in his chest, heavy with a kind of guilt he wasn't sure what to do with. Maybe he *hadn't* asked enough questions. Maybe he *hadn't* tried to understand what was going on. Maybe he was doing that again, right now.

Even if that were true ...

The guilt was replaced with searing pain, cutting through his introspection like a blade. He could question himself all he wanted, but it didn't change the reality of the situation.

Did it? What had Riley said? *Good isn't safe.*

Apparently, he had been safe enough to lie to and cheat on, though.

He couldn't see how to hold both truths at the same time—that he might have failed her, and that she had still betrayed him. That he had never really tried to understand her, to see beyond the surface of their happiness, and that she had still kept secrets from him

The contradiction of it all sat heavy. How was he supposed to make sense of something that refused to be simple? Freya placed her hand on the conference table and slid it towards him, bringing him back from his mental battle. "Maybe now?" she said, a smirk pulling at her lips as she lifted her hand to reveal the flask.

He accepted with a smile. Unscrewing the metal cap, he poured a small amount of brown liquor into his cup, more for show than for enjoyment. "If this is how all your interviewees feel, I think we should include a flask in our standard equipment checklist." He took a sip from his coffee, which now had a slightly bitter aftertaste.

"I apologize if I overstepped," Freya said.

He shook his head. "I needed it. I needed a direction to go in, even if the direction was provided via a kick in the ass. Though I have to say," he set his cup down, "I never would have pegged you as the person in my life to be making the case for love."

This got a reaction from Freya that he had never seen: she blushed. It was faint, but the tinge of color that bloomed across her face was there. "Not so much a case for love. It's more that I had the chance to, um, I mean—" Freya didn't stammer. Was she stammering? "Sometimes when I'm struggling personally, I find it helpful to examine things from a journalistic perspective, so I wanted to, you know, share that."

Even in the thick fog of his turmoil-ridden thoughts, this stood out like a beacon on a lighthouse. The blushing and stumbling over her words, sure. But even this conversation. Freya wasn't the kind to offer advice, especially not relationship advice. His mind flashed to the image of the two people he'd seen at the end of the hallway as he raced through NGN trying to find the nearest exit. He hadn't thought about it since, too consumed by his own . But now, the image resurfaced, sharper this time.

He couldn't be sure the people he'd seen were Abby and Freya. Just like he couldn't be sure what he had seen between them was a kiss.

But suddenly, it didn't just seem possible.

It seemed *likely*.

And then the moment passed. The color in her cheeks was gone and the smile on her face was as sweet and noncommittal as it always was. Had he been reading into things too much? It was entirely possible, especially in his state of mind. She was a friend and colleague trying to offer support—nothing out of the ordinary here.

Freya's phone vibrated, and she pulled it from her back pocket. As her eyes scanned the screen, she pulled her bottom lip between her teeth.

"Something important?" he asked.

When she looked up, the blush was there again.

Will wished that he could call Riley. As much as Riley had become his friend, though, he knew their deepest loyalty was with Naomi. As it should be. But that only made the loss feel bigger, stretching beyond just her. It was all of them. The inside jokes, the chaotic group chats, the late-night debates over takeout orders—he had lost all of it in one brutal instant.

But Freya was blushing, and he really, really wished he could tell Riley that something was different.

Chapter Nineteen

Naomi

"I really think it could help!"

"Would you let me handle this?"

The muffled voices were coming from outside the door. Buried under a heavy comforter on her childhood bed, Naomi opened her eyes but didn't move.

"Why do you always get to be in charge of everything?" Riley said.

"Let's make a deal. When your best friend from Hebrew school locks herself away at her parents' house for two weeks and you have to drive up to Michigan to see her, I will let you be in charge."

"But I don't have a best friend from Hebrew school!"

"So?"

"So that makes your deal null and void because I can never meet the requirements!" There was a long silence, and Naomi imagined that Abigail was giving Riley the raised eyebrow of annoyance. Her suspicions were confirmed when Riley caved moments later. "What? Why the evil eye? All I'm saying is that I can be a productive member of this support group. My advice is as valid as yours."

"Let me guess, your advice involves copious amounts of sex."

"Maybe."

"With copious amounts of people."

"Possibly."

"All of whom are strangers."

"You make it sound so awful when you say it in that tone of voice," Riley whined. "Besides, correct me if I'm wrong—"

"You're wrong," Abby interjected.

"Okay, I'm revoking your right to correct me. As I was saying, I'm pretty sure the last time we were in this situation, my advice was that she get laid and that was exactly what she did, and it worked out splendidly. Granted," they said, sounding less enthusiastic than they had moments earlier, "by setting her up on a date with Will, we created this current situation. But that's really beside the point since the point was that we solved her original problem of being sad over Simon. Which, sure, I'll admit was only a temporary fix that may have slightly blown up in our faces, but it worked in the short term, didn't it?"

"For the love of—" There was the sound of flesh smacking flesh, and since Riley didn't cry out, Naomi assumed it was Abigail smacking her forehead in irritation. "This is exactly what I'm talking about. Can you please not mention Will or Simon when we go in there?"

Naomi lay staring at the ceiling, wondering if she should let them continue, but deciding against it. Heaving herself out of bed, she shuffled to the door.

"Would you like to come in?" she said as she opened it. Her pupils protested the sudden influx of light, and she raised a hand to cover her eyes.

Abby, positioned in front of the door to block Riley, turned around with an apologetic frown. "Sorry," she said. "They showed up at my place unexpectedly as I was leaving. I told them I was going to Michigan, but apparently, they didn't care."

Riley brushed their eyebrows with the tip of their finger. "You underestimate me, Abigail. I saw it on your calendar when I was going through your computer and cleared my schedule accordingly."

The smile that made its way to Naomi's lips reminded her that even though a part of her didn't want to talk to her friends, a part of her did. "Why don't we go into the den?" she said, reaching for a sweatshirt—not her DePaul sweatshirt; that one she had thrown in the garbage.

When she got the nod of confirmation, she made her way down the stairs and into the large but homey den. Abby had been to her parents' house more times than she could remember, and they had spent countless hours together in that room. The rich wooden paneling, plush carpeting, overstuffed sofas, and soft lighting made the perfect spot for building forts, watching movies, and sleeping off hangovers. She never could have imagined she would share the aftermath of her public humiliation and heartbreak in the den with Abby too.

As Abby took a seat beside her on the sofa and Riley found a spot on the adjacent sofa, the muscles around Naomi's heart constricted in protest. She had managed to avoid talking about the wedding since her parents had packed her into their car and driven her to their house from the studio. Now, all eyes were on her, and she knew what they wanted to talk about.

She looked at the group, searching for some other topic of conversation, and settled on Riley, who was wearing a remarkably unremarkable outfit of jeans and a plain gray T-shirt. Their brown hair was gel-free, and a pair of black glasses rested on their face. "Are those glasses new?"

Riley's hands swung towards the ceiling and then back down onto their lap with a loud slap. "Thank you! How is it possible that you are the first person to say anything to me today? I'm beginning to wonder why I even spend time with you people." *You people* was directed very pointedly at Abby.

Naomi could see an amused look in Abby's eye that undermined the ambivalent shrug she gave. Perhaps as a form of revenge for ambushing her this morning, Abby was having fun giving her friend a hard time. "I just figured you were getting old," she said.

Riley gasped like they had barely made it above the surface of the water in time. "How dare you! I'll have you know I'm making a statement."

"And what statement is that, exactly?"

"That they can take my life, but they can never take my freedom. The studio cut my hair, but instead of giving up, I have chosen to embrace my mediocrity. Today, I am average. But the greatest average that ever existed."

Abby's lip twitched so hard that Naomi was sure that she would crack. But instead, she managed a reply that was emotionless but still strained with amusement. "You truly rival some of the great philosophers."

The door to the den flung open, and in burst Becca. "I didn't realize they made homes this nice in Michigan!"

For a split second, Naomi wondered if Abby had invited her. But Abby's response answered that question. "Be—what ...? How did you even find—"

"Riley told me." Becca flung herself onto the sofa next to Riley, her cutoff shorts and midriff shirt barely able to conceal what they were meant to.

"Riley!"

"Don't blame me!" Riley exclaimed, any evidence of recent offenses completely obliterated.

"Why shouldn't I blame you?"

"Because you shouldn't."

"Don't be mad, Abby. These last few months have taught me a few things. Like how I need to spend time with people who have worse lives than me. It makes me ... happier." Becca paused to apply a generous coat of lip gloss. "I mean, forget Naomi—look at you, Abby. Are you wearing the same outfit you had on yesterday?"

Naomi didn't miss that Abby's face turned a shade of bright red as she brought a hand up to her cheek. If it had been the two of them, alone, Naomi would have let it go and then tried to extract the story from Abby in a roundabout manner. But between Becca and Riley, Abby was out of luck.

Riley's eyes widened. "What's this? That's not the face of someone who forgot to do their laundry. That's the face of someone who was doing very bad things at someone else's place and didn't have time to change afterward. And come to think of it, you haven't been around at all this week."

At first glance, Abby looked affronted but once again, Naomi could see something else lingering behind her eyes. "What are you talking about? I met you for lunch two days ago!"

"Met? More like I went through your calendar, figured out when you'd be at your office, and then forced you to go out with me."

"I need to come up with better passwords," Abby said under her breath.

"Not that I would call it a lunch anyway since you hardly touched your food."

"I told you I wasn't hungry!" Abby protested.

"Hold on now." Riley used their finger like a conductor's baton, first motioning for silence and then leading the orchestra into the finale. "Disappearing all week. Wearing the same clothes. Not eating lunch? Oh my God. I've seen this before. Abby's in love!" The finger baton pointed directly at Abby.

"I ... I am not!" But the way her skin flushed scarlet across her entire face suggested otherwise.

Naomi glanced quickly at Riley and Becca, trying to silently ask, *could it be?* "Oh yeah?" she asked, turning back to Abby. "Then where have you been?"

"I was ... in ... mourning," Abby said. "For you. Who can think about a thing like clothes and lunch after what Will and Simon did to you?"

It wasn't until Naomi heard their names and felt her stomach start roiling again that she knew she had been happily distracted for a few minutes.

"You said Will and Simon. You heard it, didn't you, Naomi?" Riley sounded a little too jolly for the situation. "Abby kept telling me not to say Will or Simon in front of you, and then she's the one who goes and says it. You all heard it, right? Will and Simon? Straight from Abby's lips?"

"Yes, we get it. Thank you, Riley." Abby's red face turned a shade of gray.

"It's okay, Abby." Naomi tried to reassure her even as her meager breakfast threatened to resurface.

"I want to make sure everyone heard it," Riley said, lips pouted like a petulant toddler. "Because Abby acts like I'm always the troublemaker. But around her, everyone is a troublemaker because it's impossible to keep up with all her rules. Even she can't!"

Becca nodded. "I heard it!"

"I didn't want to bring up ... them if you weren't ready to talk about it," Abby said, giving her a woeful smile.

"But since we have," Riley said, adjusting their glasses like they were bringing the conversation into focus. "I want to know what's been going on! While Abby's been in, er, mourning, I've been out of the loop. Well, except for Team Naomi gossip, of course."

Naomi's brows knitted together, unsure what he was referring to. "Team Naomi?" she repeated.

"Well, of course! You don't think I would follow anything Team Will, would you? I mean, okay, occasionally I check out their Facebook group to see what everyone is saying. But I would never join anything Team Will-related—I don't want to bump up their numbers, which, I have to admit, are always a bit higher than the TNs. And sure, I was Will's groomsman, so it's likely I would be a celebrity among the TWs, but that hasn't stopped me from being a TN all the way."

It hadn't even been an entire minute after Will left her at the altar before the hate had started pouring in. Any online avenue for communicating became an invitation for everyone and anyone to tell her exactly what they thought of her. For her sanity, she had shut down all her social media and decided to stay off the internet. Not that it had stopped the cruelty from leaking in other ways, whether it was seeing a magazine cover at the grocery store with a photo of her stumbling after Will in her wedding dress and the headline 'Fiddler on the Run! Will abandons Naomi at the altar,' or the death threat note that found its way into her parents' mailbox. So, she knew that people were talking about it but she hadn't known that, exactly like her relationship, the Wilomi fandom had fractured and people were taking sides.

"I didn't realize all that was going on," Naomi said, her voice tired and hesitant. "After everything ... happened, I started getting all these messages. Just vile stuff, and I didn't know what to do, so I shut down my social media."

"We don't have to talk about this," Abby said. "I didn't come here to make you talk. I wanted to make sure you were okay."

As another wave of nausea rolled through her, she squeezed her fists closed and dug her nails into the palms of her hands to try and give her mind something else to focus on. "It's okay. I've been trying not to think about it too much. But maybe it's time I start."

"Have you ... heard from him?" Abby tiptoed her way through the question.

Naomi shook her head, a lump starting to form in her throat. "I can't imagine he'd want to talk to me anyway. Not after what I did."

"You can't blame yourself."

She willed her voice to remain steady even as she could feel the tears gathering in her eyes. "Sure, I can. This entire thing is my fault."

Becca clicked her tongue. "You think you could have stopped some maniacal stalker from trying to frame you?"

"Maniacal stalker?" Abby shot Becca an annoyed glance. "Please, we all know who was responsible for this."

Riley crossed their arms, apparently not counting themselves among the "we" in that sentence. "Here we go again. We were arguing about this the whole way over. I don't see why it has to be Simon simply because he was in the pictures."

"Yes, it does!" Abby said. She turned to Naomi, her gaze holding Naomi as if she had put her hands on her arms. "You know it's him, don't you? You heard him at Rosh Hashanah. He said he would do whatever it takes to get you back."

"Whoa, hold on—" Riley said, putting up a hand. "Simon showed up at Rosh Hashanah? And you never told me?"

Becca gave a high-pitched cough. "Never told *us*!"

Naomi yanked her knees up to her chest, wishing she could hide from view. "Don't be mad at Abby. I made her promise not to tell anyone. I didn't want you guys to be upset."

"He dropped by unannounced to try and win Naomi back. Said he had changed," Abby told them, the incredulity ringing clearly on each word.

Riley's laugh matched Abby's tone. "Yeah, and the Pope is an atheist now."

"But you don't think he could have masterminded this whole thing, do you? I mean, what if he was framed too?" Naomi hugged herself tighter, trying to stave off the sickening chill creeping up her spine at the thought that Simon could have been behind this.

"It's possible," Abby admitted with a shrug. "But I think the real question you need to ask is who has the most to gain from breaking up your marriage? When you consider that *and* the fact that Simon was in the pictures, then the picture starts to get a little clearer."

Riley sat up excitedly and pulled off their glasses. "Oh, try that again. Only this time, take the glasses off halfway through."

"Not now, Riley." But whatever else Abby was going to say was interrupted by her phone announcing an incoming text. Several texts. "Sorry." She picked up her phone and glanced at the screen.

Naomi heard Abby breathe in sharply. At first, she thought something was wrong, but then she noticed a small smile peek out from the corners of Abby's lips. As Abby typed out a response, she was careful to keep her phone out of view.

From their place on the adjacent sofa, Riley must not have been close enough to catch Abby's microexpressions. "I see how it is," they said with a huff. "You can get your text on during this serious moment, but if I want to help you be a little more Perry Mason, I get yelled at."

Abby locked her phone and set it face down beside her. "Okay, sorry. As I was saying. I don't know if it was Simon. But we have to start somewhere, or we'll never get any answers, and he seems like a good place to start."

The prospect filled Naomi with a sadness so deep it felt like she had sunk to the bottom of the Atlantic and would be crushed under its heaviness. "What's the point in looking for answers?" she asked them, feeling the sorrow pressing down on her chest until it was difficult to breathe. "What's done is done. Will is never going to talk to me ever again, and I'm going to die alone and hated by the entire world."

"No." At first, Naomi thought it was Abby who had made the declaration. It took her brain a few moments to process that it was Becca who had said it. Becca sat straight, eyes locked onto Naomi. "No way, Naomi. You're not allowed to give up. You're one of the strongest, most amazing people I know, and I'm telling you that you're simply not allowed to give up. Not because of a man."

Out of the corner of her eye, Naomi could see Abby looking at Becca with an expression that mirrored her own disbelief.

"This may be the first time I've ever said this," Abby said. "But Becca's right. You have to keep fighting. You have to choose yourself so that in the end, no matter what, you know you did everything you could."

Naomi's vision blurred as tears began to well up. It sounded as incredible as it did impossible. As if they were telling her to escape the dark well she had been trapped in by simply growing wings and flying out. "How? How do I do that?"

Abby sighed thoughtfully and leaned back into the sofa. "You're one hundred percent sure there's no one who can verify your whereabouts?"

Naomi could only shake her head.

"Did you snap any photos that would show where you were?" Riley offered. "Preferably a selfie?"

"No."

"Not one selfie the entire night?" Becca asked, back to her regular self. "How is that even possible?"

"Did you make a call? I'm sure they could, like, triangulate your whereabouts or something, right?" Riley said.

Under the barrage of questions, the room started to close in on Naomi, and she gripped the edge of the sofa until her knuckles were white. They had arrived at the place she had tried so hard to keep them from. She wanted to run, frantically, from the room. She gave the impulse serious consideration but then inhaled deeply and forced herself to say the words she had dreaded saying aloud to anyone. "I went out." It felt like she was screaming at the top of her lungs as she said it, but the sound that came out of her mouth was barely audible.

She didn't miss the rest of the group share a glance before Abby said, "Okay, where were you?"

Naomi felt herself sinking deeper into the cushions, wishing she could disappear. "I can't ... tell you." She dropped her head into her knees and for the first time since she arrived at her parents' house, she burst into tears. This time, there was no interrogation— just silence and Abby's hand gently rubbing her back as she let the pain and grief of the last two weeks overtake her.

Only when the sobs began to subside did Abby finally say something. "You know you can tell us anything."

Naomi lifted her head. "I know. I've been so afraid to tell you. Abby, I made such a mess of everything."

"Yeah, join the club," Abby said, comfortingly.

"As long as you don't mind us making fun of you later," Riley said.

Naomi's laugh was mingled with her tears. "That's fine," she said. In fact, it was more than fine. It was the greatest thing they could do for her. The people in this room gave her a safe place to fail over and over again and met her only with tenderness and laughter. She let out a sigh, knowing it was time to trust-fall into their support again.

"So, tell us, sweetie," Abby said. "Maybe we can help."

The sobs overtook her like a tsunami as she tried to say the words. "It was ... Simon." Even through the refracted light of her tears, she could see the look of dismay on everyone's face. She waved a hand, almost trying to dispel the thoughts they were having. "No, no. Not like that. He called me a few days before the wedding."

Abby leaned forward. "Called you? About what?"

Naomi looked at Abby. "Do you remember," she said, fighting to get each word out, "a year after he and I got married, we bought that plot of land up here in Michigan?"

After a moment, Abby nodded. "Oh yeah! You were going to build a vacation home up there. I was still living off ramen noodles in that studio apartment and wondering where I had gone wrong in my life."

"Simon was going to build the house by himself. But, no one will be shocked to hear, he never did."

"What does that have to do with anything?"

"Well, technically, my parents bought it. I mean, we gave them the money, but they put it under their name. Some stupid tax thing Simon insisted on. So when we got divorced, it was the only thing he couldn't take from me. Not that he didn't try. But he didn't have a legal leg to stand on, and I had given him everything else without a fight. I couldn't give up that silly little plot. But then, right before the wedding ... Simon ... well, he called. And he said he saw me on the news. And he said ..." She paused, trying to steady herself. "He said he could see that Will and I were truly in love and that he would leave us alone."

That day, when she sat in the parking lot of her bachelorette party, he had said the words she had waited so long to hear.

Not that he was going to win her back.

But that he was going to let her go.

It was going to be the greatest wedding gift she could give to Will. A life free from Simon.

"Let me guess. There was a catch."

"He wanted me to sign over the land to him. It seemed so easy. I should have known better. But I agreed. It was such a small price to pay." What little steadiness she had begun to dissolve again.

"But why didn't you say anything?"

Naomi put her cheek on her knee and stared at the wall, her eyes relaxing until the busy, flowered wallpaper was only splotches of pink, maroon, and brown. "I think ... I think I knew it was a mistake. But the idea of having him out of my life forever was too great an opportunity to pass up. And I knew you'd try to talk me out of it."

"Did you end up signing the papers?"

She pressed her eyes shut and then opened them again so that the wallpaper came back into focus. "I got a call from his lawyer right after you left, and he said Simon wanted the papers signed right away. And that he would meet me at a café down the street. I should have known something was up but ... you were gone, Abby, and I ... I wanted it over. I was afraid what he would do if I said no. So, I left and met the lawyer. That's why," she forced herself to finish the sentence, "I couldn't say anything at the wedding."

"What do you mean?" Abby was trying to hide her frustration, but it was simmering under the surface of her words. "You had proof!"

"Come on, Abby, proving that I wasn't cheating by admitting I was lying and sneaking behind his back wouldn't have made things any better. Besides ..." She retreated into a throw pillow, pressing it to her face. "It wasn't real."

"What wasn't real?"

Naomi kept her eyes closed as she talked into the pillow. "Him, the lawyer. I checked. I knew you were going to want to use him as my alibi, so I went to look him up, and he doesn't exist. There is no Kevin Freemont of Wilson & Ellis. There isn't even a Wilson & Ellis. It was a lie. All of it." He'd dangled the one thing he knew she wanted most—the promise of freedom. He'd given her a tight deadline, just enough details to make it feel real, and counted on all of it to keep her too distracted to ask the right questions. And she had walked straight into his trap, never once stopping to second-guess it. "Well, on the upside," Becca interjected, "that means you still have your property, then, doesn't it? Do you think maybe Peter and I could—"

Abby gave a little cry and flew off the sofa. "The alarm!"

Naomi looked up, startled.

Riley put a hand on their chest like they were moments from having a heart attack. "Sweet Mother Mary, Abigail Meyer. Is that really necessary?"

"Oh, stop acting like you tied your corset too tight today and listen!" Abby chided before turning to Naomi. "The alarm! In my office! You said it yourself, Naomi, I wasn't there when you got the call from the lawyer. You think it's a coincidence that it went off the night you needed to be without an alibi?"

"Yeah, but didn't you say it was going off all month?" Riley asked.

"That's exactly it! It *was* going off all month, but since the wedding, it hasn't been triggered once. I'll bet you anything that was Simon testing out how long it would take me to get to my office and handle things with the police. And no ..." Abby lifted a hand. Naomi looked at Riley and saw they were starting to take off their glasses again. "I do not want your glasses as I say this."

"I'm only trying to help," Riley said.

Abby was too busy following the trail to notice Riley shoot her an exaggerated pout as they pushed their glasses up the bridge of their nose. She began pacing along the square outline on the carpet. "Think about it, Naomi. Simon decides he's going to ruin your marriage by making it look like you cheated on Will. But he needs to make sure that you are totally off the radar, so no one can vouch for you during the time those pictures were taken. So he concocts a surefire way to get you to sneak away in secret. He has you meet with someone with a fake name, so even if you do admit what you were doing, you can't track them down later to prove it. Then he just needed a time when you'd be completely alone and—" Abby covered her mouth. "Oh my God, the bustle!"

"I'm not following," Riley said.

"No? I gave him the final piece of the puzzle. I told him exactly when to do it. In my interview at the bridal salon. I said you and I would be spending the night before the wedding hanging out in your apartment while I practiced bustling your dress. All the issues with the alarm at my office started *the day after that episode aired.* He knows where my office is; he's even been there—remember? He came for the little office-warming party that Riley threw me when I first started my practice there. I remember because that's right before you were going to serve him papers for divorce, and I was so afraid I would let something slip."

"That's right!" Riley exclaimed, snapping their fingers. "We even talked about how grown-up you were with your very own alarm system."

"Right! So, he knew what to do. He knew when to do it. But what I can't figure out is how he got into my office. The door was always open, but there was no sign of forced entry."

Naomi didn't even have to think about it. "I can answer that. He copied the spare key off my key ring. I can't believe I never thought of it. He was always insisting on having a copy of all my keys—Abby, remember I had you change your locks after we broke up? I didn't think about your office key. It never occurred to me ..." As absurd as it all sounded at the offset, it now was making sense. A lot of sense. Why hadn't she seen it all sooner? She had spent so much time trying not to think about everything that happened that she had failed to pick up on the obvious connection between all the events that evening.

Riley began bouncing in their seat like a yo-yo. "Of course! So, he has the key. He can set off the alarm without doing any damage that might raise actual suspicion. Then he does a bunch of practice runs before the wedding so he knows how long it takes you to get there, handle everything, and come back. Then the night before the wedding, he sets the alarm off at the same time Naomi *happens* to get a call from this lawyer."

"And then," Becca chimed in, "all that was left was to take some pictures in front of your place with a Naomi lookalike and shoot them off to NBS!"

"Brilliant!" Riley shouted. Then, more solemnly added, "Incredibly twisted, but brilliant."

A surge of excitement and hope lifted Naomi, but the wave broke almost instantly, dragging her back under. "Yeah, but even if we could prove this, what good would it do anyway?"

"There has to be something," Riley said. "Couldn't you sue Simon for slander or something?"

"For what?" Naomi felt herself plummeting back down to the depths of the ocean again. "For going out with someone who looks like me from behind? Besides, I don't want revenge. All I want is to get Will back, and there's pretty much zero chance of that happening. Whether or not I was in those pictures, I still lied to him, and he hates me for it."

Abby returned to her seat beside Naomi. "You're right, Naomi. You should give up now."

They were out of options. There was no way to prove it, and it didn't matter if they did. So yes, giving up did seem like the right call. Except she got the sense that's not what Abby really meant. "You make it sound so awful when you say it like that."

"She has a way of doing that," Riley agreed. "I think it's her tone of voice."

"It's not my—" Abby stopped herself with an exhale, then said calmly, "I'm trying to point out that this helpless maiden thing is not for you."

"Me?" Naomi pointed at herself to give Abby the opportunity to correct the mistake. "I am not being a helpless maiden."

"I see," she hummed. "So, then you're not lying locked in your room, waiting for your knight in shining armor to come to you?"

The words were like a taser sending thousands of volts through her body and rendering her muscles useless. She fell back, draping herself over the armrest of the sofa. "Why do you think I wouldn't let you see me for the last week? I don't want to hear this!" she said, burying her face in her hands.

Since escaping to Michigan, she had been hiding not only from the cameras, not only from the haters, but from the voice of reason that would tell her the one thing she already knew she had to do: keep fighting.

She had spent her whole life trying to do the opposite, trying to maintain peace at all costs. But it had never worked—not with Simon and definitely not with Will. It's what Abby had been trying to tell her all along, since the very beginning, but she hadn't been ready to listen. It had taken her two weeks—or more like three decades and two failed marriages—but she was finally, truly, ready to not only hear the message but do something about it.

She lifted her head from her hands. "So let me guess, you think that if I want to have Will in my life again, I need to win him back instead of lying around in my room feeling sorry for myself."

A smile appeared on Abby's face that made it unnecessary for her to say any more.

"I hate your advice." Almost every fiber of her being was shrieking for her to stop and leave well enough alone, except for the one, tiny, thin fiber that was tugging at her to press on. And she clung to that one. "But let's suppose, hypothetically, that you were right. What now? I mean you said it yourself: Simon went out of his way to make sure I wouldn't have any way to prove where I was that night."

"Well," Riley said. "You didn't teleport there. Somebody must have seen you go to and from your apartment."

When she shook her head, Abby took a swing. "What about at the café? Didn't you have a server?"

"I never went inside. I tried calling the attorney when I got there, and the number was suddenly out of service. I waited outside the restaurant for a while but it was pretty obvious no one was coming."

"Did you take a cab or rideshare?" Riley tried again.

"No, I walked."

"Did you stop at an ATM?"

"No."

"A convenience store?"

"No."

"Any kind of store at all?"

"And seriously, not one selfie?" Becca said, the disbelief making the words come out in a squeak.

"No!" Naomi felt the small spark of hope Abby had inspired begin to flicker and fade. "I can't believe I managed to make myself completely invisible."

"So," Abby crossed her arms and her legs, as if reassembling herself would reassemble her thoughts. "Maybe we're going about this the wrong way. Maybe it's not about proving to him that it wasn't you in those photos. Maybe it's about speaking your truth. As the adage goes, our secrets make us sick. And in the end, it was the secrets that really caused the problems, right? Simon had all the power because he was being kept a secret and he could control the narrative."

"I guess so," Naomi said. Her heart skipped a beat like she was being led to the edge of a cliff and asked to believe that there was an invisible ledge below that would catch her.

"What if you take that power away from him by not hiding or being ashamed anymore? You have nothing to be ashamed of. There's no shame in marrying a man who turned out to be something else than what you thought. There's no shame in the fact that you tried to protect Will from danger. There's no shame that you met with that lawyer, hoping it would help your marriage get off on the right foot."

"You're saying, I should tell him ... everything."

"If he's going to give up on your relationship, then let him do it with all the facts. Let him face the truth of what you've been through and what you were trying to do. And no matter what he decides, you can be free of all those secrets once and for all."

"Free." The idea of not carrying around a boulder-sized backpack stuffed with fear and shame was so exhilarating she felt dizzy. At the same time, it seemed somehow outlandish. Could it be that simple? She answered her question out loud. "Well, what I've tried up until now hasn't worked too well for me, so I guess there's no harm in trying this."

Becca spoke up. "You know, when I told Peter about those other boys, I felt so much better."

Abby gave her sister a wearied glance. "Except for the part where you didn't tell him and he figured it out on his own."

"Whatever. I told him with my *actions*, Abigail." Becca folded her arms. "My point is that once it was out, that's when things started to get better."

Naomi was deciding between letting the advice she was getting sink in and laughing at the fact that Abby and Becca were actually almost agreeing with each other when another thought entered her mind. "How am I supposed to tell him anything when he isn't talking to me?"

"Oh, that's easy. Text him," Riley said.

"I have. But he hasn't responded to any of them."

"Yes," Riley said, pushing their glasses up the rim of their nose for effect. "But reading texts and responding to them employ two entirely different muscle groups."

"I don't think it's physically possible for a person to not read a text," Becca said.

"Exactly." Riley pointed a finger at Becca for emphasis.

"What if he's blocked me?" she said.

Abby made a *nuh uh* sound. "I'd bet my therapist's license that he hasn't. He's hurt—but he loves you. I don't think he's going to cut you out of his life completely."

Naomi fished her phone out of the pocket of her sweatshirt and stared at the screen. "I just ... text him." Her fingers trembled as she hesitated over the keyboard. She looked up, her voice wavering. "And you'll help me?"

Everyone nodded in unison.

Naomi took a deep breath and started typing.

NAOMI:

My love, I want to tell you everything because I've come to realize that we both deserve the truth. You deserve to hear it and I deserve to say it.

I can't find a way to prove to you I wasn't with Simon the night before our wedding. But I'm not so sure that's important anymore. Because if you understood who Simon was and what I've been through, you'd understand why I would never have been with him.

Simon ... was my world. He was my first love, that bigger than life love that you can only have when you're young. He was charming and sweet and handsome and when we got married our future together seemed so certain and so perfect. Turns out it was none of those things. And I blamed myself for not seeing it. I mean how can you miss the warning signs of an abuser? How can you NOT KNOW? But I didn't. Even when I kept ending up in the hospital I still didn't know. I thought it was something we could work through. Until I was finally able to hear what the people around me were telling me: that it wasn't going to get better and I might die while I was waiting.

I've lived with that shame ever since. The shame that I put myself in that situation and that I stayed there when nothing was stopping me from leaving. Every time Simon reappeared in my life after the divorce, every time he threatened or harassed me, every time the police and the courts told me that there was nothing they could do to stop him, a part of me felt like I deserved it. It was my punishment. A reminder of what I had done.

And then I met you, and I felt like you shouldn't be punished for my crimes. For you, life has always been simple, filled with potential and joy. And I wanted to keep it that way for you. I wanted to protect you. And it seemed like that was what you would have wanted. Remember the night you told me you told you thought it was bad enough for people to create problems, but unforgivable to make the people you love suffer too? You were talking about a reality TV show but I heard you loud and clear.

That's why I did what I thought was best for you. I kept the problems I created, I kept him and that part of my life, as far away as possible so you wouldn't have to suffer.

I should have told you because you deserved to know. But more importantly, I should have told you because I deserve to stop punishing myself and start being myself. My whole self.

The night before our wedding, I wasn't with Simon. Not exactly. I thought I was meeting with an attorney to give Simon something he wanted and in doing so would ensure he would stay out of our lives forever. I thought I'd make my final atonement and you and I would be safe, together. But that's not how it worked out. I'd learn afterwards that the attorney I was going to meet with wasn't real and that while I was away, those photos were being taken.

Simon told me he'd do whatever it takes to get me back. And I think that's exactly what he tried to do. If I could have been open from the start, his attempts would have failed. But he relied on the fact that I've always kept him secret and I played right into that. I have to live with that. But I won't live with it like I've lived with everything else.

I am done letting Simon make me feel like I am the one who committed the crime by loving him. I am done believing that his abuse can define me or my future. I am done hiding from him or anyone else. Today, perhaps for the first time as an adult, my life is my own.

I would love to start that new life with you by my side. But even if that's not something that can happen, I hope you can move forward knowing that I truly did, and always will, love you.

Chapter Twenty

Will

Will stepped outside his apartment building. He was greeted by a crisp spring day and instantly decided the hint of frost in the air was exactly what he needed. He abandoned his original plan of hailing a cab and, securing his messenger bag more tightly over his shoulder, he set off heading straight east.

The drive would have been twenty minutes, but walking gave him an hour to clear his mind and practice what he planned to say. He'd learned from the way Riley had scripted out their scenes for Freya and Abby that having a plan was best because even when they went off script, they still had a general direction they knew they needed to go in. And although Riley's plan hadn't worked out the way they had hoped, the execution of it had been flawless—which was exactly what he wanted.

His thoughts drifted for a moment as he followed that thread.

The Plan hadn't worked out ... right?

Something had been off with Freya these past few weeks. Something he couldn't quite put his finger on. For the first time since he had met her, it felt like a part of her brain was somewhere else. In the beginning, it seemed like she was almost enjoying a joke that he wasn't in on. But in this past week, that distant smile had turned hard, as if she were gritting her teeth to get through each moment. Then, yesterday, she announced she would be out of town today. Not that last-minute travel was unusual for her, but the shroud of silence was. Something was different. But could it be someone—or even *one* someone in particular?

Riley had been convinced that the wedding would be the final piece of the puzzle for Abby and Freya. But there had been no wedding, no chance for them to walk up the aisle together at the end of the ceremony or share a microphone for the toasts. It was another dream, although one much less significant, that had been lost that day.

But if that wasn't what was bothering her, then what?

He wished she would let him help her, the way she had helped him in more ways than he could count over the past few years. But especially in this last week.

He had hoped that helping her find love would let him repay her in some small way. Thinking about all she had done for him the past few days, he realized he should probably give her a heads up about what he was going to do. He pulled his phone from his pocket and called her, but it went straight to voicemail. Instead, he began writing.

> WILL: I can't believe you're out of town today. Don't think I haven't noticed that your calendar is mysteriously absent and you haven't talked about what you're doing. We're going to be discussing this further.

As he typed out his plan, his chest began to tighten into a knot as a slough of emotions intertwined. There was a chance he was about to make everything so much worse. But it was a chance he needed to take. Still, seeing it all laid out on his screen made it even more real, and he wished Freya would answer him and tell him if he was doing the right thing. But maybe it was for the best that she couldn't talk him out of it.

> WILL: Here's the part that might give you a little heartburn. I need to do it now. I've worked up the resolve to do this and I feel like if I wait any longer, I might lose it.

He knew, even as he finished the rest of that message, that he needed to get started. He wasn't at his destination yet, but he was close enough now that he could make it there by the time he finished.

He tapped out the final words ... *wish me luck.* And then pulled up his Facebook app and, without giving his mind another opportunity to send any doubts his way, he hit "Live."

Instantly, he saw himself on screen, along with a series of icons, and a large blue button that read "Go Live."

He'd picked Facebook for two reasons. First, it was one of the only big social platforms that instantly posted the re-play, meaning he had a better chance of ensuring it would be seen right away. Second, it was also one of the only big platforms that would let people share his Live *on* the platform as it was happening. He was counting on all the Wilomi fan groups to start sharing in and out of their communities, to give him the widest reach possible. He needed to do everything he could to make sure it got circulated enough so that everyone knew. But especially one person.

Before he hit "Go Live" he clicked Tag Person. The first name that popped up was the one he wanted.

With one more tap, the blue Go Live button turned into a red End Live button.

"Okay, here we go. I'm giving this a few seconds to go live." The view counter in the upper right-hand corner showed four people were already watching, so he knew that he had done something right. He had no idea who those four people were, but whether she saw it now or on the replay, he needed her to know that this was all for her. "And hopefully Naomi will see it."

He had banked on the fact that saying her name would be a catalyst for engagement—and the payout came quickly. Almost instantly, likes and shares started climbing. More viewers wouldn't be far behind.

"Umm." He opened his mouth, ready to begin his speech. But then he realized this was absolutely nothing like what he had done for Abby and Freya. This wasn't a performance to try to trick anyone into discovering their feelings. Even though it was public, this was only for Naomi, and he needed to speak from the heart. "So, I had this whole speech planned, but now that it's actually time, I'm realizing it's all wrong and sounds so stupid. So, I'm going to wing it."

He inhaled deeply. Being on television, sharing his life with strangers, letting them witness the sweet moments and perhaps one of the worst of his life had made him vulnerable. But this was about to be so much more. He wasn't merely going to put his life out there for the world to see, he was going to put himself out there. "I know everything is a mess. And I know I'm part of the reason for that. I'm not going to act like I didn't have every reason to be angry or hurt or confused. Finding out your fiancée has been married before and that she might have been cheating on you with her ex when you're seconds away from taking your vows is, well, calling it a nightmare is an understatement. But I get that abandoning you wasn't the right move either. No matter what was going to happen next, we should have done it together." He could see the comments starting to pour in, but he knew he couldn't stop to read them. "It took me a while, but I get why you didn't tell me about Simon. After everything happened, Freya sat me down one morning and told me I needed to wake up and see that I was throwing something important away without even trying to understand it or fight for it. I didn't see it that way at first. But when I read your text, I finally started to put it all together. It wasn't only that I wasn't fighting for us now, but I had never fought for us."

He had finally come to understand what Riley had been trying to tell him that day. Good is nice. And nice is passive. He hoped, somewhere, Riley was seeing this too and would know that they had made a difference, even if it had taken a little while for the seed they planted to take root. "I was comfortable being the good guy who loved you, but good isn't safe. And I never showed you that I was safe enough to weather this with you. In fact, when push came to shove, I proved that I wasn't. I ran away without listening to you, and without trying to find out what was happening with you or why you didn't feel like telling me was an option. I won't pretend to even begin to understand what you've been through."

Comments, hearts, and thumbs up were flying across his screen, and he could see the number of viewers reaching five digits. "I've never had to run from my past. I've never had to live in fear of the next knock or text or phone call. I've never had someone go to extreme lengths to manipulate and control me. I've never been let down by a system that was supposed to protect me. If I had, it would take a lot for me to trust someone enough to share it with them, and I think I would do anything I could to build a new life without those things, even if it meant keeping it hidden from someone I loved. Once that hit me, I knew if there was any hope for us, then it was time. I needed to step out of my complacency and it was going to begin by getting to the bottom of all of this no matter what that meant."

When he had first read Naomi's text, he struggled to make sense of it and to reconcile it with the hurt he had been holding onto. It had seemed like too much to untangle—not only his pain, but now hers too. It all swirled together in his mind, making it impossible to think straight. He didn't know what to believe or who to trust.

It had taken almost a week, but then it had hit him, in an almost comic book light bulb moment. It was as if his brain had been processing in the background, putting together the pieces from Riley and Freya and Naomi, and when it had completed the calculations, it delivered the results. He had been sitting at his desk, reviewing documents, when he saw it all, clear as day. He had stood up, immediately, and walked into Freya's office.

"I need to fix this," was all he had said.

Somehow, probably because she was Freya, she knew exactly what he meant. "Finally," she had replied. "Let's get to work."

"I work in journalism," Will continued, trying his best to talk into the camera and still watch where he was going as he walked. "Finding the truth is supposed to be my job. So that's what I set out to do. Though, it was Freya—who I should probably note has no idea I'm doing this—she was the one who cracked the case. We sat and scoured those photos for any hint or clue we might have missed. She's the one who noticed that in one picture, you can see someone looking out the window next to your apartment, holding a cat. I knew who it was right away. I'm guessing you do too. So, I got her phone number and called her."

He had never been happier to talk to Mrs. Pachenkis in his life. Until the moment she picked up the phone, the only thing he'd say to her was "Hello" and "Sorry." He had said both of those things to her on the phone before launching into a rambling explanation of why he was calling. He was, admittedly, a little scared of her. But he had been more scared of what she would do when he stopped talking. She might have hung up. Or worse, told him she didn't see anything. Blessed old Mrs. Pachenkis did neither of those things, though. Turns out, despite her generally curt demeanor she actually had a lot to say.

"She doesn't have a TV, much less the internet, so she wasn't aware of what had been happening with us, but she did have a lot to tell me about that night. She said she'd heard you leave. It was dark, and she did not approve; she wanted me to tell you, by the way. She watched out the window as you headed out down the street, then she saw a car park in front of your building and a woman get out. She said she had long hair like yours. A minute later, two men showed up. They walked to the grassy area across the street, and one of the men stayed back and took pictures as the other two walked together. She didn't like what they were up to, so she wrote down the license plate of the car. From there, everything fell into place. Freya was able to help me get the license plate information."

The top of his screen was a strobe light of notifications, flashing updates so quickly his phone finally folded and gave him a generalized "Multiple Notifications" alert. But not before he spied names like Perez Hilton, DeuxMoi, and TMZ.

"The car was owned by a woman, a server and aspiring model, who'd answered a Craigslist ad for a moonlit photoshoot. She'd been given a time, date, address, and a non-disclosure agreement. When she saw the pictures and people claiming it was you, she thought she couldn't say anything, or she'd get sued. Luckily, it only took us a little digging to find out that the NDA was with a non-existent law firm; in other words, completely null and void. I can now publicly say that she has confirmed she is the woman in those pictures and that the man she was with, the man who hired her, was ... Simon Phillips."

Saying his name, knowing what this man had put Naomi through for so many years, made his adrenaline pump so fast through his veins that it was hard to keep his hand steady. On the same day she had texted Will, Naomi had put out a public statement. Will had been avoiding the news and social media, but as he stepped out of his building and saw the newspaper on the front steps, he couldn't help but pick it up. Naomi's face stared back at him from the cover, and despite his initial reluctance, he found himself reading the headline and then the article. In both her text and her public statement, her message was clear: she wouldn't hide from Simon anymore.

Now, Will had the chance to make sure that Simon didn't have anywhere to hide either. Taking photos with a Naomi lookalike might not land him in jail, but at least everyone would know exactly what he had done, and it would follow him for the rest of his life.

"Once I knew that, I needed to figure out what to do with it. I could tell you, but I felt like you deserved something bigger. No one should have to live through what you went through. There's nothing I can do to fix that, but I thought maybe I could help even the scales a little. I can't exactly recreate our internationally-televised wedding, but I figured with our current popularity, I could put this out publicly. I can also put myself out there, publicly. Which seems to be working." He stopped to look at the view count and nearly gurgled. His plan had worked. Perhaps too well. "250,000 people watching. Jesus. Okay. Um. Right. So, I'm going to try not to think about that while I keep talking."

He was almost at his destination now. He needed focus on getting there and saying the rest of what he needed to say.

"I should never have walked away that day, Naomi. I should have trusted you. And I should have stayed by your side while we figured this out together. But I ... left you in front of everyone. I want to give you the chance to do the same thing to me. I want to pick things up where we left off. I want to put everything that happened behind us. I love you, Naomi, and I want to be with you. And I mean *with* you. Every step, not only when it's easy. I'm sorry it took this long for me to find my way here. And I understand if it's too late and you don't want that anymore."

He found the spot that he'd been looking for. He set the camera on the ground, propping it against a rock so that it looked out at Lake Michigan. He'd tried his best not to give away where he was walking, and now, he hoped the featureless image of water and stones would make his final stop a mystery to everyone except Naomi. He took a seat on the ground in front of the camera and rustled through his bag as he spoke.

"Here I am. I've brought a good book and I'm going to spend the afternoon right here. Whatever my fate, it will be broadcast for everyone to see, which only seems fair. If you don't come, I promise you won't hear from me again, but I really hope you do."

Chapter Twenty-One

Naomi

Naomi lifted her eyes from her screen. Becca, Riley, and Abby were staring back at her, collectively holding their breath. Even through the sandstorm of thoughts churning in her mind, she understood why. Whatever she did next—whatever choice she made about Will—wouldn't just shape her future. In some small way, it would shape theirs too.

As if sensing the weight of their expectations, Abby reached across the booth table where they were all seated together and put a hand on hers. "You don't have to do anything right away. You can think about this and decide what you want when you're ready."

What she wanted?

The question felt like trying to take a drink from a fire hose.

It had been two weeks since she had sent the text message to Will and followed up with a public statement that laid out her past and her reasons for keeping everything secret. While the Internet had plenty to say, Will hadn't said a word. He'd remained completely silent. She had taken his silence to mean that he was moving on and that she should too.

Until today, when her phone dinged that she had been tagged on a Facebook Live video. Will's video.

She had watched the whole thing. Every word. Every pause. Every unguarded emotion in his voice as he told the world—*told her*—that he believed her. That he loved her. That he wanted to be with her.

Now, as she stared at the screen, Will sat framed by Lake Michigan, pulling a book from his messenger bag, waiting. Emotions swirled inside Naomi like a merry-go-round of feelings. Pain, joy, fear, excitement, spun around until they were a blur, and she could barely make out what her heart was saying. But even through the dizzying rush, one feeling began to take shape, clear and certain. She couldn't imagine what her future was going to look like, but the idea of it having Will in it ...

She looked up at her friends and whispered the thought, as though speaking louder might scare it away, "I want to go to him."

Her friends, in contrast, didn't see any need to contain their thoughts and began screaming with abandon. People were probably staring, but she didn't care.

"Oh, thank God." Abby collapsed onto the table in relief. "I didn't know how long I was going to be able to act neutral."

Riding the wave of their collective energy, Naomi's voice grew stronger. "I'm going to go to him." Once the words were out, they felt like they had become solid and were pushing her out of her seat. The next thing she knew, she was dashing outside, her hand shooting up to flag down the first cab in sight. It only dawned on her that her friends were following her when they all clambered into the cab, a tangle of limbs and excitement.

She could hear them talking around her—at some point, a tube of lip gloss was shoved into her hand—but her thoughts were singularly focused on Will.

She'd spent the last two weeks trying to understand if getting back together with him could even really happen. It wasn't as simple as him saying he forgave her. If this was going to work, he had to be more than the man who had once loved her. He had to be the man who stood beside her, no matter how complicated or uncomfortable things got. The man who didn't shy away when things got messy and real. The man who wouldn't *run away*.

She had changed. And if they were going to move forward, he had to change too. And he had.

She left the lip gloss and everything else as she ran from the car, across the large green expanse, until she could see the large rocky stairs leading down to the lake. To a place she had instantly recognized when he'd arrived. The place where they had had their first kiss, where he had proposed to her.

Her friends' voices trailed behind her, a distant and breathless chorus, but Naomi's world had narrowed down to a single point ahead. When she got to the top of the steps, she paused to look down. The lakefront was empty, and she had to scan for a second before she spotted Will, tucked up against a rock with a book in hand.

Without hesitation, Naomi leapt over the jagged rocks that led down to the water's edge and ran towards Will. Her feet pounded against the ground as she closed the distance between them, her heart racing with anticipation. Will's head came up, his expression, momentarily unsure, giving way to disbelief and then elation.

A burst of laughter and tears erupted from Naomi as she reached him, her pace slowing to an unsteady stumble. Collapsing onto her knees, she pulled him into a kiss that was as intense and powerful as the vast expanse of water stretching out before them.

He wrapped his arms tightly around her, breaking away from the kiss long enough to say, "I'm so sorry. I love you," before he was showering her in kisses again.

For a moment, there was nothing else but them. In truth, it may have been longer than a moment. Disappearing into their kiss, time had lost all meaning. It was only the whistling and clapping from her cheer squad that brought her back to the present.

Will released the kiss, but not her. He looked up at where Abby, Riley, and Becca were standing off in the distance and, with an enormous grin, waved at them. "I see you brought company."

She cut her eyes to his phone, still propped up in their direction. "I think my three don't really compare."

Will laughed, the sound carrying all the same feelings whirling around inside of her. "I don't know about you, but I'm so ready to be done with the audience. I want to start over. With you. And only you."

He intertwined his fingers with hers and guided her hand to his lips, the tender gesture spreading warmth across every corner of her body. "Let's do that then," she said. She reached out with her other hand and, with immense pleasure, hit the *End Live* button. "It really is only me now. There's nothing left to hide."

Will's grip on her hand tightened as if he didn't want to let the moment slip away. "Good," he murmured, gazing at her intently. "Because I want you. All of you. If I could, I would rewrite our past, make better choices, and be the person you needed me to be. But all I can do is promise to be here for you now, completely and honestly."

"I wouldn't want to rewrite a single moment." Her voice was steady. "It took each of these moments, the good ones and the bad ones, to get us here." It felt strange to say. For so long, she had wished she could make her past disappear. But now, for the first time, she understood that her past, with all its imperfections and scars, was a part of what made her whole.

Will's arms enveloped her in a warm and secure embrace. His lips met hers once again, this time with a gentle intensity, and Naomi melted into his kiss, letting the familiar feel of his body against hers wash away the hurt and loneliness of the past weeks. As they parted, he looked into her eyes, a mixture of curiosity and hope crossing his expression. "Okay," he asked softly, "so what does starting over look like for us?"

She hadn't been prepared for the question. Or the thought that followed. Something so preposterous that she bit down on her tongue before it spilled out.

Will wasn't fooled for a second. "Nice try. What is it?"

She released her tongue, and a smile crept onto her lips. All of it was preposterous. From the minute they met at her high school reunion until this moment. What was the point in stopping now? "I was thinking ... if you really want to start over, then let's do that. Let's start over."

"From the beginning?" He extended a hand. "Hi, I'm Will—can I buy you a drink?"

"No," she laughed. "No, let's start over from where we left off. At the altar."

His answer was a kiss so deep, she thought her heart might stop beating altogether. "I will marry you this instant, Naomi," he said into her ear when he finally pulled back.

Now she was afraid her heart would fall out of her chest, it beat so hard. "Then let's do it," she declared. "Right now. I don't want to wait another second."

Will reached for his phone. "Nothing involving social media, don't worry," he said, with a chuckle. He tapped something into this phone, then looked up. "Seems like there's no reason we couldn't. It says here you only need a marriage license, an ordained minister, and two witnesses."

"I have our marriage license at home. And I'm confident we can get some volunteers for witnesses." She motioned towards her friends with her eyes. "What about the minister, though?"

"It says anyone can get ordained online in minutes. Which means between Riley, Becca, and Abby we have everyone we need."

"Are we really doing this then? Getting married?"

Will looked at her, his eyes so intense they looked like they might ignite. "Naomi, before the day is over, I want to be your husband."

His words left her with no choice but to kiss him again.

Their lips had barely touched again before they heard Riley shouting at them. "We've been really patient while you made out! I need to know what's happening!"

"For once, I'm with Riley on this one!" Abby shouted.

"Because of this beautiful moment, I'm choosing to ignore how you worded that," Riley said, loud enough for them to hear.

Naomi laughed and yelled back to them, "We're getting married!" Her volume was fueled not only by the need to reach her friends, but by the sheer excitement erupting from her. "Again! Right now!"

Her friends let out ecstatic screams, rushing over to envelop her in a group hug that was as warm and enthusiastic as their shouts.

"You're getting married like now, now?" Becca asked as the group hug came to an end.

"Now, now," Naomi said.

Will put his arm around Naomi. "We already have the marriage license. We need an ordained minister to marry us and two witnesses."

"I think the three of us can handle those things," Abby said.

Will nodded. "How do we do this then?"

This was happening so fast, but at the same time, it felt like things were moving so quickly because everything was falling into place.

Naomi stepped forward, drawing eyes to her. "Here's the plan." She began, pointing decisively. "Will, you go change into your suit. I'll go home and change into my wedding dress. Riley, you're in charge of alcohol. Becca, you get us some flowers. Abby, you figure out how to get ordained. We'll meet back at my apartment in an hour."

"You've put the right person in charge of the right job," Riley said dutifully.

"I'm less excited about flowers." Becca sighed. "I'd rather be in charge of finding strippers. Are you sure you don't want a quick bachelorette party first?"

"I'm sure." Naomi couldn't help but smile. She wasn't only sure about the strippers. She was sure about all of it.

Will must have caught it too, because he bent down and gave her a kiss, saying, "Me too."

"Well, if we've only got an hour, we need to get moving!" Abby said. "Come on, Naomi. We'll share a ride back."

She wasn't positive her feet were touching the ground as she walked to the road and got in a rideshare with Abby.

"I'm no-words-for-it thrilled for you right now," Abby was saying. "This is the happiest happy ending I could have wished for you."

"It's really happening, right?" Naomi said, turning to face Abby. "I'm not dreaming?"

"I can pinch you to make sure."

"I'm good!" A burst of laughter escaped her lips, bubbling up from within her, like an uncorked bottle of champagne as the joy spilled out. "I don't know what to do with myself! Should we be telling other people? My parents couldn't make it from Michigan in time, but we could do a video call. And his parents. Oh, and what about Freya?"

Even as Abby nodded enthusiastically, Naomi didn't miss the quiet sigh that accompanied it. Not the usual dismissive and annoyed sigh she gave whenever Freya was involved. This was something else entirely. It was a sigh Naomi had been hearing from Abby a lot lately this past week. Abby had claimed it was a reaction to everything that had happened to Naomi. But Naomi had suspected there was more to it, and that sigh only served to confirm her suspicions.

She gave her friend a stern but gentle frown. "I know you're covering something up to protect me. But in an hour, you won't be able to use my situation as an excuse, and you're going to have a Confession Cam Interview, with me as the cam."

Abby met her gaze, a momentary flicker of vulnerability flashing before she masked it with a small smile. "It's nothing. I promise. All this has got me thinking, that's all. Life's funny, isn't it?" she said with a lightness that didn't quite reach her eyes. "You encounter these odd coincidences that take your life in totally unexpected directions. I mean, look at you and Will and how this all worked out. Sometimes you have to trust that even when things don't go the way you think they will, maybe a different kind of happiness is waiting for you around the corner."

As Naomi tried to decipher Abby's uncharacteristically enigmatic reply, she couldn't help but wonder if it had something to do with whoever Abby had been texting at her parents' house that day. Had Riley been right? Had she been in love with someone? And were her sighs now the sign of a broken heart?

Abby had never been one to keep her relationships secret, at least not from Naomi. Unless ...

Her mind took her back to the restaurant, to the pocket dial, to Freya. There was only one person Naomi could imagine Abby would try to keep a secret. One person she had espoused so much hate for that she might not want to admit she really loved. Could all this really be about Freya? Had they gotten together and then broken up?

She considered saying something again, really trying to get to the bottom of it. Maybe without Becca and Riley there, Abby would feel like she could talk about what was going on without the extra banter and teasing.

Naomi looked out the window. They were only minutes away from their apartment, not enough time to coax Abby into opening up. She could wait a few hours to grill her best friend. Lovingly, of course.

"You know," Abby said, obviously ready to change the subject. "My mom loves to remind me that she has the chuppah from her wedding in her basement, as if the offer of using the chuppah from her failed marriage is going to hurry me along on my search for true love. But I know she'd be equally as happy to lend it to you. If you're okay with it, I could see if she could come by with it. With the understanding that she would stay for the wedding, and the news will spread shortly afterwards."

"I'd love that." Abby's Mom had served as her second mom on many occasions. This seemed the best occasion of all.

"She's going to think this makes her the center of attention, just so you're aware," Abby said as the cab pulled up in front of their place.

A cold gust nipped at them as they stepped out of the car, and they hurried inside the lobby. "I was thinking maybe we'd try to do this in a park somewhere." Naomi shivered as she stepped into the elevator. "But inside will have to do. My place looks like a bomb went off in my living room. What about yours?"

Abby looked up at the ceiling, trying to remember. "Nothing a garbage bag and a laundry basket can't solve in a few minutes." She looked back at Naomi. "How does a wedding in my apartment sound?"

"Perfect," Naomi said. And it was.

The elevator doors opened, and Abby strode towards her apartment with purpose. Naomi followed.

"Give me a few minutes to figure out this ordained minister thing," Abby said after she reached up to touch her mezuzah. "But come over whenever you're ready."

Naomi felt something tap her shoulder and instinctively turned around.

Her mouth opened when she saw Simon's hard face staring back at her.

But her throat closed when she saw what he was holding.

A gun.

She prayed, pleading that Abby had made it inside. That somehow she hadn't noticed Simon, and he hadn't noticed her. But, then she heard Abby's voice behind her.

"What is it?" Her words dissolved into an incomprehensible gargle.

Simon flicked the gun, indicating he wanted them to walk into Abby's apartment. His eyes crackled with a terrifying intensity, a dangerous spark that Naomi knew too well. His silent fury was only the eye of the storm, a controlled rage that promised to unleash destruction. In those moments, she could only bend to his will, like a tree bending in the tornado, enduring the chaos while rooted in the resolve to survive.

And so she did what she knew how to do. She lowered her eyes and let him usher them both into Abby's apartment, moving mechanically while her mind raced for answers. She had embraced the possibility of being the person her friends saw in her—strong, deserving, capable of happiness. She had even allowed herself to dream of a fairytale ending, a life filled with love and joy. But now, as the door slammed shut behind her, sealing off her escape, she knew those dreams had been illusions.

As she turned to face Simon, she felt as if the vines of shame and sadness that she had worked so hard to throw off had grown back, entwining themselves around her, their thorns digging deep into her heart.

"Simon ... no ..." she said, her voice choked with pain.

"Shut. Up," Simon spat out, inching towards her.

Reflexively, Naomi tried to make herself even smaller. She needed to keep him calm, at least long enough to get Abby out. After that, whatever happened was of her own making. "Simon, please," she said softly. "Just let Abby leave."

Naomi hoped, for a fleeting moment, that Abby might, this one time, relent to the situation and let Simon have this moment of control.

But she was Abby. Of course she wouldn't. "Naomi, I'm not leaving you," Abby said defiantly, stepping next to her. Naomi's eyes implored Abby to stay quiet, but it was too late.

Naomi barely registered Simon's arm swinging until Abby's cry of pain echoed through the room.

"Abby!" Naomi screamed as Abby plummeted to the floor. Naomi dropped down beside her, shielding her friend with her body as she tentatively inspected the gash across Abby's forehead. The wound was deep, with rivulets of blood already flowing across her cheek. Abby looked up at her, eyes clouded and dazed from the blow.

"Get up," Simon growled behind her.

Naomi flinched at the sound of his voice. But she didn't move. Amidst the cacophony of fearful and panic-ridden thoughts echoing in her mind, a different voice emerged, clear and resolute—her own voice, echoing the words she had once written to Will.

I am done letting Simon make me feel like I am the one who committed the crime by loving him. I am done believing that his abuse can define me or my future. I am done hiding from him or anyone else. Today, perhaps for the first time as an adult, my life is my own.

She had always acquiesced to Simon's will, hoping that someday her love and obedience would be enough for him. But it never had. Her compliance had only fed the monster in him, emboldening him to go further. To go this far.

Now, as she crouched down, guarding Abby, Naomi felt a seismic shift within herself. She would no longer be the one to bend. This time, she would be the one to stand tall, to confront the storm Simon represented, not as a victim, but as a woman reclaiming her life, her dignity, and her future.

And if she couldn't stop him, she would die being her true self.

She inhaled deeply, summoning a newfound strength within herself. Then, with an exhale, she stood. Simon watched her, his expression as dark and threatening as the metal of the gun he wielded. She fixed her gaze on him, unflinching, and stepped forward until the gun pressed against her chest. Simon's face became a roulette wheel of emotions.

"Simon," she spoke with an authoritative clarity that seemed to cut through the tension in the room, "Put the gun down. It's over."

He inhaled sharply, a strangled sound of desperation and anger. "It's not over," he said as tears welled in his eyes, betraying the turmoil beneath. "Not after everything I did for you."

"You think what you did back there was for me?"

"I told you! I would do anything to get you back. It was working. I was going to get you back until *he*," he used his gun to indicate the door, as if to suggest Will's presence somewhere out there. "Ruined everything. If he could have left everything alone, it would have worked, and we would have been ... we could have been—"

"No," she assured him. "We couldn't have been. It's over."

"It's not over. You are mine, Naomi." His voice was strained. "You have always been mine."

"It's been over for a long time," Naomi spoke softly, becoming calmer as he began to unravel. "And nothing you can do will ever change that. I did love you. Nothing will ever change that either. You were my first kiss. You were my first love. I built a life with you. But that's over."

In response, Simon's thumb slipped onto the hammer of the gun. "It isn't over!"

She could feel the fear rising, but her resolve was stronger. "I think you know we can never go back."

"Stop saying that!"

Placing her hand gently on the barrel of the gun, she looked straight into Simon's eyes. "I know that you love me too. Which is why I know you won't hurt me."

Simon's body seemed to quiver, the gun shaking in his unsteady grasp. She could see the conflict in him, and she hoped it could at least buy her some time to get Abby out.

"It's okay, Simon," she whispered. "It's over now."

There was silence for what felt like hours. And then, she watched, heart pounding, as Simon's arm gradually lowered. Even as relief washed over her, she knew this moment was fragile and she needed to act fast but move slowly. If she could convince him to hand over the gun then, maybe ...

The door handle jiggled. "I can hear voices in there, Abigail Meyer," came Riley's voice, muffled but unmistakable, from the other side of the door. "I've come bearing alcohol and I won't be left out!"

Simon began to move away from the door, but before he could, it swung open, catching him square in the back of the head. His head slammed forward, taking the rest of his body with him. As he stumbled to the ground, his grasp on the gun loosened, and it slipped from his hand, sliding underneath Abby's couch.

"What the hell have you got in front of the door?" Riley asked.

Simon was still on the floor, but the momentary daze from the door hitting him was already wearing off. Whether he was still going to let them go or not, it didn't matter. He needed to be stopped until the police could come. Because this time she wasn't going to let him get away. She knew they only had seconds before their chance to subdue him would pass.

"Riley!" she heard Abby yell.

Fighting through the terror that had held her back so many times before, Naomi dove towards the couch. As she stretched her arm as far as it would go, her fingers scrambling blindly through the dust and shadows beneath the couch, she glanced beside her to see Simon inching woozily towards her, eyes blazing.

"Calm down," Riley said, their voice no longer muffled through the door. "I've brought wine. Hey, excuse me!"

She had never touched a gun before, but she knew the instant her fingers made contact with it. She gripped it tightly as she pulled it out and pointed it directly at Simon.

"Never again." The words emerged, like molten lava, drawn from somewhere deep within herself. And for the first time, Simon was the one who looked afraid.

The look didn't last long, though. Abby, clutching a wine bottle, appeared behind Simon. With both hands holding the neck like a bat, she swung it at him. The bottle connected with his head, and he dropped like the dead weight he was.

Once it was clear he wasn't getting back up, Naomi took her eyes off Simon and looked at Abby. For a few seconds, they could only stare at each other, connected in their stunned relief. Then, the door, which was only open a few inches, cracked open a little further, then came to halt against Simon's sprawled body.

"Do we need to talk about this key thing," Riley said, spryly shimmying through the available space. "Because—oh my God! Is that—are you—what the hell happened?"

As Naomi pulled herself to standing, Abby turned toward Riley.

"Abby, you're bleeding." Riley stepped forward and reached for Abby, concern etched across their face.

"I'm fine." Abby dismissed Riley with a wave, but her voice sounded thin and shaky.

Becca appeared in the doorway, the bright bouquet of flowers she carried a stark, almost comical, contrast to the scene. "I think flowers are more expensive than a stripper. I really feel like it would have been better—" Then, like Riley, she noticed the scene around her. "What's going on here? Why is there a man on your floor?"

Riley pointed at Simon. "That's Simon." Then to the gun in Naomi's hand. "And that's a gun."

Naomi had forgotten she was still holding it. The realization made her stomach churn, an instinctive revulsion urging her to drop it. But instead, she gripped it tighter.

Riley's finger, continuing its tour, now pointed at Abby. "And that is your sister who says she's fine but there's literal blood running down her face." The finger swung down. "And that's my bottle of wine, which was used to subdue him."

Becca strode towards Abby and lifted a hand as if to inspect her sister's injury, but Abby shook her head. "I'm fine," she said again. But no sooner had the words come out of her mouth than she collapsed to the floor.

Chapter Twenty-Two

Will

Will opened the door to the cab with more enthusiasm than a kid on Christmas morning.

"Where are you headed?"

"To get married!" Will exclaimed, grinning uncontrollably as he closed the door to the cab.

The cab driver lifted disinterested eyes to the rearview mirror. "Address?"

Will gave him Naomi's address and then asked, "Any experience tying a bow tie?" He tugged at the misshapen blob of fabric around his neck. After twenty minutes of swearing into a mirror and watching half a dozen YouTube videos, he'd called it quits and went outside to hail a cab.

If the driver heard him, he didn't seem to feel the need to respond.

It didn't matter. If the cab driver couldn't help him, he was positive that Riley could. Actually, he realized, Riley would probably have insisted on redoing his bow tie even if he had managed it on his own. As the cab pulled out into traffic, Will leaned back into the seat and closed his eyes, barely aware of the springs in the seat poking him in the back as he savored the moment. He couldn't wait to see his bride, but at the same time, he wanted to linger here a little longer, to take everything in. They had done it. Against all the odds, they'd found their way back to each other. It was perfect.

His eyes opened.

Almost perfect.

It was only missing one thing. Freya wasn't here.

He pulled out his phone. His screen was clogged with messages, calls, notifications and e-mails, but as he skimmed through them he could see that none of them were from Freya.

He dismissed the notifications and pulled up his messages to her, a cascade of one-sided bubbles filling the text chain. He added one more.

> WILL: OMG did you see it? She came! We're going to get married RIGHT NOW before anything else can stop us. This is killing me, where are you?

It had only been a few hours since he'd first texted her his plan. But he had no idea where she was, and since it was Freya, that meant she could be practically anywhere on the planet doing virtually anything. It was as likely that her silence was due to the fact that she didn't have cell reception because she was on a plane over the Atlantic as it was that she had her phone confiscated because she was in a top-secret government bunker. Under any other circumstances, he would have started poking around at the studio, asking his colleagues if anyone knew anything regarding her whereabouts. But he knew he wasn't going to get answers out of anyone at NGN until they got answers out of him. And he wasn't ready to talk to them yet. Not until he had said, "I do."

Sleuthing would have to wait.

As the cab pulled up in front of the apartment building, Will scanned the third floor, hoping to catch a glimpse of movement in Abby or Naomi's apartment. The lights were off in both apartments, which wasn't particularly surprising given it was still the afternoon and the midday sun brought more than enough light into the west-facing windows. Also not particularly surprising was the fact that he could make out the shadow of Mrs. Pachenkis against the light in her living room window. He waved with an enthusiasm that he hoped would translate some of his gratitude to her. On his cab ride to his apartment, he had called her to let her know about what they had learned, thanks to the crucial information she provided. He'd been prepared for her, at best, to be disinterested and, at worst, to use his call as an opportunity to reprimand him for some past offense. Instead, after he had finished talking, there was a brief silence, and then she said, "Good. She deserves to be safe and happy."

It might have been his imagination, but he sensed a faint trace of sorrow laced in the words that hinted at an untold past. Perhaps, he wondered, she had never been afforded either of those things.

Walking through the familiar lobby, he stepped into the elevator and watched as the heavy doors slid shut behind him. The tarnished and dented bronze surface offered him a final, albeit distorted reflection of his last few minutes as a bachelor. He couldn't help but grin at his slightly disheveled reflection. He ran a hand through his hair, smoothing out any stray strands, and then, with a warbly ding, the door opened and he stepped out, ready to begin his new life.

"—my God, we need an ambulance!" Naomi's shriek cut through his elation like a lance. From the elevator, he could see that Abby's door was ajar, and he immediately began to sprint towards it.

"Becca, stay with Abby and call 911," he heard Riley say forcefully. "I'm going to get something to keep him restrained on the off chance he wakes up. Naomi, keep that gun pointed at Simon."

Gun? Simon?

The shock nearly stopped Will in his tracks, but his concern drove him forward, heart racing, toward the door, unsure of what awaited him on the other side.

As he reached for the handle and tried to push the door open, it resisted him, as if there was something blocking the way. He found a way to squeeze himself through the narrow crack and into the chaos that awaited him on the other side.

Naomi stood rigid, holding a gun pointed at Simon, who was unconscious on the floor. A few weeks ago, Will wouldn't have been able to pick Simon out of a crowd. But now, his face was seared into his memory like a brand.

Naomi looked up at him, and although her eyes were brimming with tears, they were also resolute. "Stay there," she told him.

"Are you—" he began to ask, his eyes scanning her for signs of injury.

"It's over," she stated, her declaration as firm as a wall of bricks, each syllable mortared in place. Will's mind raced to put the pieces together. Naomi didn't own a gun. Did that mean Simon had shown up with one? Had she managed to fight him off?

No sooner had he started to make some sense of what he was looking at and feel a modicum of relief that whatever had occurred, Naomi appeared okay, than he noticed Abby. She was on the floor on the other side of the room, pale, unconscious, and limp in Becca's arms, as Becca frantically dialed 911.

The next hour was a frenetic blur of activity: a flurry of different colored uniforms, beeps and blips of radio communications, and the TV drama sound of handcuffs locking. As the paramedics raised the gurney and began to wheel Abby out into hallway, Naomi remained glued to her friend's side.

"We're going to need to take your statements," an officer stepped forward, their voice barely audible over the bedlam around them.

Naomi didn't slow her steps as she told them, "I'll answer any questions you have at the hospital." She looked over her shoulder. "I'll call a ride for all of us. Will, can you grab my purse before you come down? I put it on the table by the window."

He nodded and then stepped aside to allow the line of paramedics, police, and friends to make their way to the elevator. "I'll meet you down there," he said as everyone crammed in.

As the elevator doors closed, the sudden silence felt expansive, as if the departure of the crowd had somehow freed up the air in the room. He took a slow, deliberate breath, feeling as if it were his first since stepping off the elevator. He wanted to use this brief moment of quiet to gather his scattered thoughts, to try and process the events that unfolded, but instead, he felt only a numbness creeping through his body that made it impossible to do anything except focus on the task ahead.

He walked into Abby's apartment, trying not to make room in his mind for everything that had happened in the living room in the past few hours, and headed straight to the table where Naomi's purse had been tossed at some point. Outside, the sky had begun to darken, but he could still clearly see the line of emergency vehicles on the street. The whirl of ambulance and police lights cast a frenzied splatter of colors across the sidewalk, their flashes looking like some kind of macabre dance of paparazzi cameras at a scene far removed from any red carpet. Then another flash caught his eye, and he realized it *was* the paparazzi. It was only one person, but the large, high-end camera was unmistakable.

Damn, they had gotten wind of this fast. He wasn't sure who *they* were but then, he supposed it didn't matter. If there was one, more would follow. The news would surely break soon, and there would be no stopping it.

Will took out his phone and tapped Freya's name in his contacts. It went to voicemail, again.

Quickly, he pulled up his texts and typed out a message.

> WILL: Something's happened. I was really hoping you'd pick up. I want you to hear this first before it gets picked up. Naomi and Abby went back to their building to get some stuff. Naomi's ex-husband was there waiting for them. With a gun. They subdued him. But not before he hit Abby with the gun. She's unconscious and the EMTs are rushing her to Northwestern right now. We're following behind.

He put his phone back in his pocket and reached for Naomi's purse. But as he did, something else caught his eye. Next to her purse was a small cardboard box haphazardly filled with a random assortment of items. Glancing in, he could make out sunglasses, a set of keys, a pair of gold and red Lululemon leggings and a matching T-shirt, and a small book titled *Come Love with Me and Be My Life (Peter McWilliams Poetry Series #1)*. None of them on their own would have stood out, but together they told an almost unmistakable story.

He looked up and saw the paramedics loading the gurney onto the ambulance. He wasn't going to have enough time to explore his hunch so instead, he hurried out the door, typing one last message as he did.

WILL: I know it's probably not my place and maybe I have no idea what I'm talking about. But come home.

Chapter Twenty-Three

Naomi

ABBY: Even with a crack in my skull, I still somehow know that you are sitting in the hospital waiting room in the middle of the night worrying instead of going home like you were supposed to.

NAOMI: Your mom told us all to go home and get some sleep. But how can I when you're in the hospital with a serious injury because of me!

ABBY: I think you're rewriting the facts a little. I am in the hospital with a skull fracture that only requires one night of observation. Because of Simon.

NAOMI: Okay fine. But that doesn't change the fact that you're hurt because he was coming after me. I don't care about what happened—in some ways, I'm glad it did. Anything less than a literal smoking gun and he would have gotten away with it again. But he didn't and I was FINALLY able to make sure that he didn't.

But I will never be okay with the fact that you got hurt in the process.

ABBY: Girl, I've broken my pinky toe tripping on the curb merely getting out of the car, torn my ACL trying to catch a train to go get my eyebrows waxed, and gotten a black eye from a rogue tennis ball when I wasn't even playing tennis. I have been injured in so many stupid ways that have no meaning or purpose. I would, any day of the week, choose to have an injury that stood for bravery and friendship and healing and finally getting to—legally—hit Simon as hard as I possibly could. There's also a chance if I hadn't been there, you wouldn't have made it out alive. A night in a hospital seems like a fair trade for all of that.

NAOMI: Abby, I swear, only you could turn a nightmare into a badge of honor and make me laugh while you're at it. Seriously, thank you for being the most amazing friend ever.

ABBY: I will accept 51% of that compliment. I might be the majority shareholder of the compliment, but the other 49% goes to you. From the first day we met you showed me what it was to be a good friend and I've spent most of my life trying to emulate you. So, if you think I'm a good friend, then you're really talking about yourself too.

NAOMI: It's still hard to feel like a good friend. Even before you got hurt, I was feeling terrible because I know something's been going on with you and I was too caught up in my own stuff to find time to ask.

ABBY: What do you mean?

NAOMI: I think you can picture the look on my face right now.

ABBY: I can. I see your dubious eyebrow lift and I raise you two wide eyes of innocence.

NAOMI: Please, Abby. I know something has been going on, that you've been hurting, and you've been hiding it from me. Trying to hide it from me, I should say.

ABBY: Fine. If I tell you, will you go to sleep?

NAOMI: If you tell me, I will attempt to go to sleep. I can make no promises that I will actually fall asleep.

ABBY: At your parent's house in Michigan. Riley was right about me.

NAOMI: Being in love?

ABBY: Of course you knew exactly what I meant.

But yeah. I mean, no, not in love. But I was seeing someone for a hot second. And I do mean hot. Both short and intense. And then … it was over. Mutual. Sort of. I could only live in the shadow of their career and that was never going to work for me. But I'm fine.

NAOMI: Imagine the face again.

ABBY: I am! Seriously, I swear I'm okay. I have good days and bad days, but it's nothing that won't pass. And hey, here's some silver lining. Simon finally did something nice for me and took my mind off the whole thing.

NAOMI: I see your attempts at using humor to deflect and I raise you an "I will be getting the whole story out of you eventually."

ABBY: That's really the only part of poker that I know. I have no idea how to counter a raise.

NAOMI: Same.

ABBY: I think that means it's time for us to sleep.

NAOMI: I guess you're right. Thanks for telling me. And for ... everything.

ABBY: Goodnight Naomi. Love you.

NAOMI: Love you too.

Naomi woke from a brief and uncomfortable rest in the waiting room chair. Her vision was bleary, so it took her a few moments to recognize that the blob of color to her right was Will, and two seats down from him was Becca, both asleep.

"Coffee?"

She glanced to the left, where Riley was seated next to her, holding out a nondescript cafeteria cup between their hands. After a draining marathon of giving their statements to an endless parade of officers, Abby's mom had gently suggested they all head home to catch some much-needed rest, especially since visiting hours had ended and Abby's injuries, thankfully, weren't critical. Yet, as they all rose to leave, no one took a step towards the door. Instead, they all stood, feet rooted to the floor, and exchanged glances.

Finally, Naomi broke the silence. "I think I'm going to stay," she said, before adding. "You all should go, but I need to be here."

She didn't even get to finish her sentence before everyone returned to their seats. Over a dinner of mystery hospital food, they watched late-night reruns of *The Love Boat* on a mounted television that seemed nearly as vintage as the show they were watching until, at some point, they all dozed off.

"Thank you," Naomi said, rubbing the ache in her neck from the variety of strange positions she'd slept in with one hand and accepting the coffee in the other. Over Riley's shoulder, she could see *Your Chicago*, a local morning news program, on the television. Although the sound was off, she didn't need subtitles to know what they were talking about. Images of her apartment and Simon being loaded onto an ambulance under police escort were flashing across the screen. The clock at the edge of the news ticker told her it was a little after six in the morning. She looked back at Riley. "Did you get any sleep last night?"

Riley smirked. "Not really. I went to see if I could get a charger for my phone and ended up getting, shall we say, a private check-up with Nurse Michael. Wait, no, Micah. Mateo. Anyway, I didn't get any rest. Or a charger for that matter. My phone and I are going to crash hard later today."

"Bravo, Riley," Becca said, her voice heavy with sleep. Naomi turned to see Becca pulling herself up to seated and yawning. "And thank you for the role-play inspiration. We've done doctor and patient before. But comforting a loved one grieving in the halls of the hospital gives it a whole new erotic twist." She made a purring noise in her throat.

"Well, that's certainly one way to get woken up." Will sat up.

"You're welcome," Becca said. "Riley, if we don't start a podcast, maybe we can create an alarm clock app that wakes you up with sexy talk and sounds."

"Talk about morning wood," Riley said.

"Ooh, perfect name for it too."

"Okay then." Will stood up and stretched, trying to work out the same kinks Naomi had been battling a few minutes ago.

"Coffee?" Riley asked, procuring two more cups from a side table.

"Thank you," Will said gratefully, taking one. "Any word on Abby? I assume no news is good news?" he asked, turning to look at her.

"I texted with Abby briefly last night," Naomi replied. "Seems like she's doing okay."

He dropped back down into his seat beside her. "So ... then is our plan still the same?"

Naomi slipped her hand in his and squeezed. "Exactly the same."

Will squeezed back. "Only a few more hours, then."

Chapter Twenty-Four

Will

"Time for a changing of the guard."

Will had never met Abby's mother before last night at the hospital, but a lot of things about Abby and Becca began to make sense once he did. Starting with the fact that after telling everyone that Abby was going to be okay and that, since only family was allowed to see her after visiting hours, they should all go home to rest, she said, "That includes you, Becca. No one with a skull fracture needs to listen to your mishegas."

Becca's high-pitched "Moooom!" had only been met with a, "Yes, exactly that. That's not going to be helpful. She needs her whole head intact to deal with that kind of noise."

The encounter, though brief, put a whole lot of things about the Meyer sisters into place.

"Visiting hours are starting," her mom continued, standing in the door of the waiting room. "They're still planning to release her this afternoon, so I'm going to head home to get the guest room ready so she can stay with me for a few days. But you all should head in."

She had barely finished her sentence before everyone bolted out of their chairs and scurried down the hall like a cluster of pinballs, bouncing off one another. When they reached the door, Naomi paused to knock, but before her hand hit the door for the second rap, Becca had opened the door.

Needing no more encouragement, Naomi raced into, clearly over-joyed to see her friend awake and smiling back at her. Will slowed down to let Riley and Becca get in closer, but even at the back of the group, he could see Naomi begin to go in for a hug and then pull back. Instead, she leaned forward and inspected the gauze wrapped around Abby's head as if to make sure that her hugs wouldn't inflict any further damage.

Abby looked more or less the way he had expected. A little worse for wear, but in full Abby style, underneath the weariness and the bandages, her eyes still held the resilient sparkle that he had come to know.

"How are you?" Naomi asked. "They wouldn't let us in to see you any sooner!"

Becca made a *harumph* noise and crossed her arms as she dropped onto the foot of the bed. "They wouldn't let *you* in any sooner. I was allowed because I was family, but Mom said I might not be 'helpful' and went in without me."

Abby squeezed her lips together in an unsuccessful effort to hide her laughter, and Will couldn't tell if Becca didn't see it or was letting it go. She wasn't much of a letting-go kind of person, so he assumed it was the former.

Riley stepped in closer, filling in the space where Becca had been standing. "Your mother tells us they're releasing you today?"

"Finally!" Abby said.

"Finally?" Naomi repeated, giving the word her own horrified intonation. "You've been here twenty-four hours and literally have a crack in your skull."

"But," Abby held up a finger to correct her, "the non-dangerous kind."

"I don't think that's a thing," Riley said.

"Okay," she said, directing her statement to Riley, "Well, the less dangerous kind. The kind that requires brief observation, which has occurred, and then rest at home, which I happen to be exceptionally good at."

"Then, if you're feeling up for it, we were wondering ..." Naomi glanced over her shoulder, and her excited eyes met his. It took him a second to realize what she was queuing up for, but then it clicked, and with it, a jolt of nerves and excitement.

He took a step towards Abby's bed, taking his place behind Naomi. "We were wondering if you'd like to marry us."

Somewhat unexpectedly, at least to Will, it was Becca who had come up with the idea.

"I take it you two are not getting married today, then," Becca had said as they ate their dinner in the waiting room last night.

Naomi had let out a curt laugh at the suggestion. "I don't know about Will, but I'd prefer not to have my anniversary also be the day that Simon got arrested and sent my best friend to the hospital."

It was still strange to hear her talk about Simon. Yesterday was only the second time he had heard her use his name. But she now said it with a familiarity of a past that he still knew very little about. And each time she did, it sent fire and ice through his veins simultaneously, knowing that she had suffered for so many years but that now, hopefully, she was on her way to a new life. "We're on the same page about that one," he'd said. " I can imagine a lot of court documents and proceedings will refer to this arrest date, so I think I'm good not also making that our wedding date."

"Besides," Naomi added, "I can't get married without Abby."

"You should just get married in Abby's hospital room tomorrow," Becca said, punctuating her sentence with a yawn. "You two have the worst luck; if you wait any longer it may never even happen."

Will had started to laugh, but then had stopped as the idea sank in. He looked at Naomi, who looked back at him, an expression on her face that suggested she was having the same thought that he was.

"Is there any reason we couldn't?" he asked, his voice filled with equal measures of curiosity and excitement.

After a moment, Naomi shook her head. "Not that I can think of."

"Is there any reason we *shouldn't*?"

Her eyes sparkled as she replied, "None."

He wasn't entirely sure Abby felt the same way, though, as he now watched a variety of astonished looks cross her face. "Here? Now?" she asked.

"If there's one thing I've learned from all this, it's that I can't let Simon or anyone else hold me back," Naomi said. Standing behind her, his hand on her shoulder, Will couldn't see her face. But he could hear the smile lifting each word. "If I'd listened to you from the beginning, maybe we wouldn't be here today. But here we are, and I don't want to put my life on hold anymore. I don't want to let one more thing interrupt our future. We want to get married. Right now."

Abby's stare at Naomi left him to guess at her thoughts. It wasn't only impulsive, it was a lot to ask after all she had been through, and he held his breath as he waited for her response.

Then, breaking through the suspense, her laughter—tinged with joyful tears—filled the room. "I can't think of anything else I'd rather do right now."

He grinned at her gratefully and held up his phone. Unlocking it, he presented her with an online certificate from the Universal Life Church. "While we were in the waiting room, we took the liberty of registering you as an ordained minister."

"I've still got the flowers from yesterday." Becca scooted further up the bed to show Abby her handful of wilted flowers. "I would have gotten fresh ones from the hospital, but I'm saving that money for a stripper. Everyone is saying no stripper, but I think there's a stripper in our future."

Naomi reached over and took the flowers from Becca's hand. "Okay then," she said, looping her arm through Will's. She looked up at him, and her smile sent fireworks through him. "Third time's the charm?"

He answered by squeezing her arm under his, like he was locking it into place at his side, where he always wanted her to be.

Abby swiveled off the bed to take her spot in front of them, but teetered unsteadily as she tried to stand. Will reached out a hand to help her as she lowered herself back onto the bed. "Oops, maybe I'll stay seated for this." She smiled and then glanced at her hospital gown. "How do I look?" she asked, brushing out the unremarkable pattern of pale blue geometric shapes covering her legs.

"Perfect," Naomi said in a tone that said she meant it. It wasn't the wedding they'd imagined having, and it wasn't even the elopement they'd tried for. But it was perfect. Right down to their officiant in a hospital gown.

Despite not being completely steady on her feet, Abby was still up for the task. She directed Riley to stand by Will and told Becca to take her place beside Naomi. Right when he thought she was about to begin, she held up a hand. "Hang on." With a resourceful twist, she pulled the hospital sheet from her bed, offering one end to Riley and the other to Becca. "Hold your arms up. This won't be your dream Jewish wedding, but at least we can have a makeshift chuppah."

Becca and Riley obeyed, raising their hands above their head to cover Will and Naomi in a wedding canopy. "I can manage for about sixty seconds, so you'd better get a move on it," Riley said quietly, a slight strain in their voice.

"Great, let's get you married," Abby said so resolutely that Will assumed she would begin the ceremony. But then she said, "Now. Does anyone know what that means exactly? Like, what am I supposed to be doing here?"

Thankfully, as of 12:46 a.m. last night, Will knew the answer. "You have to witness us sharing our wedding vows. That's it. I looked it up."

"Like the 'I do' part?"

Will gave her an affirmative nod.

Abby let out a laugh, and Will couldn't help but join her, seeing in her delight a perfect reflection of the bizarre yet somehow fitting situation they found themselves in. Then, her laughter gave way to a bright smile. "Given your history with nuptials," she began. "I feel like I need to get to that part really fast, but I really want to say something first. You two have overcome so much, and yet you've managed to still end up here.

With each other. I can't think of any couple more prepared to face life together than you two."

Her words were brief, yet they held immense weight, and he could feel a surge of happiness welling up inside him.

"So," she continued, "Let's make that happen already. I think it goes something like this—Will, do you take Naomi to be your lawfully wedded wife? Isn't there more?"

"Something about honoring, cherishing, and dying, right?" Riley offered.

"Yes," Abby regarded them with a solemn gaze that was unmistakably tinged with amusement. "All those things. Do you?"

He turned to face Naomi, his eyes tracing the familiar lines of her smile and the curve of her cheek. As their gazes met, he saw in her eyes all the memories of their past that had gotten them to this moment and the endless possibilities of future memories yet to be made. A lump formed in his throat as he declared, "All those things and more, yes," he said with determination, knowing he would say these next words a thousand times over, without hesitation. "I do."

"And Naomi, do you take Will to be your lawfully wedded husband? And all those things?"

"I do. Absolutely," she said, her eyes overflowing with happy tears as she smiled.

"Well then, by the power vested in me by, I'm assuming, the state of Illinois, I now pronounce you husband and wife!"

Certain he knew what was coming next, he turned to Naomi, ready to kiss his new bride. But then he saw Abby's hand fly up, accompanied by a, "Wait!"

He watched, puzzled, as she grabbed a Styrofoam cup from the lunch tray beside her bed and began guzzling down its contents. As he was starting to wonder if this was an attempt to build dramatic tension before their first kiss as a married couple, she tossed the cup to the ground in front of him, turning his speculation into outright bafflement.

Then, it clicked.

This, like everything in his relationship with Naomi, was about letting go of the plan and finding the sweetness in crafting a life together with whatever came their way. He never could have imagined the path that first step into the high school gym would set him on.. He had experienced happiness and love and companionship and loss and sorrow and triumph and growth in ways he hadn't even known were possible. And every second of it was as beautiful as it was entirely different from what he had expected.

Like now.

He lifted his foot and, with a grin, welcoming a life with Naomi and everything that came with it, he smashed the cup.

Chapter Twenty-Five

Naomi

"MAZEL TOV!"

As soon as Will smashed the hospital cup turned wedding glass, Naomi didn't wait for permission. She threw her arms around Will and kissed him. Not the sweet, blushing bride version she had been coached to give by Nightly Global News. She kissed her husband with abandon, her cool tears of happiness and relief mingling with the warmth of their mouths.

Then she remembered, they technically still had one thing to do before that was true.

She pulled back and dashed to the chair where she had dropped her purse, not missing the startled looks on everyone's faces. "Quick!" she practically shouted, pulling out the marriage license Will had picked up from her apartment sometime in the middle of the night. "Everyone sign this!"

"Does that mean I can put my arms down?" Not waiting for an answer, Becca lowered her end of the sheet.

"We did make the most elegant four posts of a chuppah," Riley told her, releasing the sheet and rubbing the back of their arm with their hand. "With a little extra delt time at the gym, I think we could have an excellent side gig. Assuming the podcast and alarm app don't work out."

Naomi stepped between them, pointing to the empty signature lines on the license. "Sign!"

She ushered everyone over to Abby, who tossed the rest of her lunch into the garbage can and then flipped the lunch tray over so everyone could add their signatures.

Once they were done, she held it up in the air and waved triumphantly. "That's it! We're *married*!"

Riley followed suit, only instead of waving around a marriage license, they waved a bottle of wine that they had procured from their bag. "Time to celebrate!"

Abby's eyes went wide. "That's not the wine that I used to—"

"God no. They took that away, *CSI*-style. You didn't think I'd purchase one measly bottle of alcohol, did you?" Riley said, reaching back into their bag and—as if it were completely normal to do so—pulled out several more bottles, along with a bottle opener, and placed them on Abby's bed. "I don't do that on a boring average day, much less on a wedding day."

"Did I smash the only cup we had?" Will asked, looking at the flattened cup on the floor.

"There are some paper cups in that drawer over there." Abby indicated a small cabinet on the other side of the room. "But we'd better hurry. I'm supposed to get released soon, and I don't think they'll be a fan of our little speakeasy setup."

Will quickly walked over to the cabinet and investigated before pulling out a stack of cups and tossing them to Riley.

As the cups arced through the air, there was a knock on the door.

Everyone froze, except Riley, who deftly caught the cups, tossed them with the pile of wine bottles on the bed and then sat down on the bed and leaned backwards onto their elbows, shielding the illicit party items from view.

"Hi, Dr. Greenland," Abby said as the door opened and a woman in scrubs entered.

"Hey, Abby, I was coming with—" She stopped, her eyes scanning the room, taking an extra second to examine the abandoned chuppah/bed sheet still on the floor.

"My friends were very ... excited that I'm going to be okay," Abby said.

Dr. Greenland looked like she was weighing whether she wanted to ask any further questions, but then decided it wasn't worth it. "Well then, they'll be glad to hear that I'm coming with more good news. We'll be discharging you shortly. The nurse will be by with your papers, and then you'll be free to go."

"That's wonderful," Abby replied, employing the same tone she'd used at their Jewish summer camp when she'd convinced the counselor that the late-night giggling and flashlight flickers from their cabin were part of a study group for the next day's Torah portion quiz and definitely not a potluck of stashed away snacks. "I appreciate everything."

Like the camp counselor, Dr. Greenberg gave one more suspicious look around the room but then left. The minute the door closed, Riley, with a mischievous grin, immediately resumed their role as the unofficial sommelier, distributing the paper cups and beginning to pour the wine.

"L'chaim!" Abby said as she brought her cup forward. "To happy endings!"

"To happy endings," everyone echoed, their cups making an unceremonious clunk as they tapped together. As Naomi sipped her wine, she also drank in everything around her, her eyes roaming the room in an attempt to commit as much detail as possible to memory. She wished she could slow down time and hold onto this fleeting moment a little longer because it was all she had ever wanted. It was the wedding she would proudly tell her children about someday.

"Let's get a picture before the nurse comes!" she said, suddenly realizing she didn't only have to rely on her memory. She picked up her phone and, as everyone crowded around her, she grinned and pressed the shutter.

"Okay, let's get you out of here." They turned in a pack to see a nurse walking into the room, head down as he examined a stack of papers. He looked up. "I've got your discharge papers and a wheelchair."

"I'll take those." Becca shoved her cup into Naomi's hand and bounded towards the nurse, taking the papers in one hand and his bicep in the other as she started to guide him back towards the door. "Abby's getting changed right now, so let's give her a minute. While we're waiting, I'd love to pick your brain. See my husband and I role—"

The door shut and the group dispersed, clearing away any signs of their impromptu celebration while Abby changed into an outfit her mom had brought her. When Naomi opened the door, Becca was standing beside a new nurse.

"What happened to—" Naomi started to ask.

"I guess my questions were NSFW," Becca said, crossing her arms with a huff. "I thought medical professionals were supposed to be comfortable with the human body."

"We'd better go before Becca gets us kicked out," Abby said.

"Be forewarned," the nurse said as she wheeled the chair to Abby's bed and helped her in. "There's a little bit of a crowd outside the hospital."

Abby leaned over the side of the wheelchair to look back at everyone behind her as she was pushed into the hallway. "A crowd?" she repeated.

"Yeah, news media," the nurse nodded. "They've been parked outside for the last few hours now."

Riley practically knocked Naomi over trying to get their phone out of their pocket and Naomi sped up slightly to avoid their aggressive swiping. "Literally, what is happening right now? It's all over the interwebs! Simon's attack, the arrest, Abby's hospitalization. How did I miss this?"

"We were a little busy talking to the police and worrying about Abby," Naomi said, although given what she had seen on the news this morning, she wasn't entirely shocked.

"If you can't multi-task in the twenty-first century, you might as well be dead," came Riley's distraught reply.

Now it was Becca's turn. She dove into her purse so zealously that Naomi adjusted her pace again, this time to get out of the way of the rogue items spilling out of Becca's bag. "We're going to need lip gloss," Becca said, coming up for air with three tubes of varying shades. "Especially you, Abby. Although I'm not sure how much it's going to help. You're a mess."

"Thanks," Abby said, clearly feeling no real appreciation.

Riley began tweaking everything adjustable on their body. "You're the newsman, Will; what are we supposed to do? I am so not ready for an on-camera appearance."

"I guess we keep it simple?" Will said, his words accompanied by a shrug. "Thank them for their concern and say we're ready to move past everything. Or we find out if there's a secret back entrance."

Naomi, weary of the relentless eye of the camera, was teetering on the edge of suggesting they find a back door option when Abby spoke up. "Still," she said, as if she were finishing a conversation she had been having with herself. "There's something about closure. Like it or not, the public has been on this wild ride with us. It might help us in the long run if we let them know we're fine and moving on."

Naomi smiled as Abby, once again, helped her see things in a different light. "See, this is why being friends with a therapist is helpful. She's got a point. I know we said we wanted to leave the audience behind, but maybe this is how we make that happen."

They were nearing the glass sliding doors of the entrance. The short path leading to the sidewalk was lined on both sides with an indistinguishable mass of faces, arms, microphones, and cameras all pointed at the door.

"Then we're agreed?" Abby asked.

Naomi slipped her hand into Will's and looked up at him. He looked back and squeezed her hand tightly. "Agreed," he said to her.

The doors opened and instantly, a blast of questions enveloped them like a tsunami, the throng of reporters' voices merging into an overwhelming roar. The air was thick with the flash of cameras and the jostle of microphones being thrust toward them.

Naomi held tightly to Will as they followed Abby and the nurse out into the sunny spring day. The nurse stopped and helped Abby out of the chair, then whispered something and pattered her on the back before turning around and bringing the wheelchair back inside, leaving the group of friends to navigate the tidal wave of questions.

The uproar blended into an indistinct hum, making it almost impossible to hear individual questions. But she didn't need to hear them to know what they were asking. Feeling a sense of peace and strength, she released Will's hand and stepped forward.

As she began to speak, her voice, steady and confident, sliced through the commotion. Although she was tired of the cameras and the questions, she wasn't afraid of them anymore. She no longer had anything to hide, and she wanted the world to see that. "I think I speak for all of us," she began, and in an instant the crowd went completely quiet, as if someone had muted them. Their silence was so abrupt it was almost startling, and she paused to recalibrate. She began again, "I think I speak for all of us when I say that I'm ready to put all this behind me. We're grateful for everyone's support, but we've spent enough time in the public eye and we're really looking forward to doing whatever is next, privately."

As she finished her statement, she felt an unexpected rush of exhilaration. There was something undeniably empowering about standing there, her words commanding the crowd's attention. Will moved to stand beside her, and she glanced up at him, then back to Abby. She had said all she needed to say, but she wanted to leave the door open for them to have their own declaration moment too. "Right?"

Abby smiled at her, the pride in her eyes unmistakable. "I believe that about covers it, yeah."

That was all it took to break the spell. The reporters sprang back to life like bees disturbed from their hive, swarming them with questions.

"This is the part where we just go, right?" Abby asked Naomi, squinting as a volley of flashes flickered from somewhere in the crowd.

"I think so," Naomi said, more unsure of what route to take to get through the crowd than whether it was time to leave. The crowd had begun to bleed from the sidelines into the walkway as their eagerness for answers pushed them forward. She tried to drown out the noise and focus on their exit when a question jumped out at her from the crowd.

"Abigail, what can you tell us about your recent breakup?"

For a moment, the thought crossed her mind that Riley had gone through her phone while she had been sleeping, read her texts with Abby, and fed the question to a reporter in order to get answers. But no, that couldn't be it. While she knew the occasional snooping was greenlit by Riley's moral code, they would never share that knowledge outside of their circle. So, how did a reporter know what she had only learned last night?

She looked at Abby to see if she had heard the question too. But Abby's eyes, wide with disbelief, were trained towards the crowd. Naomi followed her gaze until she saw it too.

Saw *her*.

Emerging from the sea of reporters, eyes locked on Abby as if no one and nothing else existed, was Freya. "I ..." Naomi heard Abby stammer.

Freya, although breathless from the effort of weaving through the crowd, could be heard clearly as she asked another question. "Does staying out of the public eye mean you wouldn't date a public figure?"

Immediately, Naomi felt two hands grab her by the shoulder and then heard Riley's voice in her ear. "Oh my god. It's happening. This is it. This is *it*!"

Naomi started to turn toward them, heart pounding, but then her focus snapped back to Abby, who was staring straight at her—as if searching for an answer, for permission, for *something*. Naomi could only smile back, hoping her eyes said everything her friend needed to hear: that whatever came next, her friends would be by her side.

For a beat, Abby remained frozen, disbelief flickering across her face, her lips parted as if she couldn't quite process what was happening. Then, slowly, something shifted.

She turned back to Freya, and Naomi watched, gleefully, as uncertainty gave way to a slow, elated smile. "I think I could be talked into making an exception for the right person," she said.

Freya reached Abby, her voice growing softer but simultaneously stronger. "Can someone be the right person even if it took them a long time to get to a place where they were ready to be the right person?"

"Are you sure?" Abby asked, never taking her eyes off Freya. "Your career. Everything you've worked for. Your whole life. I know I said a lot of things, but I don't want to be the reason—"

Freya took Abby's hands and pulled her closer. "When I didn't know what had happened, when Will said there'd been an attack and you were on the way to the hospital and I didn't know if you were alive, it just ..." She stopped and laughed. "It just became so obvious that none of that matters. Abby, I don't want to waste one more moment hating you."

Riley let out a squeal that could have shattered glass. "I knew it! We made this happen!"

Naomi could hardly believe it. She'd had her suspicions, of course, but did this mean The Plan actually worked? Had Riley, had *they*, really helped bring Abby and Freya together?

"Does this mean the breakup she told me about was with Freya?" Naomi said, finishing her thought aloud.

"What breakup?" Riley said "When? You can't keep these things from me!"

"Then that actually was Freya's stuff at Abby's place I saw," Will added.

"After this, we're going to have to have a serious discussion about keeping secrets from me," Riley said.

"Shhh, later, I can't hear." Becca squeezed in, pressing up against Naomi, and hushed them.

Naomi didn't argue. She didn't want to miss another second of what was unfolding in front of her. Freya had leaned in even closer to Abby, the two now impossibly close, as if some unforeseen thread—or perhaps four loving but meddlesome friends—had pulled them to where they were always meant to be.

Even still, Naomi could make Freya's words out, clear as day.

"I love you."

Naomi couldn't stop the tears as she watched her best friend throw her arms around Freya and say, "I love you, Freya Jonsson," before pressing her lips to Freya's.

Naomi hadn't thought it was possible to be happier than she had been a few minutes ago, but standing here, watching Abby's own love story unfold, Naomi knew she had been wrong. The only thing more perfect than finding her own fairytale moment was sharing that moment with Abby. Because that's how it had always been, and it was truly the only way she wanted it to be. Their lives were inextricably connected, their friendship, a lifetime of shared laughter, dreams, tears, encouragement, and even—when necessary—fake pocket dials, all of it had led them here. Because it wasn't only Will who was her beshert. They were all her destiny. And wherever life took them next, they would go together.

Epilogue

"In five, four, three, two ..."

It had been more than two years since Naomi had been on a studio stage, surrounded by an army of cameras, lights gleaming from every angle, and shadows of crew moving somewhere behind the equipment. She had expected to find herself a bundle of nerves, the way she had the first few times she'd been in front of the cameras, but was amazed at how familiar it felt. However brief her time in the public eye had been, her body had acclimated to the experience, and she slipped back into the familiar performance without hesitation. She looked at Will, seated beside her on the plush gray sofa, dressed in a cobalt blue T-shirt, soft and worn, with a tiny watercolor TARDIS at its center. The style was unmistakably his, but the color had been chosen to match the deep blue of her silk-and-lace dress. She scanned his face to see if he was feeling the same way as her, and his smile, now hidden underneath a thick but trim beard, told her he was.

In front of her, a red light appeared on one of the cameras. The man seated across from her leaned forward, looking intimately into the camera as it began slowly moving towards him as if he were about to divulge a secret to his best friend. "From the heartwarming engagement that captured America's heart to the despair of being left at the altar," he began, "The Wilomi story has had it all. Add in a secret past, a harrowing attack, and a dramatic reunion, and you've got a season of television that's kept us all on the edge of our seats.

"After two years away from the public eye, healing and growing stronger together, Will and Naomi are back for a special episode to answer your burning questions and give us a glimpse into their journey of love, resilience, and redemption. I'm Andy, and this is Wilomi: The Tell-All. Let's dive in."

At those magic words, the camera he had been talking into swooped back, and another one came to life, sliding across the floor to capture the full stage. Andy leaned back in his chair and turned to face the sofa. Naomi shifted, crossing her legs and placing her hands on her knees. She might be used to the cameras, but she would never get used to hearing her life talked about as if it were a scripted drama.

"Naomi, Will," Andy said. "Thanks for sitting down with me today. I know a lot of people around the world are excited to hear from you, and I'd like to jump right in by addressing that—what made you decide to come forward and agree to this interview?"

While they had been warned that there was no guarantee a Tell-All would go as planned (and she suspected that they hoped it wouldn't), they had received a list of questions Andy would try to ask. Including this one, which Naomi was prepared to answer. "While Will and I are both so incredibly grateful to all the people who have watched us and supported us, this whole experience was not one we went looking for. I mean, who thinks they'll get engaged on the news and their proposal will go viral and turn into a globally televised wedding that leads to the whole world watching you face your demons and then find your way back to each other? Okay, maybe some people do, but believe it or not, neither of us are limelight kind of people. And when it was over, we were both ready to go back to our old, normally-lit lives.

"But whether or not we wanted to tell our stories so publicly, we did. And in the process, it turns out, we impacted people. Over the last two years, we've received thousands of messages from folks telling us how something they saw us go through helped them in some way. It has been really incredible. Living out your mistakes in public isn't easy but that definitely helped make it all worth it. And what's even more incredible is that the messages keep coming. Even after all this time, not a day goes by that we don't hear from people who want to share their own stories and how ours played a part in that. So," she clapped Will on the knee and looked up at him, "eventually we got to talking. We agreed that even though the spotlight isn't something we were looking for, we've been given this platform that's reached people in amazing ways. And with that comes a sort of responsibility, doesn't it? To keep speaking, to keep sharing because if our journey can help even one person, then stepping back into that light is something we're willing to do. It's about more than us now; it's about all the lives touching ours and the stories intertwining with our own."

"Wow. That's beautiful," Andy said, glancing down at a stack of cards in their hand. "Now, moving on. I think the first thing we need to do is address the elephant in the room. Or should I say ... the baby in the room."

Will reached across his body and placed his hand on Naomi's stomach, a watermelon-sized bump that was no longer able to be disguised by loose clothing. "Yep! Coming this winter!"

"Congratulations to you both! Do you know if it's a boy or a girl? Or do you want to be surprised?"

"I've had enough surprises for one lifetime," Naomi said with a laugh. "It's a girl."

"Any names picked out?"

"A few," she answered vaguely.

"Any you care to share?"

Will shook his head. "We've decided to keep her information private. She's not part of the Wilomi story, and she doesn't have any responsibility to anyone. She's Naomi and Will's daughter, and so we're going to do our best to let her enjoy life without being part of all this." He gestured around.

"Makes sense. Well, mazel to you both. I'm so happy for you, and I know everyone out there is thrilled for you as well," Andy told them, his hand motioning outwards, apparently indicating their global fanbase.

"Thank you," Naomi said, not sure that *everyone* was thrilled. She knew quite well by now that she would never, ever please everyone.

"Now, I want to bring things down for a second and address another burning question." Andy tapped his cards and the armrest of his chair, a serious look settling on his face. Naomi didn't have to think hard to guess what he was about to say next. "Simon."

She nodded, indicating she was ready for him to go there.

"Two years ago, he was arrested for assaulting you and Abby at your apartment. Since then, he was charged and found guilty of a whole host of crimes, including violating a restraining order, unlawful possession of a firearm, and assault with a deadly weapon, and he was sentenced to prison. But only a few years, right?"

"Three, but after time served and, apparently, good behavior, he's up for parole next month."

"That doesn't seem like a very long time, given everything he put you through. What has your experience been going through this, and how do you feel knowing he could be back on the streets so soon? Naomi, you first and then Will."

This was another question she'd come prepared for. "I think this outcome, his short sentence and quick release, is only astonishing to those who haven't navigated our justice system before. We've made some great strides over the years, but we still have a long way to go as a society when it comes to having the support system to help people in situations like mine. I'm beyond lucky. Being in the media meant there was pressure to act instead of brushing it under the rug. And now he'll be hard pressed to go anywhere that people don't know his face. While it doesn't insulate me from having run-ins with him in the future, it definitely cuts down on the chances. But most people in my situation don't have those things. I didn't, for years, and it was nearly impossible to get any help. In fact, I felt like I was safer not saying anything because I didn't know who would actually believe me or if it would end up making things worse. My hope is that by continuing to speak out, we can move towards a future where anyone, regardless of their situation, has access to the help and protection they deserve."

Andy's head bobbed as he absorbed, or at least pretended to absorb, her statement. As soon as she finished, his eyes flicked to her left. "Will?"

Will pulled both his arms away from Naomi and leaned his elbows onto his knees. "I'll be honest, it's infuriating. Yes, the fact that he got a slap on the wrist. But it's more than that. None of this should have happened—not the light sentence, and certainly not Naomi being unable to get help. But it's all one and the same. Sure, it's not fair that his sentence was minimal, but Simon never faced consequences before, so why would things change now? They won't unless we as a society stop turning a blind eye to these issues." He paused, looking contemplative. "And I include myself in that 'we.' My privilege allowed me to be completely unaware of what is happening to so many people. But this has been a wake-up call for me, and I hope it can be for others too. So yeah, like Naomi, I'm hoping that by talking about this we can move towards a world where no one else has to go through what Naomi did and where everyone feels supported and believed."

"I think it's noble what you two are trying to do, and I thank you for it." Andy slipped the card at the front of the pack to the end and skimmed the new set of words in front of him. His solemnity disappeared and was replaced by a smile. "Now, we want to talk about life after the cameras, but not only yours. During your time on television, viewers weren't only following your lives but the lives of your wedding party. In fact, your best woman and maid of honor almost stole the show from you there at the end. Let's hear about all of it now."

"Cut!" The director called from the darkness. "Stage crew, set up for group interviews."

There was a flutter of noise and movement, and then three individuals dressed in black came onto the stage carrying a matching sofa to the one she was sitting on.

"You're doing great," Andy said, before taking a sip from the water bottle placed behind his chair.

"And we're ready! In five, four, three, two ..." the director called before she could reply, although she wasn't entirely sure he wanted one. Instead of a 'one,' the red light flicked on, and Andy picked up where they had left off. "Please welcome Abby, Freya, Riley, and Becca to the stage."

Naomi turned to watch her friends enter, stage right, all of them impeccably styled in glamorous dresses, makeup and hair done to perfection, ready for their moment on camera. She had spent the last few hours behind stage with them, so this wasn't the exciting reunion it was for viewers, but still, she was happy to see them and she waved to them as they took their seats on the sofa beside her.

"Thanks so much for joining us today. I've got a lot of questions for you all, so let's get going. Obviously, we have to start with some congratulations."

"Yes, thank you, it's true," Riley said. "Becca and I have the number one podcast on Apple Podcasts, two weeks in a row now."

Andy laughed. "I was going to say Freya and Abby's engagement, but you're right. Congratulations are in order for you two as well. Your podcast, Take My Dicktation, has become a bit of a sensation, hasn't it? And am I right in understanding the whole podcast is about, well," Andy hemmed. "How can I put this delicately?"

"Dicks, Andy," Becca interjected. "It's okay, you can say it. We started a podcast about dicks."

"Except then it evolved into something." Riley paused. "I don't want to say better. Because what's better than dicks?"

"Nothing," Becca confirmed. Then added, "I'm thinking about my husband's right now." She wiggled her fingers off stage, presumably to where Peter was standing in the shadows.

"Let's say it evolved," Riley said when it became clear that Becca was lost to her flirting, "as we started taking listener questions, it opened new avenues for us to discuss all kinds of topics that we have expertise in. Dating advice, career advice, fashion advice—"

"And also dicks." Becca was back. "We never lost sight of what brought us together."

Riley pointed a finger towards Becca as if to drive home her point.

"I'm definitely going to come back to your podcasting success. But first," Andy turned his head slightly to look at the other couple sharing the sofa with Riley and Becca. "Abby and Freya. While we were all watching Naomi and Will, you two were having a love story of your own that none of us saw coming."

Naomi saw Riley's face twitch slightly.

"Your big moment in front of the hospital that took us all by surprise and by storm," Andy continued, "wasn't the start of your romance, it was actually the final moment. Before we met you as a couple, you two had known each other in high school, reconnected when Will and Naomi started dating, had been secretly dating for a few weeks after the wedding, and then had broken up before getting back together for all of us to see. Thank you for that, by the way."

Freya and Abby laughed together. "You're welcome," Abby said.

"As I was saying before, I understand congratulations are in order?"

Naomi looked at her friends. If she didn't know better, she would think the bright flush on their faces was purely nerves. But she had seen that look on them since the day they showed up at dinner wearing the engagement rings they now displayed for the camera. That pink flush wasn't from the interview or the bright lights overhead; they were hopelessly in love, and it radiated from every pore.

"Yep, we're engaged," Freya said.

Andy nodded approvingly. "This is a Tell-All, so tell it all. When did it all start? Because isn't it true you two were lifelong enemies?"

"I don't know if I'd go so far as to say enemies," Abby replied, intertwining her fingers with Freya's.

"Mortal enemies, Andy," Riley said. "A real Taylor Swift and Katy Perry. We're talking bad bl—"

"Okay, thank you, Riley," Abby said, a firmness unmistakable behind her smile.

Andy chuckled. "I get the picture. There was some tension between you two. But then, when did you start dating?"

After they declared their love for each other in front of the entire world, Abby and Freya chose to keep their relationship out of the public eye for the most part. So, when they both hesitated to answer, Naomi guessed they must be feeling the same discomfort she had felt talking about her relationship with Will on camera early on. "It's really sweet," she said, trying to take some of the pressure off by telling Andy what they'd told her when she'd asked the same question. "They met a few days after the wedding to talk about what was happening and try to figure out how they could help us. They came up with this plan to encourage us to stand up for ourselves so we could either get closure or answers and I guess along the way, one thing led to another."

She looked at Abby, expecting a nod of confirmation, but instead Abby had her bottom lip between her teeth. "Yeah, about that ..."

Riley sat up like they'd been given an electric shock. "Wait, what now?"

Abby looked over at Freya. "We decided on the way over here that there's enough distance between your wedding now so—"

"Yeah," Freya said, cutting to the chase. "We totally made out at your wedding."

Exclamations came from everyone on camera, and possibly some people off.

"In my defense," Abby said, laughing as she attempted to be heard over the group. "No, listen, in my defense, I went over to Freya to read her the riot act, seeing as how she was someone I disliked and was associated with Nightly Global News, who had allowed my best friend to go through all that on live TV. And then ... you know ..."

"I do *not* know!" Riley said incredulously. "We had a very formal agreement drawn up about keeping secrets in this friend group, and it has been severely violated."

"I knew I saw you in the hallway!" Will exclaimed.

"More secrets?!" Riley sounded like a pressure cooker about to explode.

"Okay, okay." Andy waved both hands in front of himself, trying to rein the chatter in. "It started with a kiss at the wedding. That brings me to my next question, then. If you two always hated each other, what changed? One make-out sesh after a wedding-gone-wrong?"

Abby and Freya exchanged glances, as if partaking in a silent rock, paper, scissors as to who would answer first. Freya must have lost because she turned to Andy. "I mean, the making out certain helped." She laughed. "But truthfully, I think we both realized the things we hated about each other were actually the things we loved about each other."

"It's funny, you say that," Abby said, looking at Freya, "I never told you this—I guess with everything else going on, it didn't seem important. But it wasn't until I accidentally overheard all of them talking about how you were in love with me that I started to realize how I felt about you. I guess that means you figured it out first and I was the latecomer to the game."

Naomi's eyes widened.

Freya shifted to look at Abby. "You overheard—but I overheard all of them talking about how *you* were in love with me. That was how I—"

Riley's hand shot out, trying to get their attention. "Never mind all that. I think what's really key here is that you two discovered your feelings and are getting your own happily ever after."

But no one was paying attention to Riley, especially not Andy. "Hang on," he said eagerly. "Are you saying you *both* overheard everyone else here talk about how the other one was in love with you? But at that point, neither of you had any feelings for each other that you were aware of?"

Abby turned to Naomi, her jaw practically on the floor. "Do you have something to tell me?"

Naomi slipped her tongue between her teeth and bit down.

"I saw that, Naomi!"

Acknowledgments

This book was written in the throes of morning sickness and the sleepless, bleary stretch of life with a newborn. In many ways, it feels like I had twins the year I finished it.

I want to extend my deepest gratitude to Rising Action for believing so deeply in this story that they invited me to turn one book into two. And for not batting an eye when my little one made it clear she had no regard for publishing deadlines and I would need more time. Thank you especially to my friend and editor, Alex, for bringing laughter and support to every step of the process.

To everyone who helped and encouraged me along the way, I appreciate you immensely. Even if my mom brain is too tired to make a list, please know how much it meant.

And to my readers, whether you're experiencing this story for the first time or returning for the other side of the hijinks and romance, thank you. This series, while far more enjoyable than actual labor, was a true labor of love. I don't know if I'll ever love another set of characters quite like these six. I'm honored you let me share them with you.

About the Author

Arden Joy turned to writing at an early age as a way to create a world as unique and different as she is. Today, she still focuses on telling diverse stories that reflect her colorful life and the beautiful spectrum of people in it. When she isn't stirring up trouble for her fictional characters, she runs Girls Who Travel, an award-winning community redefining travel to be inclusive, sustainable, and empowering for all women.

Looking for more Romance? Check out Rising Action's other love stories on the next page!

And don't forget to follow us on our socials for cover reveals, giveaways, and announcements:
X: @RAPubCollective
Instagram: @risingactionpublishingco
TikTok: @risingactionpublishingco
Website: http://www.risingactionpublishingco.com

RISING ACTION

Some loves destroy you. Some save you. Some do both.

Alex thought that leaving her Massachusetts hometown for college would help her forget Jamie, the troubled boy who was her first friend, first kiss, and first heartbreak. But five years later, at twenty-three, she finds herself back home, staring at the same yellow shutters and red door, unable to outrun the past. Forced to attend her dreaded five-year high school reunion, Alex discovers an old journal hidden in her childhood bedroom. Over twenty-four hours, memories come flooding back: the spark of young love, Jamie's chaotic family life, and the choices that shattered everything she thought she knew.
But some secrets were never what they seemed. As Alex confronts the truth about Jamie and about herself, she must decide if love can't change the past but might still rewrite her future.

Poignant, nostalgic, and deeply emotional, The Enemy of Time is a love story about the ties that bind us, the ghosts we carry, and how a single moment can unravel everything you thought you knew about love, time, and fate.

Kate Dailey's life is built on three unshakeable beliefs: Taylor Swift's music is the ultimate cure, "Happily Ever After" doesn't exist, and Jason Cole is the last person on earth she wants to see again. Growing up in a small town, Jase was her first everything—kiss, friend, and beacon of hope through her darkest days, especially with her father's battles with alcoholism. But when Jase shattered her heart, Kate left everything behind, including him and the memories of fireflies and Magnolia trees.

Now, six years later, Kate has carved out a new existence in NYC, armed with a sassy pup and a dream job. Yet, when family duty calls her back home to confront her past, including the boy next door who became the man she loves to hate, Kate's carefully constructed world starts to wobble. Facing Jase and the small-town life she escaped, Kate is torn between the safety of the life she's built and the perilous allure of a second chance with the one who broke her beyond repair.

In a story where heartbreak and hope collide, Kate must decide if she's willing to risk everything for a shot at true happiness, or if some wounds are just too deep to heal. Can the melodies of Taylor Swift guide her towards her own "Happily Ever After," or will Kate find that some things, like her love for Jase, are too persistent to ignore?